LAST VERSE

LAST
VERSE

S J Talbot

Matador
Unit E2 Airfield Business Park,
Harrison Road, Market Harborough,
Leicestershire. LE16 7UL
Tel: 0116 2792299
Email: books@troubador.co.uk
Web: www.troubador.co.uk/matador
Twitter: @matadorbooks

ISBN 978 1803132 525

British Library Cataloguing in Publication Data.
A catalogue record for this book is available from the British Library.

Printed and bound in Great Britain by 4edge Limited
Typeset in 11pt Minion Pro by Troubador Publishing Ltd, Leicester, UK

Matador is an imprint of Troubador Publishing Ltd

In memory of Detective Constable 603
Paul Hardwick, who died aged 47,
Leaving the world a much less colourful place.
Born on a different cloud…

Chapter 1

Le Papillon Bleu – shit name for a brothel. Correction: shit name for a brothel on the A630 east of Doncaster. Probably all right in Pigalle or Montmartre.

Harry Stallard smiled as he cruised past the neon butterfly. It was mounted on a steel grid by the massage-parlour entrance, and flickered blue, like it was being zapped in a giant fly trap. He swung into the car park and reversed slowly up to the front door. Two fifteen in the morning. The place empty as usual. A frost starting to silver the weeds clumped in cracks across what was once a petrol forecourt. He reached down into the footwell and grabbed the package containing the money.

A Tesco bag for life. Really? Sick sense of humour some people. Got to be one of those smartarses in TSU – pissed off at having to photograph and bundle up all those dirty, used twenties. Typical bloody techies.

The air hit him as soon as he stepped out of the car, cold enough to freeze the tits off a brass penguin. He shuddered and checked his phone was switched to transmit. No matter how many deployments he'd made as an undercover officer, this was the point when the nerves kicked in. Showtime. His heart clanged up through the gears, and sweat started beading at the base of his spine. He slowed his breathing. Counted to ten. Then he put his shoulders back and swaggered in, like the cockiest bastard since Napoleon Bonaparte.

Two men stood waiting for him in the foyer of Le Papillon Bleu. The owner, Jared Finn, was no more than forty, and weasel-faced, in a tight charcoal suit. Human Trafficking Shitbag of the Year three times on the bounce. *Nice going, Jared. Shame the empire's about to come crashing down, and you're going to rot in prison.* Next to him was Stefan. The obligatory goon with no neck and a shaved head, trying a little too hard to look the part.

Finn's hand was already out, palm up.

'About fucking time. Where's the money?'

'A joy to see old-fashioned customer service is still alive and well.' Stallard nodded to them both in turn. 'Morning gentlemen. My client sends his regards.'

'I don't want his fucking regards. I want his money – now.' Finn jabbed a finger. 'You were supposed to be here at two.' More jabbing. A tough-guy stare thrown in.

Stallard smiled. Punctuality, the thief of time, wasn't one of his virtues. He pulled the carrier bag out of his jacket, and tossed it over.

'Fifteen grand, as agreed. Now show me the goods.'

'I'll check the cash.' Finn tore at the duct tape. When he saw the money, an avaricious light pinged on inside his eyeballs, and he turned to the sidekick. 'Okay, Stefan, let him see her.' He threw the bundles of notes onto the reception desk and started counting.

'Don't forget your toes, when you run out of fingers.' Stallard, the wag.

'Get fucked, dickhead.' Jared Finn gave him daggers.

Stallard shrugged. How could he compete with such fine wordplay?

No-neck motioned him to follow, and set off down a back corridor. They went through a bead curtain and down some stairs. The old garage still smelled of diesel, but now overlaid by something a little more sweet and sour. Puke and piss. Maybe some talc and oil thrown in. They passed two doors along another corridor with a tiled floor and carpeted walls, until they reached a third that was secured by a heavy steel hasp. Stefan fumbled through a bunch of keys before undoing the padlock, opening the door, and taking a step back.

Stallard entered the room and closed the door behind him. It was a good size, but windowless, with harsh strip-lights and an old extractor that clattered along like a pair of castanets. The place was bare, apart from some mattresses scattered on the floor. The girl sat on a stained, king-size one in the corner, cocooned in a blanket and with her knees pulled up under her chin. She was supposed to be eighteen, but looked younger. He knelt down to be at her level, and softened his voice.

'Hi, my name's Harry and I'm here to help. Do you speak English?'

No words, just a barely perceptible shake of the head.

Stallard looked into her eyes and saw a distant emptiness. Whatever abuse she'd suffered had numbed her senses into submission, and now she awaited her fate with a pathetic indifference beyond her years. Somehow, that made it worse.

'Okay, no problem, but trust me, everything's going to be all right. Just trust me, you'll see…'

The girl muttered a word. A croak. It dried and crumbled on her lips.

He leaned in. 'Try again.'

'Mooser.' It was an effort. Barely audible. 'Mooser…'

He leaned in closer still, holding his breath. Silence.

And that's when it happened. From nowhere. The blanket twitched and then a flash of light on metal. A slender wrist snapping into his ribs. Bang. It sent bolts of lightning coursing through his body. *Must be a taser. Fuck. No, it's not. Shit, that hurts…*

He stood up straight. The handle of a knife stuck out of his side at ninety degrees. Up to the hilt, like a comic, magic-show prop at some children's seaside matinee. The walls started kaleidoscoping. He staggered backwards and fell over one of the other mattresses. *Come on, come on, what's wrong with you?*

Now the ground was sucking him in. He tried to push up, but gravity held on tight. White, blinding pain came in a wave and then ebbed away. It was then he could taste the blood, bubbling up fresh with iron from his lungs. It came down and went back up his nose, bringing with it the scent of an irresistible anaesthetic. The one from which none ever wake. His eyes closed. *No, don't do it – breathe. Don't do it – breathe. Don't do it – breathe. Come on, don't die on the floor of a shitty knocking shop, you bastard…*

4

CHAPTER 2

Monday morning, a little after eight.

Harry Stallard stopped outside the office door and checked the shiny aluminium plaque – *Cold Case Review Unit Manager – Gerard Hardcastle QPM*. Then he knocked and walked in. The great man himself was standing in the middle of the room, with one foot up on a mahogany coffee table, like he'd just slain it on safari and was now posing for photographs. The great white hunter. He was wearing a pinstripe suit, with a blue silk tie covered in little gold fleurs-de-lys that corresponded exactly to the little gold fleurs-de-lys on his blue ankle socks. Stallard thought maybe the old man had his foot raised to best show off this classic tie-sock combo, but then he saw the shoe brush in one hand and the tin of mid-tan Kiwi polish on the table in front of him. Shoe-shine time. A daily ritual for the anally retentive no doubt.

People mistook Hardcastle for a retired army general, because of the moustache. It was a thick wedge of slate bristles that covered his entire top lip, and bestowed upon him a demeanour of permanent displeasure. Stallard wouldn't have been surprised to see the Queen's Police Medal pinned above his jacket pocket with military precision, but there was no sign of it there, or on display anywhere in the room. What a blow. You finally meet a legend in the field of criminal investigation, and he turns out to look like your bad-tempered, but smart grandad. Life's full of minor disappointments.

Hardcastle narrowed his eyes. 'Who are you?'

'DC Stallard. Here for the welcome-to-the-department chat.'

'Except you're not.'

'Okay, I wasn't top of class at detective training school, but I always got my own name right. It was my specialist subject – rank and surname. Detective Constable Stallard – nailed it every time.'

'Don't try to be clever with me.' Hardcastle began to brush his brogue. 'I meant you're not welcome to the department.'

'This posting wasn't my choice.' Stallard shrugged. So, it was going to be like that. What had he been expecting? Ticker tape and a marching band? Speeches and waiters with little trays of canapés. He turned to leave. 'Shall I shut the door on my way out?'

'Sit down. It's not entirely your fault.'

'Wait a minute. None of this is my fault. I was nearly killed infiltrating an organised crime group.'

'Don't bull it up, son. You were stabbed by a sixteen-year-old girl.' Hardcastle nodded towards his desk. 'I've read your file. Now sit down.'

Stallard took a seat and waited. The filter coffee bubbling away behind him smelt good. It didn't seem to be on offer to passing guests. Not him anyway. Hardcastle finished buffing his brogues and put his cleaning kit away into a chintzy wooden chest that was decorated with images from The Little Mermaid. It was a music box, and when he opened the lid, it played a tinny version of *Under The Sea* for a full two minutes. Of course, it did. Perfectly normal in the office of a retired detective superintendent in a land-locked, metropolitan police force. The old guy even mouthed along to a few bars. *Under the sea, Under the sea, Darling it's better, Down where it's wetter, Take it from me…*

By the time the music had stopped, Hardcastle was behind his desk with a pair of bi-focals on the end of his nose. He sighed and frowned over the top of them.

'You see, it's nothing personal, son, but every time the HR department has a detective who is unfit for frontline duties, they send them here to me, because we're classed as a non-operational unit, and I'm fed up of my staff having to babysit the bloody sick, lame and lazy.'

'I'm not sick, lame or lazy.'

Hardcastle didn't look convinced. 'All I know, is that every month they send me some sod on recuperative duties, and they always prove to be as much use as the Pope's bollocks.'

'Good job you don't let it affect your sense of humour.'

'Are you taking the piss?'

'Me?' Stallard pulled a smile. A big cheesy one, with lots of teeth.

Hardcastle shook his head and sighed. 'To be honest, son, you look like a sack of shit – ponytail, tattoos, earrings, cowboy boots – we run a disciplined ship here. Nearly all our staff are retired, mature officers, and cold case work tends to be with professional bodies and decent citizens. Image is important.'

'Excuse me.' Stallard opened his arms wide. 'This sack-of-shit look, took eight years to perfect. Soon as I can, I shall be straight off back to the Regional Undercover Unit, where its soiled beauty is fully appreciated.'

'You've got seven days.'

'Don't I get to rest on the Sabbath?'

'That's when I'll undertake a review of your attachment.'

'Sooner the better.'

Hardcastle took off his glasses and leant back in his chair. 'Let me give you some advice, because I've read your personnel file, and it's not guaranteed you'll go back to your old job when your attachment to this unit comes to an end. It says you've got issues.'

'My only issue is I want to get back to work.'

'I've been in charge of some undercover operations in the past.' There was no stopping Hardcastle now. 'I know exactly what you UCs class as work. It's one big pantomime game, played without any public scrutiny and often any legal accountability. There's no methodical rigour.' The moustache looked particularly disapproving. 'You'll find the demands of real-world investigation far more challenging.'

'I spent three weeks on a life-support machine. Is it more challenging than that?'

The old man ignored him. 'When I ran the Burlington Estate murders, I used to remind the enquiry teams of their ABC at every morning briefing – Assume nothing…'

'Believe nobody. Check everything. ABC. Don't worry, I can be cynical with the best of them.'

'All right, you know the theory, let's see how you get on doing the business.'

Stallard made to stand up.

'Wait. One more thing.' Hardcastle slid his glasses back on his nose and picked up the file. 'The Occupational Health Unit has attached a condition on your return-to-work duties.' He scowled as he read it out. 'You must be accompanied at all times when meeting members of the public outside police premises, in case of anxiety caused by potential confrontational situations.' The glasses came off. 'Ah, bless. They want you wrapped in cotton wool.'

Stallard clamped his jaw and said nothing. So much for empathetic, modern management. But then it was probably forty years since Hardcastle nosed his way up the promotion ladder. Now he was an anachronism, pocketing a fat pension, and free to bigot at will. The rest of the Cold Case crew were probably the same.

Back out in the corridor, Stallard relaxed and smiled to himself. It would have been nice if the Head of the force's Occupational Health Unit had told him about this condition that had been attached to his recuperative duties. After all, he'd left her at home in bed an hour ago, and she'd never mentioned it. That was Doctor Laura Goody-Two-Shoes all over. Everything had to be done by the book. Work and personal life had to be separated by an inviolable, sterile corridor, even though it was work that had drawn them together in the first place.

It was three years since undercover officers had been sent for regular, mandatory counselling to the OHU, and that's where romance had blossomed over psychometric-testing forms and comfy leather armchairs. What was it the old man had said? Anxiety caused by potential confrontational situations? It made him sound like a quivering invertebrate needing protection from normal people. Just wait until he got home, then there'd be a confrontational situation. He laughed and shook his head. Shrinks.

There was a big felt-tip sticker on the main office door that said *Happy Days Nursing Home*, and a smaller one underneath that said *Department of Urology*. Stallard pushed it open with his backside, and reversed in, carrying a cardboard box of his working-life's worldly goods. He scanned his new temporary home, and saw just your average CID office – knackered corporate-blue chairs, lever arch files, out-of-date computer hardware, overflowing bins, and a tray of variegated mugs with a massive teapot. The only difference was the usual grumpy faces sat at the desks were older. Much older.

'Over here, love.' A woman stood up over to his left. Slight build. Fifty something, with steel-grey hair buzzed short at the side, and longer on top. 'Sorry, you missed the sandwich run.' She bit into a bacon and egg buttie, and a trail of yoke ran down her thumb. She chewed. 'Dump your stuff there and do us a favour – make a brew.' The yoke was licked off, and she sat back down. 'By the way, I'm Fay Nash, your supervisor, in case you were thinking of telling me to bugger off.'

Stallard shrugged for the second time that morning. The perfect start. Charismatic undercover officer to tea boy in one easy move. He navigated his way towards Nash through an obstacle course of document trolleys and abandoned exhibit bags. He was conscious that the room had gone silent, and could feel twenty pairs of eyes boring into him, and making their own tendentious evaluations. Always judge a book by its cover. That's what cops do. That's why they sit in the corner of a pub or café, so they can people-watch with prejudice.

As he got closer, he could hear the giggles behind him. Then stifled laughs and whispers. He plonked the box down and spun round. All eyes reverted to their screens, but some shoulders were still bobbing. He threw open his arms, and addressed the room.

'Go on then, take a good look at the freak.' He pirouetted and shook his ponytail. 'Roll up, roll up. The circus is coming to town. Lock up your daughters.'

Nobody spoke or looked up. Sod it. He sat down.

Fay Nash rolled up close to him on her chair. 'Okay, you're different. Well, so am I.' She put her half-eaten buttie down. 'But they're good people, so don't treat them with contempt.'

'Sorry. Twenty weeks off work has left me a bit twitchy.'

'How did you go on with Hardcastle?'

'I think someone must have pissed on his Coco Pops.'

'He's a cuddly grizzly bear.'

'No, he's a miserable bastard.'

'Just old school.' Nash picked up her sandwich again. 'How many times did he mention the Burlington Estate murders?'

'Only once.'

'That's a record. He must like you.' She took a big bite and chewed. 'Tea. You're supposed to be mashing.'

Stallard took a tray from the windowsill, and found a small kitchenette down the corridor. It looked like the first mash since Friday. The mugs had thick tide-marks, and the carton of milk was lumpy and rancid. When he got back there was a box on his chair, tied up with red legal ribbon.

Fay Nash said, 'Present for you.'

'It's not my birthday.' He put the tray down and picked it up.

'It's your first case, courtesy of Mr Hardcastle.'

He read the typed label: Misper – DOANE, J.N.M. 'A missing person? Why can't I have a juicy unsolved murder?'

'You know what they say, every misper is a potential murder.'

'Yeah, like every fart's a potential turd, but most of the time it's just wind.' He untied the tape and removed the lid. The original handwritten missing-from-home form was paper-clipped to the top bundle of documents. 'Wait a minute. This case is only five months old. I thought reviews were done after a year.'

'They are, unless fresh evidence comes up in the meantime.'

'So, what's come up?'

'A body in the Humber estuary. Literally.' Fay Nash laughed, showing off a silver tongue-piercing. 'Though it won't be exactly fresh after this long. Post mortem's in Hull at half ten, and Mr H wants you there. How strong is your stomach?'

'I thought you said he liked me?'

She wrinkled her nose. 'Guess I was wrong.'

'And I don't need a baby-sitter?'

'Dead bodies and pathologists aren't the general public. Is it a problem?'

'No, I can't wait. Who doesn't love the scent of rotting flesh on a Monday morning?' Stallard picked the tray of mugs back up, and trudged over to the window. So much for being eased back into work through recuperative duties. This could be the longest seven days of his life.

Chapter 3

Stallard emptied the box onto his new, temporary desk, and rifled through the documents. Nothing was numbered, categorised or cross-referenced. 'Where are you supposed to start?' He threw a statement onto the pile and flopped back in his chair. 'I give up. It's a crock of shit.'

'Welcome to the world of the cold case review.' Nash raised her mug in a mock toast. 'The detectives on the Major Crime Team think they're film stars, hence filing stuff in a proper manner is beneath them. If you're in a hurry, just read the CSR.'

'The what?'

'The Current Situation Report. Every case is filed with one, and we update it after every review. If you can't find the hard copy, have a look on the system.'

Stallard leafed through the papers looking for it twice, then gave up again. 'Do me a favour, Fay. I'm a bit rusty on the force IT. Please…'

'You want me to print you the CSR?' Nash was typing. 'Anything else boss? Grout your bathroom?

Wipe your bum?' She rolled her eyes and tutted. 'Give me a minute.'

He waited. The clock was ticking. The dead body in Hull mortuary wasn't going anywhere fast, but he didn't want to give Hardcastle any excuse to do him down. Mention of his possibly not going back to the undercover unit had come out of the blue, and unsettled him. Being a UC was his dream job. It was the only thing he'd ever been good at, though admittedly it had come at a cost – mentally over the years, and then physically at the Blue Butterfly.

The thought that at the end of his recuperative duties he might get posted back to a general CID office made him feel angry and on edge. Why had nobody in HR sat down with him and talked through what was happening? Mushroom management at its finest – kept in the dark and fed shit. All he'd had was one welfare visit from his UC inspector, and a call from a personnel clerk saying he wasn't fit for frontline duties.

Now, here he was in geriatric wonderland. He looked round the office, and it could have been a building society or insurance brokers. People were just sitting at workstations on the phone or tapping away at keyboards. Battery detectives. He preferred to be out and about, free-range, bouncing off human contact in all its glorious forms.

Eventually, Nash finished what she was doing and printed the CSR. Stallard grabbed it and jogged the back staircase down to the car park.

The Cold Case Unit didn't have their own pool vehicles, so he jumped in his personal chariot – a battered Jeep. The bodywork was half rust, half fibre-glass patches, but it never needed cleaning and the engine would run another hundred years. It suited him. The last thing he wanted was anything approaching ordinary.

Rush hour had tailed off, and traffic was flowing freely on Sheffield's southern ring road. He followed it along the valley side, with its blocks of post-war maisonettes, and then cut off through a faceless retail park, and dropped onto the road heading out east into the sun.

The day was already hot. June had broken all records, and now July was shaping up to follow suit. On the radio, The Beach Boys were picking up good vibrations, and because there was no air-con, all the Jeep windows were down, and half the city was getting drenched in Californian surf.

Soon, yellow diversion signs started to appear at the side of the road, and then the vehicles up ahead began to bunch. Roadworks. Things slowed to a walking pace. He reached for the Current Situation Report on the passenger seat, and hitched the mirror sunglasses up onto his forehead. Turned the radio down so he could concentrate.

DOANE, Joseph Noel Michael, aged 21 years. Reported missing on the fourth of February by his sister. His vehicle, a Ford Pickup, registered number RG06 STR had been found by council workmen the previous day near to the Humber Bridge, apparently abandoned. CCTV footage for the relevant 24-hour period has been checked and is negative.

On the 17th of October last year, divisional drug-squad officers executed a search warrant at the home address of DOANE, and recovered 60 grams of what was believed to be heroin. He was arrested, and exercised his right not to comment during subsequent police interviews. He was bailed to return to the police station on the 5th of December, pending forensic examination of the drugs. Following representations from his solicitor, this date was extended until Monday the 3rd of February this year, which is the day his vehicle was found abandoned in the early hours.

Something about the name seemed familiar. He was busy rifling through his brain's filing cabinets when there was a shout in his right ear: *Hey, tosser. Watch the road.* He turned to see a cyclist, ginger dreadlocks pouring out from beneath her helmet. She had a smartphone pointing in his face through the window, and took a snap, before cycling off. Great. That would be on Driving-Like-a-Twat.Com later or some other website. To make it worse, she wore a circle-A T-shirt, showing off her anarchist credentials, while acting as the self-appointed enforcer of petty, authoritarian state rules. Bloody hypocrite.

Tests on the powder recovered from DOANE's flat confirmed it to be a controlled opiate drug. Had he answered bail on the 3rd of February, the Crown Prosecution Service had taken a decision that he would have been charged under the Misuse of Drugs Act 1971. He had no previous convictions, and no other matters pending.

Following extensive enquiries, summarised later in this report, it is believed that DOANE took his own life. This is despite information indicating that he had

been murdered, which led to the case being referred to
the Major Crime Team. To date, a body has not been
recovered. Searches of the…

Traffic started to move. It was like the stopper being pulled from a bottle. In no time, he coasted past the Rasta cyclist, and gave her a friendly wave with his middle finger. Then took a left and looped round to join the link road heading out towards the motorway. Just as he was merging into the nearside lane, it came to him out of the blue.

JOEY. Of course, it was bloody Joey. Joey Doane, the frontman with The Magic Rats, who everybody said were going to be the next Arctic Monkeys. Not that this counted for much, because every time a half-decent band appeared on the Sheffield music scene, they were always going to be the next Arctic Monkeys. It had been the same now for the past ten years. The next Arctic Monkeys – instant kiss of death. Never fails.

One junction down the M1, he peeled off onto the M18. There were a lot of wagons heading out towards the container ports, and a few caravans on their way to resorts a little further up the coast. The landscape soon became flat. Field after field had been scorched straw-coloured by weeks of south Mediterranean weather.

The disappearance of Joey Doane was bothering him. Why didn't he know about it? The Magic Rats weren't the biggest band in the world, but locally they were right up there. Since last summer there had been a buzz about them. They were the band to see, and he had seen them. It was part business, part pleasure, and he smiled at the memory. Fucking great band. Now it looked like their leader had topped himself over a few bags of smack. It must have been in the news. Why didn't he know about it?

The miles rolled by, and gradually Stallard realised what a sizeable chunk of the year he'd missed. It felt like the blink of an eye, but the reality was different. Three weeks in ICU, followed by four on a general ward. Then a month laid up at home, and a fortnight at the police convalescence home in Harrogate. When he got back from that, Laura took her entire year's annual leave, and stayed with him. He trained outside four hours a day, and was fitter than he'd ever been before, but inside his head there was a black hole. A chapter of life he'd simply skipped. Missed and gone forever. No flicking back through the pages.

He picked up the signs for Hull and veered right for the M62. The traffic noise went up a few notches, so he wound up the windows, and instantly felt the back of his shirt become sticky.

He tried to picture Joey Doane, and saw a fuzzy image of a curly-haired kid with slightly buck-teeth. No looker, but attitude in spades. Funny thing was, Stallard had only seen him the one time, but had identified with him straight away. There was an instant connection. Maybe it was because he recognised one of life's fellow misfits, or maybe it was more personal.

Stallard cast his mind back to his own youthful exploits on guitar. The band he formed at school were just skateboard punks, who morphed into half-competent rockers, and who knew where music might have taken them? *Phff…* He snorted a laugh. Probably not very far, but that wasn't the point. When you reach one of life's T-junctions and turn left instead of right, you'll always wonder where the other road went to. A shithole or stardom? He'd always regretted taking the safe route of university and steady employment. Maybe that's why he was getting more reckless as he got older.

Would he recognise Joey if the body on the slab was his? Unlikely, after five months marinating in mud and diluted sewage. There was a strength and spark in Joey that shone out and lit up a room. He was definitely not the sort you'd think would dodge life's troubles by ending it all, but then they seldom are, the desperate souls who see no alternative. Still, for some reason suicide didn't seem likely. It didn't feel right.

Who would want to kill Joey Doane? Lead singers can be annoying arseholes. It goes with the territory. Look at Liam or Van the Man. But mild annoyance is not usually a motive for killing someone, otherwise the prisons would be full. Joey must have done something else. Stolen the wrong person's money or girlfriend. Disrespected the wrong psychopath. Become embroiled in a vendetta between two feuding families or warring gangs.

Stallard was curious. Eighty miles an hour was too fast to be reading at the wheel, so he took the next exit, and found a shaded layby on the B1230. There was a caravan that catered for truckers, and he bought a bacon bap and a black coffee. The Current Situation Report was written up in the usual police jargon. He sat with it and his breakfast on the bonnet, and skim-read until he found what he was looking for.

Within 48 hours of DOANE being reported missing, information was received from a source to the effect that he had been the victim of a contract killing. The two men named as taking out the contract were Brandon QUINN and Baxter QUINN, brothers who run a company called Southpaw Investments and Management. In October last year, this company had become agents for The Magic Rats, a band fronted by DOANE, and recently secured a recording contract with a multi-national label.

Stallard re-read the paragraph. No, his eyes had not deceived him. His old friends, the fraternal scumbags Brandon and Baxter were managers of The Magic Rats, and purportedly legitimate, musical impresarios. Pigs might handglide. He read on.

The informant believed that the QUINN brothers had supplied DOANE with the heroin seized by police in a raid on his flat. They feared that when DOANE answered bail at the police station, he would name them as the source of the drugs. Extensive enquiries were carried out to corroborate this information, but to date, there is no evidence or intelligence to support it. Telecoms analysis, CCTV, house to house, witness interviews...

Blah, blah, blah. Why is everything about drugs? He checked his watch. Shit. What was left of the sandwich went in the bin.

The mortuary at Hull Royal Infirmary was split on two levels. A duplex of death. The main cutting room, with five tables, was downstairs, but the specials' suite was on the floor above. Specials were forensic or high-risk cases, and that's where Stallard found the Home Office pathologist already masked up in her scrubs standing in the doorway. All he could see were her eyes, but they looked pretty sparky for ones that spent so much of their waking hours staring at the obscenity of unnatural death, and bearing witness to man's cruelty to fellow man.

She had her hands on her hips.

'You're late.'

'Late is such a judgemental, little word. I prefer chronologically challenged.' Stallard smiled.

'I prefer drinking cocktails to dissecting cadavers, but guess what, here I am, on time and waiting.'

He couldn't tell if she was smiling back at him, but there was a bit of crinkling at the sides of her eyes, so he kept his own ticking over. 'I'm a professional drinker, but even I don't start this early.'

'Good time-keeping is good manners.'

'I know. Better three hours too soon than a minute late.'

'Did you get that in a fortune cookie, or a self-help book?' She started to swap her slip-ons for a pair of white Wellington boots.

'Merry Wives of Windsor, Act two, Scene two.'

'Ooh.' She looked up. 'A cop who quotes Shakespeare. How quaint.'

'And you thought I was just a pretty face. Go on, admit it.' He went all wide-eyed and innocent. 'I'm offended.'

She said something under her breath, but he couldn't hear it for the industrial extractor fans that had kicked in. First day back at work, and he was flirting with the Home

Office pathologist. It was like riding a bike. No stabilisers, just straight back in the saddle. Shame he'd fallen off so many times in the past, but it was all part of life's bumpy journey. He started to follow her into the room, but she stopped him.

'You need a forensic suit and hairnet or observe from next door. It's your choice.' She pointed to a window.

'I'd look stupid as a giant tea bag.' He was glad of the excuse to get out of smelling distance before the ominous parcel he could see on the slab was unzipped, so he backed out into the corridor.

The adjacent room was much better. As well as the viewing window, it had a monitor which relayed live footage from a ceiling camera directly above the autopsy site. A bird's eye view of the main event. He took a seat and watched as two police Scenes of Crime officers came in, booted and suited. One to video, the other to take stills and exhibits. They agreed a plan of action with the pathologist, and approached the stainless-steel table.

At first, the bag was unzipped, then cut away with scissors and rolled up, before being sealed in its own exhibit bag. There was still no sign of the body. It was wrapped in thick plastic sheeting, tied up with nylon rope. The ropes and the sheeting were cut, and slid away, to be sealed in a separate bag. Water ran off into the gullies of the table. Stallard felt cold. The body wasn't much more than a torso with one and a half legs. No head or arms. The skin was ivory and wax-like, and a femur poked out from an area of discoloured tissue.

The pathologist with the nice eyes walked around the body, and bent down a few times to enable a closer examination. Then she came over to the viewing window, and spoke through a filter-covered hatch.

'Relax, it's not your guy.'

Stallard walked over. 'How can you be so sure?'

'Because of the vagina.'

'Really?'

'Do you want to come in and check for yourself?'

'No, I just thought someone might have noticed before now.'

'Take it up with Humberside's Body Recovery Team, but they'll tell you it's not their job to make any kind of initial assessment.' She seemed to be smiling again behind the mask. 'And this body hasn't been in water for a few months. I would say more like years, but it's hard to be definitive.'

'Thanks. Whose time has been wasted now?'

'Quid pro quo. Perhaps we'll meet again when another one washes up.'

'Next time, I'll be three hours early.'

Stallard was already out in the corridor, when she called him back.

'There's one thing you might want to check,' she said. 'Three weeks after your man went missing, a body was found on the north shore, and I did the PM. Massive organ failure caused by impact onto the water. Even though there'd been some bloating and decomposition, the initial feeling was that it could be the missing musician from Sheffield, but then your detectives came back and said it wasn't.'

'Do you know who these detectives were?'

'It'll be in the file. See the mortuary manager downstairs.'

The mortuary manager was called Scott. Stallard found him in the main body-storage area. He had dark rings round his eyes, and pink hair that made him look like a punk panda. Scott remembered the case. The client, reference number 4659, was still upstairs, taking up one of his eight, precious long-term freezer spaces. It was unusual for clients to remain unidentified for so long, but occasionally it did happen. The last one was a seasonal fruit-picker from Romania, who clocked up twenty-seven months. Talk about overstaying your welcome. It all depended on whether families or friends contacted the police, and whether the right lines of communication were then followed.

Stallard nodded. Calling them clients made it sound as though they were booking in for a stay at the Holiday Inn. Perhaps it was a mortuary-technician joke. Something to lighten up the chilly atmosphere of constant cadaver-handling. He asked if he could view the client, and Scott said he was welcome, but there were photographs of the deceased in the file, and he was probably better looking at those. Excellent idea. They went to Scott's office and he pulled the file of client 4659.

As soon as he saw the first photograph, doubts came crawling into Stallard's mind. He'd seen a photograph of Joey on the original missing-from-home form back in the cold case unit, and he'd seen him on stage in the flesh, but he just couldn't be sure. The face in the PM photo was puffy, with cuts and abrasions; the hair was lank and straggly, and the last time he'd seen eyes like that was Sainsbury's fish counter. Still, he wasn't sure. There's nothing like death to drain your features of their recognisable quirks, and transform you into a stranger.

A buzzer sounded in the office, and a CCTV screen showed an undertaker's van waiting outside the roller-shutter doors. Scott said he needed to go. Stallard borrowed a pen and paper, and rifled through the file for the name of the police contact. There it was. On the 9th of March, Detective Sergeant Coleman from the South Yorkshire constabulary had contacted the mortuary, and informed them that following DNA checks, it had been established that the deceased was not Joseph Noel Michael Doane. Definitive and final.

Stallard took one more look at the photograph before he put it back in the file. Funny. Now he was sure that corpse 4659 was Joey from The Magic Rats. But that was impossible, wasn't it?

CHAPTER 4

There was a little square bag stuck in the middle of the Jeep's windscreen. A fixed penalty notice. 'Guess it's going to be one of those days,' said Stallard to no one but a seagull that was picking over a discarded Styrofoam chip-tray on the pavement. He tore the parking ticket off, and threw it onto the passenger seat. Back in the undercover unit, they had a secret slush fund to take care of such mundane irritations, but he knew there wasn't much hope of Hardcastle dipping into the corporate coffers to pay a fine. More chance of squeezing milk from a rattlesnake's breast.

When he switched his phone back on, there was a message from Laura. *How's it going?* He started the engine and fired one back. *Expensive, but haven't been stabbed yet.* To which he added three smiley faces and two hearts. Then he remembered the condition that had been added to his recuperative duties, aimed at protecting him from confrontation. As head of the Occupation Health Unit, Laura wouldn't have been directly involved in the practicalities of his return-to-work plan, but she must have been aware of it, and yet chose not to say anything to him. Her professionalism was so irritating.

The sun was overhead. The lady voicing Google Maps told him to keep straight ahead for the M62, but he saw the north tower of the suspension bridge looming in a haze on the left, and decided to turn off and loop back around, so he could take a look at the potential site of Joey Doane's death.

Signs took him to the Humber Bridge visitor centre, where there was a free car park, and he made the rest of the way on foot, safe in the knowledge there were no hit-and-run fixed-penalty bandits. It was hard work in the heat and fumes. The pedestrian walkway was a few feet below the main carriageway, and stretched off south into the distance, a curving ribbon of black, flanked by grey steel cables and railings. He walked slowly and deliberately, trying to picture what it would have been like in the middle of a February night. Black and icy. Not like now, when wagons thundered past, and the tarmac was hot enough to fry onions.

Where would Joey have done it? Bang in the middle, or closer to one of the banks? It had to be the middle, where the drop was greatest, and a despairing mind would see symbolism in its equidistance from human refuge. It was a mile and a half, and felt further. By the time Stallard reached it, a breeze coming up the estuary had dried the sweat on his face, and his eyes were stinging with salt crystals.

He stopped and faced the railings. They came up to his chin, to make sure nobody was going to go over the side without making a real effort. He grabbed hold of the bars and felt their reassuring stability. Two or three times in his own past, he'd had dark thoughts, but had never got this close to a place where they could be carried out. It was a strange feeling. He pulled himself up, so that the top of the railings wedged in his stomach, and his upper body pivoted out over the abyss.

He closed his eyes and thought about Joey Doane. The brash showman with so much living still ahead of him, and the coquette fame beckoning him with her faithless finger. Would he really have taken his own life at that point in time? How fucked up would his head have been to even think about it?

When he opened his eyes and looked down, all he saw was deep blue. He closed his eyes again, and imagined how Joey might have given himself another push, and tipped into the void, his body rolling head over heels in freefall. What would he have felt? Panic or calm resolve? Then the impact, as skull, torso and limbs hit a wall of water at ninety miles an hour, and shock the vital organs into hoped-for instant and final failure. No more life. Just a beat-up carcass, like the one labelled 4659 in the long-term freezer cabinet.

Stallard felt himself fall, and his bloodstream flooded with an overdose of hormones that whacked his heart muscles like a steam-hammer. Bang. Bang. Bang. When he opened his eyes, he was face down on the pedestrian walkway, and clinging to it like it was the deck of a ship in a biblical storm. He was dizzy and hyperventilating. After a while, he crawled a few paces, and rolled over onto his back, trying to take slow and shallow breaths. Fuck.

Imagination is a great thing, but too much can cause problems. He looked up at the big sky and began to laugh.

A shadow fell across him. 'Are you all right, mate?'

Stallard screwed up his eyes, and saw a middle-aged couple, with rucksacks and floppy hats. The man coughed and spoke again. 'Sorry, but are you all right, mate?'

'Never better, pal,' said Stallard. 'Never better.'

The couple hesitated, then continued on their way across the bridge.

Stallard stood up, and dusted himself down. The funny thing was, he did feel good. Sometimes, there's nothing better to pep you up than looking death in the eye. It gives you the kind of kick up the arse that makes you feel good to be alive, and puts the rest of the world into perspective. The problem is, it doesn't always last too long.

The walk back along the bridge to the car was surreal. Nothing significant in the universe had taken place since the time he strode out to the middle, but something intangible had changed. He felt different, and it wasn't just the adrenalin levels settling back down. It was the settled belief that Joey Doane had been unlawfully killed at this very spot. Sixth sense? Educated hunch? Call it what you want. Stallard was new to this cold case malarky, but he knew you don't get a feel for a job just sat in an office.

When he got back, it was feeding time at the old folks' home. Everybody was at their desks with lunch boxes, and soft fruit and cups of tea. The sun had moved a few degrees around the building, and was now gently baking the oversize windows that ran the full length of one wall, turning the office into a greenhouse. No air-con or blinds, just a few vintage fans whirring back and forth, and a message someone had scrawled up on the white board – *Club Tropicana, drinks are free...*

The place stank of egg mayo and chicken tikka. Stallard gave it a few minutes, and then slipped out, taking one of the Joey Doane files with him. He needed fresh air and cold beer. The Cold Case Unit shared a shabby, concrete cop-shop with the uniform response team that covered the south of the city, and it took him a while to find a pub in the suburbs.

When he did, it was a soulless all-day eatery, but Guinness is difficult to screw up, even for crap chain-joints, and especially if you add some dry cider, so he took a pint of the stout, with a spare glass and a bottle of Bulmer's into the beer garden, and mixed his own cocktail in the sunshine. Black Velvet a la Stallard. The first didn't touch the sides, so he ordered two more and settled down to read some more about the mysterious vanishing act of The Magic Rats' lead singer and songwriter.

Before he could open the file, his phone buzzed with a message. It was from Frank, wanting to meet up as a matter of urgency. Everything was urgent with Frank – all capital letters and exclamation marks. He was Stallard's Cover Officer in the UC Unit for the past eight years, so they'd lived in each other's pockets, and become closer than brothers. It was the primary role of a Cover Officer to keep his UC safe, and the incident in the Blue Butterfly had hit Frank hard. Failure wasn't something he was used to, so for the last five months he'd been over-compensating, and pestering the life out of Stallard with endless visits and phone calls. Guilt is a hard task master.

Stallard thought about ignoring it, but gave in, and replied with his location. Fifteen minutes later, Frank slapped him on the back.

'How's it going with the old gimmers?'

'Laugh a minute. That's why I'm sat here on my own getting spannered.'

'Do they let you park in the disabled bay?'

'Piss off.'

'Same again?'

'What do you think?'

Frank disappeared inside. He was the size of a double-decker bus, and had to duck through the doorway. When he came back with the drinks, he had his game face on.

'I've got some bad news.'

'There's no more Guinness?'

'It's serious, Harry.'

'The doctor's put you on a diet?'

'Karina's gone missing.'

'Thank fuck for that.' Stallard sighed and shook his head. 'I thought you were going to tell me that they'd filled my place in the unit, and there was no way back.'

'You're not bothered that the girl who nearly killed you has buggered off?'

'She was a victim.'

'No, an illegal immigrant.'

'Who was trafficked into the UK to be a sex slave.'

'She should have been in a secure detention centre instead of a refuge.'

'How would that have looked in court? Locking up a witness?'

Frank smacked the table. 'She should have been charged.'

'It was self-defence.'

'Was it hell. You were trying to help her. I heard it all on the audio feed, remember?'

'Look, forget it, Frank. It was me she stabbed, not you, and I forgive her. The only thing I want is my old job back.' That wasn't strictly true, thought Stallard, because he also wanted Jared Finn to go to prison for a long time, and it would also be nice to know what Karina had said just before she put a knife in his ribs, but sometimes in life you can't have everything.

Frank shook his head and took a long pull on his pint of lager. Then he took a few deep breaths and puffed. He wasn't built for heat, and tears of sweat were bursting from his hairline and rolling down his face. The hair itself didn't move. He was older than Stallard, and liked to keep his pitch-black hair looking good with plenty of products. Nobody at work said anything, because it was his one and only touchy area, and he could be a nasty, violent bastard. Gentle giants are for fairy stories, not specialist police units tackling organised crime.

'Thought you were Premier League, anyway,' said Frank.

'What do you mean?'

'Best UC in the region.'

'I am, but keep it to yourself. Nobody likes a bighead.' Stallard grinned. He knew where this was going. They'd had a permutation of the same conversation every day for weeks. Ever since he'd been well enough to receive visitors.

'So, how come a girl got you with a sucker punch?'

'You know why.'

'Do I?'

'Someone fucked up.'

'Yes, it was you. Bloody amateur.'

'You had one job.'

'You walked straight into her trap.'

'Don't be daft.' Stallard skimmed a beer mat across the picnic table, and got Frank on the side of his head. He laughed. 'You're still bitter because you never had the brains or physique to be a UC.'

'I'm glad I don't look like a heroin addict.'

'If we ever have to infiltrate a gang of thick-as-pig-shit pie-munchers, you're the man.'

Frank leaned over and grabbed Stallard's collar. 'You calling me fat?'

'And stupid. Don't forget stupid.'

'Think you're clever, don't you?' Frank pulled him across the table, so they were nose to nose.

'Yes.' Stallard puckered up, and tried to kiss Frank on the lips.

The big man let go and pushed him away, shouting, 'Get off me, you mad chuff.'

Two men in shirts and ties on the next table looked askance and edged further away. A girl collecting glasses froze, and then scuttled back inside the pub, as though she was going to tell the manager. Stallard smiled. It was like old times.

The afternoon drifted on. Frank filled Stallard in on the latest gossip in the unit – who had left their wife or husband, and who had gone back home – and what the latest operations being developed were. They were busier than ever. The main job was a firearms importation from Ukraine, being facilitated through a private airfield, and they had some web-based extortion cases bubbling. It made Stallard realise the world hadn't stopped, and someone had stepped into his shoes. The king is dead, long live the king.

He told Frank about Joey from The Magic Rats, but it didn't mean anything to him. Music was for wimps, and putting ringtones on his phone.

'We saw them at the Shapeshifter Club last year,' said Stallard. 'I was working and you called in to check up on me.'

'It was just noise.'

'Old git.'

'I remember the girl. Bit of a looker.'

'Joey's sister on keyboards.'

'She can tickle my ivories any day.'

Stallard shook his head. 'Thought you'd packed that game in?'

'I have,' said Frank. He checked his watch. 'Shit, got to go.' Drained his glass. 'Meeting an informant.'

'Yeah, pumping her for information.'

'Shut up. It's not like that.' Frank hoisted himself up, and headed off between some bushes towards the car park. A lumbering bulk on a mission.

The Joseph Doane file was still lying closed on the table, like it had been for the last few hours. Stallard was feeling drowsy, from booze and the heat. He opened the file, and finished reading the Current Situation Report. There wasn't much extra of interest, just a list of routine enquiries that are carried out for any long-term missing person, copied from a national template. Policing by numbers. It was signed off at the end by Detective Sergeant

1139 Coleman, the same officer who had eliminated the corpse in Hull mortuary.

Then he thumbed through the rest of the file, and soon realised most of it comprised a series of thirty or forty typewritten letters, all addressed to DS Coleman. Page after page, in the same small font and each with the same five-word heading: The MURDER of JOSEPH DOANE. They were sent by Shannon Doane, who had signed each one, and added handwritten postscripts emphasising the need for urgent action. That was back in March.

Stallard poured the last of the cider into the stout, and watched it froth up. It was time to go home, but something about the case had got under his skin and given him an inquisitive itch. Perhaps it was just that he'd been off work for so long, or maybe because he felt this strange, personal connection to Joey, purely on the basis of seeing him perform on stage a total of once. The fact that the Quinn brothers were involved was ominous and in his own mind, made it personal. He still couldn't believe that those two psychos were managing a band like The Magic Rats.

Should he call it a day and go home, or try and find out a bit more about Joey? *Fuck it.*

He picked up his phone and rang Shannon Doane.

CHAPTER 5

It was pushing six, when Stallard slipped the mirror shades into his top pocket and plipped the locks on the Jeep. The car was a pile of shit, but in this area nothing was safe. It was a part of the city that estate agents called *up-and-coming*, but a more objective epithet might be The Land That Time Forgot. It was a warren of narrow streets, lined with terraced houses that had their numbers daubed on the brickwork in white paint to match those on the bins blocking the pavement. A continental grocer's cowered behind steel shutters, and a couple of other corner shops were boarded up, and covered in graffiti. It was where second-year university students used to live, before new apartment blocks sprang up down by the river, and lured them all away with promises of a trendy, urban vibe. Now the area was just rag-tag mix of private renters and rehoused asylum seekers. A place people didn't stay long.

Stallard hadn't forgotten the restriction imposed on his return-to-work duties by the Occupational Health Unit – no unaccompanied contact with the general public.

What the hell? Anybody would think he was mentally fragile and who exactly was he supposed to get hold of to come and chaperone him at this time? The rest of the Cold Case Unit would already be at home eating their shepherd's pies, or other easily chewed TV meals.

Shannon Doane opened the door with a scowl, and looked him up and down.

'Are you a real detective or what?'

'I'm a *what*.' He smiled. 'All the real detectives are busy cleaning their massive magnifying glasses.'

'Very funny. Now show me some ID.'

'I don't carry any.'

'A police officer without a warrant card?'

'It's a long story.'

'Goodbye.' Shannon started to close the door.

'Wait.' He held up his hands. 'I have got a warrant card at home, but it spoils the cut of these jeans.' He didn't want to tell her that UCs never carry identification. Never, ever, ever, for fear of being found out, and getting both legs broken or worse. 'Ask me a question. Go on, one that only a real detective would know the answer to.'

She peered through the gap in the door, and the scowl softened. 'What am I supposed to think? You ring me out of the blue, then turn up looking like the bastard child of Lemmy from Motorhead and Joan Jet, with no form of ID.'

He laughed at the description. 'Sorry, I just want to help find Joey.'

'Come in.' The door opened.

The last time he'd seen Shannon Doane, she'd been on stage and looked different – letterbox-lipstick and beehive hair, with big black mascara eyes, and a short, spangly dress straight out of the sixties. That was a special night. Stallard had worked at the Shapeshifter Club for a couple of months to develop his UC backstory or *legend*, as they call it in the unit. The place was a rundown dive, and most of the bands pulled in a handful of students and bohemian weirdos. Probably their own friends and long-suffering relatives. That day The Magic Rats played was different. It was packed, and the crowd bounced along to every number, mouthing lyrics of songs that had never been released by a record company, just uploaded to YouTube. Yet, they knew every word. There were crowd-surfers, flying plastic glasses, and sweat, sweat and more sweat. It was electric.

Now, she was in a vest, shorts and flip-flops. He followed her through towards an off-shot kitchen, where she went straight to the sink, and began to fill the kettle.

'Tea or coffee?'

'Coffee.' He stopped in the dining room that had been turned into an office, and began looking at the photographs pinned to a corkboard. There was one of Shannon and Joey, with an older couple arm in arm on a windswept beach. 'Is that mum and dad?'

'Yes, they still take us away once a year. That's Whitby.'

They looked a proud couple, but older than Stallard had imagined. Mum was petite with a silver bob, and dad was tall, with a shock of wavy hair, and a bit of a stoop.

'Which is the most recent one of Joey?'

Shannon stepped back into the office and pointed at one with the spout of the kettle.

'That's the day The Magic Rats signed their first recording contract. Look at his face, and tell me that's someone who would throw themselves off a bridge two weeks later.'

Stallard studied the seven by five print. Joey wasn't the greatest looking kid. His hair was too curly, and his front teeth needed a bit of work, but he had *it*. Like Lydon and Morrissey had *it*. In the photograph, he was standing on the tail of an old Ford truck, with a Fender Jazz bass in one hand, and a tin of Carling in the other, screaming down the lens. There was something that looked like the pure love of life burning in his eyes. The camera never lies, or does it? Maybe on the other side of the mask was a dark, troubled soul.

Funny things, genes, thought Stallard, and took another glance at Shannon. Her brother was an ugly kid, whereas she had more the classic good looks. Huge hazel eyes and cheekbones that could chop onions or peel a Granny Smith. Perhaps her mouth was a bit big, and her nose a bit snub, but perfection is subjective. In another life, he could have seen himself falling for her, especially when she scowled at him from behind the Chrissie Hynde fringe. But this wasn't another life, and he had a job to do.

'Maybe he was worried about answering bail, and getting charged with drug offences?'

'Joey?' Shannon laughed. 'He couldn't give a monkey's. The biggest danger was that he'd forget to turn up.'

'Then court appearances, and possibly prison?'

'Both his solicitors said that the worst he would get was community service.'

'Both?'

'He sacked his first one.'

'Because?'

'No reason.' She shook her head. 'That's Joey – he can be a prick sometimes.' Her lip wobbled. 'I mean he could be, past tense.' She went back into the kitchen, and sat the kettle in its base. 'I guess that's lead vocalists for you.'

Stallard's mind's eye went straight back to the Shapeshifter gig, and saw Joey and Shannon harmonising together, like great sibling songsters of the past: The Everly Brothers, the Jacksons, the Carpenters, Ray and Dave Davies, Donny and Marie. Okay, maybe not Donny and Marie.

'Did that cause tension in the band?'

'Yeah, we all hated each other. Is that what you want to hear?' When she turned around, she was dabbing her eyes with a piece of kitchen roll. 'And before you ask, I wasn't shagging either Tyler or Mickey.'

'I'm not interested in that.' Stallard quickly tried to picture the other two band members. Tyler was the guitarist, with an Elvis quiff, and an annoying habit of standing with one foot on the stage monitor, and waggling his backside towards the audience. Mickey, he couldn't recall in any great detail – just your average Duracell bunny bashing away non-stop all night in a cap-sleeved T-shirt to show off his biceps. That's drummers for you.

'DS Coleman seemed to be more interested in my love life than finding Joey's killers.'

Stallard shrugged. 'Perhaps he was looking for possible motives.'

'He wasn't going to find any staring at my chest, was he?'

'Tell me about the drugs.' Stallard was quick to change the subject.

'It's a rock and roll band, not a church choir.'

'So, you were all using?'

'Not me.' Shannon took a coffee jar out of an overhead cupboard. 'They used to call me Mother Teresa.'

'Because you're a saint?'

'It's my middle name, and I'm so, so old. Joey's seven years younger than me – so are Tyler and Mickey.'

'But the rest of the band were doing heroin?'

Shannon slammed the coffee jar down on the worktop. 'Forget the rest of the bloody band and drugs. It's not important.'

'Let me decide.'

'Please yourself.' Shannon took out a couple of mugs and banged them down. Her hands were shaking. 'All I know, is that we'd just finished our first proper tour, and there'd been no problems. Whatever happened off stage, it didn't affect anyone's performance.' She stared off into space. 'We were tight... buzzing... on fire... night after night to full houses, and at proper venues, not pokey, little places.'

'That must have been some feeling.'

'It was like walking on air. It's hard to describe. Joey said he felt like a god or king of the world. That's all he'd ever wanted, so why would he...' She drifted off.

Stallard saw something move on her cheek, and it took a moment before he realised it was a teardrop.

'Had he done anything like it before?'

'What?'

'Gone missing?'

'No.' She wiped her eyes. 'Not like this.' Blew her nose on the kitchen roll. 'Sometimes we couldn't get hold of him for a few days, but he always turned up.' She laughed and sniffed. 'Been on a bender somewhere – he didn't do things by halves.'

Stallard smiled at the thought of a kindred spirit. 'You wrote letters claiming to have evidence he'd been murdered?'

Shannon reached for the coffee jar, but caught it with the back of her hand, and it tipped over, emptying granules all over the steel draining board.

'Shit.' She started to scoop it back in. 'Sorry.' Water in the ridges soaked into the granules. She stopped and put her hands in front of her face. 'Why does everything go wrong?'

'Don't worry about the coffee. It's overrated.'

'Sod it.' She opened another cupboard, and pulled out a bottle of Jack Daniels. 'This is my drug of choice.'

He made his voice an octave lower, and threw in a bit of gravel. 'Stand aside coffee – this is a job for alcohol.'

She held up two glasses. 'Do you like whisky?'

'We've got a relationship, but it's on the rocks.'

'You want ice?'

'I was trying to be funny.'

'Do you want some or not?'

'Go on then.'

Shannon poured two generous glasses and took them into the dining room cum office. She passed one to Stallard, and then pointed at a pine bureau, and two full-length bookcases that were crammed with A4 files. They appeared to be colour-coded, and some had dividers, separating them into sub-sets.

'There's your evidence.' She took a large swig of the Jack Daniels.

'All I can see is folders, arranged in a pretty pattern.'

'It's what's inside that will prove Joey was killed by the Quinn brothers.' She spat out the name. 'Our own management company – the horrible, lying pieces of...'

'What's inside?'

She opened the leaf on the pine bureau, and took out a MacBook. 'I've got a website called Justice For Joey, and those files contain hard copies of all the information that people have posted during the last one hundred and twenty-seven days.'

'Posted?' A deep valley appeared between Stallard's eyebrows. 'Are we talking eye-witness accounts from real people, or tittle-tattle from anonymous trolls and bored teenagers sat in their bedrooms?'

Shannon looked down, and nibbled her bottom lip. 'Maybe some real people.'

'No signed confessions then, or photographs or metaphorical smoking guns?'

She looked up, defiance now burning in her eyes. 'I read somewhere that circumstantial evidence can be as compelling in criminal trials as direct evidence.'

'It's true that witnesses can lie or be genuinely mistaken, whereas facts speak for themselves.' He took a drink of Tennessee's finest, and felt it warm his throat. 'Do you have any facts, Miss Doane?'

She held his gaze for a few seconds, and then fetched an armful of folders from the nearest bookcase. She dumped them without ceremony on the table and opened one. For the next fifteen minutes, she went through the contents, eagerly scanning each paragraph, only to sigh in frustration at the end of each page, and turn over to the next one and start again.

Stallard watched her, unsure if she was mad or just desperate. The obsessive and over-organised collation of data was probably displacement activity for something else, but he had no idea what. Maybe it was a coping mechanism or a screen to hide behind.

Finally, she looked up, and the air of defiance had gone. Tears were flooding her eyes and red blotches had spread up her neck and cheeks.

'Please help me find out what happened to my brother.'

Stallard looked at her, and wasn't entirely sure that she wasn't putting on a bit of a performance for his benefit. All the world's a stage, and some are better at acting than others. He should know. Besides, the last time he'd donned his armour and tried to save a maiden in distress, she'd inserted a stiletto knife between his third and fourth rib, and he could still feel it burning. But there was something about the woman in front of him that made him want to try and help. The problem was, she had no evidence, and he only had seven days.

CHAPTER 6

Stallard climbed out of the Jeep and smiled. He couldn't help it. It was the same every time he returned home, even though he was standing in front of a crumbling wreck in an overgrown jungle. Imagination is a powerful tool.

Three years ago, he'd invested an inheritance in a property with a parcel of land in the shadow of the Pennines. It was an old bungalow, which needed knocking down and completely rebuilding, but ever since then he'd been busy. That was why he still lived on-site in a static caravan, while bindweed and dandelion gradually colonised the whole plot, and his planning permission drifted inexorably towards its expiry date. The caravan itself had also seen better days, but he told himself it was just a temporary fix, and one day he'd start the grand redevelopment project. *One day* – those two words that preface many of life's most casual lies.

Laura kissed him on the lips and ran her fingers up and down his ribs.

'How's the war-wound?'

'Killing me.' Stallard kissed her back. He could see a half-drunk bottle of wine on the outdoor table and an open book. He put his arms around her, and squeezed her into him, but there was a wooden feel to her. A tell-tale sign of resistance. 'What's the matter, and don't say *nothing*?'

'Nothing. Tell me about the new job.'

'Is it because I didn't call in at the curry house?'

'No, not really. Although I am bloody starving.' She backed out of his embrace. 'Why do you never keep any food in this place? I'm not cross, it's just, you know...'

'What?'

'I thought the new job was nine to five.'

'Eight until four.'

'Whatever.' She threw her arms up. 'Office hours. An eight-hour period during the daytime that most normal people work.'

They were standing outside the caravan on a square of recycled paving slabs that served as an uneven patio. Stallard shrugged. 'I've never been a nine-to-five man.'

'Master of the under-statement, as ever.' She pulled a sardonic smile. 'There's been weeks when I never heard from you, and had no idea whether you were dead or alive.'

'I was a UC when we met – you know how it works. Some operations I have to go in deep.'

'In who?'

'Stop it, you know it's not like that. We're professionals.'

'Aren't you forgetting that I give counselling to undercover officers, and some of them actually tell me about what they get up to for queen and country, warts and all.' She snatched her glass up, and took a drink of wine, as

47

though it was needed to cleanse the vivid recollections. 'You know, those mandatory counselling sessions that you called a load of bollocks and refused to talk in?'

'I chatted you up, didn't I?'

'God knows how.'

'Okay, so it was just physical attraction.' He stepped nearer and opened his arms to take her in another embrace.

'Oh, no you don't.' She backed off and put out a flat hand. 'The point is, for the last four months it's been like having a proper boyfriend. We've been together, instead of just like passing ships in the night, and I've enjoyed it.'

'I enjoyed it, too.' He risked a little smile.

'Then the very first day back at work, it's like you've never been away.' Her face hardened. 'You roll home four hours late, stinking of booze, and expecting things to go straight back to the chaos of the old days.'

'Is there a problem?'

'You've not changed one bit.'

'Why mess with perfection?'

'You're sad and deluded.'

Stallard was tired. He sat down on one of his plastic, garden chairs, and took off his boots. It was a sticky evening and the light in the caravan windows was starting to attract flying visitors. After a moment, his brain processed what Laura had been saying, and a dark thought crawled out from the crepuscular reaches of his mind, all on its own.

'Did you have anything to do with the decision to put me in a nine-to-five job?'

Laura's eyes flared up. 'You know I don't take personal issues into the workplace.'

'Just a coincidence.'

'Give me a bit of credit.' She went inside the caravan and came back out with her overnight bag. 'I had nothing to do with your return-to-work posting, but I know it was done with your best interests at heart.' She unzipped the bag and put her book inside. 'You nearly died, you idiot. Nobody comes through the trauma you came through without bringing some baggage out the other side. Grow up.'

'Sounds like it was done with your blessing.'

She stopped and stared at him, with a mix of anger and pity. 'I thought losing a few pints of blood and having a brain seizure might have changed you, but no, one day back at work, and you're just exactly the same.'

'The same what?'

'The same dreamer, who buys a dump like this. The same fool who's frightened that other people might think he's normal, or – shock-horror – average.'

'This dump has got potential.'

She finished zipping the wheelie-bag, and pulled out the telescopic handle.

'You're a bloody cliché, Harry – a detective with commitment issues, who drinks too much – it's been done before.' She tilted her head, and pulled a mirthless smile. 'Do yourself a favour and try playing another character.'

'Harsh.'

He watched her go down the path, and out onto the lane where her car was parked. Sometimes it's tough dating a psychoanalyst. Even one with shiny, chestnut hair, and big green eyes, and a body honed tight in the gym. They're always going to win an argument with their penetrating and cruel reasoning.

Next morning, Stallard was in the office by seven-thirty. There was a thrash-metal band playing a gig inside his skull, and three Nurofen hadn't made any difference.

Fay Nash was already at her desk. 'You look like shit.'

'It's a gift.'

'Here, guaranteed hangover cure.' She pushed a tray-bake of brownies, cut into squares, across the table. 'Take a couple.'

He chewed on the thick chocolate, and brought Nash up to date with the Joey Doane misper case. He told her about the distraught and slightly manic sister, Shannon, who had been mounting a one-woman crusade to prove her brother had been murdered, and about the only suspects, Brandon and Baxter Quinn, who fancied themselves as the northern Ronnie and Reggie. She laughed when he told her about the torso with female genitalia and frowned when he got to the bit about the body in the long-stay freezer that fitted the age and description. There was something not right about the case, he told her. Suicide didn't stack up.

When he'd finished, Nash said, 'Could he have staged his own disappearance?'

'I don't think so.'

'Why?'

'Because I think he's dead and somebody killed him.'

'We don't do gut feelings in the cold case unit.'

'Why not? There's plenty of guts.'

'Stop it. I'll die laughing.'

'Okay, call it a hunch.'

'We leave subjective guesswork to investigators who haven't trained their minds to process information and make logical deductions.'

'Thick bastards?'

'We prefer to say valued colleagues. Without them we'd be out of a job. Now, when you've got a minute, go and see Myers.' Nash pointed across the office to a large, corner workstation. 'The orange-haired kid – if a missing person is still alive, he'll know.'

'Supernatural powers?'

'No – a big computer and he knows how to use it. The point is, don't rule out a staged disappearance just yet.'

Stallard swallowed the last of the brownie and could already feel the cocoa solids emulsifying his gut acid, getting his metabolism back up and running with the help of lots of sugar. Not healthy, but effective. He wiped his fingers on some blue roll.

'Where will I find DS Coleman?'

Nash's left eyebrow immediately arched up. The right one never moved. 'Why do you want to know?'

'There are a few things I want to clarify about the initial investigation.'

She shook her head. 'Send him an email.'

'Really?'

'Yes, really.' She folded her arms, and her face turned serious. 'What you have to understand is that the relationship between the major crime team and the cold case review unit is a minefield, because all we do is check their work, and second-guess their decision making – all with the benefit of hindsight – they hate it.'

'We're all professionals, aren't we?'

'Some in the MCT are easier to deal with than others.'

'But not Coleman. He's an arse, right?'

'Fancies himself – the smart murder squad detective – be careful, and if you can, use email, because it gives you an audit trail that might prove handy in the future.'

Stallard nodded, and thanked Nash for the advice. Back-covering audit trails didn't bother him, because he didn't plan on being around longer than necessary. Soon as he could, he would be back in the world of undercover policing, which was completely different to what he was doing now. Chalk and cheese.

He spent an hour drinking black coffee and dipping in and out of the Joey Doane file. It was a mess. At some point, the Major Crime Team had obviously decided this was a simple suicide case and lost interest; hence the lack of structure and investigative rigour. Enquiries had been actioned out from the HOLMES computer, but then either ignored, or if they had been carried out, there was no result recorded. Statements hadn't been cross-referenced, and there was no definitive timeline showing the missing person's last known movements or sightings.

Fay Nash had been right. It wasn't hard to find the unit's analyst, Myers, because his hair was the colour of a fluorescent carrot. He could have been a teenager doing his homework, dressed in T-shirt, baggy shorts and Converse High Tops, with a face full of freckles. There was a poster above his desk – *Have You Tried Turning It Off And Back On Again?* Hardware humour. Stallard smirked, despite its overworked and banal usage. He introduced himself, and soon established that Myers didn't have a first name, and that he was a frustrated maths' graduate, who wanted to be a detective. He oozed a naïve enthusiasm, like an oversized puppy always wanting to play ball and please.

Myers knew his stuff. Within a couple of minutes, he'd pulled up on screen what was needed, and sent a copy to the printer. The intelligence report was brief, and stated that Joseph Doane had been the victim of a contract killing, ordered by Baxter Quinn and Brandon Quinn, following a dispute over a drugs debt. The information had been received three days after the last confirmed sighting of Joey, and it was this that had escalated the case from being just a simple missing person enquiry into a potential homicide investigation. The important bit was where the intelligence had come from – it was an untested source, which meant it could be Crimestoppers or a member of the public.

'Thanks,' said Stallard. 'Just one more favour. I'm kind of new to this cold case business, but is there anything in place to keep tabs on what's still going on? I mean, how do we know Joey Doane isn't sat with his feet up in a bedsit in Camden?'

'There's a checklist on the system,' said Myers. 'It can't rule out that someone has acquired a brand new identity, with the new appearance and means of support to go with it, but it makes sure we've got covert flags on anything IT-based, which may indicate an individual is still alive. Here, let me show you.' He made a few keystrokes. 'Bank accounts, NHS, mobile phone, social media, passport, DVLA, email addresses, HMRC...'

'Okay, thanks, I've got it.' Stallard tapped him on the shoulder. 'What about facial recognition?'

Myers shook his head. 'Nope, not yet. There's a load of CCTV out there, but it's not linked. Having said that, if you brought me some footage that wanted checking I could do something with it.'

'Thanks, I'll bear it in mind.'

'Is there anything else I can help with?' Myers looked up with eager eyes.

Stallard felt guilty walking away without giving Myers more work, but it was time to go and reacquaint himself with Baxter Quinn, who he hadn't had the pleasure of seeing since he left Beechthorpe council estate at the age of fifteen. When he got back to his desk, there was a message on a pink Post-it: Shannon Doane had rung the office, wanting to speak to him, and saying it was important. He had a nasty feeling that these calls were going to become a regular event. She was a trier, that was for sure, but she'd have to wait, because people like that soon think they own you, and expect you to jump up and down at their beck and call. He stuffed a few papers in his leather satchel, and got halfway to the door, before he heard a voice.

'Oy, where are you going?'

He turned back, and saw Fay Nash standing hands on hips. She was in a pair of skinny jeans and monkey boots, which seemed a bit racy for an old-timer like her, and definitely not in keeping with the rest of the place.

'Me?' said Stallard. 'I'm going to check out a couple of leads.'

'First off, you're supposed to be reviewing the case, not reinvestigating it from the beginning, and...'

'Aw, come on, Fay. I can't sit behind a desk all day. You've no idea how difficult it is for me.'

'And second, if you do have to go out, then you need a partner. I'm ignoring the fact that you met one witness yesterday on your own, but I can't let it happen again.'

Nash motioned towards the corridor. 'You know what'd happen if Mr Hardcastle found out.'

'Fantastic.' Stallard shrugged, as though he couldn't care less. 'Who's going to hold my hand?'

Nash cupped a hand to her mouth. 'Hey, Keith, over here a minute.'

Two desks down, a papery-faced man with wispy hair stood up, and shuffled towards them. He was wearing beige slacks, and a light mustard shirt with the sleeves rolled up. His forearms were covered in liver spots, and he had a pair of gold-rimmed spectacles on a lanyard around his neck. When he got close, the spectacles became positioned on the end on his nose. 'Yes, Fay?'

For a moment, Fay Nash looked like she was having a hard time trying to stop the corners of her mouth twitching upwards. She turned back to Stallard.

'Meet your new partner.'

Stallard stared at Nash to see if it was a wind-up, but her face was now straight and serious. Then he looked around the cold case office at all the grey hair, and realised there was never any prospect of getting paired up with Mel Gibson or Sandra Bullock. It was always going to be Keith or someone similar, and it wasn't for ever.

CHAPTER 7

The Quinn brothers were notorious in the shadier parts of the city. A couple of spoilt brats, who'd pupated into small-time gangsters, and then shed their chrysalis to fly off into the beautiful world of business. At first, it was security, then boxing and snooker, and now music. Whatever they did was always tainted by recurring rumours of drugs and money laundering, and wherever they went, they always took along a bad smell of menace and violence. Along the way, there'd been a few run-ins with the local CID, but no charges or convictions ever materialised, because potential witnesses always preferred to keep their leg bones in one piece, and a functioning hand on the end of each arm.

The original investment capital had come from old man Quinn, who was a scrap-metal dealer, and when Stallard was growing up, he'd lived round the corner from them. Theirs was the only house on the council estate with a Bentley Convertible parked outside, and a hot tub steaming away in the front garden, part shielded by a pallet fence on one side, and a wall of tyres on the other. Classy. Baxter was in his year at school, while Brandon was in the year above, and a couple of sisters, Bethany and Brooklyn, made up the rest of the clan. One or other of the two sisters was always squealing that some boy at school had called them *an ugly slag*, and the two Quinn brothers, both in matching haircuts and Doc Martens, would kick the crap out of the poor kid in front of the bus queue at 3.45pm. It was like Groundhog Day meets Clockwork Orange.

One particular day, Stallard had been the victim. His crime? To be the copper's kid. Brandon, two years older, had sought him out one lunchtime, and toyed with him like a cat does with a mouse. Now and then slapping him across the face, and sometimes throwing in the odd punch to the stomach. What made it worse, was that Baxter just stood there and laughed. Stallard and Baxter were in the same class together and supposed to be mates.

Baxter and Brandon had come a long way since Beechthorpe Secondary School. Their company SIAM – Southpaw Investments and Management – had its offices on the other side of town, in a stone-built, Victorian villa, which stood proud in its own grounds and overlooked the Botanical Gardens. It exuded an old-fashioned feel of respectability, more in keeping with a longstanding accountancy business, or a family law firm, rather than a Johnny-come-lately outfit acting as agents for sport-jocks and pop stars.

Stallard whistled at the cherry-red Ferrari in the car park, and crunched his way up the gravel path to a heavy front door, guarded by more CCTV than most financial institutions. Despite the handicap of a heavy migraine, he'd managed to remember his warrant card, and hoping that nobody looked too closely at the clean-cut recruit in the photograph, he held it up to one of the cameras and buzzed. He waited a couple of minutes, and buzzed again. Nothing. He looked at Keith, but his new partner was too busy studying his iPad. It was glued to his hand, like a kid with a new Nintendo. Stallard tried the door, but it wouldn't budge. He was about to try knocking instead, when they were buzzed into the entrance, only to be confronted by another locked door. Finally, after the external door had closed, they were buzzed through the new door and into the building.

After such difficulty, Stallard was expecting the classic Rottweiler on reception, but the woman standing there could have stepped straight from the front page of a fashion magazine. Her badge said Melanie, and her face said Botox. She was tanned and smiling.

'Good morning, how can I help you, gentlemen?'

'We're police officers,' said Stallard, 'here to see Baxter Quinn.'

'I'm sorry.' Melanie smiled. 'Mr Quinn is not in the office today.'

'So, whose is the car?'

'That's Brandon's – Mr Quinn's brother.'

'He'll do,' said Stallard, and watched as she made a call without the smile flickering a fraction of an inch.

A few minutes later, they were shown into an oak-panelled room. Brandon Quinn was sitting at a modern L-shaped desk, with a couple of monitors, and a bowl of fruit. He was thick-set, with a square, bald head, and a tufty soul patch of copper hair on his chin. Some more copper hair was bushing up over the V of his black vest. The walls around him were covered in memorabilia: a Ronnie Sullivan waistcoat; a Jimmy White cue; a pair of silk shorts signed by Tyson Fury, and a host of black and white boxing prints. Pride of place was a poster for the Anthony Joshua vs Wladimir Klitschko fight at Wembley, with a sharpie dedication, *To Brandon…*

Quinn said, 'This is a waste of time. You've got two minutes.'

'I've got thirty-six hours if I arrest you, and take you back to the station.' Stallard smiled. 'Your choice.'

Brandon Quinn bulged his eyes. 'You wouldn't be so stupid.'

'Watch me.' Stallard pulled the mobile from his shirt pocket, and started to dial. 'Do you want a marked car with blues and twos or the riot van?'

'Okay, ten minutes, and then I'm calling my legal team.'

Stallard hung up, and sat down. The green, leather Chesterfield was soft and uncomfortable. He watched Keith sink down alongside him, with a look of mild terror frozen on his face. So much for the chaperone who'd been tasked with protecting him from potentially confrontational situations.

'What happened to Joey, Mr Quinn?'

'He's dead.'

'How come you're so sure?'

'You coppers couldn't find your own arse with a mirror on a stick.' Brandon Quinn laughed. 'But these days, even you lot can find missing kids, because they can't live without their fucking mobiles.' He extended his thumb and little finger to make a phone, and held it to his ear. 'I'm right, aren't I?' The soul patch nodded in agreement.

Stallard smiled back. The box-headed thug behind the desk was right, but he didn't want to show any acknowledgement. Locating mispers by tracking their phone was like shelling peas. If a missing young person's SIM stopped pinging off the nearest mast, it was either a case of dead battery or dead kid.

'Did you supply Joey Doane with drugs?'

'Have you come here just to annoy me?'

'Answer the question.'

'No. I do not supply drugs to anyone.' Quinn's voice was ice-cold, but a vein in his left temple had started to jiggle.

'Seems a coincidence he disappeared the day he was due to answer bail at the police station.'

'Lost his bottle.'

'Addicts often want to do a deal and give information to shorten their sentences.'

'What are you implying?' Quinn's teeth were grinding together. The vein in his right temple joined in with the left. A Mexican wave of blood vessels.

'Did you and your brother kill Joey to stop him grassing you up?'

'Okay, so now I know why you're here.' Quinn shook his head. A snarl of disgust creased his top lip and nostrils. 'The mad bitch has got you to reopen the case. I'm right, aren't I?'

'Not unless the mad bitch is the name of a headless corpse in Hull mortuary.'

'I mean Shannon, the sister.'

Stallard looked into Brandon Quinn's eyes, and saw the wild hatred. Whatever Shannon Doane had done, she'd made an ugly enemy, and one with money and unsavoury connections. The worst sort.

'Were The Magic Rats about to break through and make you millions?'

'Music management is Baxter's part of the company.'

'What do you think?'

'Who knows? The pop industry is a shitshow, and talent is optional.' Quinn gestured to the walls of his office. 'That's why I prefer sport.'

'The recording contract must be worth something?'

'Null and void. Some twat in a suit told us it was like getting The Arctic's without Alex Turner. Humpf.' Quinn snorted air down his nose. 'To be fair to the smarmy bastard, he was right.'

Stallard stood up and bent over the desk. 'May I?' He took a pen and scribbled his details down on a pad of SIAM-crested paper. 'Tell Baxter to give me a call.'

Brandon Quinn looked at the paper and then squinted back up.

'Where do I know you from?'

'I'm the ghost of Christmas Past.' Stallard pulled Keith up out of the sofa. 'And this is Jacob Marley. Together we fight greed and selfishness around the globe.'

When they got outside, big splodges of rain were falling at random from a bright, cloudless sky. How's that happen? They ducked their heads and walked a little quicker towards Stallard's Jeep down the street. By the time they reached it, everything was dark, and water hammered down from the heavens. Stallard de-misted the windows, and eased out into the main road. Then someone flipped a switch, and the rain turned into hailstones the size of marbles that threatened to crack the windscreen. Summer in the Steel City.

Stallard had no choice but to pull over into the kerb and wait it out. It gave him chance to call Shannon Doane.

She answered in a suspicious tone.

'Is this you on a new number trying to catch me out?'

'It's DC Stallard.'

There was silence, so he elaborated.

'The bastard child of Lemmy and Joan Jett? You rang the office asking for me.'

'Sorry, I thought you were someone else.'

'No, it's definitely me.'

There was a little throat-clearing cough. 'What are you doing tonight?'

'Erm, I'm not sure yet...' If all else fails, tell the truth. Still no word from Laura, so probably be sitting in a caravan, eating tinned spaghetti and watching The Sweeney on box set. The thrilling, high-rolling life of a real detective.

'Pick me up at nine from my mum and dad's – I'll text you the address.'

She sounded earnest. Maybe a touch strident, but he knew she was fighting for a cause she cared about.

'Where do you want to go?'

'I'm going to show you I was right about Baxter Quinn. I've got evidence.'

'Like I said, there's a good chance I'm not...' He stopped talking, because he was talking to himself. She'd ended the call.

Five minutes later, Keith pointed to the screen of his iPad, and said, 'Looks like SIAM are layering.'

They were sitting outside a Costa, tucked in the corner of a bijou shopping precinct. The air was warming up again after the storm, and a wagon-train of SUVs was slowly circling, waiting for precious parking spaces to become free, and allow mothers and toddlers to join those brunch-timers already grouped outside the pavement cafés and coffee shops.

Stallard frowned. 'Try again in English.'

'Layering is when an organisation has a lot of companies set up,' said Keith. He was softly spoken, almost diffident, with something of Mrs Tittlemouse about him. He took a serviette, and brigaded crumbs into little piles on his plate. 'See, if you move money around multiple companies, it's difficult for law enforcement to know where that money originally came from.' He pushed a big pile of crumbs right to the edge. 'Especially if one or more of those companies is located off-shore, in certain countries where financial transactions are, shall we say, more opaque.'

'Sunny places for shady people,' said Stallard. 'I know a bit about it. One or two laundromat schemes featured on the periphery of undercover jobs I worked on.'

'Except Quinns' companies aren't in the usual dodgy jurisdictions, like Central America or The Caymans, they're in Vietnam and Thailand, which is strange. I would not expect to see that.'

Stallard said, 'How come you know so much?'

'Twenty-five years in the fraud squad, with the last three spent setting up the new Financial Investigation Unit.' His nose twitched with pride, and he tapped his iPad. 'I can still use the force's direct portal to Companies House, and access our account with Equifax and Dun and Bradstreet.' He leaned over the bistro table, and lowered his voice. Perhaps to avoid being mobbed by over-zealous fans. 'I'm now the longest serving member of the Cold Case Review Unit.'

Stallard tilted back in his chair to get away from Keith's breathless enthusiasm. It's true what they say – weak chin, strong halitosis. He drank some coffee. 'Any tips for the latest recruit?'

'Always remember Locard's principle.'

'It's engraved on my frontal lobe.' Stallard let his eyes drift behind the mirror shades, to follow a pair of tanned legs. They were in a pink and purple mini-dress, and moved slowly and rhythmically like they knew he was watching them. 'This Locard. Just remind me of the main principle bits – broad brush.'

'Every contact leaves a trace.'

'What if there's no body, no crime scene, no weapon and no formal suspect?'

'We call that an undetectable.'

'I call it a challenge.'

'Good for you.' Keith gave a weak fist-pump. There were dark mustard sweat-patches under the arms of his shirt. 'As your new partner, I will provide all the assistance I can in rising to the challenge.'

'Temporary partner.'

'In return, I would like your help in a small matter.'

Stallard folded his arms. 'No promises.'

'In your previous role, would I be right in assuming that you were trained in covert-method-of-entry?'

'How many times do I have to say it? The undercover unit is my current role, not previous role.' Stallard unfolded his arms, and pretended to tear at his hair. 'This cold case appearance is temporary, and within a short space of time will have faded like an insubstantial pageant, leaving not a rack behind.'

'Are you CME trained or not?'

'Yes, I did the buggers and burglars course. What do you want doing?'

'I want you to break into a house, and steal a certain lady's panties.'

Stallard grinned. 'Keith, you dark horse.'

'It's not what you think.'

CHAPTER 8

Stallard found DS Coleman in one of the three Major Incident Rooms on the top floor, in the company of a sidekick called DC Katz, who was stocky and mean looking, with a face like a warthog sucking piss off a thistle. They were strolling out of a midday briefing, with matching man-bags, and litre bottles of mineral water. Coleman himself was more cultured and chiselled, with slicked-back hair, and a made-to-measure suit that nicely complemented his aura of self-confidence.

Both seemed a little surprised when Stallard introduced himself, and told them he wanted to pick their brains regarding the Joey Doane case. They ushered him into a side-room that was used by exhibits officers to bag and tag the weird and wonderful things that always get seized on any major incident: mobile phones, used condoms, odd shoes, tab ends and clothes. Lots of clothes. Three walls were racked out with metal shelving, the other had a worktop bench.

Coleman and Katz took the only two stools, and sat with their arms crossed.

'Relax,' said Stallard. 'I come in peace.'

'Share,' said Coleman.

'Share?'

'The Doane case isn't up for review until February next year,' said Coleman, 'which means there's been a development. I'd like to know what that development is.'

'A torso washed up on the banks of the Humber.'

'Our man?'

'No, definitely not.'

Coleman smiled. 'End of story then, my friend. Return the file to the archives, and move on to the next one.'

Stallard stood his ground. 'There's a couple of loose ends I'd like to tie up.'

Coleman spun his stool to look at his partner. 'Did we leave any loose ends? I don't remember leaving any loose ends.'

Katz didn't look back at his sergeant. He just stared at Stallard. 'It's our job to wrap cases up tight.'

Stallard held his gaze. 'Maybe there aren't any loose ends, and it's just the paperwork that's incomplete.'

Katz bristled. 'Are you criticising my paperwork?'

'We're all busy, and sometimes other things come along and take priority. I understand.'

'Don't patronise me, pal.' Katz flared his nostrils. 'There's nothing wrong with my paperwork.' He shook his head, and mouthed under his breath. 'Tosser.'

Stallard had heard enough. 'Shall we go downstairs now, and I'll show you the total crock of shite that some clown thinks passes for a case-file?'

Katz sprang up, and jabbed a massive finger. 'Who

the fuck are you? Another one of Hardcastle's invalids too shit-scared to go back on the frontline?'

'Got me in one.' Stallard smiled.

The smile made things worse, and Katz stepped in close, with a puffed-out chest and flecks of spittle in the corners of his mouth. 'What makes a wuss like you – with no experience of murder investigation – think you can come here and tell me how to do my job?'

Stallard looked at Coleman. 'Tell sausage-fingers to get out of my face, before I lose my temper and put him on his arse.'

Silence.

There was a stand-off for a few seconds, and then Coleman laughed. 'Sit down Katzy. Our friend is trying to do what he thinks is best.'

Katz backed off, still staring.

Stallard said, 'You guys have got a great good-cop-bad-cop routine going on. Why don't you save it for some criminals?'

Coleman brushed some lint off his jacket sleeve. Nonchalant. 'What are these two loose ends?'

'There's a body in Hull mortuary that matches the description of Joey Doane, but their records show it was eliminated by DNA.'

'Correct.'

'But Joey's DNA isn't on the national database.'

'Ah, but his sister's is.'

Stallard paused. 'Shannon?'

'The one and only. Isn't she something?' Coleman cocked his head, and half-winked. 'But she obviously didn't tell you about her conviction.'

Stallard watched Katz and his sergeant exchange knowing glances. Self-satisfied and in control of the information flow. 'She seems very determined to find her brother.'

'She's mentally unstable and vexatious,' said Coleman. 'We had to block her emails and stop responding to her letters. Don't give her any encouragement.'

'Sometimes it takes a crazy person to get things done. To change stuff...'

Katz snorted. 'She's certainly fucking crazy.'

Coleman raised a laconic hand to signal that he wanted to hear no more of Shannon Doane, and stood up. 'We need to be going.'

Katz glared. 'Yeah, we've got a real murder to investigate. Off you go, back to the cripple squad.'

Stallard watched them leave and called after them. 'Keep that routine going – I love it.'

When he got back down to the office, Keith was tucking into a potted beef sandwich, and a bag of Mini Cheddars. He'd got a small transistor radio on the windowsill, and was listening to something on earphones. Stallard tapped him on the shoulder, and Keith pulled them out, complaining that the England bowlers were pitching too short outside off-stump. It was a common error apparently.

Stallard yawned and told him he wanted to know about the panties. Keith's face lit up. It was a cold case murder from the nineties that he'd been working on for weeks. A barmaid strangled with her own tights and dumped in a skip. There was no hit on the national DNA database, which meant that the offender had never been previously charged with an offence. Not since 1995 anyway.

Several times, in his boyish enthusiasm for all things deoxyribonucleic acid, Keith started to fly off at tangents, wanting to explain Short Tandem Repeats, alleles, and Low Copy Number, and each time Stallard had to haul him back. Being concise can be difficult for people with a passion. The point seemed to be that even if an offender isn't on the national DNA database, it's sometimes possible to identify them, if one of their close relatives is recorded on there. In the world of cold case review, they call it familial searching.

Keith explained how the result of a familial search was always just a starting point, and that there always followed a great deal of research.

'Cut the crap. Where do the knickers come into it? Stallard helped himself to a handful of Mini Cheddars.

Finally, Keith mentioned a woman who might be a suspect, but was out of the country for the summer. If she had left laundry in her basket, the knickers would be the surest bet for getting a DNA profile. It just needed someone to get into her house, and retrieve the contents. A search warrant wasn't an option, because the link was too tenuous.

Stallard was in the process of explaining that covert entry requires specialist resources, when the office door opened, and Hardcastle summoned him into the corridor.

The cold case manager looked stern behind his Stalinesque moustache. 'I've had a call from the head of the Major Crime Unit.'

'That was quick,' said Stallard. 'Has somebody run crying to their daddy?'

'He rang to remind me that our job is to review unsolved cases, and identify potential new lines of enquiry

– not reinvestigate them by interviewing original witnesses and suspects.'

'What if I think something's not right?'

'Then do your job.'

'What does that mean?'

'Don't listen to old men like me.'

Stallard looked for any sign of humour behind the grumpy façade, but there wasn't any. Hardcastle turned on his heel, and went back to his office.

Myers was also lunching when Stallard sat down next to him, but the young man was still working away, inputting data into a spreadsheet with one hand, eating a slice of cold, veggie pizza with the other. Stallard felt guilty asking Myers to run basic nominal checks on the force IT systems, but he was out of practice.

He watched the analyst open up another window, and key in the details of Shannon Doane. There was only one with an address in the force area, and the date of birth looked about right. Nothing listed on the local intelligence system, but one record on the custody handling system, and one conviction listed on the Police National Computer.

On the 10th of September last year, Shannon Doane had appeared at the Magistrates Court, for an offence of criminal damage, and been sentenced to two hundred hours' community service. Stallard read it again. It seemed a bit steep for an offence of simple damage – one not aggravated by hate-crime factors – and for a first offence.

Then Myers opened up another tab, which showed the whole of the written charge, and it became clear why Shannon Doane hadn't just received a fine or a conditional discharge. The damage was to a Lamborghini Huracan, and valued at £37,000. Stallard smiled to himself. That must have been some scratch. Maybe she bent the aerial as well.

CHAPTER 9

It was nudging 1.15pm, when Stallard swung his Jeep twice around the traffic island at the university, and left by the same road that he'd entered. He was on his way to meet Frank at India 3, which was a UC Unit safe house, and so counter-surveillance techniques were good practice, even though he wasn't currently deployed in the field, and hadn't been for five months. It felt strange. There was no indication of suspicious activity behind him, so he cut left over the tram tracks, and out towards the north of the city. The sun was baking the road again, and the inside of his car was hotter than a smack head's spoon.

Stallard wiped the sweat from the back of his neck with a shift cuff. A few years ago, he'd been infiltrating a gang of Geordie gun smugglers, when one of them had held a pistol to his head in a hotel room, and made him chase the dragon to prove he wasn't a copper. These things happen. He was about to do it when the hotel fire alarm went off, and there was shouting outside in the corridor. Frank to the rescue. One of many times he'd saved Stallard's skin.

The Met called their cover officers *uncles*, but Frank was more of a brother.

In the undercover unit, the UCs counted their time on deployment in dog years. Twelve months in the field was the equivalent of seven years normal service. It was the pressure of constant risk that did it. By the time Stallard got himself stabbed in the basement of the Blue Butterfly he was an old dog, and the law of averages said his luck would soon run out, even though he and Frank were a good team. It was just the source of the danger that proved surprising. Frank had kept him safe from Albanian drug barons, coked-up Russian gangsters and a host of homegrown psychopaths, but not this girl, Karina. The absurdity was annoying.

Traffic was moving freely, and he performed one more manoeuvre to make sure there was no tail, then cut through a narrow rat-run from the dual carriageway into an area where the roads became lined with cherry and lime trees, and soon he was there. He parked up, and travelled the last fifty yards on foot, so that his vehicle was not seen near to the building.

The safe house was actually an apartment. A fairly new block of about thirty, mainly rented out to young professionals, who didn't have the time or inclination to pry into their neighbours' business. If anybody did check out who the tenants at 6b were, they would discover it was on a long-term lease to a company called Star-time Promotions. They would not discover anything else. The Regional Undercover Unit used it mainly for briefing and de-briefs, but also for putting-up out-of-town UCs, who were passing through, or who'd come to play a bit-part in one of the ongoing operations.

Frank opened the door. 'What can I say?' He curled his top lip. 'Wankers.'

Stallard squeezed past him into the hallway, and then straight into the kitchen, where he took a bottle of Budweiser from the fridge, and flipped the top. He collapsed onto a battered old sofa, and took a drink.

'They're definitely going to withdraw the prosecution?'

'That's what Deano says,' said Frank, sitting down to a half-eaten sandwich at the table. Deano was the detective in the regional ops team, who had interviewed Jared Finn and submitted the file. 'He had a case conference with CPS and the barrister first thing this morning, and they're both of the opinion that without the girl's evidence, it's a non-starter.'

'That's why they're called the Criminal Protection Society.'

'You mean the Can't Prosecute Shitbags.' Frank was eating a brie and bacon baguette, and bits of crust flew across the room.

'We've got to find her.'

'There isn't time. She could be anywhere.'

Stallard chewed on a mouthful of Bud. 'Let's start at the last place she was seen.'

'The refuge?'

'Unless you've got a better idea, Einstein.'

'Sergeant Einstein to you, cheeky git.' A splodge of cranberry sauce fell from the sandwich onto Frank's shirt. 'Bastard.' He pulled it up to his face and licked it off. 'Good as new.'

'Still not house-trained then?'

'Piss off.' Frank shot out a grin but then let it fade and became serious. 'Are you sure you want to do this?

Sometimes it's best to let things go and move on. You know, don't give them head-space, especially when your head's full of other stuff.'

'Are you questioning my mental capacity?'

'I mean you need to focus on getting yourself back to what you were, not worrying about other people's problems.'

'Like Jared Finn.'

'Yes, like Jared Finn.'

'But that's why we do this job, isn't it? To worry about other people's problems like Jared Finn, because if we don't, he'll be trafficking some more young girls, and there will be more victims and more misery. The world will be a worse place.'

Frank rolled his eyes. 'Okay, let me check out the refuge. You get back to your missing person case.'

'It's a murder.'

'Whatever. I'll find Karina.'

Stallard thought about it, and made a decision. The quickest way for him to get his old job back was to do his new job well, and prove he was mentally and physically fit. That meant leaving Frank to try and rescue the Blue Butterfly case. That might be a big mistake.

CHAPTER 10

A little after 9.30, Stallard's smartphone sat-nav took him into a cul-de-sac and told him in a very polite voice that he had arrived at his destination. Joey Doane's parents lived in a bungalow on the site of an old pit. The slag-heaps had been landscaped into a grassy park, with footpaths and a visitor board that explained how coal miners had once lived and worked in the olden days of the twentieth century. The development was all done in soft pastel brick, with cycle lanes and little roundabouts painted on the road.

'I thought you weren't coming.' Shannon answered the door, and invited him in. 'Would you mind.' She pointed to his feet. 'Mum's a bit precious about her carpets.'

Stallard slipped his cowboy boots off, and followed her into the lounge, where he saw Jim and Elaine Doane surrounded by photographs of Joey. Dozens of photographs. Some were in frames, but lots were scattered loose on the floor, and some were in albums propped up on a coffee table. Elaine Doane had red, blotchy eyes, and a pile of scrunched-up tissues next to her on the sofa.

Jim Doane stood up, and offered his hand. 'Sorry about the mess, we were just reliving a few memories.'

'That's okay,' said Stallard, and shook Jim's hand. It was strong. The old man still looked like the photo on Shannon's wall – big and mop-haired – but now even older and gaunt. The broad shoulders were sagging, and the skin on his neck hung like the jowls of an ancient bulldog. He had an old-style tattoo on his forearm, faded and fraying into weathered skin a little around the edges. It was a dagger and a laurel wreath, on top of a scroll, *Per Mare Per Terram*.

'You were a Royal Marine?' said Stallard.

'Seven years,' said Jim. 'I left after the Falklands.' He looked out of the window, as if it was a portal into the past. His eyes filled with water. He blinked and brushed away the tears that squeezed out. 'I'm sorry. I was thinking about Joey. He's the same age as I was back then.'

Stallard didn't know what to say. Losing a child at any age shouldn't happen to anyone. He spoke for a few minutes, which felt like an eternity, and reassured them that he'd do all within his power to find out what happened to their son. He couldn't do any more, or say anything else. It was easy in an undercover role to rattle off something that sounded good, and he didn't need a script or prompt in the wings to help him do it, because improvisation came easy to him. But when he was himself, it somehow sounded insincere and forced.

Standing there and witnessing their pain, he realised why Shannon had asked to be picked up from her parents. She'd wanted him to see first-hand the effect Joey's disappearance had wrought. The perfect lives that it had poisoned, and caused to wither prematurely. How it had ripped the heart out of a family, and left in its wake a black hole of suffering and confusion. It was a set-up, and he'd walked straight into it. The photographs had probably been got out especially for the stage-managed occasion. It was the sort of theatre he was used to orchestrating for other people, not being on the receiving end of, and it was disconcerting. So what? Their suffering was real.

When they left the bungalow, Stallard was struck how good Shannon was looking, and that unnerved him too. Was that all part of the plan to reel him in? She wore tight jeans, with a slinky low-cut top, and her hair was up in an untidy bun that must have taken a lot of work to make look so dishevelled. And when she slipped into the passenger seat next to him, she brought with her a scent of wild flowers and reckless nights.

He said, 'So where are we going?'

'To see our drummer, Mickey Flint.' Shannon buckled up. 'He's playing in a new band.'

'On a Tuesday?'

'Yeah, it's a crappy covers band,' she said, wrinkling her nose. 'They're doing a private function in town by the river. Some poncey food place with its own micro-brewery.'

'Mickey didn't waste much time then, did he, before he moved on to pastures new?'

'Money.' She shrugged.

'He's your new witness?'

'A few days before Joey went missing, I heard him and Baxter arguing in the storage area of the rehearsal room, and when I walked in, Joey was holding a brown-paper package, like Baxter had just handed it to him, and Mickey was there, pointing a finger and joining in the argument.' A shiver seemed to go down her spine. 'Baxter said, *I'll fucking kill you,* and Joey laughed like it was all a big joke.'

They took the slip road onto the M1, and after a couple of junctions, picked up the link road that ran straight through to the city centre. The air was hot and humid. Stallard had the driver's window down, and his elbow out. He needed air to clear his head of a sense of worry that he couldn't distil into words. Maybe it was Laura. She'd not replied to his voicemails, and he'd taken refuge on a bar stool, drinking pints and shooting the breeze with a motley crew of vagrants, loners and drunken businessmen. Textbook stress-reduction therapy. It hadn't worked.

Shannon was chatty. Music was her passion, and always had been. She'd grown up listening to her dad's albums, and while her friends were into boy bands, she was playing along to the Stones, The Who and The Jam. As the older sister, she in turn had influenced Joey's taste and got him into guitar-based groups. For a second, Stallard thought about recounting his youthful exploits in a band, but thought better of it. She was in a different league.

He slowed down for the traffic lights by the city incinerator, and turned left across an iron bridge over a weir in the river, and onto a road where ancient cobbles peeped through bare patches in the tarmac. Most of the old factories were now apartments, but some had been converted into brasseries, and sold street food and craft ale. He pulled up. 'Why didn't you tell me about the criminal damage conviction?'

Shannon was quiet. Then she took a deep breath. 'You never asked me, and it's on record. I assumed you knew.'

'Those Italian sports cars are expensive.'

'I was engaged to a man who turned out to be an ignorant bastard.'

'So, you trashed his motor?'

'You won't believe me, but I didn't do it.'

'Your record says you pleaded guilty.'

'I did, but I swear I never touched his bloody car.' She smiled, with a hint of sadness. 'I just wanted to forget the relationship and move on.'

Stallard watched her face, and for some reason believed her. He didn't know why. Then he climbed out and patted the bonnet of his Jeep. If Laura ever attacked his car, she'd struggle to cause a hundred quid's worth of damage.

The Stainless Kitchen and Tap had a spit and sawdust bar at the front with barrel tables, where a dozen or so couples perched with drinks and leftover gastro nibbles. The music was coming from a function room at the back, with a handwritten sign hung on the door that said, *Alan's Leaving Do*. They bought a couple of beers at the main bar, and walked through to find what looked like the remains of an office party, with one guy the wrong side of sixty – no doubt the eponymous Alan – bare-chested on the dancefloor doing some ska moves to *Too Much Too Young*, while the rest cheered him on. Stallard thought the band were pretty good, but the look on Shannon's face showed she wasn't impressed.

After another couple of numbers, it was all over, and the lights went up. Piped pop music kicked in, and before the room had emptied, the band had started to break down their gear.

'Let me introduce you to Mickey.' Shannon took hold of Stallard's arm.

'Thanks.' Stallard gently eased away. 'But I need to speak to him on my own. If you want to wait for me in the bar, I won't be long.'

Shannon's face turned dark. 'What's the matter, don't you trust me?' She didn't wait for an answer, and stormed off.

He found Mickey Flint collapsing cymbal stands into a long canvas bag with wheels at one end. He was a stocky lad in Hawaiian shorts and a white, sweat-soaked vest, with matted, wiry hair that could have been used to scour saucepans. Stallard waited for him to look up,

'Did Shannon tell you I was coming?'

'Yes, I told her not to waste your time, mate. There's nothing I can tell you that I didn't tell the others.'

'So, you told the police officers who did the initial investigation that you'd heard Baxter Quinn threaten to kill Joey Doane?'

'No, I didn't, but I mean, it wasn't like that.' Flint wiped away some sweat that was hanging over his left eye. 'There was nothing to tell, mate. Baxter might have said something like, *I'm gonna bloody kill him*, but we all said, *I'm gonna bloody kill him*. That's the sort of kid he was. Typical screwed-up singer – it's all about *me, me me*.' Flint pointed to the back of the stage. 'Do us a favour, mate, pass us that cymbal case…cheers. Anyway, why don't you ask Vinegar Tits what she did to upset Joey?'

'Vinegar Tits?'

'Shannon. Her and Joey hadn't spoken to each other since they had the big bust-up, and if you ask me, the only reason she's going mental now, doing this single-handed crusade shit, is that she feels guilty, because she's the one he's running away from.'

'You think he's run away, not killed himself or been killed?'

'He's not dead.' Flint laughed as he zipped up the last of his cymbals. 'I'm telling you, it's all about *me, me, me* with Joey. He'll be on a Spanish island, waiting until he thinks he's punished his sister enough, and the world of music is ready for the miraculous return of Joey Doane and his Magic Rats.' Flint shook his Brillo-pad head. 'Did you know that he wanted to change the name of the band to *Joey and The Magic Rats*? Unbelievable. Can you believe it? What a knob.'

Stallard noticed there was still a stencilled rat holding a wand spray-painted on the bass-drum skin, but the band's name had been covered by masking tape. The same rat with a magic wand had been stencilled on a couple of other equipment boxes.

'If you think Joey is going to come back, and carry on where he left off, turning The Magic Rats into the next big thing, why have you joined another band?'

'Cash.' Flint didn't hesitate. 'Being an arty-farty musician don't pay the bills, know what I mean?' He stopped folding the legs of a little leather-seated stool, and looked Stallard in the eye. 'This may sound daft, but I'm not really into music. I learnt drums when I were a kid, because our old man wanted me to, and now this is my job

– not my life, my job – I'm a drummer. Mainly, because I can do fuck-all else. Now, if Joey comes back, and he manages to stay out of prison, then I'm a Magic Rat again, because that's where the big bucks will be. Call me a slag, but there you go, I couldn't give a shit.'

'What about the drugs though? Joey might avoid a prison sentence, but if he's back on the heroin, there isn't going to be any big bucks for the band, because it will scramble his brains. That's what you were arguing about at the rehearsal room, isn't it? You and Baxter Quinn thought Joey was back on the smack, and going to ruin your big payday, just at that one moment when it was within touching distance. That is what happened, isn't it?'

'No,' said Flint. He looked surprised. Sweat ran down the furrow he'd just made between his eyebrows. 'Why would we be angry with Joey? We were all using, apart from Mother Teresa.'

'I still don't understand why Baxter would give Joey a load of gear, just at the moment he needed to stay clean, when you were about to–'

'You what? What're talking about?'

'Shannon saw it, in the backroom where you store the equipment,' said Stallard. 'Baxter gave him a brown package, and you don't need X-ray vision to know what was inside it, do you? It might as well have had *Skag – The UK's Favourite Opiate* printed on a flashing label in block capitals.'

Flint grabbed a towel, and balled his head dry in a flurry of hands. When he came back out, there was a smile on his face.

'It was a passport. Joey wanted his passport back, 'cos we'd all handed them in to Baxter at the start of the tour.

Joey said he needed it for something and swore he wasn't going to leave the country, but me and Baxter thought he might piss off and leave us in the lurch. That's what we were arguing about, and do you know what?' He hoisted a massive holdall up onto his shoulder, and a look of derision contorted his face. 'It seems like we were right, doesn't it? That prima donna, diva shitbag has sold us a dummy and done one.'

Stallard scribbled his number on a Carlsberg beermat, and handed it to the drummer. 'Call me if you hear anything.' Then he picked his way back across the dancefloor, through spilt drinks and empty glasses, wondering why the supposed next big thing in the world of popular music would want his passport back. The obvious answer was to leave the country, and if that was the case, it wasn't the actions of a man contemplating suicide. Things didn't stack up. He looked around the bar area, but there was no sign of Shannon.

Outside, he strolled towards the Jeep, the smell of the club's sweat and stale booze dissipating off his shoulders into the warm night air. He stopped. An irrational notion that he was being watched had prickled the back of his neck. He turned, just in time to see headlights reverse down the street, and disappear into a side road. Coincidence or had he got a new stalker? Nobody knew he was going to The Stainless Kitchen and Tap, and he'd not been followed there, had he? Surveillance-consciousness was something all UCs prided themselves on. It had to be coincidence, or he was losing his touch.

CHAPTER 11

Stallard rolled out of bed, and padded two yards of linoleum to the bathroom, arms out in front of him like a zombie. He kept his eyes screwed up, because he could sense the sun shooting deadly laser-rays through the gaps in the caravan curtains, and any light on his retina would definitely be fatal. Once inside, he bent over the sink, and coughed up a ball of mucus, which tasted a lot like the bottle of Jameson's he'd drunk as a nightcap six hours ago. Then he cupped cold water into his face and made snorting noises. Last night had been a car crash, with Shannon marching off in a strop, and Laura still not answering his calls or messages. What was it with Laura after all this time together? He managed a one-eyed squint in the mirror. *Ever thought it's because you look like a bag of shite?*

Three Nurofen and a can of Pepsi later, he put a new elastic band in his freshly brushed hair, and got dressed. Another double-black-denim day in paradise. He'd just squeezed into his boots, when he heard the saxophone solo from Lou Reed's *Walk on the Wild Side,* and went to look for his mobile phone. He found it shuddering around in circles on the bedside table, and when he picked it up, it was a number he didn't recognise, but answered anyway.

'Hello?'

'It's Baxter Quinn. You wanted to see me.'

'Yes, what about later?' Stallard's brain hurt. What time was it? What day was it? Come on, pull yourself together. He cleared his throat. 'Shall we say two o'clock at your office?'

'What about right now, Harry? Have a look through your front window.'

'What...'

Stallard's spine went cold. This must be some kind of wind-up. There's no way anybody could know his home address, least of all a pseudo gangster like Baxter Quinn. He ripped open the threadbare, flowery-print curtains, and there sitting on his rattan patio chairs were two men, laughing at him. Bloody laughing. He must be still asleep and this was one of those nightmares. He bit into his cheek, and it hurt. Bastard. It was real.

In the past, his training would have kicked in, and he'd have assumed a façade to shield his personal turmoil, but he was rusty and this had caught him off-guard. He didn't think. He bowled out of the caravan, and round to the front, where the dozen concrete slabs served as his outdoor seating area, and gritted his teeth.

'Get off my land. Now.'

The two men stood up, but didn't move. Baxter Quinn looked like the same slob of a bully from back in the day, but a bit chubbier, with little, darty rodent eyes, and bald head. His laughing-partner looked like a flyweight boxer, who'd lost more bouts than he'd won, with a flat nose and scars where his eyebrows should have been.

'Your land?' said Quinn. 'I've got a swimming pool bigger than this.'

'I'm not joking.' Stallard fixed a stare on the bigger man's face, and walked towards him, steadily picking up speed. 'You don't scare me, so I'll tell you again, leave my property. Last chance.'

'Calm down, Harry,' said Quinn. 'We're not here to try and intimidate anybody, are we, Woodsy?' He turned, and smirked at the boxer, who grinned back, like he had just witnessed great comedy genius at work. 'We're here, as they say, to help with enquiries.'

Stallard stopped himself. Wrong place, wrong time. 'You still haven't got the balls to do anything on your own, have you?' He went back inside the caravan, and put the kettle on. The sense of panic had gone, but it had shaken him. He watched the two men share another joke as they walked away to a waiting car, and wondered how they knew.

Fay Nash tore a square off the jumbo blue roll, and wrapped it round a piece of millionaire's shortbread.

'Here, guaranteed to make you feel better, but if you're late again tomorrow, Gerry's definitely going to put you on a fizzer.'

'Ta.' Stallard took it, and sank his teeth into the soft toffee top. He chewed. Mmmm, sugar. 'So, what if Hardcastle does give me a written warning? Big deal. It might get me straight out of here, and back to my old job.'

'Do you think?' said Nash, showing again how she could arch one eyebrow without the other moving.

Stallard didn't reply. Things were slipping out of control. He'd been confident of walking straight back into the undercover unit, as soon as his period of recuperation was over, but now he wasn't so sure. UCs are supposed to be unidentifiable and untraceable, but Baxter-bloody-Quinn had just tipped up at his home address.

Nash stared at him, and steepled her fingers under her chin. 'There are very few people who can get away with wearing sunglasses indoors, and you're not one of them.'

'I know.' Stallard lifted the sunglasses up, and showed her his eyes. 'Have sympathy.'

The Nurofen were doing their best to gently launder the inside of his head, but it was still a dirty, dull ache. So what, it could have been worse. He could have flipped completely and ended up brawling with Quinn and his sidekick, the laughing pugilist. He guessed they'd made their point by being there, and that was enough. A show of knowledge and statement of intent.

Something else champing away at his brain was the lack of news from Frank. What about his visit to the refuge? One minute he's never off the phone, the next it's radio silence. The desktop monitor flickered into life and lit up with the SYP corporate screensaver. He logged onto the network, and fired up the Internet. Every now and then during his recuperation he'd run the same search or a variation of it, trying to find meaning behind that word Karina whispered. Mooser. He googled it again without thinking and scrolled through the results. The usual stuff.

He changed the spelling a few times and re-ran it. The same random nonsense.

Then he saw it and froze. Musor. Not a word found in dictionaries, but Russian slang for a police officer. Not complimentary either. It meant garbage or shit. He read it three times to be sure, and still didn't believe it. There was no way Karina could have known he was a UC when he went into that basement. Absolutely, no way.

CHAPTER 12

'Don't you have any pool cars?' said Stallard, chewing gum.

'No,' said Keith. 'We use our own, and claim mileage at the end of the month.' He checked the junction twice, and pulled out onto the main road. He was driving a '01 plate Nissan Micra, mint, with less than 50K on the clock. 'Who did you say we're going to see?'

'A kid who calls himself Tyler Montage, but whose real name is Kyle Salt. He's the only one of Joey's band I've not seen yet.'

Keith was quiet, until the penny dropped. 'So, he's changed his name to become a pop star like Gary Glitter and Alvin Stardust?'

'Spot on, but don't mention Paul Gadd. He's a kiddy-fiddler.'

'Shame, I used to be rather fond of the Glitter Band.'

Stallard tried to picture Keith in a silver jumpsuit, with platform boots, but it was too incongruous an image to conjure up, so he gave in and checked his watch. 'Any chance of breaking the twenty mile an hour barrier? It's just that we're supposed to be there at twelve.' He chewed some more. 'And I'm going to get cramp soon.'

'There's plenty of time. I was rather hoping we could agree a plan of action to get those panties I'm after.'

'Pervert.'

Keith pursed his lips and ignored the taunt. 'How much do you know about DNA?'

'I know it stands for the National Dyslexic Association, that's all.'

Keith gave a withering sideways glance. 'And familial DNA?'

'Look, I'm not interested in all the boring stuff, just tell me about the knickers.'

Keith sighed. 'So, the problem in this case, is the relative whose DNA I need to check, is a lady who spends all summer at her apartment on the Costa Brava. Now if she doesn't come back to the UK before October, that means I've got approximately four months in limbo, because I can't eliminate her from the enquiry, and I can't establish if she is the offender, but...' Keith pushed his shoulders back a little, and smiled with pride. 'I have a plan. What does everybody do on the night before they go away on holiday, whether it's six months in Spain, or a weekend in The Lakes?'

'Get pissed?'

'They put the clothes they wore that day into the laundry basket, don't they? Think about it.' Keith tapped his thin, yellow-tinged hair with his left forefinger. 'Nobody travels in dirty clothes, and nobody packs dirty clothes into their suitcase. So, if I can access said lady's laundry basket, I can get a DNA sample.'

'It won't be admissible as evidence in court.'

'I'm not bothered, because if it doesn't match the outstanding suspect's profile, then I can eliminate her, if it does – bingo – wait for her at the airport, and obtain an evidential sample from her. Either way, I win.'

Stallard chewed. 'Devious old bugger.' Then he checked his watch again. 'Does this sardine tin go any faster?'

Keith kept his eyes on the road and his mouth shut. Some comments didn't merit a response, verbally or physically.

After a while, the suburbs gave way to urban sprawl. The road became lined with terraced shops, takeaways, and patches of wasteland that had been colonised into coach parks and hand car-washes. Parked vehicles lined the streets. Traffic lights on every junction. They skirted the new university buildings, and cruised past the diesel fog of black cabs that snarled up the railway station entrance.

The flats where Tyler Montage lived were a 1960s brutalist block of concrete. Not long ago, this monolith menaced half the town centre from their stronghold high on a grassy hillside. They were built by post-war idealists, to replace the inner-city slums, and create wonderful estates in the sky with new close-knit communities. They were so wonderful and close-knit that occupants could hear their neighbours fart or fornicate, and smell whether they were having fish or bacon with their chips.

Over the years, they'd turned into bigger slums than the ones they'd replaced, with the lifts becoming urinals, and the walkways strewn with hypodermic needles and dog muck. There was a time, when the residents often felt the need to test Newton's Law of Universal Gravitation by means of a high balcony and household appliances, such as big, old, cathode-ray TV sets and knackered microwaves, and sadly, accidents did occur, particularly to panda cars parked below, which had been lured there on false calls.

But now, it was all different. Thanks to an EU grant, some developer had gentrified the shit out of the place. There were creches and cucinas, and the vast swathes of naked concrete had been clad in soft, pretty colours to give the impression of a Tuscan hilltop village shimmering under the hazy, midday sun.

Tyler Montage's flat was on the top floor, and when he answered, Stallard flashed his badge. 'Mind if we come in? I've brought my dad.'

As he walked through to the hallway, he could hear Keith whispering to Montage behind him. 'I'm not his dad. I'm Keith Blenkinsop, an investigator from the police cold case review unit.'

The living room was a mix of bohemian tat and hi-tech paraphernalia, with a few arty prints on the wall, and a bank of serious music stuff, that included mixing desks, amps, synthesisers, a couple of laptops and three Fender Stratocaster guitars – red, blue and butterscotch.

Stallard whistled. 'Bet the neighbours love you.'

Montage held up a pair of headphones. 'My music is for my ears only.'

There was a pile of black cases and boxes in the corner, each with the same logo stencilled on in white paint. The same one he'd seen before – a rat holding a magic wand.

'You've not formed another band then?'

'Why should I?' said Montage.

Stallard wondered how long he'd spent practising that top-lip curl. More Billy Idol than Elvis, but not bad. He shrugged. 'Because if Joey's dead, you're going to spend a lot of time waiting for him to turn up.'

'Who says he's dead?'

'The odds.'

'I don't need Joey Doane, and I don't need another band.' Montage was restless. His right leg was jigging up and down, and sweat was marbling his top lip. 'Why are you here?'

'I want to know where The Magic Rats got their drugs from.'

The sneer came back on Montage's face. 'We didn't do drugs. I already told all this to the other two coppers.'

'Yeah, but did they do this?' Stallard flat-handed Montage in the chest, and knocked him backwards, off his feet into a striped arm chair. 'And this?' He went to the chest of drawers, and pulled the top one all the way out, before tipping it over and emptying the contents on the floor. Pens, plectrums, CD cases, phone chargers, disposable lighters, batteries, bits of paper and some Indian takeaway menus – they all went flying.

'What the fuck are you doing?'

'I'm ripping this place apart until I find your stash.' Stallard shot him a grin. 'Then I'm going to drag your scrawny arse down the nick, and lock you up until you start rattling good and proper.'

'You can't do that.' Montage looked over to Keith, but he'd become interested in a Great Gatsby print that was hanging in a frame by the window. Nose pretty much glued to it.

'Yeah?' Stallard pulled the next drawer out. 'Keep watching.' He flipped it, and there was a tumble of books, cards and small electrical items. The bottom one was heavy. He dragged it open, and emptied it by hand: more books, an old printer, power leads, some loose tools and a biscuit tin full of screws, string and fuses. Then he went to the black boxes in the corner of the room, with the white, stencilled Harry Potter rats.

'Okay, that's enough.' Montage wiped his nose on the back of his sleeve. 'It was Joey. He used to sort me and Mickey out.'

'Who did he get the gear from?'

'I never asked.'

'Heroin?'

'And coke sometimes. Joey loved a massive speedball.' Montage laughed, and his face changed. He turned from a surly poser into a happy-go-lucky kid, with dimples and gleaming eyes.

'What do you think has happened to Joey?'

'Dunno.' The face shut down again. Just like a switch had been flicked. 'At first, I thought Baxter must have got him locked away somewhere, to try and straighten him out.' Montage shook his head, and ran a hand up his forehead to restore the lank quiff that had fallen across it. 'The recording sessions were coming up, and Joey's habit was spiralling out of control. We'd always just smoked and snorted after gigs to chill, then he turns up at the rehearsal room with needle marks on his arm, and says he's been giving blood. He thought we were idiots. I mean, who the fuck wants a junkie's blood?'

'That must have caused bad feeling in the band?' Stallard walked over to the wall, where the three Fender Strats hung in a line on Y hooks. 'Losing potential money is worse than never having had the hope or prospect of it – Mickey seemed really pissed off by it.'

'Ha. The whole band were. We hated Joey, we loved Joey. Hated him, loved him, hated him, loved him and then just hated him. That's what it's like in a band, you know – it's a family. A screwed-up family of control freaks. Did Mickey tell you about the royalty splits?'

'What about them?' Stallard lifted a mid-blue Stratocaster down from the wall, and ran his fingers along the maple neck.

'Hey, be careful. They're not copies.'

'What about the royalties?'

'Joey was on the contract as sole songwriter.'

'What's the problem, if he wrote the songs?'

'This is the twenty-first century, dude.' Montage raised his voice. 'All bands share the credits these days – even Coldplay which is basically Chris Martin.'

Stallard nodded. He wouldn't recognise the other members of Coldplay if they were standing in a police line-up with flashing arrows over their heads, and holding boards in front of them that said, *Member of Coldplay*. 'I guess that's where the real money is.' He put the guitar back, and took down another, this time candy-apple red. 'These Stratocasters must have cost a bomb. Bank of Mum and Dad?' He held it in front of him and strummed a few barre chords.

'You play?'

'In a different lifetime.'

'I'm still paying off the loan.'

'That can't be easy with no income.'

'Baxter has been cool about it.'

'You borrowed money from a shark like Quinn?'

'It's not like that.' Montage took the guitar and carefully hooked the neck back up on the wall bracket. 'They invested in us. They took us on when nobody else gave a shit about The Magic Rats, and stuck with us, and turned us into...'

'What? What did they turn you into?'

'It doesn't matter – you wouldn't understand. There are people out there in the music business who know how good we were, and what we could have achieved.'

'So, what now?'

'Every man for himself.' Montage knelt down, and started putting things back in the overturned drawers. 'Joey's probably dead in a ditch somewhere with his veins full of scag, and the band's fallen to pieces.'

'Is that what you think has happened to him?'

'Maybe.' Montage shrugged. 'I don't know.' He picked up a blank CD with *Demo* felt-tipped on it, and dropped it in a drawer with a rueful look. 'Like I said, Joey was going off the rails.'

'Is that why him and Shannon fell out?'

'No, that happened before we saw the needle marks. It was something personal that neither of them spoke about with us.' Montage looked up. There was a tinge of bitterness in his face. 'They were a family within a family.'

Stallard fingered the two silver rings in his left ear.

Shannon Doane seemed to be keeping something else from him, other than her penchant for trashing expensive cars. It was time she told him everything, if she really wanted to find out what had happened to her brother. She'd stomped off in a huff last night because she didn't feel trusted, but trust works both ways.

When they left Montage, he was still scooping up relics from his short-lived career, and cramming them back into the wooden drawers. He cut something of a forlorn figure. The quiff had once again lost its shape to dangle over his eyes, and the paleness of his skin was accentuated by angry red pimples. Stallard remembered the popinjay that had strutted around on stage at The Shapeshifter Club, but now there was no exuberance or pride left. Just bitterness and regret. A nascent taste of fame snuffed out by the inconsiderate disappearance of the band's creative soul and driving force. No coat-tails to hang on to.

Halfway to the lift, Keith produced a paper bag of mint humbugs from his pocket, and held it out.

'I'm not sure I'm altogether comfortable with this aggressive style of investigation – it's not how we operate in the Cold Case Unit.'

'You surprise me.' Stallard popped a humbug.

'I'm here because you need to be protected from confrontational situations, but you seem to be the one who creates confrontational situations. It's a conundrum, and I'm not sure what to do.'

'Relax, I'm fine.' Stallard put his arm around Keith. 'And don't go telling tales, or you'll have to find someone else to steal panties for you.'

CHAPTER 13

Mickey got the text. *Delivery in ten minutes.* What had taken them so bloody long? He was sitting on his own in the smoking shelter of The Greyhound, a skanky estate pub in the north of the city, chaining Bensons and picking scabs off his elbows. He itched all over and hadn't had a shit in three days, but so what? Nothing good comes to you in this world without a few consequences.

It was Joey had introduced him to it. He called it Apache or China Girl, and said it was the best thing since sliced heroin. He wasn't wrong. The only problem was, it didn't come cheap. That's why Mickey had to keep working, because he knew what would happen if he had no money. He'd have to go stealing or dealing. The two career paths of the skint smackhead. The wad of notes he'd got stashed behind the cistern at home was already getting smaller.

There was a squeal of tyres, and a black Audi Sport bounced into the car park to some booming drum and bass. Not a circumspect entrance. Mickey knew that people like them didn't need to be careful. Showing off in broad daylight was all part of their plan to instil fear and demand respect in the marketplace. Their own customers and the competition. Fuck the coppers – they didn't even count.

The driver's door opened and Woodsy got out. Mickey watched him walk straight past without a glance in his direction. All part of the choreography He gave it exactly thirty seconds and then went inside, and found Woodsy in the Gents, checking the cubicles were empty by booting each door open

Mickey was hopping with impatience. He already had the cash in his hand. 'Give me the gear, mate.'

Woodsy span round and pushed his flat nose up into his face. 'What did you say to him?'

'Who?'

'The ponytailed pig, Stallard, who do you fucking think?'

'Nowt he didn't already know.'

'Why have they reopened the case?'

'Dunno. Maybe something to do with Shannon.'

'Did you tell him about Joey?'

'I've no idea where Joey is…'

'What the three of you did?'

'Course I didn't. Do think I'm crazy?' Mickey was fidgeting and his palms were sweaty. 'Look, can I just have the China Girl?' Six twenty-quid notes fell from his hand onto the tiles bordering the urinal. He dropped to his knees, ignoring the piss-splashes and peeled them up. 'I can get clean ones. Don't go. I can get clean ones. Please…'

'Put your money away, these are on me.' Woodsy pulled two blister packs from his back-left pocket, and handed them over.

Mickey couldn't believe his luck. 'I owe you, mate.'

'I ain't your fucking mate. Remember that.' Woodsy's top lip was pulled tight across his teeth in a canine snarl. He held it a moment for effect, and then left.

There was a Spanish-Mexican takeaway place in a row of shops around the corner. Mickey bought a chipotle-chicken burrito with a small Pepsi, and took them into the recreation ground opposite. There were some bushes off the footpath there that he'd used before to score, when he couldn't make the journey home. He wasn't proud of it. That's what this stuff does to you.

The camping knife he used to cut up the pill was one he'd had since school. He took the foil off the burrito and the straw out of the Pepsi, and fired up his lighter. This is what it had come to. From the brink of stardom to chasing the dragon in a clump of council rhododendrons amongst the mounds of dogshit and discarded johnnies. He waited until the powder melted into a liquid, then sucked the vapour up into his lungs.

Now he could relax. He took a few more hits and let his mind wander off on its own. He's back on stage with The Magic Rats, and the crowd are going mental. Jumping and screaming and moshing into each other. Fast, then slowing right down into a drowsy blur. The drumsticks are like two long feathers in his hands, and a tender perfume is wrapping itself around the lobes of his brain.

Joey turns round from the mic and beckons him to the front of the stage. Shannon and Tyler smile encouragement. *Don't worry, everything's gonna be okay.* Mickey leaves his drum kit and moonwalks through maple syrup, between two monitors, laughing at the greatest joke he's ever heard. Tears are pissing down his face.

As he gets close, Joey takes his bass off, and rams the headstock through the front of the nearest speaker cabinet. There's no skull-splitting howl of feedback, just the sound of Mickey's own breathing getting longer and deeper. He watches as Joey climbs onto the sub-woofer and mouths something. *Follow me.* Then he lifts his arms to form a crucifix and falls backwards off the stage into a sea of arms. Somewhere, far away, there's a ripple of whoops and cheers.

It's Mickey's turn. He knows his family are out there. That's his mother waving like she did at his first school concert, and blowing her nose, pretending not to cry. He climbs onto the PA stack and steadies himself. He needs to be quick. He can feel himself going. Don't panic and fuck it up. Will they catch him? Can he trust them? Quick. Decide. His body stiffens, and he tilts back until he reaches the point of no return. Then he relaxes and lets nature do the rest. He falls and the lights go out.

CHAPTER 14

'Yes, number twenty-nine, that's the one.' Keith removed his spectacles, and let them swing on the lanyard round his neck. A look of twitchy excitement lit up his face.

Stallard examined the house. It was big for a semi-detached, brick-built with a protruding gable at the front, and a driveway that led to a rear garage. Two problems: the first was that the front garden had no fence or hedge cover, and the second was that the back door was actually at the side of the house, facing onto the driveway, and visible from the pavement. Everything was too open.

'What do you think?' said Keith. 'Can you get in?'

'Easy, but half the street would be dialling three nines.' Stallard turned round to the back seat. 'What do you think, Frank? If you were prepping this as a covert entry job, would it be achievable?'

'Okay, this is what I'd be looking at, if this was a regional op.' Frank cradled half a jumbo sausage roll and licked his thumb. 'I'd have the house itself under technical surveillance for 48 hours before, to make sure there's no movement inside, and I'd have this estate covered by a full surveillance team of twelve in six cars and a motorcyclist to eyeball any potential approaching target, and then I'd have a team of four dressed as workmen, with a tent and a big chevroned van, blocking the view of the house from the street. That's the minimum.' He bit the sausage roll, and bits of pastry flaked down his chin. 'What resources have you got?'

Stallard nodded towards Keith. 'Him.'

'Forget it,' said Frank, dispatching the remaining roll in one, and smearing crumbs and grease in his stubble with the back of his hand.

'Let's have a walk up the road together, Frank,' said Stallard. 'I want a private chat.'

They left Keith in the car, and strolled up the pavement. Stallard was uncomfortable. The estate was too middle class. No empty lager cans wedged in the privet hedges, and not a single mattress littering a front garden. Or a double. No dog shit on the verge, and no knackered white vans with rust bleeding through the paintwork. The cars here were smart and shiny, with a few droll bumper stickers, like *If You Can Read This – Thank a Teacher*. It was the sort of place that had a Neighbourhood Watch committee, run by a retired civil servant called Clive, and kids still did the Brownies and Cubs thing. Exactly the kind of community where people paid attention, and where a ponytailed and tattooed vagabond stuck out like a turd in a bowl of tomato soup. Even if the ponytail and tattoos suited said vagabond and complemented his natural rugged good looks.

'How close are you to finding Karina?'

Frank sucked his teeth.

'That means nowhere near?'

'You know what it's like.'

'No, tell me.'

'We don't have a mobile number, address, associates. Nothing.'

'Get something then.'

'How exactly, smartarse?'

'Cash, subterfuge, brute force – all your usual personal dating techniques.'

'Stop it.' Frank grabbed his belly and bent over. 'Oh, please, stop it, stop it, my sides are hurting so much. The pain, arrrgh.'

'Funny.' Stallard straight-faced. 'I'm telling you – she knew.'

'Bollocks. Forget that mooser bullshit.'

'It's musor.'

'Mooser, musor – same difference. Don't overthink it. Come on, let it go.'

'Piss off. Let me remind you who got stabbed, and whose job it was to prevent it.'

Silence.

Stallard clenched his jaw. Too late. The words were out. It wasn't the actual words, more the way he'd said them. Serious, not teasing. Tone and facial expression make all the difference at times like this, and they don't lie. Something had changed. What was it? He didn't really blame Frank for what happened in the basement of the Blue Butterfly, did he? Course not. Probably just frustration then. Not at Karina, against whom he bore no grudge, but at the thought that Jared Finn might walk free if she couldn't be found. Justice. A lottery where the prize is freedom.

Maybe he was still shaken by Baxter Quinn rocking up unexpectedly at his caravan? These things don't happen to undercover operatives. What next? A leaflet drop across the city emblazoned with his photograph and resumé – meet Harry, your personal, covert law-enforcement officer. Available for drug-buying, extortion-negotiation, ransom delivery, sting operations and all your long-term OCG infiltrations. Forget the rest, hire the best. Go on, you know it makes sense.

When he was about thirteen or fourteen, he used to hang about the skate park in town. Weekends and long summer evenings. He'd take his deck on the 52 bus with a couple of mates, and spend hours practising the moves. Jumps, kickflips, railslides, nosegrinds, the whole works. Carefree times. The kids came from all over, and formed their own community. The older ones looked out for the youngest. Someone always had music, and often there would be girls, either boarding or just hanging out. He liked that, because he could show off.

One day, a gang of older lads turned up. No skateboards. Just tins of cider and a Staffy on a thick chain choker. It was obvious what was going to happen. They started off asking to borrow money for cigarettes, then demanding, then threatening and then flat-handing kids across the face. When it was his turn, he was ready. One thing his father had drilled into him – always stand up to bullies. Get the first one in, and make it count. So, he did. Pretty soon he was on the floor getting his head kicked in. Cheers, Dad.

After that, he only went back to the skatepark on a few occasions. He wasn't scared, but something in his world had changed, and he couldn't figure out what exactly. It wasn't the same. Sometimes fate gives you a clue that it's time to move your life on to the next phase. Maybe that was happening with Frank.

The afternoon was hot and sticky. Stallard found himself at a familiar crime scene. The police station canteen. Today's victim was a ham and asparagus quiche that had been burnt to death in a horrific arson attack, before being served with new potatoes and salad. Cruel and heartless. The suspect was a middle-aged woman called Angela, whose psoriasis would have precluded her from handling food in most other walks of life, but this was South Yorkshire Police. Nobody gave a shit.

He was sat squeezing a third sachet of mayo onto the deceased, when Coleman and Katz came up to his table, carrying their plates.

'Got room for a couple of proper, frontline detectives?' It was Coleman, smiling.

Katz didn't wait for an answer. He sat down.

Stallard looked back over his shoulder to the door. 'When are they coming, the proper detectives?'

Coleman draped his jacket over the back of the chair opposite, and tucked the end of his tie inside his shirt. 'How are we doing with the misper case?'

'We? Thanks for trying to get it put back to bed, but it didn't work. It's still active and I'm on it.'

'I know,' said Coleman. 'Our gaffer says Hardcastle is way past his sell-by date.'

'By about fifty fucking years.' Katz didn't look up. He ate with his face directly over the plate, spooning chilli and rice straight up.

'Why don't you just get it served in a dog bowl?' said Stallard. 'Then you wouldn't need the cutlery.'

'Piss off.' Katz carried on spooning.

'The question is,' said Coleman, 'would you be so keen on pursuing this futile exercise if it wasn't for the delightful Shannon, who happens to be the missing person's sister?'

'What's it matter to you what I do?'

'If you were a proper frontline detective you'd understand.' Coleman just had a small piece of salmon, with a few leaves. 'It's about professional pride and etiquette.'

'Look, I'm not out to do anybody's legs.'

'Excellent.' Coleman ate the salmon. Knife and fork chinking on crockery. After a minute, he said, 'We wouldn't like it if someone tried to undermine or tarnish the reputation of the Major Incident Team.'

'That's not what I'm about.' Stallard ignored the grunt from over the chilli.

'Good.' Coleman chinked more salmon. Then. 'The last time someone tried that was at the CID Spring Ball, and it resulted in a very ugly incident.'

Katz dropped the spoon into his empty bowl. 'It was literally like the Battle of the Alamo.'

'Really?' Stallard stopped eating. 'There were two thousand Mexican soldiers at the CID Spring Ball?' He screwed his face up in astonishment. 'What about Davy Crockett, was he there as well?'

'Piss off.' Katz. Master of witty retorts.

Coleman wiped his mouth on a napkin, and checked his watch. 'Come on Katzy, we don't want to keep our guests waiting.' He stood, shot his cuffs and eased back into his jacket, before turning to Stallard. 'Please excuse us, Channel 4 are making another documentary on murder investigation, and seem to have taken a shine to us.'

Katz said nothing. Turned his back and walked off.

'Brilliant.' Stallard clapped. 'Keep the double act going. If you don't get your own series, there's something wrong.'

Coleman bent down, and lowered his voice. 'Shannon Doane is trouble.'

CHAPTER 15

B axter Quinn lived on an exclusive enclave in the west of the city. The houses, although each slightly different, were all big, five-bed beasts, with mock Palladian pillars at the front, and acres of lawn, undulating but flawless behind wrought-iron electric gates. His mock mansion backed onto a newly planted copse of rowan and wild cherry right at the end of the lane, and had its own outdoor pool and stool-lined bar. There was a quadruple garage, which had a terracotta-gravel turning circle in front of it, and in the middle of the circle was a fountain, where a stone cherub stood whistling and nonchalantly recirculating water through his modest penis. Class.

A little after 5pm, Baxter Quinn pulled up to the gates in a black BMW with the hood down. He used a remote to open them, and drove along the driveway lined by bright green, dwarf box hedging. The day was still hot. After he'd parked in front of the garage, he got out and tugged at the shirt sticking to his back. Then he did the same with the seat of his trousers, before grabbing a sports bag from the passenger seat, and heading for the house. All the time, he was unaware of the eyes watching him on his own CCTV system.

Stallard was sitting at the kitchen island. When Quinn walked in, he raised a half-drunk bottle of Peroni. 'Hope you don't mind, but I was parched.'

'What the fuck are you doing in here?' Quinn's voice was quiet, but he looked like a grenade with its pin just pulled.

'We never got round to having a chat this morning, so I thought I'd drop by.'

'Whose fault was it we didn't talk? You had your chance to have a chat this morning, and you missed it. Now you can piss off, I'm calling my solicitor.'

'Tell him to meet us at police headquarters.' Stallard fished in the pocket of his denim shirt and pulled out three small bags of white powder. 'While I was waiting, I thought I'd check the usual cocaine-stashing places, and before you say I planted them, may I introduce you to Keith, who filmed the search.'

Keith waved his iPad and gave a nervous smile. He looked like he might pass out any minute.

A cloud of indecision appeared on Quinn's face. He stood there clasping his mobile phone, in a rapidly sweating palm. Not so cocky now.

Stallard saw it. 'But I'm happy to forget about three fifty-quid bags of Charlie, if you're happy to answer a few questions about the disappearance of Joey Doane.'

'How do I know I can trust you?'

'Watch this.' Stallard emptied one of the bags out onto the marble worktop and marshalled the powder into a line with a coaster. Then he unscrewed a pen, and using the bottom half as a tube, snorted it in two hits, one up each nostril. 'That good enough for you?'

Quinn laughed. 'You were always fucking crackers, Harry.' He pocketed his phone and got himself a beer from the fridge. Relaxed but cautious.

Keith was quiet. He had his elbows on the table, and his head in his hands. The end of civilisation had just come early. Beam me up.

Stallard wiped his nose. 'Two days before he went missing, you gave Joey a package in the back room of their rehearsal place. Was that drugs as well?'

'It was an envelope, not a package, and don't listen to that sister of his, she's as loopy as you.' Quinn twisted the cap off his bottle and took a drink. 'And you already know it was his passport, because Mickey's told you. We collected all the band's passports for the tour, since sometimes the hotels get a bit funny, and Woodsy, that's the tour manager, has to provide ID for everyone.'

'Why did Joey want it back?'

'Said his solicitor wanted it. Said he might have to surrender it to the police or the court or something, and if he did, there was a better chance of him not getting locked up.'

'And did you believe him?'

Quinn tumbled a mouthful of beer in his cheeks. 'I don't know. I had a nasty feeling he might bottle the whole court thing, and piss off abroad somewhere, and that was the last thing we needed right then. It wasn't just the recording contract, we'd got interest from all over the place – promoters, sponsors, Internet-advertising agents…'

'So, is that why you threatened to kill him?'

'Yeah.' Quinn laughed. 'I threatened to kill the curly-haired, little bastard, in the same way as I could murder a plate of pie and chips. It's a figure of speech, isn't it?' He took another drink. 'I've got nothing to do with him going missing, but I'll tell you one thing, if he does ever turn up, I will bleeding kill him.'

'Is that because he owes you money?'

'Not the way you mean it.' Quinn's shaved head shook. 'We're a business, and we invested in these young kids, but without Joey, they're worth nothing. Zero. Zip. Nada. There was a period of a few weeks, when we thought it might all be a big set-up, and Joey would suddenly reappear from nowhere in a puff of dust – the original magic rat – and with that stroke of genius the music world would go crazy, and we'd all be raking it in. But that's not going to happen now, is it? Fat fucking chance.'

'Does that mean you think he's dead?'

'Yes, I think he's dead, and all thanks to his big sister. The one time in his life when he needed help, and she turned her back on him.'

Stallard's phone buzzed. He checked the message. 'I've got to go, but I'll swap you one more piece of information for these two remaining bags of coke.' He jumped down from the stool. 'How did you find out where I lived?'

Quinn looked puzzled. Genuine. 'My mum still lives next door to your auntie Jean.'

'Thought so.' Stallard lied. He dropped the two bags into a swing bin on his way out and cursed his own stupidity. Still, it could have been worse. The main thing was that there was no link to what had happened at the

Blue Butterfly or any publicity that followed. It wasn't some criminal mastermind or gangland overlord who'd breached the integrity of what was supposed to be a highly secure and robust system. It was good ole auntie Jean. But then, that's what always happens with highly secure and robust systems – someone's auntie Jean comes along and fucks them up.

The Nissan Micra was parked fifty yards away on the next lane. As they walked back, the lines in Keith's forehead were deeper than usual. Stallard guessed what was troubling him.

'Look.' He took a clear bag of white powder from his pocket. 'You don't really think I just did a line of Class A, do you? It's an old UC trick – snort some inert white powder to gain instant credibility in the seedy underworld in which criminal lowlife operate. Works every time.'

Keith didn't look convinced. 'What is it?'

'Talc, corn starch, maybe a bit of glucose. Nothing that a good sneeze won't sort out. Fancy a go?'

Keith shook his head. Stallard swapped the dealer bag for his mobile and rang the number which had just messaged him. An excited voice answered.

'It's me, Myers. The analyst. The one in the Cold Case Review Unit. The one you spoke to yesterday...'

'It's okay, Myers. I remember who you are. What are you still doing in the office at this time?'

'I'm not. I'm at home. But I have alerts set up that email me if there's any activity on any of the flags or hidden markers I've got in place, and I thought you might want to know that Joey Doane is still alive.'

'You sure?'

'He logged onto his Facebook account forty minutes ago, and sent private messages to two of his friends – a Tyler Montage, and a Mickey Flint – both of which appear to be in the same band…'

'Yeah, I know, but how quick can we get a location trace on this?'

'That'll take 24 hours, maybe more, because the case is no longer classed as immediate threat to life.'

'Shit.' Stallard looked skyward.

'But we might not need it…' Myers' voice was even higher than normal.

'Why not?'

'The three of them have arranged to meet tonight.'

CHAPTER 16

The Trattoria da Valentino was empty, apart from two tables. It was an old-school joint, with lots of red sauce, and schmaltzy soft furnishings to counteract the hard, wooden chairs. The tables had candles in Chianti bottles, which were covered in layers of waxy lava, and the walls had gilt-framed paintings by Raphael and Caravaggio. A little bit of Rome right here in the heart of the Steel City.

'I'm sorry. What did you say?' Laura's eyes never left the menu.

She'd chosen to meet there to discuss their relationship, because it was neutral territory. It made it sound as though they were at war, and this was a break from the trenches, thought Stallard. Perhaps he should have brought a football so they could have a kick-around. He took a hefty swig of house red, and leaned across the table.

'I've got to leave in a couple of hours – work – I'm sorry.'

Laura sighed. 'That's okay.'

What sort of response was that? Good or bad? Who knew? He'd expected more of an eruption, followed by a rant about how his work always came first. Hold on. This must be the latest psychological tactic: the aura of apathy.

'Look, I am sorry. It's just that I'm investigating a cold case, where this singer called Joey Doane has been missing for five months, presumed dead, and from nowhere he's arranged to meet his bandmates at ten o'clock tonight.' Stallard widened his eyes to add emphasis. 'It could be big. It could be the re-birth of The Magic Rats, and the solution to a puzzle the like of which has not been seen since Richey Edwards vanished.'

'Who?'

'The guitarist from the Manic Street Preachers.'

'Oh.'

'This is a massive deal. What I'm trying to explain about The Magic Rats is that they're...'

'Okay, okay, it's important, I get it' Laura studied her menu. 'Even I've heard of The Magic Rats, and I don't like music.'

What? Stallard couldn't believe his ears. Has the world gone mad? Since when did she not like music? How many hours had they lain in bed together listening to his stuff? Why hadn't she said anything when he'd been talking her through his vinyl collection, and linking each record to events in his teenage years? Wait a minute. Everybody likes music. Just another tactic to piss him off.

'Except I don't think he's still alive.'

'Really?'

'He's been murdered.'

'How awful.' Laura's eyes never left the menu.

'Did you actually hear what I just said?'

Laura nibbled on her bottom lip. 'I can't decide whether to have a starter or just some olives.'

Stallard let his look of amazement fade away. Was this to be his fate? Casually tortured by indifference. Why not just get up and walk out now? Thanks for the memories, love, but I'm off before I become completely emasculated by insouciance. No, that would be unworthy. She'd nursed him through week after week of convalescence and deserved better. He could still hear the never-ending rain on the roof of the caravan, and her laughter as they played Dirty Scrabble. Smell the Thai pork buns she'd steamed on his crappy electric stove, and taste the sweet and spiciness on her lips. He poured himself a refill, and tried to build a smile. It was a weak effort.

'Please don't be like this. I am sorry. Whatever I've done, I'm sorry.'

'All right, I shouldn't tell you this, but I'm desperate.' She fixed him with a solemn stare. 'Somebody rang the office yesterday to tell us they believed you were unfit to be at work.'

'Don't worry about it. That will be Keith, the old guy they've paired me up with. If he's fit enough to be at work, then I definitely am.'

'Not *physically* fit for work, *mentally* fit. People are worried about you, Harry, and so am I. We're worried that you're going to have an accident, or do something which puts your recovery back to square one.' She reached across the table and touched his hand. 'Don't forget, dealing with stress is my job, and I'm good at it, the same way you're good at being an undercover cop, so listen to me – if you don't slow down, those scars on your brain aren't going to heal, they're going to be burnt in there and keep flaring up for the rest of your life.'

It was difficult for Stallard to explain. Mainly because he wasn't sure himself of what churned round in his head. Life's dirty washing, that he had no desire to tumble dry and iron. All he knew for certain was that the training he'd been given was designed above all to instil in him one overriding quality – the strength to never show weakness. It's a UC thing. On the national undercover course, he'd been kidnapped by Special Forces playing the role of terrorists. They'd tied him to an old iron gurney in an aircraft hangar, and interrogated him on and off for twelve hours. It was an exercise that had since been stopped, after one recruit sued for false imprisonment and mental distress under the Human Rights Act, but Stallard had passed with flying colours. It just didn't seem that bad. He put it down to grit and bloody-mindedness inherited from his mother. The SAS were no match for her, even now.

'I need to get back to the Unit. The longer I'm away, the less chance there is of me being able to do it.' He put his hand on top of hers. 'You know what they say about falling off a horse, jump straight back in the saddle.'

'Sometimes it can be the worst thing you could do.' She slipped her hand away from under his and shook her head. 'Sorry.'

'What's the matter?'

'*You*, that's what. You've given me an ethical dilemma.' She took her first drink of wine and pulled a face, as though it was lemon juice. 'Really I should report yesterday's phone call to your line manager and the HR department, and look at setting up a case conference to discuss whether you should be at work at all.'

A waiter lolloped up to the table. He was a short, grizzled guy, with a chin that needed shaving twice a day. Laura ordered prawns and risotto, and Stallard followed suit. That was because he'd not looked at the menu. Then he ordered another bottle of house red, because the first was somehow empty, and after the waiter had grizzled off towards the kitchen, he grabbed Laura by both hands.

'There's no dilemma. You've got to make that report to my line manager, the same as you would for any other member of staff, and I'll take whatever comes my way. Hey, I'm ready for a holiday – two days back at work and I'm knackered.' He squeezed her hands tight. 'But forget about all that crap, what do you want to do about us?'

She was quiet for a long time. She took a deep breath, and glanced around the room, then out of the window, and then back around the room again, before finally looking him in the eye.

'I'm really not sure.'

'What if I stop being The Cliché? What if I build the new house for us?'

'It won't happen. You're stuck in your own world.'

'Try me.'

'I can't stand the thought of being let down again.'

'Are you saying we're finished?'

'I need trust.'

'It's my middle name. We're in luck.'

'You're doing it again, aren't you? Playing a part for the benefit of some imaginary audience.'

'Wait a minute. What if this is really me?'

'That's the problem – even you, the great Stallard doesn't know who he is.' Laura pulled her hands away. 'I need you to promise me that you'll never go back to the undercover unit.'

'Hah, I knew it, you're jealous.'

'The job's going to kill you. Just stop it.'

Stallard's chest went tight. 'I'm not sure I can.'

CHAPTER 17

Stallard got to the rendezvous point early. The location where Joey Doane had arranged to meet his erstwhile bandmates was out of the way and unusual for a social get-together. Alarm bells rang. What was the kid frightened of, or who was he hiding from? The place was a disused cricket pavilion, gently rotting in one of the city's municipal parks, flanked by woodland to the rear, and looking out over a two-acre patch of scrubland, where the old pitch was now overgrown. Once the site of epic battles between pub teams resplendent in white flannel, it was now a canine toilet. No more fours and sixes, just number twos.

He'd constructed a makeshift hide behind the pavilion on the edge of the woodland. Eat your heart out Bear Grylls. It was a lean-to structure of fallen branches, and green sack-cloth webbing that he carried in his go-bag. There were only two routes to approach the RV, and from the hide he could observe both. The first was a cinder track that snaked up from the park's main entrance, past a fenced-off square of tennis courts, and ended at a small overgrown car park alongside the pavilion. The other was a trodden-down path made by dog walkers, that emerged from an adjacent estate, and performed an oval around what had once been the perimeter of the pitch.

Before becoming a UC, he'd worked in Covert Ops, and they'd sent him on a CROP course – Covert Rural Observation Post. Run by ex-military. It's where they train a small cadre of specialists to undertake static surveillance in the great outdoors for days on end. Usually dug into a peat bog or perched up a tree like a twelve stone squirrel. No visible movement or sound allowed. Hours of fun. Especially trying to perform ablutions. It was the only course Stallard had ever actively wanted to fail, and he'd managed it. Easy. But he'd kept the go-bag that was personal issue to each student, and it included a pair of night-vision goggles. He used them now to survey the approach routes. Nothing, but it was still early.

Question. Why had Joey fixed up to see Tyler an hour before he met up with Mickey? Made no sense. Unless he had some information he didn't want both of his friends to know. Such as what? All three were in the same band, and shared the same hopes and dreams. No obvious secrets. Maybe something had happened in the five months since Joey disappeared that changed the dynamic? Or was it more basic that that – did it link back directly to the reason why he went missing in the first place? And why hadn't he arranged to meet Shannon? Whatever had driven those two siblings apart must have been bad.

Stallard checked his watch: 2145 hours. Another fifteen minutes before the first of the meetings was due to take place. He scanned the plot. Still nothing. No movement, human or otherwise, just the hum of traffic in the distance, and the lingering, pungent smell of skunk weed that some scallywags had been smoking earlier. Wow. That was an aroma that clung like fox shit to fur.

To pee or not to pee, was the question. His bladder was full, but he didn't move. Sod's law something would happen if he did. Hold it in. Think about something else – football, sex, Descartes's principles of philosophy. What about which toad had rung the Occupational Health Unit and reported him mentally unfit? Plenty to think about there. Sneaky bastards. Probably Keith, but you never know. Perhaps as a precaution, he should ask Fay Nash if she could swap the Boy Wonder for someone else. Younger. Less snitchy. Someone not obsessed with stealing dirty knickers. Who did that leave in the Cold Case Unit? Probably not many. Wait, what about…

Shit. Stallard jumped and his neck snapped back. He'd been on the verge of sleep, with his eyes closed, when some sort of internal alert system had injected a massive dose of adrenalin straight into his left ventricle. He shook himself, and checked his watch again. Settled down to concentrate once more on the landscape. Senses still tingling.

And that's when he saw the two figures. They were coming along the grassy path used by dog walkers, treading gingerly between the clumps of turf, and skirting the saplings that had over-spilled from the edge of the woodland. Dressed in all black, they occasionally glanced behind them, to make sure they weren't being followed. One was twice the size of the other. The big one was carrying a stick, and the smaller one was wearing a pork-pie hat. They got closer, and just before they disappeared around the front of the pavilion, Stallard recognised the big guy, and what he was carrying. *Oh, come on, tell me this isn't what I think it is…*

The hide that Stallard had constructed was about fifteen yards from the back of the pavilion, and it only took him a few seconds to walk round to the front, and climb the three steps onto its wooden veranda, where he came face to face with the giant.

'Hello, Mr Doane. Didn't know you were a fan of the Red Sox.'

'Uh?' Jim Doane stood there like a big startled rabbit.

'You've got a baseball bat, and apart from the fact that this is an old cricket ground, I'm guessing you weren't planning on using it to play sport.'

Jim Doane dropped the bat. 'I'm really sorry.'

Stallard turned to the smaller figure, standing to one side in the shadow.

'And I'm guessing you knew Joey's password, so logged on as him and invited the rest of the band to come and meet him.'

Shannon gave a little grin. Embarrassed. 'You are a real detective after all.'

'What were you two thinking of?' Stallard, raised his voice. 'You can't take the law into your own hands and beat the truth out of people, just because you think they might know something that you don't. That's not how civil society works.'

'What if it was your brother?' Shannon had regained her vim. 'What happened to Joey has something to do with the band. Or Baxter Quinn. Or both. So, what do you expect? What chance have we got trying to get information out of Quinn? Hmmm. Tell me that.'

'So, you decided to pick on the easy targets?' said Stallard. 'Well done.'

Shannon took off the trilby, and shook her hair loose. 'Look, it's not like we were going to work them over or anything like that. My plan was to see if Tyler and Mickey turned up, because if either one of them knew for certain that Joey was dead, then they wouldn't turn up, would they? They'd know straight away that it was something dodgy.' She fiddled nervously with the band of her hat. 'And I wanted to know if I could trust my bandmates to share information with me, and now I know the answer. They've both had all evening to ring me and tell me about this supposed meeting, and I've not heard a thing from them. It's not like it was a minor detail – they got a message from my missing brother and they never even told me.'

'Nice try.' Stallard picked up the baseball bat. 'But what about this?'

'Stop it.' Jim Doane stuck an arm out. The one with the tattoo. 'I wanted to protect my daughter.'

Shannon went and linked arms with her dad. 'Like I said, I can't trust Tyler and Mickey. They could run straight to the Quinns, and if Baxter turned up, things could have turned nasty.'

'So why here?' Stallard gestured across the moonlit wasteland. 'Ever heard of pubs? They have people in. Safety in numbers.'

'Blame me, it's my fault,' said Jim Doane. 'I've had enough, and I've got to do something. I've got to know what happened to my son, and if that means breaking a few arms, then so be it. Let's see how they play guitar or drums with a plaster cast on, and a…'

'Dad, shut up.' Shannon tugged at his sleeve.

'I saw this film once.' Jim Doane again. 'They got the piano player to talk by crushing the bones in his fingers with a hammer, because being a musician he…'

Shannon hit him with her hat. 'Dad, shut up. Just leave it. You're making it worse.'

'Sorry, love.' Jim Doane put an arm around his daughter, and turned to Stallard. 'And I'm sorry about causing you this trouble, officer. Just take me down the station, and do what you have to do. It doesn't matter anymore.'

'Go home,' said Stallard.

A train of cloud chugged across the moon, and in the distance the whoop of a siren in the night air signified another potential tragedy for a family just like the Doanes. Over on the far side of the old cricket pitch, a couple of spaniels appeared with their owner for a final ball-chase of the day, and beyond them in the housing estate, a drunken man was shouting an ode to his favourite football team. Life goes on, even when someone else's personal world has stopped.

Jim Doane and his daughter looked at each other and hugged. Then reluctantly, they let each other go, and trudged across the veranda towards the steps. As they passed by, Stallard tapped Shannon on the arm.

'Not you. We need to have a serious talk.'

'About what?'

'For want of a better word, let's call it the truth.'

CHAPTER 18

Tyler Montage turned up at the pavilion bang on ten o'clock. He arrived alone on foot, and hung around for five or ten minutes, kicking the dirt and checking his smartphone, before realising he'd been spoofed, and marching away. Pissed off. Stallard and Shannon watched it all from inside the woods. They waited another hour and a half, but Mickey Flint never showed. What did that prove? That he realised it was some sort of wind-up? That didn't mean he knew Joey was dead.

A little after midnight, Stallard wasted a bit of breath blowing on his black coffee before taking a sip. It still burnt the tip of his tongue. He cracked open a bottle of mineral water, and added a few splashes to his cup, before trying to swat away an oversized bluebottle that was buzzing around his head.

The café was an all-nighter down the east end of town, used mainly by road sweepers, cops and homeless alcoholics, a few of who were there now. The plastic chairs had been bolted to the floor so they couldn't be nicked and sold for cider or used to dash out the brains of fellow customers. That's the sort of establishment it was. A place that kept the underbelly of the city alive while the rest slept in their beds.

Stallard pushed a giant plastic tomato filled with ketchup across the Formica table.

'Never let it be said I don't know how to treat a lady.'

'Lady?' Shannon made a throaty laugh, and squirted a circle of thin cash-and-carry sauce onto her burger. 'I'm bloody starving, aren't you having anything?'

'No.' said Stallard. 'I'm more interested in hearing what it was that you and Joey fell out about before he went missing. The big argument.'

'Sorry? Fell out? I think you're...'

'Stop. Don't deny it. Witness, phone records, social media – they're not all wrong.'

Shannon lost her appetite. She put the burger down, and was silent. Then her face crumpled and tears started to flow. She snatched a handful of serviettes from a dispenser on the table, and dabbed her cheeks.

'What he did was so unfair. It was...' She had to stop, because the sobbing was taking her breath away. After a minute, the spasms died down. 'What he did was so unfair to our parents, after everything they'd done for us, that I couldn't forgive him. I'm sorry, that's the truth. I couldn't forgive him, and now I don't know whether I'll ever see...' The convulsions started again.

'It's okay, take your time.' Stallard scanned the café. Nobody seemed to care what the commotion was. That figured. 'What did he do, Joey? What did he do to your parents?'

'I still love the ungrateful little shit…' She sniffed. Blew her nose again. 'Sorry, it's too painful.'

'Whatever's happened to him, I'm sure it's not your fault. A problem shared is a problem halved.' Stallard – smooth talker and confidant to the general public.

Shannon took a deep breath. There was a blotchy rash coming up from her chest, and her eyes were black smudges.

'We're adopted me and Joey. Mum and dad couldn't have kids. They tried but realised, after a lot of years and heartbreak, that if they wanted a family, they'd have to go down the adoption route. I mean, why not, they had a lot to offer and a lot of love to give?'

Stallard nodded. It explained why Jim and Elaine Doane looked a little older than he'd expected.

'We were from different natural parents, and I was a few years older, but from my earliest ever memories, we were always a proper family. Mum and dad were just mum and dad. I think they told us about the adoption thing when we were quite young – probably before we started school – but after that it never got mentioned, and we had childhoods as happy as any I can imagine.'

Stallard risked another sip of coffee. 'They seem good people, your mum and dad. I'm sure they loved you as their own flesh and blood.'

Shannon gave a faint smile, and nodded. 'Absolutely. Me and Joey felt the same way about them, or at least I thought *he* did until that day he…' A fresh wave of tears came. 'He told me he'd found his birth mother. I'm not sure how – on Facebook I think, not through any official channel – and discovered that he had another brother and sister. Can you imagine? I said, what the hell do you think you're playing at, and he said he was just curious, but do you know what, he'd never even mentioned trying to find his birth mother before, and then as soon as we start getting a bit of success, *bang*, he's straight onto it.'

'What do you mean?'

'You don't know Joey, do you? All he ever wants to do is be showered in praise, and show people how talented he is – he craves approval and adoration all the time. So, what better person to get that from than your own natural mother? I said to him, isn't it enough to make our own parents proud, without you having to find the actual uterus that spawned you?'

'What did he say?'

'He never spoke to me again.'

'Do your mum and dad know about this?'

'Sort of. They know about Joey finding his birth mother.' Shannon prodded the forlorn burger with a finger. 'But not about the argument between the two of us. They're already heartbroken – that would make it worse.'

'Did he ever meet his birth mother?'

'Yes, I've got it all written down in the files at home.' Shannon looked like she might give the burger one last chance, but decided against it, and pushed the paper plate to one side. 'As you know now, I have Joey's password details for just about everything. It wasn't difficult to log into his Facebook, and see who she was, and find out that they'd already met.' She looked round the café, until she saw the toilet sign. 'Excuse me, I need to go and fix my face.'

When she'd gone, Stallard sat back, and tried to piece it together. If there was something in the original

132

investigation file about this, then he'd missed it. He couldn't have, could he? No, it definitely wasn't there. Coleman and Katz, those sticklers for detail strike again. Thanks guys. Probably too busy getting make-up applied for their next starring role. Or maybe Shannon and her parents had deliberately held back for personal reasons. Problems in the family, stay in the family.

One thing it didn't explain was how Shannon and Joey could do the sibling harmonies so perfectly without being genetically related, but then again neither were the Righteous Brothers. Or The Ramones. Not like they harmonised much. What it did explain was how Joey was a bog-ugly kid with an exaggerated sense of his own importance, while Shannon was attractive and self-sufficient.

On the next table, a tramp with a patch of soiled gauze taped over one eye, drooled tea down his scabby chin into a polystyrene cup, and recited random snatches of scripture. Hair like a roadkill badger, and a thick army overcoat, even though the air was hot and sticky. Every thirty seconds, he looked over his right shoulder and shouted, *for God's sake, leave me alone, Tony-fucking-Blair, or I'll cut you to ribbons, man…* Nobody batted an eyelid. Stallard made a mental note – great persona to adopt if you ever get back to the UC unit.

Shannon reappeared. She had the pork-pie hat back on, and her face was restored to near perfection. A table of council workmen in vests and orange trousers, stopped playing cards to watch her walk by. When she got back to the table, she didn't sit down, but walked around it and yanked Stallard to his feet by the wrist.

'Come on. I want to show you something.'

CHAPTER 19

'Give me a clue.' Stallard was steering his faithful Jeep back towards town. The roads were empty, apart from the odd black cab or private hire, and the air was wet and heavy like a late-summer night in New Orleans.

'Head for the university. It's a little club called *The Wild Tulip,* and every Wednesday night is *our night.* The guy who runs it, Leo – who's a friend and massive fan from the early days – he puts on a special *Magic Rats* fundraiser event. He started it a couple of weeks after Joey went missing, and for a while other bands came and played for free, and the place was rammed, but now, you know, it's kind of dwindling as each week passes.'

'Time is a thief. You can't stop people moving on.' Stallard slowed down to let a Battenberg traffic patrol car fly past. 'So, this event of Leo's, what is it raising funds for?'

'At the start we used a big chunk to set up the *Justice for Joey* website, but now it's used to keep the push going on social media, mainly Instagram where we can target the right bracket of young people who are into indie music.'

'Is it worth it after so long?'

Shannon bristled. 'Yes, of course it is. We're still getting sightings all the time from all over the world. People send us photos from their smartphones. Okay, most of them are holiday selfies showing some random guy in the background with curly hair, but it only takes one photograph to be a game-changer. The main problem is, we have to put up with all the sad bastards who pretend to be Joey and send us stuff saying, *I'm living it up in the Hotel California – piss off and stop trying to find me,* or *I'm working down the chip shop, I swear.*'

'If you think Joey's been killed, why are you putting yourself through all this? Trawling the Internet is only ever going to attract a load of bottom-feeding idiots.'

'The appeal for sightings of Joey is aimed specifically at the two days after he went missing, and before his car turned up at the Humber Bridge. Nobody knows where he was during that time, and obviously that's where the answer to all this lies. Those 48 hours are crucial, They're the key...' Shannon swallowed hard, and chewed on a bit of thumbnail. 'And until I see his body, there's always hope, right? That's why I examine every stupid selfie and read every stupid message.'

'Sorry.' Stallard sensed the pain. His questions were poking around inside the wound and it was time to let it rest. 'Maybe I could get one of our analysts to look at what you've collected, and see if there's anything in there for us to prioritise. You know, what we real detectives call *fast-track actions.*'

Shannon smiled. 'I'd appreciate that.'

The Wild Tulip was just off the tram tracks that ran out from town centre towards the university. It was a pop-up venue that specialised in live music, and 2-4-1 booze deals guaranteed to attract students and schoolkids with their fake IDs. It had popped up between a kebab shop and a bookie's, in premises that used to be an old-style boutique over two floors, and still had the swirling marble staircase and stained-glass chandeliers hanging from the ceiling. It all added some art deco pizazz to an otherwise charmless building.

'He's with me,' said Shannon, to a young guy with a big beard on the door, who stamped the back of Stallard's hand with a splodge of purple ink. It was supposed to be a tulip, but it looked more like a phallus. With a bit of luck, it'd wash off before work. Tattoos of bell-ends were likely to be frowned on in the Cold Case Unit.

There was no band playing, but a DJ on a podium was filling the room with early '90s grunge. A handful of kids were throwing shapes on the dancefloor, and another dozen or so were just hanging around in knots of two or three. Stallard couldn't help noticing that most of them were wearing the same fluorescent yellow T-shirts, and there was a lot of facial hair. Shannon took hold of his arm, and escorted him up the marble staircase to where a bar lined one wall, and where the noise-level was less damaging to the inner ear. Again, there were only another dozen or so customers up there, nearly all sporting the same fluorescent uniform.

The girl behind the bar came round and kissed Shannon, then went and fetched a bottle of Jack Daniels and a jug of ice cubes. She set them down on a stumpy table made of reclaimed planks, and Stallard poured two generous helpings onto the rocks. He'd just chinked glasses, and swallowed the first mouthful, when another bushy beard appeared. This one belonged to a stocky man in shorts, with his hair scraped back into a sumo top-knot.

'This is Leo,' said Shannon. 'Leo, this is DC Stallard, the officer I told you about.'

'Nice one.' Leo did his own fist-pump in the air. 'Any friend of the band is welcome here, and as a new disciple to the cause may I present you with this gift on behalf of Joey.' It was the fluorescent yellow T-shirt.

Stallard accepted it with a suitably solemn and grateful nod. *Disciple to the cause?* Blimey, Joey had skipped sainthood and gone straight up to being the new Messiah. Funny how popular some people became once they're dead, even though in life they'd been obnoxious pillocks who nobody'd liked. Not Jesus Christ, but maybe Joey Doane.

'Put it on then,' Shannon smirked. 'Come on, make sure it fits.'

'Come on, man,' said Leo. 'Join the club.'

'It'd be a privilege,' said Stallard, teeth gritted, already regretting the decision to allow himself to be dragged there. Now he'd been pressured to swap his vintage black denim shirt and its classy, embroidered piping for something that looked like a hi-vis safety vest. He ran his hand down the studs to unfasten his shirt, and took it off, pleased to see Shannon give him a sidelong glance to admire his tattooed upper body. Then he pulled on the neon yellow T-shirt, and looked down at the black lettering on his chest – *Who the fuck are the Magic Rats?*

'Nice one,' said Leo. 'Give me a shout if you want anything.' And the beard was gone.

Stallard looked at the slogan. 'I don't get it.'

'Have you never heard of *Who the fuck are Arctic Monkeys?*' said Shannon. 'It was their first ever EP, and because someone once joked that we were the new Arctic Monkeys, Joey thought it was hilarious to get this T-shirt made up, and wear it on stage every night of our tour...' She drifted off into a memory somewhere, and shook her head. 'That was the silly bugger all over. Anyway, it's become a sort of tribute to him, and we try and get as many people as we can to wear them, because it keeps his story current and stops people forgetting he ever existed. It's like our new brand.'

'Okay, I get it now.' Stallard swirled the ice in his glass and took a drink. Whatever the backstory, the crap shirt was going in the bin as soon as he got home.

Shannon leaned closer and he felt her breast brush across his arm.

'Here's a little test for you. Name one frontman or woman who was a good bass player *and* singer, and you're not allowed Paul McCartney, because obviously he was a genius, and don't say *Sting*, because obviously I said *good* bass player.'

Stallard sucked his cheeks. It wasn't a subject he'd ever given any time to, but thinking about it now, all his favourite frontmen were guitarists, not bassists. He took a drink. Played for time, savouring the hot, oaky smoothness, until he had a flash of inspiration.

'Phil Lynott.'

'Well done.' She patted him on the thigh. 'The point is this – it's virtually impossible to sing the melody of a song and simultaneously play a bass-line which is following a completely different rhythm, but Joey could do it better than anyone.'

Stallard creased his brow. 'Are you saying Joey was a genius?'

'Not really.' She laughed. 'Just some kind of freak.' Her face dropped. 'It makes you wonder what gets passed down to us in our genes...'

Stallard had a good idea what he'd got passed down. He'd got his mother's stubbornness and love of the arts, and his father's cynical selfishness and love of booze. A great combination. Didn't really explain how much was nature and how much was down to nurture. *They fuck you up, your mum and dad. They may not mean to, but they do...*

What would Larkin have made of the mess inside Joey Doane's head? A kid who wasn't happy being fucked up by one set of parents, but wanted to find some more to fuck him up even worse? What was it about gifted people, that they often turned to drugs, or was it all part and parcel of how their brains were wired up? Genius and madness – the bipolar brothers in arms.

He realised an hour had passed. They'd spent it escaping their troubles, by talking about anything other than The Magic Rats or police work. Shannon had regaled him with tales of growing up listening to her dad's record collection, and long drives to Cornwall for family holidays. Stallard had preferred to talk about the future, because that's what dreamers do. They'd swapped *favourites* – favourite band, favourite single, favourite album track, favourite guitar solo, favourite live performance by a band or solo artist.

Now, he got the urge to try and explain why he was so committed to Joey's case. Tell her the story of a long-haired teenager in a rock band, who joined the police, and became afflicted with regret. How he gravitated to the undercover world, because it was role-play and the next best thing to being on stage. But he didn't. The whole thing would have sounded stupid and disrespectful. He still had a vocation, whereas Joey's had been snatched away.

Time to leave and he still couldn't decide if he was being deliberately schmoozed. Whether Shannon was softening him up, so he'd be more pliable when she wanted to manipulate him in whatever way suited her private investigation into Joey's disappearance. Or was she genuinely interested in him? Bit of both? He was happy with that. He didn't mind giving the impression of being a dolt, as long as he remained in control. Any suggestion that the relationship was clouding his judgement, then he had to make a clean break.

In the Regional Undercover Unit, he'd always had Frank to watch his back. Every deployment was debriefed, and every contact discussed. They would have talked about Shannon at great length, because she was the kind of woman that could cause problems. Frank would have advised him on what was acceptable and what was not acceptable, and made a written record for the file. This methodical approach helped Stallard, because it gave him a clear, objective framework to operate within, and it helped the organisation, because it gave them the means to cover the corporate arse. That was the trade-off.

This time, he was on his own, and there was no cover officer to debrief him. What would he have said if there was? That the witness Shannon Doane was a determined and resourceful woman, with a magnetic charm she switched on and off at will? That she didn't trust the police? She held information back for her own purposes, and wasn't afraid to use unconventional tactics to achieve her objectives? She loved her brother, and deeply regretted arguing with him? Yes, he would have told Frank all those things, but there was something else, and Stallard knew he would have struggled to explain it at the debrief – a feeling that the argument between Shannon and Joey was somehow linked to his death.

Stallard followed Shannon out of the club and found the night air still warm and clammy. After the intimacy of their conversation inside, there was now an awkward silence. She stumbled and laughed. He caught her arm, and thought he saw a look in her eyes asking not to be left alone. Maybe she really was *trouble* like Coleman had said, and he had been genuinely trying to warn him? It seemed unlikely, but Stallard hailed a passing cab before anything else could be said, and opened her the back door. Then he watched it drive away, and couldn't decide if he'd done the right thing.

Chapter 20

Modern managers set great store by their open-door policy, designed to make them more visible and approachable. Gerard Hardcastle was the opposite. That's why Stallard had to knock and wait until Mr H pressed a little button behind his desk, which turned the red light on a panel outside his door to green. Enter now underling, into the palace of the great emperor. QPM.

Stallard walked in with his hand raised. 'Yes, I was late. My fault, no excuses.'

Hardcastle peered over his bi-focals. 'Late? I don't know what you're talking about. I don't expect my staff to work until midnight, and then turn up at eight next morning.' The moustache twitched. 'Yes, yes, I know about Joseph Doane's supposed resurrection on Facebook. There's nothing happens in the Cold Case Unit that I don't know about.' He picked up a sheaf of papers on his desk. 'I have morning prayers every day, where the team leaders brief me and the analysts prepare updates, so my finger is always firmly on the pulse.'

A cloud fell on his eagle-like features. 'No, it's not timekeeping I wanted to see you about. I had a call first thing from the HR department – they want to set up a case conference with me and the Occupational Health Unit to discuss your fitness to remain at work. I thought you ought to know. Have the opportunity to make any representations you consider pertinent.'

Stallard shrugged. It hadn't taken Laura long to shop him. She must have typed it on her smartphone on her way home last night, the taste of tiramisu still fresh on her lips. Frailty thy name is woman.

'The thing is,' said Hardcastle, 'I detest the HR department. They're about as much use as a johnny machine in the Vatican. Shit-scared of their own shadow, the lot of them, so if they want to place you on mandatory sick leave, I'm inclined to object. But first, I need to know what you want to do.'

'Stay at work, naturally.'

'Because of the Doane case?'

'I don't want this to sound immodest, but I'm onto something.'

'Did I tell you about the Burlington Estate murders?'

'Yes, great detective work.' A white lie. Whopper.

'Every now and then, a case comes along that defines us as individuals for the rest of our service and beyond. The Burlington Estate murders was mine.' Hardcastle pointed to The Little Mermaid music box on his coffee table. 'The Doane case could be yours.'

Stallard stared at the music box. Nope. Still didn't get it. Must remember to ask the old man about it one day. Scrub that. Life's too short. 'I will find out who killed Joey Doane, if you make sure I don't get put back on the sick.'

The Cold Case Unit didn't have their own briefing or meeting room. They had the use of one on the ground floor, which belonged to the Neighbourhood Policing Team, and with whom they shared the building. It had a giant, oblong beech table surrounded by corporate-blue swivel chairs, and the walls were covered in traffic-light crime charts, coloured red, amber and green, depending on the seven-day rolling performance against each target. This week was mainly red. That would be kicked-arses all round, and lots of self-flagellation.

At one end of the room was an old touch-screen Smartboard, with a laptop hard-wired into it. Myers was sitting at the controls, trying to stop his hands shake with nervous excitement. The only other people in the room were Stallard and Keith Blenkinsop.

'So, when I got to work this morning.' Myers. Helium-voiced and a hundred miles an hour. 'I didn't know that Joey Doane hadn't turned up last night – I'm still under the impression he's resurfaced – and that gets me to thinking – if that's the case, then he must have staged his own suicide.'

'By abandoning his car next to the Humber Bridge?' Stallard helped himself to a Jaffa Cake from a plate leftover from the earlier performance meeting.

'Correct.' Myers made a couple of keystrokes and silent video footage appeared on the screen. 'I got this digital file from the original investigation. This is the M18 north of Sheffield. There's ANPR running full-time on these cameras, which is how we know that at 0127 hours and 43 seconds on Monday the 3rd of February, Joey Doane's Ford Pickup travelled towards the M62.'

Stallard chewed on tangy orange and watched the video. It didn't give away much detail. The camera must have been mounted on a bridge over the motorway, and it showed a steady but randomly interspersed stream of headlights approaching at speed and disappearing directly below. All strangely silent.

'That's the day he should have answered bail, and the same day his car was found abandoned.'

'Yes...' said Myers. 'Just another couple of seconds. Here, this is it.' He paused the video. 'There, that vehicle in the inside lane is Joey Doane's pickup. The original investigative team viewed this footage, and concluded that it supported the suicide theory.'

Stallard squinted at the screen. The image was fuzzy. Totally dominated by the light coming from the headlights. It was only just possible to make out that the vehicle in question was a pickup truck, rather than a regular saloon, so there was no way of identifying the driver, not even using the best enhancement techniques.

'So, what did the original team miss?' An image of the Coleman and Katz double act flashed through Stallard's mind. 'To be fair, it doesn't look like they could have done much more with that footage, given the quality of the recording.'

'The other car,' said Keith Blenkinsop, removing his spectacles. 'They missed the other car.'

Myers beamed.

'What other car?' Stallard, mouth full. Behind the game.

Keith explained. 'If you are going to abandon your own vehicle at two o'clock in the morning, pretty much in the middle of nowhere, how are you going to get back?'

'I'm with you.' Stallard stopped chewing. He'd caught up. It had taken a while. 'If there's another car, being driven by his mate, they're probably travelling in convoy on the way to the drop-off zone, but then only one comes back, and if the Humber Bridge is about an hour away, then his mate's car should make another appearance around 0330 hours.'

Myers' grin was wider than the Humber estuary. 'It's actually 0342…wait…' He ran the video another second. 'There, in the middle lane. Not quite in convoy, there's one vehicle between it and Joey's pickup truck. The registration number is HG17 EWA.' He opened up another file, and ran a new video. 'Here we go. The ANPR picks up the same number, HG17 EWA, travelling southbound at 0342 and 10 seconds.'

'Of course, it could be coincidence,' said Stallard, sensing that the analyst was still holding something back. 'Whoever was driving that car might have just travelled to somewhere else roughly an hour away and be driving home again. Who does the car belong to?'

'This is why it's highly unlikely to be a coincidence,' said Myers. 'The number HG17 EWA has never been registered. Whoever helped Joey abandon his car was using false plates.'

'Wrong.' Stallard jumped up. 'You mean whoever *killed* Joey was using false plates.'

'That too,' said Myers.

Stallard charged round the table and hoisted Keith up in a bear hug. 'What did I tell you? This is not a bloody suicide.'

'Put me down.' Keith landed breathless, and tucked his shirt back in. 'You may be onto something, but our way is to be methodical and meticulous. Slowly, slowly, catchy monkey.'

The initial rush of excitement drained from Stallard's body. How long had he got until the case conference met to discuss his mental state, and what if they decided he was unfit to remain at work? That meant he might not have the luxury of a slow and methodical approach in his quest to catch Joey's killers. It was time to pick up speed, and he knew where he heading next.

Nobody had mentioned Joey Doane's girlfriend to him. It was like she didn't exist. That was strange, because sexual partners can often be the depositories of someone's innermost thoughts and feelings. Their desires, their fears, their hopes for the future. And yet from Joey's parents, his sister and his bandmates not a word about the young woman he slept with. Like the curious incident of the dog in the night, they had all remained quiet.

CHAPTER 21

Joey Doane's on-off girlfriend, Rosie, lived in a modern townhouse on a bright red-brick estate that looked like it had been clicked together by toddlers out of Lego. It was a social housing development, which nestled incongruously in the middle of a swathe of tired, grey maisonettes. An oasis in a desert of drabness.

She answered the door in pyjamas. 'Have you come about the cats?'

'Police.' Stallard badged her. 'We want to talk to you about Joey Doane.'

Rosie leaned forward and used a suspicious frown to scan left and right. 'Come in quick, before the cats see you.'

She waved Stallard and Keith Blenkinsop through to the kitchen, and quickly slam-bolted the door shut. An attack of feline commandos was clearly imminent. Then she padded barefoot to a smoked glass table, sat down on plastic garden chair and lit a cigarette.

'Has he found himself then?'

'I can't do cryptic clues. Give me an easy one.' Stallard stood in the middle of the room, so as not to touch any of the surfaces, all of which were covered in grime. Even the clean glasses on the draining board had a film of grease and dust. Gross.

Rosie sucked hard on the cigarette's filter, making her sunken cheeks even more cadaver-like. 'Has he come back from wherever it was he went to find himself?'

'Is that what he said?'

'That one and a lot of other lies.' Rosie exhaled through her nose.

'Tell me about them.'

'Oh, there's so many.' She posed a second in contemplation. Rodin's The Thinker with a JPS Superking. 'Like the one about how he was suddenly rich, and the one about how he had to go away.' She took another drag. 'And best of all, the one about how, when he'd found his feet, he'd arrange for me to join him.'

Stallard looked at Rosie. What did Joey see in her? She was emaciated, with oily, lank hair, and lips thinner than a pair of paper cuts. Her skin was flaky with an unhealthy tinge of yellowness that went nicely with her teeth. So what? Beauty's on the inside. Or maybe when your veins were shot through with heroin, there was a puff of smoke – *poof* – and she turned into Marilyn Monroe. That would be magic.

'Tell me something. Did the Quinn brothers supply Joey with the heroin found in his apartment?'

'No comment.' Rosie chewed on where a fingernail had once been.

It confirmed what he already suspected. *No comment.* It still didn't mean much. The Quinns would have never been hands-on with the gear. It would have always been an intermediary doing their dirty work. 'Why did he have to go away to find himself?

'Something to do with the money. Like too good an opportunity to miss.' She stubbed the cigarette out in an overflowing saucer. 'Bastard. I'm better off without him.'

Better? What had she been like when they were together? He didn't feel like hanging around too long. It was either Rosie or the place, but something gave him the creeps, and he craved fresh air. On the way to the front door, he hesitated.

'Did Joey ever speak about his family?'

'Heeeeee… heeeeee.' A laughing wheeze, and Rosie's frame rattled with mirth. 'He's too selfish to talk about anything but himself.' The wheeze turned into a cough. A lung-wrencher. It doubled her over and she hacked away for a full minute. When she came back up for air, there was a look of bitterness in the red, watery eyes. 'The only thing he said about his family was he was glad that bitch wasn't his real sister.'

'Sounds like a great guy.'

Rosie opened the front door, and her demeanour instantly changed again. A wary scowl appeared and her head darted from side to side. 'Quick, as fast as you can before the cats see me. Go, go, go…'

No sooner had Stallard's back foot hit the path, than he heard the door slam shut behind him. He looked around the garden, and in those of the neighbouring houses, but the whole area was a cat-free zone. When he reached the pavement, he noticed Rosie standing in the front room window. She'd lit another cigarette, and was back on watch, scanning the world outside her house for an unseen enemy. Maybe it wasn't the cats she was really frightened of, but some other savage animals with less fur, and more bags of white powder.

He'd gone two yards on the pavement when he heard something in his head that turned his blood to ice, and stopped him dead in his tracks. SPLAT. The sound of a massive bollock being dropped from a terrific height. At least a mile. What the fuck? Why had it taken him so long to see the obvious? How could he have not made the connection when Shannon told him about the two of them falling out? Idiot. He felt sick. The great detective fails to spot a scientific non-sequitur that a schoolchild would have picked up every day of the week. What had Rosie said about Joey? He was glad that bitch wasn't his real sister. REAL SISTER.

Coleman and Katz had used Shannon's profile from the DNA database to eliminate the body lying in Hull morgue. The lazy, posing bastards. Problem was her and Joey weren't blood relatives, which meant one thing. Cadaver client reference number 4659 in the long-term freezer cabinet was probably Joey Doane. He'd been lying there for months, because the fancy murder squad detectives tried to short-cut the system, instead of putting in the leg-work required to get a full sample relating to their missing person. Suicides aren't sexy. Simple as that. Now he was going to have to pick up the pieces.

CHAPTER 22

Problem. How to get a sample of Joey's DNA to run checks against the body in Hull? In the olden days, dental records to establish ID might have cut the mustard, but not now DNA was top dog. Someone must have got a bag of Joey's belongings, and no doubt his DNA would be all over it, but so would lots of other profiles. Messy and time-consuming. More to the point, Stallard didn't want to alert the family to what was happening. There was a slight chance that client 4659 was not Joey, and while ever that remained the case, things were best kept on a need-to-know basis. No point advertising the existence of a huge fuck-up if there was still a glimmer of hope. Even a tiny one. The reputation of the force was at stake, or what was left of it.

Next best option was tracing and obtaining a sample from the birth mother. He didn't much fancy that either. No guarantee she wouldn't go running to the press. *Body left on slab due to police incompetence.* The local rag would have a field day, and Coleman and Katz would get their backsides busted into uniform. Okay, so maybe not a bad idea. He was warming to it.

He sat in the Cold Case Unit office, and stared off into space, while twiddling the two rings in his left ear with the fingers of his left hand. That's what he always did when he needed a plan, and it seemed to work most times. Perhaps he should patent it. The earring-twirling decision-making model, courtesy of Harry John Stallard.

'Penny for them.' Keith rolled alongside in a blue swivel.

'How can I get my misper's DNA, and don't say dirty boxer shorts. None left.'

'Hairbrush?'

'We're talking about a man.'

'Torch, then.'

'Eh? Where do you think he's put it to get DNA on it? Up his back...'

'Low Copy Number DNA from where he's handled the batteries.' Keith's nose did a little twitch. Pleased with itself. 'Batteries are ideal, because they're usually only handled once straight out of the packet or box.'

'Brilliant, except nobody under sixty-five owns a torch. They've all got smartphones...'

Stallard stopped. Joey's phone was missing, but Keith was onto something. The old fox. He made a call to Tyler Montage, and fed him a line about trying to track down some concealed drugs. It didn't take long to establish that Joey had three things that took batteries. A chromatic tuner, which he used to set the pitch of his guitar strings. The bass guitar itself, which had an on-board pre-amp to boost the signal before it reached the pickups. And something called a Big Muff – yes, a Big Muff – which was a distortion pedal he played his guitar through.

Within an hour he had all three batteries and was in the forensic submission unit of the Scientific Support building. Doing all three was probably overkill, but if the same profile was found on all of them, it was Joey's. Happy days. Or maybe not. It would mean extinguishing the last flicker of hope for the Doane family. Young Joey wasn't sunning himself on a tropical beach. He was just lying around in a freezer waiting to be collected and cremated. Win some, lose some. At least there would be closure, and the investigation could focus on how he got there. Shame about Coleman and Katz, and their budding career in fly-on-the-wall documentaries.

Stallard smiled. Gary, the old guy on the forensic submissions desk was ex-job and grouchy. He said sending all three batteries for profiling was too expensive. Likewise, fast-tracking was an added cost, reserved only for suspect-in-custody cases and life at risk. No exceptions. It was like Gary had to pay for everything out of his own salary, and his grandkids would starve. Stallard explained about the body in Hull and asked Gary if he wanted to be complicit in the biggest balls-up since The Yorkshire Ripper turned out not to have a Geordie accent. Gary didn't. So, all three batteries were premium fast-tracked.

It would still take twenty-four hours to get the results. No point mooching around killing time. One good turn deserves another, so he made a phone call, then drove back to the Cold Case Unit, and handed Keith his jacket.

'Okay, let's go and steal some knickers.'

'Seriously?'

'Bottle gone?'

'I wasn't expecting…'

'Now or never. I've got my secret weapon in place.'

They went in the Nissan Micra. Less of a sore thumb than the Jeep, and it meant that while Stallard was doing the business, Keith could sit outside behind the wheel. The world's oldest getaway driver. What could possibly go wrong? Nothing, as long as it didn't require speed, quick reflexes or a strong bladder.

The street was quiet on arrival. Stallard showed Keith where to park up, and then settled down to wait. The pantie-woman was called Amanda Paice. She might be summering on the Costa Brava, but Stallard wanted to make sure there wasn't a cleaner or relative inside the house before he made an approach. Tradecraft. The thing that burglars and covert cops have in common.

When Stallard judged the time was right, he opened the car door. 'Wish me luck.'

'Shall I honk the horn if anyone approaches?' Keith, panicking.

'If you want me to beat you to death for advertising our presence.'

'Please yourself.' Keith, sulking.

Stallard carried a shoulder bag and clipboard. It was a long time since he'd done his buggers and burglars training course, and things felt a little rusty. He knocked on the front door and waited. Nothing. He knocked again, and gave it few seconds before walking round to the back on the house. There was no alarm box. Good.

He peered in through a gap in the lounge window curtains, careful not to put his fingerprints on the glass, and didn't see anything to suggest recent occupation. Good. He came back round to the driveway, and checked the bins, finding all three empty. Good. Then he retraced his steps to the front door, knocked one more time for good measure, and peered in through the letterbox. There was a pile of junk mail, indicating to the trained detective that nobody had been home for a long time. Good. The only worry was the garden looked tidy, meaning somebody was visiting regularly, but probably only once a week at most.

Things were as good as they could be. He tracked back round to the side of the house, and checked the pavement up and down the street. All clear. The back door to the house was clearly visible from the end of the driveway, so it didn't give him long. It was a wood panelled door with a both a mortice and a Yale lock. Standard stuff. He did a quick assessment of what was required. His bag contained a wide selection of skeleton keys, picks and jigglers, and it was important to narrow the choice down.

The scene was set. A few deep and slow breaths to get in the zone. It instantly intensified his senses, and he heard a song thrush, and could smell that somebody nearby had recently cut their grass with a two-stroke petrol mower. He worked quickly. Sweat soon ran down his back. He prodded and poked, wiggled and waggled. Garlic and onions came from a kitchen somewhere, so powerful it made him feel sick. Sensory overload. Keep your focus and work quickly.

Then he heard a car in the street, and stopped breathing. It was coming closer, and slowing down. He stood up at the door, clutching his clipboard. Just one of those regular and annoying door-to-door canvassers. The car didn't stop, just carried on past the end of the drive. He breathed again. You owe me for this Keith – nearly had a bloody heart attack there. Sweat was pooling on his top lip, and he wiped it away.

Thirty seconds later the mortice lock rolled over. Yes, get in. And then the Yale gave way quicker than a division of French infantry. Ready. He cricked his head down and spoke quietly into the top pocket of his shirt. 'Entry has been gained to the target property, and I am going in. Repeat, I am going in.' He snapped on a pair of white latex gloves.

The house felt cool. All the windows had their curtains three-quarter closed, and it had kept the summer heat at bay. The obvious place to look was in the utility room. He found it next to the kitchen, no bigger than a cupboard. There was a washing machine, and a folded-up ironing board. No linen basket.

He walked through the lounge-diner to the stairs. It was a clean and stylish house, with plenty of family photographs on the fireplace and a coffee table. Amanda Paice didn't look like an evil killer. She looked like a middle-aged lady, with a liking for floaty purple-pink clothes, and with a wrinkly face from too much sun. Still, it takes all sorts, and anyway the chances were that DNA would eliminate rather than convict her. People forget that about DNA. It's also the friend of the innocent.

Upstairs, all doors were closed. Stallard tried the first, but it was just a box room. The sort of place everyone stores their life's flotsam and jetsam. No basket. The second was the bathroom. Again, no basket. He walked into the master bedroom, fearing the worst, but there in the corner, tucked down alongside the dressing table was a wicker basket.

Stallard walked round the king-size divan, his feet sinking into the spongy carpet, and lifted the lid. The basket was half full. He fished around, and straight away found what he was looking for. A pair of white knickers. *Keith, you are a genius.* He unzipped his satchel, and took out a clear plastic bag. He gingerly dropped the knickers in the bag, and sealed it with tape.

He was carefully placing the bag in the front pocket of his satchel, when a voice behind him said, 'What are you doing in my bedroom?'

Shit a brick. Stallard spun round, heart doing somersaults. It took a split second to realise where the voice was coming from. There was a white plastic sphere sat in a stumpy holder on the dressing table. One of those cheap internet systems.

'I said, what do you think you're doing in my house?' Cyclops spoke again.

'I think I might need help.' Stallard into the top pocket of his shirt.

'Get out, before my neighbour makes you wish you hadn't been born.'

Stallard ran out of the bedroom, and tore down the stairs, but it was too late. The neighbour was standing in the doorway. He was wizened and grey, but he'd brought his wife as back-up. Together they couldn't have stopped Stallard barging his way past them, and legging it down the street, but accidents happen, and he didn't want some pensioner risking their health.

Before he could say anything the sound of a siren and

screeching brakes came from the road. Heavy footsteps and a familiar voice.

'Stand back, let me take care of this.'

Frank appeared in full police uniform, and ushered the neighbours out of the doorway. He grabbed Stallard by the arm and twisted him round, so his face was pressed up against the wall. Then he roughly yanked his wrists back, and ratcheted on a pair of cuffs.

Stallard yelped. 'Hey, watch it, fat pig, that's excessive force, that is.'

Frank turned to the neighbours.

'You've done a good job. We've been after this pervert for a very long time. Thank you, on behalf of your local constabulary.'

Then he frog-marched Stallard down the driveway to the panda car, grabbed his pony tail and threw him into the back seat, deliberately scuffing his head on the door-arch. The secret weapon overplaying his role.

CHAPTER 23

'Are you sure?' Tone of bafflement. 'One hundred percent?' Higher-pitched with a hint of challenge. 'I mean, there can't have been a mistake? Okay, I understand.' Resigned but still bemused. 'Thanks… Have a nice day yourself.'

Stallard put the landline back in its holster, and stared out of the window. Unbelievable. Client 4659 in the long-term storage suite of Hull morgue was not Joey, frontman of the promising band, The Magic Rats. Definitely not. The same profile had been found on all three batteries and it didn't match. Just as well he wasn't a betting man, because he would have lumped bottom dollar, mortgage and shirt on them being one and the same. Goes to show gambling is a mug's game, and his mother had been right. Again.

Good news for Coleman and Katz. They lived to fight another day, and fuck up some more investigations. How come so many truly useless people lead charmed lives, and nothing ever sticks to their Teflon backsides, whereas good, hardworking staff get punished for one mistake?

Outside, a tanker delivering petrol for the police station fuel pumps blocked the car park exit, and stopped two Panda cars leaving on emergency calls, sirens blaring. There was a lot of arm-waving.

Stallard watched, distracted. Where did this latest DNA development leave the Joey Doane case? Back to square one? No, not quite. The good work by Myers had moved things on. Two cars went to the Humber Bridge, and only one came back. A staged suicide or murder? He knew what he thought, but the alternative had to be eliminated.

'What do you know about passports?'

'Passports?' Keith had bagged Amanda Paice's underwear and was writing a bright yellow exhibit label. He looked up. 'I like to think I'm an expert.'

'Is there anything you don't know?'

'I was head of the fraud squad's financial investigation unit. Every case we dealt with crossed international borders.'

'How can I tell if Joey Doane is abroad or in the UK?'

'You can't.' Keith finished the label and taped it to the brown-paper exhibit bag. 'The system doesn't track people. That's Big Brother territory.'

'Bugger.'

Keith rummaged around in his desk drawer and brought out a tatty paper bag of mint humbugs. He inspected one for hairs, popped it in his mouth and nursed it in his cheek.

'If your man left the country it was before he was due to answer bail.'

'Sure?' Stallard waved away the offer of a sucky sweet.

'When he didn't answer bail, his PNC record would show him as *wanted*, and the ports' IT system would have picked that up.' Keith paused. The humbug swapped cheeks. 'Of course, he could have travelled on a false passport.'

'He wanted his own back from Baxter Quinn.'

'That suggests he left the UK before the bail date.' Keith ruminated. One end of the humbug peeped out between his lips like a shy tortoise, then shot back inside. 'Of course, he could have wanted his passport back at the request of his solicitor, to surrender to the court, if they intended another bail application.'

'That sounds too sensible for Joey.' Stallard checked his watch. Outside, the tanker driver was face down on the concrete, being speed-cuffed by two uniforms. Served him right. 'No, my guess is Joey wanted his passport back for another reason. Something to do with his argument with Shannon.'

'Such as what?'

'I don't know. It's a work in progress.'

Joey Doane's birth mother was called Kate Munday. She lived in an old cutlery works that had been converted into apartments, with a cobbled square and its own vegan café. Newsflash: Steel City surges into twenty-first century. Stallard had spent over an hour listening to her talk, and she was still going. It made him appreciate how guilt can defy reason and inveigle its way into the brain of otherwise resilient people. How it can frighten you and make you overcompensate, so you spoil the ones you love, instead of helping them, and how easily it can become an excuse to avoid facing up to the truth.

No mother wants to give their baby away, and Kate was no different. The fact was, Joey was a mistake. Kate and her husband, Ashley, already had two children: a son aged 16 and a daughter aged 14. But they embraced their mistake, as the genuine gift it was, and never dreamt about a termination, even though it meant Kate's career would be put on hold again. Then one day, Ashley was killed in a car accident, and the world changed.

Grief can affect people in different ways. The two teenagers pushed the boundaries more than ever, rebelling against everything and everyone, but in reality, against the futility and injustice of their father's death. Kate bore the brunt. She had no close relatives, and felt weak and isolated. The pregnancy and suffering had left her exhausted, but she knew she had to be strong, and do what was best for all her children. So, she made the decision to give the baby up for adoption.

The guilt hadn't hit her too hard in the early years. She'd been too busy fighting to make sure her older kids fulfilled their potential, and didn't succeed in screwing their own lives up. It was a tough battle, but she'd won. Oliver was now a successful lawyer, and Naomi ran her own business. Going back to work had also helped her, once the kids left home. She switched careers, and became the chief executive of a homeless charity, devoting more time to the never-ending round of meetings and fund raising events. It wasn't altogether altruistic. Doing good deeds made her feel better. It was a degree of penance for the bad thing she had done by giving up her baby, but never enough.

She hadn't ever tried to look for a new partner, believing that it would betray the memory of her husband. At 57, she'd retired, and gone back part-time as a volunteer. That was two years ago, and now the arrival of grandchildren had helped fill the hours, and given a new perspective on her own life as a parent. Things were ticking over, as good as they could, and then came that message from Joey out of the blue.

Stallard was sitting on a tweed sofa, and looked at Kate Munday. She'd taken care not to let herself go over the years. Like Joey, she wasn't a classic beauty, but she had a gap-toothed charm, and eyes that could light up or soften down her features, as she chose. She was intelligent and strong.

He leaned forward, anxious to move the story on.

'What did you think when he first got in touch with you?'

'That it was all too soon,' she said. 'For both of us, but especially for Joseph. It was a day I'd dreamt of for a long time, and I wanted so much for it to happen, but I knew that at twenty-one he wasn't ready, especially with the… mess… you know, the–'

'He told you about the drugs?'

'Yes, the first time we met.' She laughed. 'It was a pub lunch. I took Oliver and Naomi with me for moral support, and he came bowling into the room like a gust of wind, hugged everyone, and gave us his full life story. Just like that.'

Stallard nodded. Joey talking about his favourite subject, the great Joey Doane.

'Did he tell you why he wanted to meet you?'

Kate Munday massaged her earlobe while she thought. A kindred spirit. Stallard noticed she was still wearing her wedding and engagement rings.

'No, not really,' she said. 'I got the impression that he's an impulsive young man, and he hadn't given it much thought. I'd like to think that one day we can talk about it, but...'

'When was the last time you saw him?'

'A few days before he went missing. I bumped into him at Naomi's.'

'How did he seem?'

She stroked the same lobe again. 'Distant. I felt a little disappointed. Like he'd already lost interest in me. Though he and Naomi seemed at ease together.'

'Did he talk about going away?'

'No,' she said. 'He was preoccupied or distant. I don't know whether it was the drugs, or the prospect of going to prison. When I'm working, I talk to addicts on the street sometimes, and they have the same vacant look.'

Stallard noticed there was no piano or guitar in the room.

'Did Joey get his musical genes from your late husband or you?'

'Neither. We couldn't hold a tune between us.' She laughed, and then became more earnest. 'Is it true that Joseph was going to be a successful musician? It's just, I'm not sure I could take every word he said as gospel.'

'Yes, it's true. He was an amazing musical talent, and destined for undoubted success.' Stallard knew it might be an overstatement, but he remembered what Shannon had said about Joey wanting to make people proud. 'Who knows, he might still do it one day.'

She fixed him with wistful eyes. 'What do you think has happened to him?'

165

'I don't know.' He held her gaze. It didn't feel right to tell her that the baby she gave up was as good as dead.

He drove home in a downbeat mood, ably assisted by Johnny Marr's melancholy chords jangling from the Jeep's speakers. Not the best day of his working life, but not as bad as being knifed in the ribs. Frank said the search for Karina wasn't like looking for a needle in a haystack, it was like looking for a tiny piece of hay in a haystack. That's Frank. Always the optimist.

Laura wasn't returning his calls again, and he didn't know whether that was for personal or professional reasons. Nobody had bothered to tell him when his case conference was coming up, but then it was only his future they were discussing. Nothing important. The three missed calls on his mobile were from Shannon Doane, but she'd have to wait. He still wasn't sure exactly how guileless she was.

The evening sun was still strong. It was angling over the Pennines, getting ready to dip and turn the sky into a pink and purple sea. Stallard swung left off the main road, and cut down past the reservoir. It was a longer route, but it wound its way back up through limestone farms and hamlets, and he liked to see the cows chewing the cud over five-bar gates, and the geese protecting their territory like parading dervishes. It was only just outside the city, but a world away.

Once home, he took a long shower, and put on some shorts and a khaki cotton shirt. The one with an embroidered horseman about to hit his left nipple with a long mallet. It was a clothing brand he wouldn't have chosen for himself, but Laura had bought once it in a futile attempt to make him look conventional.

He fried up some sausages, eggs and beans in one pan, and ate them watching junk TV, with half a bottle of Johnnie Walker's Red Label. Supper of champions. Then he streamed some Catfish and the Bottlemen through a Bluetooth speaker, and started washing up.

Cutlery done, there was a brief knock on the caravan door, and it swung open.

Laura walked in, and laughed when she saw him. 'I can't resist a man in Marigolds.'

Stallard pulled off the rubber gloves, and tossed them in the sink.

'Too late. You've just missed a treat. I did Tournedos Rossini in a Madeira jus.'

'Really, it smells like burnt bangers?' She walked up and put her arms round his waist. 'Is it okay if I stay tonight?'

'You rang HR and told them, didn't you?'

'Yes, and I've felt shit about it all day.'

Stallard kissed her and squeezed her close. Not all guilt is bad.

Chapter 24

Stallard was hovering somewhere in between the land of Morpheus, and that of the living. There was a magical sound, mellow and rich, like the song of a blackbird on a languid day, wrapping itself around his brain, soothing and soporific, and coaxing him back down into deep slumber. *Be not afeard. The isle is full of noises.* Then he realised. Bollocks. Jumped out of bed in search of his mobile. It was where he'd left it. On charge in the kitchen, and he reached it one second before the saxophone cut out.

'Who is it?' His voice scratchy.

'Chris Block. Drug Squad. I think we worked on a job together a hundred years ago.'

Stallard rubbed an eye, and tried to place him. Big lad, bit of a mullet. He caught sight of the clock – *0600* – and stifled a yawn.

'Yeah, I remember. Thanks for the wake-up call.'

'I'm down at the mortuary and the lad on the slab has got your name and number in his pocket. I thought you'd want to know.'

'Does he have a name?'

'Mickey Flint.'

Stallard had given him the beermat, as he packed away the drum kit. Poor kid. 'I'll be there in half an hour.'

Radio 2 was playing in the mortuary. Just loud enough to be heard over the extractor fans that struggled to suck out the stench of human transience. The resident technician, Colin, dressed in scrubs and white Wellington boots, used a hose to chase bodily fluids with a jet of water across the tiles into stainless-steel sluice channels, and whistled along to Freddie Mercury, wanting to break free. He even threw in a bit of the push-pull vacuum cleaner dance, grinning and playing up to the gallery. All he needed was a pair of fishnet stockings.

Stallard and Chris Block stood and watched in the viewing area, separated from Colin in the PM room by a Perspex screen. On the other side of the screen, a corpse lay on the gurney in its post-autopsy state, like one of Victor Frankenstein's less successful creations. It had big bootlace stitches up the front of the torso, where the chest cavity had been opened up and closed, and smaller stitches under the neck, where the face had been peeled back to access the skull, and then tacked back down once the brain had been removed. It was Mickey Flint.

'Looks like an overdose,' said Block. 'But we won't know for sure until the tox results come through.'

'Where was he?'

'Scrubland. A black Lab called Albert found him.'

Stallard scanned the body. Just a young man. Twenty-one at most. 'I thought the days of fatal overdoses were behind us?'

Block shook his head. The mullet was starting to grey at the temples. 'Ever heard of Fentanyl?'

'Isn't that what killed Prince?'

'Yes, and about 20,000 Americans last year.' Block pointed over his left shoulder, as though the Atlantic Ocean was right behind him. 'Do you remember that operation we worked together on a few years ago? The multi-kilo heroin importation through Immingham container port? Well, that's chicken shit compared to what's going to happen soon. The world's changing and synthetic opioids are the future. Do you want to know why?'

Stallard shrugged. 'Sure.'

'Come on, let's get some coffee. I've been up all night.' Block motioned towards the door, and slouched off. Mr Grumpy in search of caffeine.

The Medico-Legal Centre housed the city mortuary, the Home Office pathologists, the Coroner's Court, its bereavement counsellors and the police coroner's officers. A one-stop shop for all your unexplained deaths. They made their way back through the main storage area, where the bodies were filed away in a bank of refrigerated drawers, and were buzzed past a security door into reception.

The mess room was tucked away down another corridor. It had a fridge, and a sink with a water boiler, but visitors had to use the vending machine. They sat down at a trestle table. Block clicked a couple of sweeteners into his coffee, and stirred it with a biro.

'It started last year. We got a cluster of deaths, which was strange, because there was nothing anywhere else in the country. Not even in London.' He wiped the biro on his sleeve and put it back in his pocket. 'And I'd never heard of Fentanyl, so I started to do some research, and what I found scared the shit out of me. Have a guess how much stronger than morphine it is.'

Stallard blew on his coffee. It was hot enough to blister onions. 'No idea. Twice as strong?'

'Fentanyl is over a hundred times more powerful than morphine. Think of it.' Block blinked his eyes a few times for added emphasis. 'The US military looked at using it as a chemical weapon, it's that strong. The only legitimate use it has, is to relieve the chronic pain of people in the advanced stages of cancer, and even then, it's used in tiny quantities on patches applied to the skin. That's all it takes, a patch on the skin. Imagine ingesting a few milligrams direct.'

'How do users score?'

'The usual – inhaled or intravenous. Strange thing about this case is the vast majority of overdoses are needle jobs, whereas your Mickey Flint was tooting.'

'Because smoking is more gradual than whacking it straight in a vein?'

'Correct. Same as heroin. The big difference is how it's imported.'

'Because the quantities needed are smaller?'

'Partly.' Block blinked again and nodded the mullet. 'It's not a crop. You don't need poppy plantations or forests of coca plants, with lots of labourers and processors, and a complex network of storage and distribution. You just need a lab and a post box.'

Stallard ventured a sip from his Styrofoam cup. It tasted of chemicals and sour milk.

'Why the post box?'

'To post the drugs, obviously.' Block smiled. He'd misplaced a couple of teeth over the years. 'The days of mules swallowing packages or sticking them up orifices are gone, mate. Thanks to the Internet, there are millions of packages sent to the UK every year now, so only a miniscule fraction can ever be checked by law enforcement agencies, and because the synthetic drugs are so cheap to produce, it doesn't matter if a few consignments get intercepted or go missing.' He rapped the trestle table with his knuckles. 'I'm telling you. Our biggest drug traffickers will soon be DHL and Parcel Force, and do you know where it all comes from?'

'Naughty elves?'

'It's all manufactured in China.' Block did the blinking eyes thing again. 'Lots of pharmaceutical labs sprung up there in the noughties. Some legal, some not, and the majority on the spectrum in between. They're massive. They produce most of the chemicals used in the world's prescription drug industry, but then these are shipped to other countries for processing into the final product. The Americans think most of their Fentanyl comes from pill factories in places like Thailand and Vietnam.'

Stallard blinked himself a couple of times. Maybe it was catching. He thought of Mickey Flint lying two rooms away. 'What are we doing about it at a national level?'

'No idea. I'm just local drug squad. I guess nothing much will get done until the kids of rich people in London start dying. That's what usually happens.'

Cynical, but true. *Plus ça change, plus c'est la même chose.* Stallard tipped his coffee down the sink, and crumpled the cup into a bin.

'So much for the classless society.'

CHAPTER 25

Eight-thirty, Stallard sat in the police station canteen, furring up his arteries with a full English. There were a few uniform cops breakfasting, and a couple of Community Safety Officers, still wearing full hi-vis in case any stray motorists drove in and needed flagging down. They probably wore them in bed at home to impress the wife. It's always the same with some men. Give them a neon tabard and they think they're demigods.

Three mouthfuls into the fry-up, Stallard pushed the plate away. The egg was latex, and the mushrooms a strange compound of black rubber and sweaty flesh. He knew that it was his mind playing tricks, but he could still smell the mortuary. It was as though the odour of Mickey Flint's innards had melded itself by a chemical reaction to his clothes, and every now and then they squirted a little whiff out in front of his face for him to sniff, like one of those plug-in Air Wicks. *L'odeur de la mort.*

What if he got posted back to force fulltime? Being an undercover cop wasn't a job, it was his life. Laura was right when she complained about him not wanting a *normal* relationship, because that implied a kind of lifestyle that he dreaded. Shopping together in Sainsbury's, and saving up to start a family. Fuck that. He and Mickey Flint were the same – they just got their rush from different things.

A few years ago, an op had gone tits-up, and he had unexpected time on his hands. Take a holiday, they said. Two days after he touched down in Cyprus, he was on his way home. An incident on the beach with some Russians hadn't helped, but the reason for cutting his stay short was boredom. Two full weeks and he would have drunk himself to death. Or killed a Russian.

Strange how people have a different perception of risk. He watched a young PC walk up to the counter in the canteen. The kid was about 6'5" and built like a shithouse on steroids, but he was wearing enough body armour for a whole battalion, and he had one of those belts covered in pouches that held every non-lethal option available to the British police. Talk about safety first. He was probably patrolling an area full of 99.9 percent law-abiding folk, who wanted to see the reassuring presence of a friendly bobby, not a cross between RoboCop and the Terminator.

Stallard glugged some black coffee, and mused how far this could go before the pendulum started swinging back, the other way. These things always did. That's when the doors flew open like a wild-west saloon, and Myers squeezed and shimmied his way past a queue of uniforms.

'I've got something.' The analyst had eyes big as saucers. 'The file that Shannon Doane sent. It contained a lot of reported sightings of Joey, and I've done a bit of work on one of them that might have led onto something

174

else, and I think that if this one is developed further, it might lead on to something else even more significant, but in order to do–'

'Whoa, stop.' Stallard held up a hand. The kid obviously thought he'd struck gold, but the excitement had spawned a stream of consciousness. 'Let's go back to the office.'

Stallard finished his coffee and put his breakfast on a trolley of other leftover plates that were congealing nicely under the fluorescent lights. As soon as they were back in the CCRU and Myers was seated behind his extensive workstation, he immediately calmed down, and the game face descended. It was like James T Kirk assuming his position on the bridge of the *Enterprise*. The universe is once again in safe hands.

'Okay,' said Myers. 'So, I downloaded the council CCTV, and used it to either verify or disprove the sightings of Joey around the relevant two or three-day period immediately prior to his disappearance.' He got busy with the mouse. 'That's the crucial period.'

'Are the timings so specific you can do that?'

'No, they're not.' Myers tried to look serious. He struggled. A pleased-with-himself grin kept tugging up the corners of his mouth. 'But the first time we met, you asked me about facial recognition, so that got me thinking, and the very first section of footage I ran it on, I got a hit. Here we go, Friday the 31st of Jan. The last day before he disappeared.'

The giant 32" monitor showed a busy pedestrianised area of the city centre. It must have been a cold day. People were walking quickly, wrapped up in big coats, woolly hats and gloves. Clear and sunny, but cold.

'Watch that doorway there.' Myers fired a red laser-pointer at the top left of the screen. 'That's Revolver Records, a vinyl shop where one of the assistants remembers Joey going in. She's a big Magic Rats fan, so I guessed she wouldn't mistake him for someone else, and I was right. It was just the time she was sketchy on, but thanks to the FR software, I nailed it down to 1429. Here he comes.'

Myers froze the image. The camera had captured Joey leaving the shop, and pulling on a baggy, crocheted Rasta hat. He was empty-handed. No bags or packages, and he was wearing a donkey jacket, with a retro CND badge sewn across one shoulder.

'Yep, that's him.' Stallard stuck out his bottom lip and nodded. 'Good work, Myers, finding our man on what might be his last public appearance, but it's not going to win *Breakthrough of the Year* at the annual Police Breakthrough Award Ceremony. Probably not even runner-up.'

'Patience, Mr Stallard.' Myers smiled. Ran the footage on. 'Once I'd got a positive ID on Joey, I used the network of council CCTV to track his movement through the town centre. He walked up from the markets, called into Greggs, where I presume he bought some type of puff-pastry slice, because that's what he ate as he made his way past the Town Hall and dropped down to the Crucible. He screwed the used paper up into a ball and dropped it in a planter, and kind of strolled around for a minute or so on his mobile phone, before cutting through to High Street and crossing the tram tracks by the cathedral, where he disappeared into those little lanes that run down towards the Crown Court.'

'His solicitor's maybe. There's a lot of law firms down

there, and it was his last chance for a consultation before he answered bail on the Monday.'

'Possibly.' Myers ran the video on. 'There's no coverage, but he reappears fifteen minutes later, and comes back over the tram tracks. Here he comes...'

The monitor now showed another scene. It was the junction of two streets. One, a cobbled pedestrian zone, with benches and a Big Issue seller on the corner, and the other was a wide road with a steady flow of buses and black cabs.

'I see him,' Stallard pointed. The excitement was infectious. He was starting to feel it. Somewhere beneath the ponytail, hairs on the back on his neck prickled.

'Watch him.' Myers grinning. Not trying to hide it any longer. 'Watch what he does.'

Joey skipped across the road, between some slow-moving traffic. His shoulders were hunched against the elements. When he reached the corner of the pedestrian precinct, he stopped and took something out of his trouser pocket. It was impossible to tell what it was. The angle of the camera meant it was obscured by his back, but whatever it was must have been relatively small. Then he vanished.

'Where's he gone?' Stallard cranked his neck towards the screen.

'In the shop he was standing in front of.' Myers stopped the video and reversed it. 'I'll slow it down this time.'

Stallard watched Joey turn on a sixpence, push on a plate-glass door and disappear on the other side of it. 'What shop is it?'

'That's the interesting bit.' Myers beamed. 'It's a travel agency.'

CHAPTER 26

The traffic had lightened. Stallard gunned the Jeep up the link road that hugged the valley side, and then swooped down towards the centre of the Steel City. Dark clouds were bunching above the hills over to the west, giving notice of summer rain, and the trees were starting to sway and shimmer in a lithe, presaging storm-dance. He crested the brow by the old castle, and began the descent beneath the electric wires of the tram track. They buzzed and crackled on the car radio.

He called into a filling station and bought fuel and a bag of sweets for Keith. The old guy was wearing a different shade of mustard shirt today. More phlegm-coloured. Then he pulled back out onto the road, and coasted down the hill. He'd gone about fifty yards, when he saw something in in his rear-view mirror. A silver Hyundai SUV pulled away from the kerb, and dropped in behind him two cars back. He'd seen an identical car when they'd left the police station. One and the same? If it was, the driver knew what he or she was doing. Tailing someone's not easy, especially when that someone is an undercover cop, trained in anti-surveillance techniques.

Stallard cursed himself under his breath. He should have spotted it before, but he was out of practice. Working in the Cold Case Unit had made him professionally flabby. But who'd want to follow Dad's Army? They were hardly cutting edge, covert operatives targeting organised crime groups, were they? He looked at Keith for instant confirmation. Correct. Just a man with the face of a walnut enjoying a Werther's. All he needed was a tartan rug on his knees. Not exactly Jason Bourne. So, what was going on? Was he imagining it?

One way to find out. Hold on tight, kids. There was a side road coming up on the nearside. He accelerated towards it, and at the last moment, hit the brakes and hangered left. A blast of horn from the car behind. Two women crossing the road grabbed each other and jumped back on the kerb. Sorry. Then he booted the Jeep flat out in a short burst, and spun into the next side road off to the right. Parked up and waited.

He watched in the wing mirror. The snout of the silver Hyundai appeared at the junction behind. It hovered there for a second, undecided. Would it take the bait? Not this time. There was a squeal of rubber on tarmac, and the SUV shot off.

Stallard knew the inner-city backstreets like the back of his hand. He shot forward, took the first left, and pushed the Jeep to its limit on a wider, straight stretch of road.

They hurtled towards the upcoming T junction, and saw a flash of silver fly across from left to right. Stallard stood on the brakes and threw the back end out. It slewed round, and he corrected it, as they sailed past the Give Way markings, and joined the next road in a cloud of dust. Now they were behind the Hyundai that had been tailing them. Time for the hunted to do a bit of their own hunting. He glanced across at Keith, expecting him to be frozen in terror, but the old guy looked calm, and had a biro poised over the back of his hand to make a note of the number when they got close enough.

Before they could get nearer, the Hyundai realised what was happening. Black smoke blew from its exhaust, and it bulleted down the middle of the street lined with parked cars. Stallard followed as fast as he could, given the poor visibility of what was happening on the pavements. The Jeep helped with a throaty roar. Loud enough to wake the dead, and warn the living of its presence within a two-mile radius. Beware the beast.

Taillights up ahead. A crossroads was approaching and there was a crawling line of cars backed up. The Hyundai had nowhere to go. Time to find out who was playing games. Stallard bore down on his prey, getting ready to pounce. What? Before he got there, the silver SUV mounted the kerb, ploughed across a flowerbed planted out with miniature roses, bypassed the standing traffic and careened back onto the carriageway up ahead.

Stallard blasted his horn, and full-beamed his way down the outside, making cars coming the other direction pull over into the edge. Beyond the crossroads, he started to make ground on the target. Next up was a major intersection controlled by traffic lights, and clogged by queuing vehicles. *Nowhere to go this time, pal.* Except the

Hyundai didn't hesitate. It swerved across the road onto the pavement and disappeared, as if by magic.

Whoever it is knows this city, thought Stallard, as he followed suit. It was an old pedestrian underpass. A throwback from the seventies lined with white urinal tiles covered in graffiti. Two schoolkids having a crafty fag plastered their backs to the wall and breathed in. Up the ramp on the other side, and the Jeep barrelled out onto a service road that fed into the main dual carriageway towards town.

On the wide, open stretch of road, the newer car in front had the edge. The gap grew and Stallard saw his quarry slipping away. There was one trick left up his sleeve. He knew the layout up ahead, and the likely route a pursuee would take. With the help of an outrageous short-cut, he could get there first and be waiting. Worth a risk? Course it was.

He bumped over the central reservation, shot across the oncoming traffic and up onto the pavement next to a Pelican Crossing. Then he nosed the Jeep to the top of a flight of concrete steps, took a deep breath, and bounced his way gently down them one at a time. A few students laughed and took smartphone photos. That would be another appearance on his favourite website, Driving-Like-A-Twat.Com. Two in a week. Legend. There was a horrible metallic scrape as the Jeep tackled the final step and his bumper met the paving-slab walkway at the bottom.

Fifty yards he cruised on a footpath that meandered through a grassed area of benches and flowerbeds, and he was at the main road. Time to wait and see if it worked.

Shit. It had worked. The Hyundai flew past. One occupant. Male Caucasian. No other details. Stallard pulled in behind and floored it. He looked up ahead and saw a convoy of double-decker buses. This was the chance to strike.

Instead of slowing down, the Hyundai accelerated, then braked and peeled off left into a pedestrian precinct. Big mistake. Now Stallard knew he had him. Today was market day and stalls and vans would make it impassable. He turned to follow, when something entered his line of vision from the right. What the flaming fuck? A massive spoked wheel. He slammed the brakes on, yanked the steering wheel, and screeched sideways to a halt. He'd managed to stop short of it by a matter of inches.

It was a penny farthing being ridden by a man dressed in Victorian breeches, tweed cap, and a flannel shirt. He wobbled a bit, and jumped off, blocking the way. Passers-by stopped and gathered round. Beyond them, Stallard saw the silver SUV negotiate its way out the other end and escape to freedom, and he sighed. Thwarted by a Dickensian caricature. A regular occupational hazard for the detectives across the land no doubt. Bastard.

'What the heck was all that about?' Keith smoothed back a few strands of hair from his forehead.

'We were being followed.'

'By who?'

'Aliens who want to use our bodies for experiments and then kill us.'

'Pardon.'

'How should I bloody know?'

They backed out and re-joined the main carriageway, then drifted along into the town centre. Stallard was pissed off at losing the Hyundai and changed the subject by asking how the pantie case was going. Keith said the DNA results wouldn't be in for a few days. Gary on the submissions desk had said no to fast-track, and Keith had let it slide. Too polite to kick up a fuss.

When they reached the giant roundabout on the edge of town, Stallard made two full laps to make sure they weren't still being tailed, before ignoring a *Bus Only* sign, and swerving off to take the bridge that crossed the spot where the River Sheaf meets the River Don. The spiritual home of the city. Now overgrown with foreign weeds in a way that symbolised how the steel industry had succumbed to invaders from abroad.

Keith pointed out of the window. 'Policeman's Helmet.'

'Where?'

'On the bank there. Himalayan Balsam or as it is commonly known, Policeman's Helmet.'

'Flora as well as financial investigation – you're a revelation.'

'Don't you have any hobbies?'

Stallard thought for a moment. 'Just drinking.'

The travel agency was quiet for a Friday morning. Four women sat at computer screens in an open-plan space, all wearing navy blue suits with cream piping, and canary yellow scarves. Let's do the time warp. A bureau de change booth stood empty, next to an electronic board of currency exchange rates. There was no apparent hierarchy, so Stallard badged the first suit he came to, who was a smiley lady with painted-on eyebrows that gave her a look of permanent surprise. Her badge said *Zoe*.

Stallard explained they were investigating the disappearance of Joseph Doane, and had reason to believe he visited the shop on the 31st of January. Would it be possible to check their systems to see if he made any bookings with them?

Zoe looked surprised. 'Yes, of course.'

She alternated between mouse and keyboard, clicking and tapping. Zoe liked to talk herself though a task. A running commentary to give herself moral support. 'Now if I just enter this... not forgetting to come out of this... make sure this field is checked... before pressing enter...'

Stallard caught the other three suits exchanging glances. It clearly pissed them off. Working in the office all day with the verbal incontinent. If looks could kill.

'Select date and press enter again, then scroll down.' Zoe said to herself. She scrolled down. 'Yes, here we are. Joseph Doane booked flights through us on the 31st of January.'

'Where to?' Stallard's heart did a little hop.

'Vietnam. We booked him Air France from Manchester to Hanoi, via Charles de Gaulle, and then an internal flight from Hanoi to Danang with Vietjet Airlines.'

'What date?'

'Depart Manchester at 9.20am Monday the 3rd of February, and returning same route, due to land at 5.30am on Tuesday the 18th of the same month.'

Stallard stroked the silver tiger tooth in his left lobe, as he assimilated the new information. Sometimes, he twirled the gold hoop that sat alongside it, but right now he chose the tiger tooth. Okay, the flight was in the morning, a few hours after Joey's truck was found abandoned at the

Humber Bridge, and before he was due to answer bail at the police station. That figured. He wouldn't have been circulated on PNC at that time, so he was free to leave the country unhindered.

'Can you tell if he made the return flight?'

'No. We just made the booking as a third-party agent. You need to verify with the airline to see if he actually checked in and took his seat on any of the flights.'

'I'm guessing he paid cash.' Stallard knew no transactions showed up on Joey's cards.

'Over twelve hundred pounds.'

'Economy?'

'It would have been half that if he'd not left it until the last minute.'

'Kids, eh?'

'Don't know they're born.'

'Youth's wasted on the young.' Stallard kept rubbing the tiger tooth. One day a genie was going to appear, and grant him three wishes. Two would be rude, but his third would be money. He pointed to the bureau de change. 'What about currency? Did Mr Doane change any sterling?'

'That's a separate system. Give me a minute.' Zoe disappeared into a back room and reappeared with a key for the booth. She secured herself in, and narrated her way through logging in to the new system. More sour glances from the other three. After ten minutes, she looked surprised and nodded.

'Yes, we took a copy of his passport as proof of ID. He bought just over two thousand pounds worth of US Dollars.'

'Dollars?'

Keith coughed. 'The Vietnamese Dong is highly volatile and not widely stocked, and because the exchange rate is so poor, most travellers take US Dollars. They're accepted in all parts of the country.'

'Thanks,' said Stallard. 'Would the resident travel expert know how Joey could have obtained a visa?'

'Vietnam operate a visa-on-arrival system, in addition to the standard application route.' Keith put his shoulders back. The font of knowledge. Not just the fatherly chaperone.

They left the travel agency, and drove back out of town, following the tram tracks. Stallard knew there was no point ringing Air France's UK office. He'd only get through to a call centre, where staff had been brainwashed into believing the Data Protection Act was a law compelling them to be uncooperative with everyone, and especially the police. So, he rang Briggsy, who was a Special Branch officer at the Ports Unit of Manchester Airport, and asked him to make the necessary enquiries on his behalf. It was one of those calls you make, knowing that you'll answer the phone one day, and it's Briggsy wanting his favour back. Debts are incurred and paid off. Backs scratched. That's how it works.

Briggsy said give him an hour, so Stallard drove up towards the ring road, to see what Shannon Doane was wound up about this time. The video of Joey going to the travel agents was replaying slow-mo in his mind. Whatever he'd taken from his pocket before going in must have been cash. Over three grand, and even in twenties a fair wad. Where did a musician scratting round for his next fix get that sort of cash? And why Vietnam?

Could he have just been running away? Maybe the thought of going to prison had overtaken him, and forced him to abandon his dreams. But that didn't make sense. It was obvious to any rational person that if he pleaded *guilty*, he was going to get a slap on the wrist. Probation or community service. Maybe *rational* was the clue. No saying what goes off in the addled mind of a skaghead. Except…

The Magic Rats had just signed their first recording contract. Repeat. The Magic Rats had just signed their first recording contract. Stallard knew what this meant to Joey. What would have happened if the roles had been reversed? If he'd had a shot at a career in music instead of choosing to put a uniform on and go and work for the clampdown? Would he have fled the scene to avoid an awkward court case? No fucking way. Wild horses wouldn't have got him on an aeroplane. Come on, this was a critical moment in the evolution of the band. You have to snatch the chance and roll with the impetus, because it's never going to happen again.

Stallard found it easy to put himself in Joey's head. They were cut from the same shabby but stubborn cloth. Whatever made him leave the country at that time must have been something huge. More to the point, it wasn't a one-way trip. Joey was always coming back. For some people, the drug of performing is more powerful than anything you can snort up your nose. He knew Joey was one of those.

Traffic was heavy, as people headed home to beat the storm. They skirted the retail park, with its crap shops and fast-food drive-throughs, and re-joined the tram-tracks. The radio station hummed.

Stallard fiddled with the stereo controls. 'What music do you like?'

Keith was concentrating on something, head down. 'I'm a middle-of-the-road-man.'

'You'll get run over.'

'Easy listening.'

'For the hard of hearing.' Stallard tried a couple more FM stations before he found one with a clear signal. Bonnie Tyler was lost in France again. 'No...' He switched it off, and a roll of thunder shook the sky.

'I thought so.' Keith was still staring into his lap.

'Genital warts?'

Keith lifted his iPad. 'SIAM are linked to companies in Vietnam and Thailand.'

'Doing what?'

'Sports gear. Snooker cues, boxing gloves, clothing...'

'Any mention of illegal drugs?'

'No.'

'Funny that.'

Stallard pulled up outside Shannon Doane's stone terrace. He switched off the engine, and realised it was the first time he'd seen her since Mickey Flint's death. They'd had a brief phone conversation when he left the Medico-Legal Centre, but it had been stumbling and stilted. How was she coping?

At that point, the first drops of rain splodged heavy on the windscreen, and within a few seconds water was cascading down from a treacle sky, and the gutters were running with fag ends and the dead blossoms that had lain there since late spring. The circle of life. Mickey was gone, but maybe Joey was still out there and about to be reborn. That would be some rock 'n' roll comeback. Better than AC/DC after Bon Scott died of alcohol poisoning in a Renault 5 somewhere in East Dulwich. What are the chances? Okay, they were slim. Stallard knew Joey was still dead.

CHAPTER 27

Shannon Doane had been crying. There were red patches under her eyes, and she had a runny nose and wobbly mouth. Stallard could see Jack Daniels had made an early appearance. The naughty boy. There was a bottle on the kitchen table, and a single glass. Her hands were trembling, and every surface was covered in a jumble of souvenirs of the past: photos, board-games, scarves, badges, school books, CDs, hats, music books and the assorted bric-a-brac of life that everyone keeps for no good reason. Laziness disguised as sentimentality.

The two of them went through to the small sitting room. Keith had stayed in the car. It was then that Shannon opened up for the first time. Spoke of the mess she was in, because she'd never properly grieved for Joey. Why would she? She'd never believed that he'd taken his own life, and in the early days always thought that she'd open the door one day, and he'd just be standing there with his stupid grin. Days turned into weeks. She knew somebody must have done something to him, but still she hoped. She hoped for his safe delivery from whatever or whoever had taken him away.

News of Mickey's death had hit her like a sledge-hammer. It had made her realise that her brother wasn't coming back. He was gone, like Mickey. How could she have been so stupid? An hour or so ago, she'd been sick in the toilet. Was that shock, or was that drinking at nine in the morning? She didn't know, but she felt alone. She had nobody to talk to. Her parents were only down the road, but talking about Joey to them, only made their pain worse, and she couldn't bear the thought of doing that to them. Joey was dead. What was there to say anyway? It wouldn't bring him back, would it?

Stallard started to say something comforting, but Shannon hushed him up. She hadn't finished. She told them how she thought she knew Joey. He was her kid brother. She knew how he liked to dance as soon as he could walk. Before he even started school, he'd put on her ballet shoes, and spin round the bedroom, with his arms above his head, humming nonsense. His favourite dressing-up costume was Superman, and if he wasn't allowed to wear it, he wouldn't eat his dinner. He hated boiled carrots, and couldn't pronounce cucumber. She knew that his first crush at junior school was a girl called Chloe Watson, and he would go beetroot-red if anyone said her name. When he had his first proper girlfriend, Shannon was the one he confided in. She knew him better than anyone.

Then he got older and became the Joey he wanted others to see. The first kid in class to smoke a reefer. The one who was always showing off on his bike in front of the shops, and giving lip to anyone who complained. The joker. The cool dude who could play guitar and sing, and make it look easy, because he'd spent hour after hour in his bedroom working on making it look easy. Brash and big-headed.

Yes, she thought she knew her brother, but then she didn't. It wasn't the drugs. It was meeting his real mother. Or both? He changed, that was for sure. It was like she, his own sister, wasn't good enough for him anymore. He'd discovered something better in a different world, and which he believed he belonged in. It was his birth right. Of course, Joey had denied it, but she'd seen the look of contempt on his face, and hated him for it. She told him so. Now he was dead, and she wished they'd not quarrelled.

Stallard waited until she'd finished. Spilling out your feelings can be cathartic, but it can also make things worse when you articulate the conflict in your head. Either way, it didn't help him decide whether or not to tell Shannon about Joey's trip to Vietnam. She'd finally accepted her brother's fate, and would it not be cruel now, to confuse her by offering false hope? To tell her that he might still be alive? Seeing her now in front of him, the temptation was to tell her about Joey's trip to the travel agents. It might salve her suffering. But if it came to nothing – pow – back to square one. Or worse. It would be like losing her brother twice. He decided to shield her, until he had more answers, but that meant asking questions.

'Was he much of a traveller?'

'You're joking. Brittany was as far as he ever got.'

'With the band?'

'No, family holidays, three years running.'

'Nice.'

'Bloody bunk beds.' Shannon sobbed and laughed at the same time. 'Weather just like this.' She pointed out the window. 'Pissed it down.'

'Did he talk about going anywhere?'

'Maybe Nashville one day. Dolly Parton at the Grand Ole Opry.'

'Not the Far East?'

'No.' She half-blew her nose, and stopped. Her eyes narrowed. 'What's all this about?'

'Routine.' Stallard, the great dissembler. Remember – cruel to be kind. 'Could he have afforded to travel?'

'What do you think?'

'That any spare cash he got went straight on a ten bag?'

'You should be a detective.'

'That's a good one. Never heard it before. What did Joey like in his ten bag? A bit of Fentanyl?'

'What?'

'Fentanyl. The stuff that killed Prince.'

'Yeah, I know that. Everyone knows that.' Her mouth went tight. Mistrust or irritation. 'Is that what killed Mickey? Is that what this is all about?'

'It's just routine.'

'The needle's stuck. Change the record.'

'All right, there's been some overdoses in the city, but we're waiting lab results.'

'Thank you.' Shannon looked down at her hands. She tore the tear-stained tissue into tiny shreds. Slowly and deliberately. As though imagining what could have been with The Magic Rats if things had turned out different. A sad smile flickered and faded. Then her eyelids closed like the curtain coming down on a final production, and she was quiet. After a while, she looked up. 'Sorry I can't help with the drugs. Was there anything else?'

'You said you had something for me.'

'Of course.' She ruffled her hair, and brightened up. 'I found it yesterday when I was going through Joey's things for one last time. Can you believe his bloody landlord just chucked everything into bin-liners?'

They went back into the off-shot kitchen, and Shannon dropped the leaf down on the pine bureau.

'Here,' she said, holding out a business card. 'I've no idea why Joey would have this.'

Stallard took it. The card was a fancy, embossed one, with a violet heart-shaped logo, and gold lettering. *The Willows. Private Clinic. Moorgate, Rotherham. – Your wellness is our business.*

Shannon said, 'I thought it was maybe a rehab clinic, but when I looked up their website, it's a boob jobs and liposuction place.' She gave a little snort. Disapproval. Easy when you're perfect. 'Oh, and hair transplants, but that's the last thing our Joey needed.'

'I'll check it out. Take it easy on the booze, and be careful.'

Halfway to the car, she called him back.

'There's a band called *Flat Pack Philosophy* play every Friday at The Atlantic Club.'

'What about them?' Stallard hunched to stop rain going down his neck. It had eased. Gone from torrential to steady.

'I like them, and I've got no one to take me tonight.' She looked him straight in the eyes. Gauntlet thrown.

'You're big enough to go on your own.'

'You'd like them.'

Stallard held up his hands. Mock surrender. 'Look, I can't socialise with someone who is a witness in an investigation. It's ethically wrong, and a misconduct offence under Police Regulations.'

'Is it because you're in a relationship?'

'That's none of your business.'

A fire appeared in her cheeks. 'The same way that my brother's connection to the Far East is none of my business. That's bullshit – I have a right to know what's happening. Why can't you be honest? Why is it always such a bloody fight to find the truth?'

She slammed the door.

Stallard walked back to the Jeep, wiping rain from his brow. *It's ethically wrong, and a misconduct offence under Police Regulations.* Where had he pulled that one from? It had never worried him before. But then witnesses never looked like Shannon Doane. They were always sixteen-stone psychopaths called Tyson, or emaciated meth-users with open sores and no teeth or arse. So, Shannon looked different. What was he worried about?

CHAPTER 28

The roads were flooded. Some of the puddles were as big as lakes, and manhole covers were jagged up at angles, spouting water like iron geysers. It had snarled up the traffic. Local radio said the road underneath the railway bridge up ahead was totally submerged, and vehicles had been abandoned. Somewhere else, a landslip had blocked the bus route. Watery chaos. They'd been stuck on the same sodden stretch of road for over an hour. The roof of Stallard's mouth was starting to feel sore from all the hard, caramel candies, and he was busting for a piss. Welcome to the glamorous life of a real detective.

The mobile in his trouser pocket vibrated. That didn't help.

'Watcha, it's Briggsy. I've got the result of the DP request to Air France.'

'And?'

'It was a no-show.'

'He didn't make the flight?'

'Affirmative. Joseph Doane checked in online on Sunday the 2nd of February. Paid for an extra suitcase. Selected seats for both legs of the outward journey. But never caught the flight from Manchester.'

'Could he have turned up at Paris, and taken the connection to Vietnam from there?'

'Nope.'

'Thanks, Briggsy. I owe you one.'

So much for Joey still being alive, and enjoying the life of a beach-bum in Vietnam. It was never a realistic scenario. Five months is a long time to be off the radar, and remain anonymous. In that kind of situation, the biggest threat comes from the person themself. Boredom, loneliness, self-doubt, and the basic human need to communicate, usually with relatives, but sometimes with just anyone. We're social creatures. It takes a certain special sort of hermit to be able to survive without contact for any length of time. Normal people simply can't stand it.

A few years back, Stallard had a walk-on part in a witness protection job. It was a case being run by the PSNI's Historical Enquiries Team, which was set up to investigate the 3,000 undetected murders during the Troubles. They had an ex-IRA foot soldier who was willing to take the stand and testify against his old comrades, so they gave him a new identity, James Keane, and relocated him to a comfortable cliff-top estate just south of Scarborough. He lasted six months. That's how long it took before he realised that he couldn't take it any more. James Keane went back to Belfast and took his chances of a bullet in each knee.

So, Joey wasn't shacked up eating Pho in Hanoi. It only reinforced the bad feeling he had that the kid had been killed. Stallard found it difficult at times like this. Things were starting to happen from an investigative point of view, and he was juiced up by the direction it was taking. He loved it. A murder enquiry is the zenith of the detective world. A gold disc at The Grammys or a number one in the download charts. It's what you desperately want, and yet it comes with a cost. Someone has to be a victim, and the more you identify with them and their family, the higher the price you pay. Excitement and pain. Another of life's strange paradoxes.

It had been the right decision not to tell Shannon about the flight booking, and worth getting the door slammed in his face. Now all he needed to do was find out why Joey had booked the flights in the first place. More to the point, what had stopped him making it to the airport.

The mobile in his pocket vibrated again. Someone was determined to make him wet himself.

'Mr Stallard. It's Myers.'

'Hi Myers. What've you got?'

'Remember on the CCTV, a few minutes before Joey goes to the travel agents, he's hanging around near the Crucible, looking like he's on his phone?'

'Uh-huh.'

'I've checked the time against his billing, and it's a call to a Vodaphone number, the subscriber of which is an Oliver Munday of 2 The Oaks, Old Mill Lane. No trace of this nominal on PNC or the local intel system.'

'Joey's brother. By birth anyway. What about other calls?'

198

'I'm still waiting for a few subscriber checks to come back, but there's nothing much. There's a couple more calls to Munday in the preceding two weeks, and the rest are his usual contacts – his band mates and Baxter Quinn.'

'Thanks, Myers. See you later.'

'Wait. I got a result back from that company we use for image comparison. That car on the false plates, which follows Joey's truck to the Humber Bridge, it's a Mitsubishi Lancer. Apparently, they can tell from the shape of the rear light clusters.'

'Thanks, Myers.' Stallard was about to hang up, but a thought occurred. 'Am I right in thinking you want to join the job?'

'Being a police detective is my number one life goal.'

'It's not all pretty girls and hanging out in bars.'

'I want to send serious criminals to prison.'

Stallard smiled. How sweet. 'Let me see what I can do.'

The gridlock eased, and they made it to a pub. It was an old-style inn, with stone flags on the floor and the heads of animals sticking out of wooden plaques on the walls. Stallard gave Keith his order, and found the Gents, before settling down on a copper-topped table beneath a snarling fox. The fox looked really angry. Who could blame him? The Guinness and cider tasted good. It had the solid, burnt maltiness of the stout to line his stomach, and the fruity fizz of the cider to get some alcohol back into his bloodstream, and kickstart the weekend. That's what Friday lunchtimes are for. Keith had half a mild. The man was an animal.

Stallard was looking forward to a weekend of boozy relaxation and sex with Laura. Lots of booze and sex. It was his first proper weekend for months. While he was on sick leave, the days of the week just drifted into each other and became the same, but now he'd spent a full five days back at work, and he was ready to make the most of two days off. *Whay-hay...* He took another drink, and closed his eyes.

Keith put his iPad down on the table, and gestured towards it with his spectacles.

'Danang has some of the best beaches in Vietnam, and is five minutes up the coast from Hoi An, which is the main backpacker area for young people from around the world.'

'Fascinating, Mr Tourist Information. Are you trying to tell me that Joey could just have been going there to chill out?'

'It's also the biggest city and port in Central Vietnam.' Keith did the nose twitch. Loving it. 'With a thriving chemical and pharmaceutical sector.'

'That doesn't help. He could have been going then for either business or pleasure. But maybe the two suitcases suggest he was planning a longer trip.'

'Or smuggling?'

'No, Block was definite. These synthetic opioids are posted. It's like getting your gear delivered by Amazon.' Stallard swilled another mouthful of drink. Brain fuel. 'The extra case could have been for cash to pay for the drugs. Not stuffed full of cash, obviously, but hidden among a load of clothes and other crap. Still a bit risky though.'

Keith pursed his lips. 'No. That's what the Quinns would have a company out there for. They can transfer money from the UK to their Vietnamese business, and then they don't have to worry about moving cash out of the country.'

'They just need someone to take possession of the goods and post them back?'

'Yes, if they can't trust the seller out there, and if the goods need concealing in something else, such as a pair of boxing gloves or a box of snooker cues.'

A waitress pulled up at the table, with two plates of steak pie and chips. Big Jenga-sized chips fried in beef dripping, and thick, gelatinous gravy. The pie steamed and Stallard salivated. He cut a big chunk of crust, and piled some gooey steak on top. The fork was fully loaded when his mobile went.

It was Block. The toxicology prelims had come back. Mickey Flint had synthetic opioids in his blood. It wouldn't be confirmed officially as cause of death until further tests had been done on the liver and brain, but these would take a few weeks. That was a technicality. The fact was Mickey Flint had died from an overdose of Fentanyl.

Block explained he'd snatched a few hours' sleep and done some more checking. Deaths from Fentanyl were around 120 per calendar year for the whole of the UK, but in the past twelve months, the Steel City on its own had seen 32. No other hotspots in the country. Something was going on. The same thing had happened in the US, two or three years ago, and they were still trying to figure it out. A localised spike in Fentanyl deaths, with no associated intelligence.

Stallard could see the pie getting cold, and tried to end the call, but Block hadn't finished. He'd done some checks on one of the blister packs found on Mickey Flint's body, using a drug field-test kit. It was negative for heroin, indicating that the pills were one hundred percent pure Fentanyl. This was unusual. Most pills are a mixture of heroin, bashed with an inert powder, and a small amount of Fentanyl. It might explain how he'd managed to OD without injecting. It might also explain the strange localised spike in deaths.

When the call ended, Stallard had lost his appetite. Did Mickey Flint know the pills were pure Fentanyl, and not the more common mixture of powders? It was unlikely that stuff like this came with a full list of ingredients on the packet, with a best-before date and a government warning. *Caveat emptor* never rang more true. Suppliers of this shit had a huge moral responsibility to know exactly what they were selling, or accidents would happen. But what if they did know? What if they let their customer believe it was the same substance and strength that they'd had in the past? That could be a fatal omission.

Back in the Cold Case Unit, people were already starting to leave for the weekend.

Fay Nash had her arms crossed. 'Sit down. This is where I'm supposed to officially ask how your first week went back at work.'

'I'm not some kind of invalid.'

'Hardcastle will want something in writing Monday.'

'Give him Jane Eyre – it's a classic.'

'What about I put that you're an insecure chauvinist, with an overinflated opinion of his own ability and charm.'

'Stop it, you're making me blush.'

'Who hides behind childish humour when confronted by something he doesn't like.'

'Don't forget I'm rude to vicars and disabled people. Do the full hatchet job.'

Nash laughed. 'I'll just put you're doing okay.'

'For an arrogant tosser?'

'Something like that.'

'Cheers.'

Nash sat and typed. Every now and then she stopped, and stuck her tongue out. Stallard saw the silver piercing. It made an appearance every time her forehead creased. It's not easy saying nothing in words. She caught him watching her and stuck two fingers up. Now who's childish? She looked at the clock. Friday afternoon. Better things to be doing. She said, 'How do you spell pathological narcissist?'

'Delta, India, Charlie, Kilo.'

Laughing. 'That'll do.' Finished. Logged out of the network. Desktop closed down. Jacket on.

Stallard saw a bunch of flowers in her tote bag. 'Who's the lucky girl?'

'Third wedding anniversary. Got a dirty weekend booked at a five-star hotel in York.'

'Enjoy.'

Sounded very much like his own weekend plans. Except for the five-star hotel. That reminded him – the sheets in the caravan needed changing. First, he had a bit of tidying up here to do. The business card from The Willows Private Clinic was on the desk in front of him. He used a landline to call the number. It rang four times, then tripped onto answerphone. The recorded message was a woman with a cut-glass accent. Maybe she was from

Rotherham, but it seemed unlikely. She invited him to leave his details, and promised to ring back. *Remember*, she said, *your body is our business.* Scary. He hung up. No one was using his body for their commercial purposes.

Next, he tried the mobile number for Oliver Munday. This time a real voice answered. It too had a lot of cut-glass mixed in with it. What was going on? Was there an elocution bug going round and he was the only one with immunity? Should he try and up his game? Put on that telephone voice his grandma used, which made the queen sound like an east-end scrubber? No. Stick to talking like a thick copper. Nobody will be disappointed.

'I'm calling about Joseph Doane.'

'Well, officer, I do appreciate you getting back to me, but it must be five months since I gave the information.'

'Sorry?'

There was a sigh on the line.

'I only gave one piece of information. About the Quinn brothers...'

CHAPTER 29

Tyler Montage was in the zone. He was playing his guitar through an audio-interface box straight into his laptop, where he'd just installed some new multi-track recording software by Propellerhead. It wasn't cheap, but way better than the old Apple Garageband that he'd downloaded for free years ago. Money was still okay, but it wouldn't last forever. You can only sell your soul once.

That's why it was important to start making music again. Writing and performing or even selling his songs on for other artists to record. An old band called The New Misleaders had asked him last month to go on tour with them as their guitar technician, but he wanted more than just employment and a minor role in the music business. That had always been Mickey's problem – no ambition.

Tyler looked across at the colour print that he'd had blown up, and stuck on the wall. It was the last night of their first and only tour. The four of them were standing on stage with their arms around each other, wide-eyed and drenched in sweat. The fact that their career was cut short was cruel, but in his heart, he wondered how long they actually would have survived together if they had been given the chance? How long could he have put up with Joey always having the final say on whose song made the cut? Maybe success would have helped assuage his ego. It seemed to work for a lot of big-name bands. The insane thing was, The Magic Rats were so close to making it, they could smell it.

The memory faded. Tyler slipped his headphones back on, and a familiar wave of sadness washed over him. Whatever their faults, the band were the nearest thing he'd ever had to a family, and he missed them. Even Shannon. Where was his own father? No idea. Mother? Living with a violent and controlling prick somewhere in Spain. Sister? Dead at seventeen from a fucking eating disorder.

The song he was working on today was a kind of tribute to Mickey. He'd laid down drums and bass using loops on the software, and was now adding the guitar lead. He'd called it *The Beat is Dead*. It was about Joey as well, but because nobody was sure what had exactly happened to him, the lyrics didn't mention him by name.

It stemmed from the idea that something had killed the beat. Drums and bass. The pumping heart of a band that drives the music and gives it life. The verses told the story of friends who answered each other's ads online and formed a band. They clicked and became a unit. Surprised people by how good they were, and started to get talked about.

Then came the fateful day. No plane crash or overturned sports car. It was more gradual, but nevertheless they were killed and it wasn't natural causes. They put their trust in the wrong people to guide them on a perilous journey. Naïvety or naked ambition? History will decide. Soon they were seduced, and then enslaved. The China Girl had them wrapped around her little finger, and could make them do whatever she wanted.

The chorus was just four words. *The Beat is Dead.* Repeated six times. It wasn't quite scanning with the melody, and needed some filling out, but he was working on that. He took a deep breath and puffed. An hour was all he could concentrate for these days. Then he became drowsy and befuddled.

Tyler took his headphones off and sprawled out on the sofa. Sleep came swiftly. When his smartphone woke him, he'd no idea what time it was, and his neck was cricked. The number calling him wasn't one that was stored in his contacts, but he was used to that. Their dirty phones were always burners.

'Have you got me sorted?'

'What did you tell the coppers?'

'Ugh?'

'The new one. I know he's seen you.'

'Didn't tell him nothing.'

'Liar.'

'Please, I need the gear.'

'What did he ask you?'

'Nothing, he just pushed me about and emptied my stuff all over the floor.'

'Find anything?'

'Course not.'

'Plugged it up your arse like you did on tour?'

'Come on, I'm rattling.' Tyler's knee jiggled up and down.

'I don't know if we can still rely on you.'

'Please, I've never told anybody and I never will.'

CHAPTER 30

Oliver Munday lived on a smug cul-de-sac of four-bed houses. It was a prime spot at the southern tip of the city. In Anglo Saxon times, it had been the boundary between Mercia and Deira, but now it was where Yorkshire cosied up to the Peak District National Park, and houses came in at close to a million. The place was built on an old lead-mining area, and in the field beyond, you could still see the humps and hollows formed by the extraction and smelting of ore.

There was a sleek, new Range Rover on the drive, but when Munday answered the door, he was wearing full Lycra, and still sweating. The bike and helmet were propped in the hallway. Stallard took a dislike to him straight away, and the hairs on both forearms stood on end. No reason. That's what happens sometimes. Armhairs know their stuff when it comes to judging character. Fact.

Munday said, 'Sorry, I cycle to the office and back every day.'

'I thought you'd been skiing.'

'In July?' Munday pulled a face. Confused.

Stallard shrugged. Whooosh. What's that? The sound of a sarcastic rocket zipping straight over someone's head. That's the trouble with introductions, you never know what wavelength a person's on. 'What's the job?'

'I'm a solicitor.'

'You know what they say – make crime pay, become a lawyer.'

Munday looked down his nose. 'We don't do criminal actually. We specialise in industrial disease.'

'An ambulance chaser?' Stallard smiled. That explained it. No sense of humour, and a big house.

'I think you're getting confused with personal injury firms, who do a lot of business around motor vehicle accidents.'

Munday's voice was calm and low. He purred. He had a voice that could charm the pants off a widow, and make her change the beneficiaries of her will. Maybe he did Probate as well.

Stallard said, 'Do you do *no win, no fee*?'

'We do.'

'Sounds like ambulance chasing to me.'

Munday looked like someone had just sellotaped a dollop of fresh dog muck under each nostril.

They went through into the kitchen. It was the sort of big, hand-built temple of good taste that you'd see celebrity chefs sashaying around in, when they're relaxing at home with a camera crew. It had an island, with an induction hob and double sink, and lots of stainless steel and quartz.

There was a fridge the size of a double garage. Munday opened it, and poured himself a glass of something sludgy green from a plastic jug.

'Can I get you something to drink, detective?'

Stallard shook his head. 'Tell me about Joey Doane.'

'It's all the rage these days, isn't it? Everybody wants to know who they really are, and where they came from.' Munday took a gloopy drink, and started stretching off his calf muscles. 'Mother said it was something that she'd always hoped for, and so we were happy for her. *We*, as in me and my sister Naomi.'

'Weren't you worried that he was just after money?'

'Of course.'

'You're a lawyer, I forget.'

Munday smiled. Oily and unctuous. 'Yes, at first we were worried, because when father died, mother received a lump sum payment, which was invested rather wisely, and now she's sat on a sizeable nest-egg.' He swapped from calves to hamstrings. Bent forward at ninety degrees. 'I soon realised Joseph wasn't interested in the family estate. He never asked about it or showed the slightest interest in it. He just wanted to impress us.'

The back door slammed shut, and there was the sound of children. A woman's voice said, 'Daddy's busy.' Through the kitchen doorway, Stallard saw a pair of shapely legs usher a couple of kids straight upstairs. *To the tower, young princes.*

'It's the boys' cricket practice tonight, and I need a shower,' said Munday. 'So, I'm afraid I can't spare you oodles of time. You wanted to know about the Quinn brothers?'

210

'That's right.'

'I only met Joey three or four times, and I think it was the third time…' Munday paused, and closed his eyes, as though wanting to be certain. 'Yes, he rang me at work, and said he wanted to meet for a *bit of advice*, as he called it. He also kept addressing me as *bro*, which I found disconcerting.'

'You are his brother.'

'I know, but I wasn't sure if he was using it in that context, or as some hip-hop greeting. I'm not a fan of popular music. Anyway, I took him for lunch to a sushi place round the corner, and he started to tell this laborious story about these two hoodlums who managed his band.'

'The Quinns.'

'I tried to shut him up.'

'Why?'

'He was the same as you.'

'Irresistible to women?'

'He also wrongly assumed that because I'm a solicitor, I practise criminal law. It was clear that this sorry saga was going to involve something illegal, and I didn't want to be put in the awkward position of personally having to do something about it.'

'Not even for your long-lost brother?'

'Never act for family or friends.'

'Because they don't pay the bills?'

'No.' Munday shot a look of contempt across the island, then grabbed a towel, and draped it around his shoulders. 'I referred Joseph to a colleague of mine called Ben Phillpotts, who's a partner at a firm specialising in criminal law.'

Stallard blinked and thought he saw for a split second, the genetic resemblance between the man opposite him and Joey Doane. The same pointy jaw-line and low forehead. It was hard to compare hair, because Munday's was plastered down with sweat. Dried out, it probably had the same natural curl.

'Joey never got to tell you about his problem with the Quinns?'

'Not as such.' Munday made a big deal of looking at his watch. 'Look, I know that biologically he was my brother, but he was a very insecure and damaged individual. I think he was suffering from some kind of drug-induced paranoia or psychosis, so I wasn't entirely surprised when I heard that his vehicle had been found at a notorious suicide spot.'

'If you thought he'd taken his own life,' said Stallard, 'why call the police and tell them the Quinns might be involved?'

'Suspecting is not the same as knowing. You should know that, detective. And then there was the phone call. The last time he made contact.'

Stallard flipped through his notepad. 'Friday the 31st of January, about half past two?'

Munday shrugged. 'Possibly. It's so long ago now. He was rambling about the Quinns, and how he couldn't trust Ben Phillpotts, because he might tell the police, and it was all very bizarre, but there was one thing he said that stuck in my mind. He said, *they want me to do it again.*'

'And he was talking about the Quinns?'

'Without doubt.' Munday downed what was left in his glass of liquified vegetation, and used the towel round his neck to wipe his mouth. 'Got to freshen up before nets,

I'm afraid. Give me a ring in the office one day, and we'll meet up for lunch.' The slimy smile came back. A hand was extended to signify the conversation was over.

Stallard shook it and smiled back. *Meet up for lunch? No thanks. Rather slash my own arse and sit in vinegar. Ambulance chaser.*

The drive home was depressing. What if that's what Laura wants? The show-home with marble worktops. The perfect 2.6 children. The husband who cycles home at five o'clock, and juices his own energy drink. The gleaming 4x4 to run the perfect 2.6s to their pointless activities. On a constable's wage?

Okay, so Munday had done well for himself in a material sense, but what price spiritually? Running compensation claims for retired miners and steelworkers. What sort of job was that? Filling forms in and stealing half their money. Nice work, Oliver. If that was success, Stallard didn't want any part of it. That's why he was driving home to a 1970s caravan in a Jeep that smelt of mould and cat piss. The joys of being virtuous.

The road ahead forked. He drifted left, and started the final ascent out of the city. West into the sun. He slipped on the shades, and checked the mirror. Gotcha. The tail was back. A silver Hyundai SUV was tucked in a string of half a dozen cars behind him. Big mistake. This was Stallard's home turf, and he wouldn't let them get away from him again. He fired the Jeep up the hill to create distance, then as soon as he crested the brow he slewed left onto the verge and waited. The string of cars passed by. No Hyundai. Either they were really good, or he was starting to imagine things.

CHAPTER 31

Mid-morning, Stallard was down to shorts and flip-flops, doing some easy stretches on the mats. Lavender and honeysuckle drifted from the old, overgrown garden, and mixed with the mint that had colonised the border. Bottle it, and you'd make a fortune.

Laura was reading a magazine. She called over.

'Don't forget we're at Tom and Helena's this afternoon.'

'How could I? I love barbecues.'

'Don't start.'

'Warm lager. Shit food. Gobby kids…'

'You promised.'

'Yes.' Stallard shut up, and rolled over into a plank. A bit of pain to wash away the thoughts of an afternoon being nice to strangers. Not his forte. He could see it now. The usual bunch of professionals, who thought all police were dim Nazis. In terms of jobs, a copper was somewhere between potato-picker and the man at roadworks who twiddles a sign from *stop* to *go*. Maybe not even the stop-and-go man, because there's a lot of responsibility riding on getting the timing right with your fellow stop-and-go man at the other end of the roadworks. Especially if there's a bend in the road, and they can't see each other, so walkie-talkies are required. Huge responsibility, coupled with technical know-how. The human traffic light. He laughed. That's what he'd be this afternoon when he got the inevitable *what-do-you-do* ice-breaker question from Laura's snotty friends. *I'm a human traffic light actually.* He liked it. Not one of his usuals. Marine biologist. Male model. Ice sculptor. Earwax-candlestick maker.

Undercover work was a reason to avoid social gatherings. The Cold Case Unit less so. Laura wouldn't be fobbed off with an excuse about protecting his identity. The muscles in his stomach screamed for oxygen. He held his breath, and let them scream some more. And more, and more, until… failure. He flopped down, face burning and rolled over. A few heavy breaths.

'The thing this afternoon. Is it people from your office?'

'Mostly.' Laura looked up from the magazine. She was wearing a polka dot blouse, and big square sunglasses. 'Are you worried about your case conference?'

'No.'

'Just break the habit of a lifetime – act normal.'

'Ouch.'

The rest of the workout was silent. Stallard took it steady, with a few light weights and some old-fashioned burpees that he'd learnt at police training school. Yesterday's conversation with Oliver Munday was bouncing around in his head every time he squatted, dropped his hips and then sprang back up to make a star. Especially the bit about Joey's last phone call. The one where he was mooching around by the Crucible, and just before he went to the travel agents. The one when he said, *they want me to do it again.*

What again? Vietnam? Had the Quinns sent him out there before for something? It had to be the *F*-word. Fentanyl. Shannon had mentioned about Joey going missing once before. Ten days or so, last year. That could have been it.

But if Keith was right, there was no easy way of checking. No computer system. Just the airlines own records, and without any date parameters, it would be impossible to ask Briggsy to make enquiries. And which airline? It could be one of many that flew to the Far East. That's if Keith was right, but he would be, wouldn't he? Old Wiki-brain.

It was probably time for Baxter and Brandon Quinn to see the inside of a police cell, but then there was no evidence to put to them in interview. They'd be fully lawyered-up with a team of fancy solicitors, who thought that the rights of criminals were more important than the rights of victims and society in general.

Stallard took a shower. He dressed in black jeans, and a black shirt with a black bootlace tie. He could have been going to a rockabilly funeral, rather than a barbecue, but so what? Style is subjective. He even thought about wearing his old Texas Stetson with silver buckles. If people thought looking different was wrong, that was their problem. You have a choice of two ways to go as an undercover cop. You can either be the chameleon, who blends into any background and remains anonymous, or you can be the oddball: the one that people remember, but would never suspect of being a copper in a month of Sundays. Stallard was the oddball. It was the quickest and easiest way to get accepted by organised crime groups, or evil psychopaths who wanted to hire a hitman to kill their business partner. It was just a lucky coincidence he'd always been an oddball. Round peg, circular hole.

While Laura took a shower, he sneaked a bottle of pink wine from the fridge, and poured himself a big glass with two lumps of ice. Pre-loading is better than looking like the only alcoholic at the party. The weekend was in full swing, so his phone was on silent. Bzzzzzzzzz. Second gulp, he saw the Samsung skittering around on the kitchen worktop like a dying bluebottle. It was Shannon. Should he let it trip to voicemail? That would be the smart play. Trouble was, he felt really bad about holding back on Vietnam yesterday. Conscience doth make cowards of us all.

He swiped the screen and answered.

'Hello, you're through to the real detective agency. May I help?'

'Don't mess around, please. It's Tyler. He's not answering, and I've been trying for hours.'

The tone of her voice made Stallard put his glass down on the side. She sounded close to breaking down.

'Give it a couple of days. He'll turn up.'

'Like Joey did?'

Good point. 'Have you tried his girlfriend?'

'Tyler? He's gay.'

'Okay, boyfriend then. Or his parents?'

'There is only Tyler, and he's never not answered his phone before. I've got a key for his flat, but I'm scared to go in on my own.'

Stallard was quiet a moment. The shower had stopped, and he checked the clock. Still plenty of time. *Fuck it.*

'All right. Meet me there in twenty minutes. Don't be late.'

CHAPTER 32

Shannon Doane was waiting. She was hanging around at the edge of the car park, next to the lift shafts. A summer breeze had sprung up in the shadow of the giant block of flats, and sweet wrappers and crisp bags were skipping and chasing each other round in circles under the corner of the concrete walkway. She was in a pair of baggy combats, with a matching olive-green top. It looked like she'd put eye-liner on with a creosote brush, and combed her hair with an angry ferret. The dishevelled Cuban-revolutionary look.

She said, 'I've been up all night trying him. Tyler's a jerk, but he was the most reliable member of the band.'

'Don't worry, he'll be fine. There will be some kind of explanation. There always is.'

They rode the lift in silence. At the top, they emerged into glaring sunlight. Stallard took the key, and they squinted their way along the walkway past apricot, peach and saffron-coloured doors, sequenced to co-ordinate with the cladding. They stopped at a peach one, and he knocked. No answer. He knocked again. Still nothing, so he tried the key in the door. It didn't budge. It took him upwards of a second to realise the key didn't budge because the door wasn't locked. Basic physics. He nodded and made out that he'd known this to be the case all along. The professional – just following standardised MOE procedure.

He led the way inside. No dead-person smell. Good sign. They looked in the kitchen. Empty. Just a few pots corralled nicely by the sink, waiting to be washed. Good sign. He reversed into the hallway, and looked in the living room. Nothing. Just the same music gear he'd seen on his previous visit. The three Strats hanging from y hooks on the wall, and the black boxes stencilled with white Harry Potter rats. Good sign.

Then he found the bedroom. Clear. Just a neat and tidy three-quarter bed, and a lot of clothes on open rails. Good sign.

Last, he checked the bathroom. There was a naked body in the bath. It was Tyler Montage and he was very dead. Bad sign. Really bad sign. There was a second, equally dead body on the floor, but this one was female and clothed. Really, really bad fucking sign.

Stallard spun round to try and stop Shannon following him in. Too late. Her knees buckled, and he caught her. Steered her back through the hallway into the living room, and sat her down. The colour had gone from her face. She was trembling. So much for *don't worry, he'll be fine.* Nearly as good as, *there will be some kind of explanation.* Yes, it's that dead people are shit at answering their phone. Way to go, Sherlock.

'Who… is… the…?' Shannon's voice was broken.

'The girl is Rosie Chadwick.'

'Didn't… recognise… her…'

'That's what Class A does to your complexion. Thought you said Tyler was gay?'

Shannon closed her eyes. Recalling better times. 'Tyler and Rosie liked to get together sometimes to bitch about Joey… and me…'

He went back in the bathroom. There was no indication that Tyler had drowned. He was on his back, head fully out of the water. Eyes wide open but cloudy with death. The skin had marbled, and there were signs of washerwoman's hands, with some goose-fleshing on the arms. Significant exposure to water, but hours not days. The pathologist would know more. No sign of gases building up, and no discolouration, other than the normal lividity, caused by blood pooling, as gravity took its course. Tyler had died in that location.

A kid whose real name was Kyle Salt. Who'd dreamt of glamour and stardom, and changed his name to Tyler Montage in the hope that it would be the start of a journey that would take him around the world, selling-out stadia, shooting videos and rubbing shoulders with the stars. Now, he was Kyle Salt again. Death, the great leveller.

Rosie was crumpled up on her side on the floor, rather than stretched out. She was wearing jogging bottoms and a Nike sports top. Satirical given the likelihood she ever exercised, but also sad. Her right arm was stretched out, and just beyond it, a smartphone lay on the tiles, as though she could have dropped it there. Maybe she'd tried to call for help when Tyler's breathing started shutting down, but then hers had gone quick-time too. That was something for the divisional team to look at. Suspicious deaths were theirs.

A blister strip of pills lay on the lid of the toilet cistern, with only one missing. Next to it, a small ceramic pestle and mortar, and a pipette containing clear liquid. A single shared needle to administer the last fix. There was another mobile phone, presumably Tyler's, on the side of the bath, and Stallard was itching to check it for recent calls, but every sudden death is a potential crime scene, so he stuck his hands deep in his pockets, and went back outside.

He rang the local uniforms first, then put a call in to Block. No answer. It was Saturday, so maybe the drug squad were in somebody's garden drinking warm lager and making small talk. The curse of the barbecue. He left a message, and found Shannon crying in the doorway.

She said, 'There's only me left.'

Before he could say anything, she buried her face in his chest.

He stood there, letting his shirt get wet. No point saying everything will be fine. Already tried that one, and look what happened. In ten minutes, the uniforms arrived, then local CID. They insisted Shannon go down the station to give a statement. No arguments. They also wanted a statement from Stallard, but being a cop, they said he could type his own on Monday morning and email it through. Big of them. What to do? Shannon was clinging to his arm as though her life depended on it. He checked his watch. Still plenty of time. The chivalrous thing to do would be to accompany Shannon to the police station, so that's what he decided to do. Maybe he could polish his armour on the way.

Stallard parked the Jeep in a bay that said, *Reserved – Divisional Commander*. No insubordination intended – the big wigs never work weekends. The foyer was typical of any city-centre nick. Hard benches on a tiled floor, and a wall covered in out-of-date posters and appeals for information. The usual mixed bag of clientele: a lad with a bloodied tea-towel on his head; a woman taking to a spider in the corner; a man dressed as a nun. There's always a man dressed as a nun. They sat and waited. Detective Constable Godot would be with them shortly.

Meet you there. Half an hour. Stallard sent Laura a WhatsApp. She fired one straight back. *Don't let me down.* Classic blackmail. Time passed, and nothing happened. Even the spider looked bored. Finally, there was a buzz, and a young detective held open the door for Shannon. She clung onto Stallard.

'Do you have to go?'

She was still shaking. He gently peeled her hands off his arm, and watched her disappear into the back corridor of the station. He felt shit. The Magic Rats had been a proper band. The time-travel switch in his brain flicked on, sending him straight back to The Shapeshifter Club, and he saw them tearing the place up all over again. Incredible night. But right now, two were in the mortuary, and one was missing, presumed dead. The last surviving member was still standing, but only just, and he couldn't help thinking that this fragile soul might soon be damaged beyond repair. It was as if the band was cursed. Or was it to do with something more terrestrial, like the fact they'd got involved with a pair of full-weight shitbags?

He stroked an earring as he walked back to the car. Three people dead since he started reviewing the Joey Doane case. Coincidence? Bollocks. What if the pills found in Tyler's bathroom proved to be pure Fentanyl as well? Could they be verified as being from the same batch as the ones that killed Mickey? Was there any way of finding out if Tyler and Mickey had been accustomed to using pills that were only a fraction Fentanyl, and their supply had suddenly switched?

Hold on. Now we're bordering on the perfect crime. Even if he could ever prove that Tyler and Mickey's usual gear had been upped in strength, nobody made them buy it. Nobody made them inject it or snort it up a straw. Everything that happened, they did freely to themselves. They probably never even asked what was in the pills. Kids like that never do. It's not how the seedy drug-world works, and bastards like Brandon and Baxter Quinn know it.

Even if something like that had gone down, the question was why? Three young people losing their lives still attracted attention. It had to have some connection to Joey's disappearance. Fuck it. Stallard yelped and let go of the earring before he ripped it clean through his lobe. The last thing he felt like was faux bonhomie at a barbecue.

Okay, he was pissed.

Laura was driving them home and not speaking. Things had got a little messy when he switched from beer to red wine. Why had he done it today? The middle-class friends hadn't been so bad. Nobody had called him names or tried to have a serious conversation about why the police picked on motorists. None of the usual. They seemed like decent people trying to have a good time. Apart from the kids. They were little bastards.

So why get blitzed? It helped blank out the vision of dead kids in the bath or on mortuary slabs, but those mental bumps and scrapes were part of the job, and they'd be back tomorrow when he sobered up. What an idiot. Maybe it was the thought of what might happen to Shannon. Some knocks are harder to take than others.

Laura got out and slammed the driver's door. Stallard went after her, one step at a time. Slow and careful. He found her in the caravan, packing her bag.

'What you doing?'

She stopped and stared at him.

'I've had enough, Harry. You turn up late, and get shit-faced. I might as well have not been there.'

'I was talking to your friends.' He swayed a bit. Leant on the door. 'I think they like me.'

Laura's eyes fired up. 'How long have we been together, and it still feels like we're two individuals, who just happen to have sex occasionally.'

'It's great, isn't it?'

'No, I wanted us to be a team, and live like a proper couple.'

He shrugged. 'We can work on the team thing.'

'Forget it. You always just bat for yourself.' She zipped up her bag.

'Root or Boycott?'

'Bye.' She brushed past. 'Have a good rest of your life, Harry.'

'I've got a great slow left arm delivery.'

'Too late – it's over.' Into the car and gone.

'Over?' Stallard slumped onto his vinyl banquette, and stared after her through the open door. Dumped by a cricket metaphor. Fuck. He was tired.

CHAPTER 33

Monday morning, Stallard was in the office early. Some automated bot had taken advantage of the weekend to fill his inbox with corporate excrement: online health and safety refresher module; mandatory self-defence refresher training; Taser refresher course; level one surveillance refresher training; operational risk-assessment and CHIS-handling refresher. How could one person need so much refreshing? Was he curling up at the edges? Or had the decision to post him back to force permanently already been made, and this was what regular detectives had to put up with on a daily basis?

He sipped on the large Americano he'd collected from a new drive-through on the way in, and hit the button, *delete… delete… delete… delete… delete…*

Fay Nash breezed alongside, and slid a box of chocolate-coated flapjack on the desk.

'Good weekend?'

'Not bad.' He didn't look up. What was he supposed to say? Found two dead bodies, got wasted, got un-coupled, spent Sunday in the hangover from hell? 'What about you? How was York?'

'Didn't see much of it.' She winked and went off to wash some mugs.

He gave a grudging thumbs-up. Glad someone had fun. What's the time? Still only 7.30. No point checking in with Frank yet, but time was running out. Somewhere around 9.30, CPS would drop the charges against Jared Finn if Karina hadn't been found. What can you do? Sometimes, in the real world, the bad guys walk free, and go on to bigger and better criminal enterprises, because they've learnt from their mistakes, like clever little children. It shouldn't happen, but it does.

Keith came in. He was wearing a beige linen jacket with matching trousers, and carrying a cotton tote bag. The jacket had a lot of pockets.

'Morning, Harry.'

Stallard looked up. 'Doctor Livingstone, I presume.'

'What?'

'The safari suit.'

Keith tutted, and rose above it. 'Did you have a pleasant weekend?'

'Shit, but thanks for asking.'

'Any joy with Oliver Munday?'

'Kind of.' Stallard helped himself to a corner chunk of flapjack. 'If Joey had been to Vietnam before, how could we find out?'

'Check if he got a visa.'

'With the authorities in Vietnam?'

'The embassy in London. Would you like me to do it for you?'

'Do flies eat shit?'

'No, technically, that's not really correct. Flies lay their eggs in faeces and it is the grubs that use it as a source of food.' Keith gave a little peppy cough. 'Most common flies actually prefer to eat rotting fruit or sugary liquids.'

'Okay, let me rephrase this. Yes, I would very much like it if you made enquiries on my behalf with the Vietnamese embassy in London.'

'That's better.' Keith nodded.

Stallard chewed on the syrupy oats and chocolate. Some tastes and textures are made for each other, and even better than that, they drive away the remnants of a stubborn hangover to aid concentration. *Okay, think. What's next on the investigative action plan?* No point rushing anything. The enquiry with the Vietnamese embassy would take time. Probably a byzantine process involving carbonated forms in triplicate and carrier pigeons. Suit Keith down to the ground.

Fast forward. What if Joey had been to Vietnam before? Then it had the Quinns' pudgy fingerprints all over it. *They want me to do it again.* What else could it mean? But why would they send him out there when The Magic Rats were about to go into the studio? Was Fentanyl that lucrative? If it was, why not send someone else? Why Joey?

Myers was at his desk. Stallard checked in with him to see if there'd been any more developments. No, nothing new. Just confirmation that the car shadowing Joey's to the Humber Bridge was a Mitsubishi Lancer, and a boatload of subscriber checks on numbers that Joey had called from his mobile. They were the typical dead-ends. A guitar shop. A taxi company. Guys from other bands. Casual acquaintances and the usual percentage of Mickey-Mouse fake details that would never be traced.

As well as subscribed checks, Myers had done cell-site analysis to establish Joey's location when he made the calls. Most of the time, it looked like he'd been at home. There were some calls he'd made, which correlated with his being at his girlfriend's house, and a couple which showed him in the east end of town. That was where Naomi Munday lived. Stallard recalled that Kate Munday had seen Joey for the last time there, when he'd appeared stoned. One call was covered by the mast half a mile from Baxter Quinn's home address. Coincidence? The rest showed Joey in and around the town centre.

Stallard asked Myers how his application to join the job was going. The kid said there was a fitness test to pass, and then an assessment centre in a few weeks. He was nervous. He'd never been the sporty type, and the bleep-test was supposed to be mega-tough. His younger brother had got a stop-watch, and been helping him practise every evening in the park. Stallard told him to keep working hard and go for it. He didn't have the heart to tell him that being a detective isn't the right job for everyone. It steals your innocence and blights your faith in human nature, while slowly but steadily turning you into a sad, cynical and mentally damaged bastard. It also happens to be the best job in the world.

Eight o'clock, his mobile rang. It was Block. They exchanged notes on the deaths of Rosie Chadwick and Tyler Montage. Block said that in police headquarters a huge pile of faecal matter had collided with the rotating air-conditioning unit. The whole Fentanyl thing had become political. The Chief Constable wanted to go public, and try to reduce harm by highlighting the dangers, but the Police and Crime Commissioner didn't agree. She said publicity would be counter-productive, and entice more users to try it out. It was better to contain the situation and ride it out. Politicians. Always working the angles.

Block said he would try and get the drug squad to do some surveillance on the Quinn brothers, but it would be difficult. Their priority was still gun and knife-related crime. That's what gets in the papers, and panics Joe Public into thinking civilisation is about to end, not a few junkies taking a one-way trip to paradise. People think they deserve it. What they don't realise is that the victims of the gun and knife crime are often the actual drug dealers. They deserve it more.

Bang on 8.30, Hardcastle requested his presence. The seven-day review. Fay Nash had defused the bomb by submitting a glowing report, and if the old man was disappointed, he didn't show it. He blathered something about the Burlington Estate murders, and told him to keep up the good work. Crunch-time would be on Wednesday, because that's when HR had fixed up the case conference. He came out of Hardcastle's office not knowing if he'd been pardoned or reprieved.

A little after 8.45, Stallard and Keith set out for The Willows Private Clinic. It was in the green bit of Rotherham. Not the industrial sprawl that runs down one side of the M1, and scares passing motorists. The clinic was located close by the general NHS hospital. Possibly so that obese patients didn't have far to go for their liposuction, but more likely so the doctors could make money in their lunch break. A win-win all round. It had a nice car parking area, with pink rhododendron bushes, and an alpine rockery with purple aubretia and ground-covering perennials. High-class vegetation.

The reception area was smart. Two rows of chunky, new fabric chairs, where you could watch day-time TV, while waiting for your hair transplant, and there was a nod to the past with a sleek, well-stocked aquarium. Perhaps they used the piranhas to nibble the fat off patients. Everything gleamed. It took a while to convince Genghis Khan on the desk, but eventually they were ushered through to the manager's office.

Jenny Schmidt was smart and business-like. She had her hair lacquered into a formidable helmet, and her nails were immaculate, with little sparkles in them. Stallard could see that Genghis Khan had already told her their business, and things looked promising. There was a buff-coloured file on the desk, with a typed label, *Doane, Joseph Noel Michael*. Stallard did the introductions, and explained why they were there.

There was a pregnant pause. Then Jenny Schmidt shook her head, and said, 'I'm afraid medical information is confidential. We can't release anything without written consent, signed by the patient.'

'What if the patient is missing?'

'Same applies.'

'What if the patient can't sign a medical release form, because they've lost the use of their arms due to death?'

Jenny Schmidt smiled. 'I'm sure you know, that you'd need a warrant under Section 8 of The Police and Criminal Evidence Act.'

Stallard smiled back. Full wattage. 'What if I said, getting a warrant would take time that I haven't got, and that the lives of millions of innocent people across the planet are at stake?'

Jenny Schmidt laughed. Her hair never moved. 'Would you like a cup of tea?'

'No, thank you.'

She said, 'Are you sure you wouldn't like a cup of tea?'

'No, honestly. It's okay, thank you.'

'Only if you wanted a cup of tea, I would have to go into reception, and leave that file on my desk.'

Stallard could have kissed her. He didn't, because she looked diligent and methodical. She reminded him of an old girlfriend who always started sending emails as soon as they'd finished making love. Difference was, Jenny Schmidt looked like she probably sent them during. It didn't matter. He loved her, and what's more it was the old magic smile that had done the trick. *He hadn't lost it. Of course not. Who said he had?*

'Just milk in mine, thanks.'

Keith looked askance. Like he knew something was happening but wasn't sure what. 'One sugar for me, please.'

Jenny Schmidt clicked out of the room in a pair of high-heeled sling-backs. Stallard went round and sat in her chair with the buff-coloured file. It wasn't thick. There was a standard welcome questionnaire that Joey had filled out, with his medical history, and a list of disclaimers and small print that he'd signed. Then there was a single sheet. It was a print-out from a database. Joey had given a sample of blood. It was dated the 23rd of January. There was bumph attached, with the name Bell-Bio Inc, and a couple of bar codes, but nothing else.

When Jenny Schmidt came back in, she said, 'I'm sorry, we seem to be all out of tea today.'

Keith looked genuinely disappointed.

Stallard wrinkled his nose. 'I don't think I understand. I thought Mr Doane would have been seeking treatment for drug addiction or some other physical condition. It looks like he just gave blood.'

'I can't comment on Mr Doane's case,' said Jenny Schmidt. 'Hypothetically speaking though, we do act as agents for an increasing number of Internet-based companies, who provide a variety of biological and genetic services. All we do is take the blood sample. What it is then used for is between the individual and the company.'

'Thank you. I appreciate your help.' Stallard signed off with another big smile. A belter. One of his best.

The shortest route back from Rotherham was to cut across Junction 33 of the M1 motorway. It was a snarled-up intersection of wagons, cars and caravans, getting baked in their own fumes, and bombarded by electro-magnetic waves from the pylons that converged at the centre of this island. Officially the best place in the UK to go if you want cancer. So, he dropped the Jeep down a narrow rural lane that ran under the motorway, and looped around a reservoir and through some old villages that had been subsumed into the greater metropolitan area.

Keith had a fresh quarter of mint humbugs on the go. Stallard sucked on one, and tried to decipher what Joey Doane's visit to The Willows Private Clinic signified. It wasn't to try and find his birth mother, because by the 23rd of January, he'd made contact and they'd met up. Whatever the reason, it explained the mark on his arm that his bandmates had seen, and caused them to assume he'd been shooting up. Didn't he tell Tyler he'd been giving blood? Joey had been telling the truth. Except he'd not been donating it to the NHS for transfusions. So, why else would he do it?

Stallard was turning right past the reservoir, wondering if Bell-Bio Inc might have the answer, when he saw something familiar two cars back. A silver Hyundai SUV. *Coincidence? The South Korean manufacturer is taking an increasing chunk of UK market share these days, and silver is a popular colour.* He kept driving steady, and took a left onto an estate of retirement bungalows. The Hyundai turned left. He carried on past an old Working Men's Club that was now a nursing home, and an old bingo hall that was now a Co-op, and turned right at the next roundabout. The Hyundai turned right.

Stallard wasn't going to make any mistake this time. No dramatic, high-speed Bond-esque chases through shopping centres and markets. Definitely no penny-fucking-farthings. He took another right, and pulled up at the T-junction. They were now back at the main road that they'd turned off half a mile back. The silver SUV pulled up behind him, still two cars back. He waited until more cars had pulled up at the back of the line, and then turned his engine off. Nobody was going anywhere. Time for some fun.

After a minute, one driver started honking a horn. Someone else joined in. He got out of the car, and held his arms out in frustration to the driver behind, as though there was nothing he could do. *Sorry. The knackered old Jeep has given up the ghost.* Then he casually walked down the street, spat out the humbug, and climbed into the back seat of the silver Hyundai before the driver knew what was happening. He was an older guy. Bald patch and the sort of stubble that's not fashionable, just scruffy.

Stallard hooked his right arm around the man's neck, and yanked it back. He leaned forward between the two front seats.

'I suffer from recurring nightmares. One of them is being followed. I don't like it, and I get very angry.'

'Ugh, ugh. Strangling me…' The man just managed to say.

'I get violent. The aliens who are following me are trying to kill me, and I have to kill them first.'

The man's face was red. His eyes were popping. He tried to talk, but his mouth made a squelching sound. Some gurgling came from lower down.

Outside, the car horn started up again. Stallard eased up on the windpipe, and waited. The man still couldn't speak. He pointed to the console between the driver's and passenger seat. There was a wallet tucked in the cubby hole. Stallard flipped it open with his left hand, and saw a business card. Oh, great. He let go of the driver, and fished it out, so he could read the full thing. *Lawrence P Maggs. Private Investigator. Discreet and Trustworthy. Over 30 years' law enforcement experience. All types of investigation undertaken.*

Stallard put it in his back pocket.

'Okay, I won't kill you, but I'm still angry. Who are you working for?'

Maggs choked and massaged his throat. He took a couple of deep breaths and coughed. Then he wiped two trails of snot from his top lip.

'Shannon Doane.'

'What happened to *discreet and trustworthy*?' Stallard prodded him in the ribcage. 'I ask you once who your client is, and you blab it out straight away. Show some backbone.'

'I thought you were bloody killing me.'

'We need a chat.'

CHAPTER 34

They found a garden centre with a café. It was the sort of place old people take their parents. Stallard got a round of coffees and buttered toast. Maggs still had the bullfrog eyes, so it was the least he could do. There were fake oak beams, and shelves of botanical books, and piped music of Michael Bublé's Greatest Hits, floating between the potted succulents.

'Begin at the beginning, and go on till you come to the end: then stop,' said Stallard, deploying the interview technique first used by Alice's King of Hearts.

'Shannon engaged my services about a month after Joey went missing.' Maggs spoke quietly. His voice brittle. 'My remit at that time was to follow up the sightings that came in from the Justice For Joey website, and all the social media ads. It was busy. Stuff was coming in from all over. But it was all crap, and as the weeks turned into months, things started to thin out. I was wasting time, and she didn't pay well.'

'I've told you before, Larry – stop dissing your client. Show a bit of loyalty.'

'It's Lawrence.' Maggs chewed on some toast. 'It wasn't her fault. The money came from fundraising events, and they were hit and miss, so I had to drop my hours down. Work a bit smarter.'

'Be more selective on the follow-ups?'

'No. I scrapped them altogether. Like I said, they were all crap.' Maggs took a drink to help the toast down. 'Listen, I was a copper for 30 years, so I knew what to do. I went proactive. Instead of waiting for dead-end leads to come in, I switched to looking at who might have killed Joey.'

'The Quinns?'

'That's who Shannon said.'

Stallard nodded and brushed toast crumbs off his chin. 'And did Shannon ask you to follow me?'

'No, that was my idea. She thought you were holding back on her. That there was some new information. The only way for me to find out was to hold onto your coat-tails, because I've not got access to all the IT systems, and the magic warrant card that opens doors. You've no idea how difficult it is being a PI.'

Stallard bit his tongue. *PI? Where does he think he is? Streets of San Francisco? Easily confused with the outskirts of Rotherham. They've both got trams and hills. End of.*

Keith had wandered off to browse a display of bird-feeders and gift sets of secateurs and gloves. The lesser-spotted Blenkinsop in his natural habitat.

Stallard said, 'What did you find out about Baxter and Brandon?'

'Plenty.' Maggs opened a notebook. 'They still operate their old man's non-ferrous scrap business.'

'Not scoop of the decade.'

'And supply door staff to nightclubs and events management companies.'

'Still fascinating. I'm gripped. Is this all kosher?'

'Her, her, her.' Maggs laughing. A throaty rasp. 'Do you know any scrap business or security firm that's totally legit?'

'What about their sports and music management business?'

'Do you know what I think?'

'Yeah, I'm a fucking mind reader.' Stallard rolled his eyes. 'Don't know why I bother asking questions.'

'I think all that sports and music management crap is just a hobby for them.'

'Or a front.'

'They like to mix in those circles. To see and be seen.'

'Except this is the Steel City, not exactly wall-to-wall glitterati.'

'Big fish, little pond.'

'I didn't know PIs were such gifted sociologists.'

'Her, her, her.' Maggs popped in the last bit of toast, and licked butter from his thumb. 'Do you want a tip?'

'You do financial advice as well?'

'They've got a place that would be worth turning over on a warrant.'

'What's the reasonable grounds?'

'I followed Baxter there after he left SIAM head office, and then kept the place under static obs for a full week.'

'Impressive.'

'I've got my own Transit kitted out for those kinds of jobs.'

'A regular one-man surveillance machine.'

'You know what it's like – eating sandwiches all day and pissing in pop bottles.'

'I could talk for hours about which is the best impromptu container of urine, but let's get back to reasonable grounds.'

'There were boxes being delivered dawn til dusk.'

'Maybe it's what's called a business.'

'I tried to take a closer look one time, but a guy collared me by the gate. It was like he was acting as look-out.'

'Safeguarding your own premises is not a crime.'

'You get a nose for these things in our job, don't you?'

'Can I borrow your nose to put on the application for a search warrant?'

'Check it out yourself, and see if I'm right.'

Stallard drained the dregs of his coffee. 'Address?'

'The Quinns own a snooker hall down the east end. It's on an industrial estate round the corner.'

'You don't know the address?'

'I'll take you there. I feel really bad about letting Miss Doane down.'

'Maybe you should, Mr Maggs. Maybe you should.'

The rest of the drive back into the Steel City was uneventful. It was sunny. He didn't have to stop off and throttle anybody. There was that feeling in the air, just before schools break up for the summer holidays, of excitement and anticipation of long, hot days to come. It was the week kids took games into class and watched DVDs. The older ones, who'd done exams, were already out getting drunk on cider and exploring each other's bodies. The joys of youth.

Keith had bought a pair of mauve gardening gloves, and had them on, flexing his fingers. 'Soft and supple, but at the same time extremely hardwearing.'

'Can't beat real leather.'

'They're suede actually.'

'Same thing.'

'Not strictly.' Keith cleared his throat. 'Look, these have a napped finish because it comes from the underside of the animal skin.'

'Forget I mentioned it.'

'The word itself comes from the French phrase *gants de Suede*, which literally translates as *gloves from Sweden.*'

'Keith, shut up.'

Stallard checked his phone. There was still no message or missed call from Frank. Nor was there a voicemail from Laura, saying that she'd made the biggest mistake of her life, and pleading with him to take her back. Maybe the battery was dead. Nope. The little icon was still standing tall. Maybe there was no mobile signal. Nope. Three bars. Strange. He rang Shannon, because he had a bone to pick with her called Lawrence P Maggs. She was at her parents. The regeneration project where they lived was two minutes west, so at the next island, he swung the Jeep right, and found the Doane cul-de-sac.

Shannon met them at the front door. She lowered her voice.

'Please don't say anything about Tyler and Mickey. I haven't told them yet.'

Stallard thought she looked better than when he'd left her on Saturday. No make-up, and a little delicate, but more in control. He saw over her shoulder that there were suitcases at the bottom of the stairs. He pointed to them with his eyes.

'Going away?'

'Not me. Mum and Dad booked a last-minute all-inclusive to Kos. They need a break. I've been on at them for ages to do it.' She stepped back. 'Do you want to come in?'

'No, we're okay here.' Stallard remembered Elaine, the carpet Gestapo. Taking off his cowboy boots in this heat might cause offence. Worse than actually walking on the Axminster, unless Elaine had her own breathing apparatus handy.

Shannon twirled some keys on a finger. 'I said I'd run them to the airport. We probably should be going soon.'

'I stopped by to apologise for not telling you about something,' said Stallard. 'Two days before he went missing, Joey booked a flight to Vietnam. It was for the Monday, but he never made it.'

Shannon looked puzzled. 'Why would he do that?'

'I don't know, but I remember you saying that he'd gone missing once before. Can you remember when it was?'

'No, not really.' She shook her head. Her fringe fell down in strands over her eyes. 'Possibly this time last year. I'm not sure. But I don't think he will have been anywhere like that. Joey liked to make out he was worldly-wise, but with some things he was clueless. Like, he couldn't boil an egg. He didn't know where the oil cap is on a car, and there's no way he could have got himself to somewhere so foreign. Even in this country, he couldn't even book his own hotel.'

Stallard wasn't so sure. It was a trick as old as the hills. Make out you're useless, and someone else will do it for you. He himself was a grandmaster of the ancient art. The Stallard-meister. If he put his mind to it, he could be useless at absolutely anything. Bloody useless sometimes. He also thought that there was a good chance that Joey might have confided in his other bandmates more than his sister, but there was no way of asking those guys. Not without a Ouija board.

'One more thing. Why didn't you tell me about the old gumshoe?'

'Ugh?' She cocked her head in puzzlement.

He pulled the card of his pocket. 'Lawrence P Maggs. All types of investigation undertaken.'

'Oh, him.' Going bright red. 'Sorry.'

'Why didn't you tell me?'

'I didn't know if I could trust you.' She couldn't look him in the eye. 'Or Maggs. I thought it was better to have two dogs in the race.'

'You can be manipulative. It's not a pleasant characteristic.'

'I'm trying to find out what happened to my brother, not be a nice person.' She spat out the words like orange pips. 'And I don't give a shit what you think about me.' She slammed the door in his face.

Stallard stood there. That's two women he'd upset in the course of two days. It was becoming a habit. He checked the time on his mobile. He'd got an appointment to see Naomi Munday at midday. Maybe he could make it three in a row.

Keith coughed. 'I didn't like to say anything while you were talking to the young lady, but I have a result on the request we put in this morning to the Vietnamese embassy.' He tapped his iPad.

'What?'

'It's all computerised. All they had to do was check, and I put the request through a good friend of mine in the City of London fraud squad, which will have greased the wheels.'

Stallard smiled. Old boys' network. Literally. 'And?'

Keith coughed again. For a man who ate so many sucky-sweets, he coughed a lot.

'Joseph Doane entered Vietnam on the 15th of June last year, and left two weeks later on the 1st of July.'

'He had been there before. Fuck. I was right.'

CHAPTER 35

Naomi Munday lived by the canal. She was mid-thirties, with frizzy hair fastened down by a rainbow bandana. Her body was the shape of a pear, and her teeth were spread out at intervals, like fence posts on moorland. In Chaucer's time, she would have been a great beauty, but nowadays she didn't quite fit in with conventional aesthetics. Times change.

She said, 'Welcome to Bedlam,' and invited Stallard in.

The place where she lived was an old workshop. A brick building that would have manufactured knives or sickles back in the nineteenth century. Now it looked as though it was both apartment as well as workplace. It reminded Stallard of a studio in the Lower East Side of Manhattan, or somewhere a Dutch post-impressionist might have cut their ear off. The only natural light came from narrow windows above head height, but to compensate, there were lots of industrial pendants and angle-poise lamps.

Paintings filled the room. A couple of them stood on easels, but most leant against walls or were laid out on picnic tables. There were lots of shelves with jars, and pots, and brushes.

'You're an artist,' said Stallard. Strike one to the great detective.

'That's my website.' She handed him a card. 'Ten percent discount for government workers. Not that you look much like a copper.'

He read the card. *Bedlam Art. Born of Confusion.* Looking at the paintings, that explained a lot. Put them over the mantlepiece if you wanted to frighten the crap out of the kids, or just keep them away from the fire. Scenes from science fiction book covers or old prog-rock album sleeves. You know the stuff. Woman with lizard's tail fights dragon with three heads, and man dressed in Edwardian shirt and breeches rides horse across futuristic moonscape. No thank you. If I want retro on my wall, I'll go for something plain and simple. Tennis girl scratching bum, or Debbie Harry by Warhol.

Naomi cleared away some magazines, and made space for him to sit on a stool. He waited while she went and made coffee. The kitchen was separated from the studio by a freestanding folding divider. Beyond that, he could see a bed and piles of clothes, and in the corner, a tiny bathroom. Working from home, hard-core. She came back with two mugs and two orange Club biscuits.

Stallard sat and listened to her story. Everyone has a story to tell, if you are prepared to listen, and eat thick chocolate-coated biscuits with them. He liked Naomi. He didn't like her art, but he liked her. She was warm and open, and not afraid to either cause offence or laugh at herself. There was an air of mischief about her, and a sense of

247

strong loyal and moral values. She reminded him of some old friend who you'd want to spend all day with in the pub, getting steadily more and more sloshed. She was good company. The opposite of Oliver, the ambulance-chaser.

The back-story flowed. She told him about growing up. Camping holidays in summer, so they could afford to ski in winter. Big parties. The ritual meal at six, at the table, no TV dinners. The pets. They were a good family and they were good times. Mum could be pushy, but which mums aren't?

When she was about fourteen, mum said she was pregnant. There was initial revulsion at the thought of her parents having sex, but other than that, she quickly accepted it as a fact of life. Rather looked forward to having a baby in the house. Oliver didn't say much. He was sixteen or seventeen. Typical boy. Out with his mates.

Then dad died. Weeks that followed were hell. Pain, anger, numbness, despair. Mum tried to hold it together, but she was physically ill as well. Oliver had good predicted grades for his A levels, but now he was up all-night partying, like he was on a suicide mission. None of them knew at that time how the family finances would work out. They were scared.

Naomi had to stop and blow her nose before she carried on. She didn't know why, but this was the time in her life that something changed inside her. Blamed her mother for dad's death. Started to resent the unborn baby. Became withdrawn. Then she began to go out, and got noticed by older lads. She took up with one of them called Max. They became an item. No big deal. Except Max was twenty-one and into drugs.

Her mother had never told her why she gave the baby up for adoption. Didn't need to. She was trying to salvage what was left of her existing family. It worked for Oliver. He got his grades and went to Warwick. It didn't work for Naomi. You can't save people from drugs. Only the addict can save themselves, if they want it badly enough, and not always even then. She'd been in and out of rehab over the years, and done the Methadone scheme.

Painting was cathartic and helped pay the bills. She'd seen it on a TV documentary. It was about soldiers suffering PTSD from Iraq or Afghanistan. Painting was good for their mind. She'd been doing it ten years, and accepted there was never going to be a Bedlam Art exhibition in a major gallery, but it worked for her. Sometimes she lapsed. She had no idea why. Just the demons, and the boredom and the futility of life. Even then, she carried on with her art. Like the Romantic poets and painters who worked through a haze of opium. Sometimes drugs made the art better.

She'd been nervous about meeting Joey. Mum wanted her and Oliver to be at the first reconciliation. The nerves had been misplaced. Joey and her were kindred spirits, and met up a few of times on their own afterwards. He wanted her to do the artwork for The Magic Rats' album. Maybe it was the drug connection. She could tell Joey was an addict too, but they never really talked about it. One of the times, he came to the studio, they shared a spliff on the canal bank, but that was it.

Only once during Naomi's monologue did he think she was hamming it up. There was just one blow of the snuffly nose too many. But he gave her the benefit of the doubt.

Some people like to dramatise their personal misfortunes and feel sorry for themselves.

She stood up.

'Do you fancy a little stroll on the towpath? I'm busting for a ciggy.'

They went outside. The stretch of canal bank was shaded by the red-brick factories that butted right up to the towpath. Some were renovated. Some still had cracked sky-lights and weeds growing out of the walls. The water was black, but clean. There were a couple of men fishing, watched by a heron that sat patiently on a corrugated roof. Everything was still. Over the tops of the chimneys, you could hear engines and the whoosh of air-brakes.

Stallard stepped back to let a jogger pass, then fell in beside Naomi.

'Why do you think Joey got in touch?'

'I've got a theory, but it's probably bollocks.' She cupped her hands and lit up. 'I think he knew he wasn't normal, and wanted to find out why. Like, was it something that he'd inherited?'

'What did Oliver think?'

She stopped. Bristled and became immediately defensive. Then she relaxed and puffed smoke down both nostrils. 'What do you think? He's a solicitor. He thought Joey was after money.'

'It sounds like you and your brother don't get on.'

She smiled. There were lots of gums. 'We argue like hell about politics, but he's a big softy. I love him. He's smart and generous. It didn't take him long to work out that Joey wasn't after money. That's when he paid for his treatment.'

He wondered if the smile was forced. 'Treatment?'

Naomi took a deep drag and held it in, letting the nicotine work its magic in the little nooks and crannies of her lungs. Then she tilted her head back and exhaled.

'Drug treatment. Oliver paid for mine a few years back. It's not cheap. Residential costs a bloody fortune.'

Stallard nodded. Good old Oliver. Saviour of the downtrodden addicts. Still didn't like the robbing bastard, no matter what he did in his spare time.

'Where was it?'

'Joey told me, but I can't remember. Some place I'd never heard of.'

'Did Oliver give him cash?' Stallard knew where this was going.

'Yes.'

'But Joey never made it there?'

'No. That's when he went missing.'

Stallard stopped walking and stroked his chin. 'Is it just me, or does anyone else think that giving a junkie a wad of cash is a stupid idea?'

Naomi turned round. 'You think he ran off with the money, don't you?'

He pouted. Let me think. 'Does the Pope shit in the woods?'

She laughed. 'I guessed you'd jump to that conclusion. But you're wrong.'

'I am? It would be a once in a Millennium event, but I'm prepared to listen to a well-reasoned counter-argument.'

She drew on the cigarette, and then chucked it in the canal.

'He didn't run off with the money, because he jumped off the bridge. It's sad. Life sucks sometimes.'

'I think somebody killed him.'

Her face changed. 'Don't say things like that.'

'It's my opinion.'

'Do you have proof?' There was a new edge to her voice. Almost threatening.

'If I did, somebody would be sat in a cell.'

'Then keep it to yourself, and let people have closure.' The tone was firm. Borderline aggressive. No more discussion was to be had on this subject.

Up ahead, a road crossed the canal, and the bridge was low and tight. Just enough to get a barge through. They made a U-turn, and strolled back on the towpath. Naomi lit and smoked another Marlboro Light. The talk of Joey being potentially murdered had darkened her mood, but gradually it lifted. By the time they reached the studio, she was bubbly again. At the door, he thanked her for being honest and forthright.

She looked at him and smiled. 'Come back if you ever want to show me those tattoos.'

He put a hand up to his chest, self-conscious, and smiled back.

She gave him the fence-post smile again. 'I can do portraits.'

'Thanks. I'll bear it in mind.'

He walked back to the Jeep. *Note to self – keep away from mad artist. Fancy sitting bollock-naked, and being painted in some weird human form, with serpents' heads and a unicorn's legs? No, thank you, I'll pass on that one. There are better ways to spend an evening. Eating burnt pizza and making pyramids out of empty Stella tins. That's what will be happening later chez caravan Stallard. Can't wait.* He blipped the driver's lock and climbed in. Put his phone on charge, and saw there was a message. Wait a minute. From Laura. What the…

I'm going to ring you at 4pm. Be somewhere on your own. It's not what you think.

This is not about getting back together.

He knew it. She wanted to get back together. The cunning reverse logic of a psychiatrist. He put his shades on, and pointed his trusty steed back towards the nick.

CHAPTER 36

Myers was eating pasta salad from a plastic container. When he saw Stallard approaching, he opened a drawer, popped it inside and wiped his mouth. It was that time of day. Around the office, there were Tupperware boxes on desks, and pieces of fruit and bags of crisps. Most were doing Sudoku puzzles, or checking out the BBC news website, but Myers was working on a spreadsheet between mouthfuls of penne and rocket. That was Myers. The kid was relentless.

Stallard threw him another task. Find out as much as possible about Oliver and Naomi Munday. He gave him the *Bedlam Art, Born of Confusion* card, and told him not to look up the paintings. They'd give him nightmares. Myers said he was always up until the early hours playing *God of War* and *Resident Evil 3* on Xbox, where he put people's heads into meat grinders, and chopped their limbs into bite-size pieces with a chainsaw. They did the same back. So, he didn't think paintings would be scary. Smart lad.

When Stallard got back to his own desk, he logged on, and went online to find Bell-Bio Inc. They had a fancy website. They were fast, accurate, confidential and competitively priced. They were also UK-based and experienced in their field. It looked like their field was mainly paternity tests. Send little Jimmy's blood sample off together with that of a potential father, and they'll give you an answer. But what if there's three or more potential fathers? No problem here at Bell-Bio Inc, madam. We're not judges of morality. If there are three or more possible fathers, you can send extra samples at a super-discounted rate. The more you send, the more you save. Go on, sleep around. *Stop it.* He slapped himself on the forehead. *Stop being such a cynical prick.*

There was a number with a London area code. He dialled it, and a woman with a mid-Atlantic accent answered. She was sorry, but they couldn't deal with police enquiries over the phone. They had a legal department, and he would have to submit a request in writing. She was sorry again. Stallard was sorry. Everyone was sorry, but it didn't help. If they'd been in the room together, he would have given her one of the megawatt smiles, and things could have got sorted out. That's the problem with the phone. It's the curse of the good-looking, charismatic detective. *Stop it.* He slapped himself on the forehead again. *Stop it with the fake irony.*

Keith ambled over. He'd been working on the Vietnamese visa angle, trying to link it back to a particular airport or airline. No luck. They needed more details from the Vietnam end. Stallard had a brainwave. Brainwaves were things to be cherished in the world of real detectives, because they didn't happen often. He remembered what Shannon had said about Joey, not being able to boil an egg, and how he wasn't exactly a hardy traveller. Ergo, he was inexperienced and a creature of habit. Perhaps he'd used the same travel agents?

The answer was yes. It took a while to get there. He had to hang on the line, while Zoe talked herself through how to use the computerised booking system. Like it was her first time. It turned out that Joey had booked the same route last year: Manchester to Danang, via Paris and Hanoi. It also turned out phones can save good-looking detectives a lot of time. They were redeemed. *Hallelujah*.

The Cold Case Review Unit office had once more turned into Club Tropicana, as the afternoon sun hove into view. It had gone from defrost to full power, missed out the reheat button altogether. Stallard slipped out of the door, and drove to The Three Feathers. He needed somewhere cool to think, and a drink to help him do it. He ordered a Guinness, and drank a pint of lager while it settled. Then he did the same again, because thinking wasn't coming easy. Eventually, the grey cells realised they'd better start doing some heavy-lifting before alcohol killed them off one by one.

Joey had travelled to Vietnam last year, but his sister didn't know about it. It was well before they fell out, so if it was a holiday trip, he would have told her. That meant it must have been drugs. Joey had no money back then, so somebody must have funded it. He didn't know Oliver Munday at that time, so he couldn't have conned cash out of him using the old rehab routine. That left one possibility. Everything came back to the Quinns, and their links to the

Far East. He needed to check one thing with Block – when did the first cases of Fentanyl start showing up?

At precisely four o'clock, his phone showed an incoming from Laura, and he answered straight away.

'Hi, this is The Cliché himself speaking.'

'Give it a rest, Harry. This is not a phone call I want to make.'

'Is someone coercing you to make it? Have gangsters taken your mother hostage at gunpoint? Go on, ring the detective or the old gimmer gets it.' He did The Godfather accent.

'Shut up and listen. Don't tell anybody I made this call, and if anyone finds out, I shall deny all knowledge.'

There was something in the tone of her voice. It made the hair twitch on the back of his neck. He shut up.

'Not everyone is like you, Harry. When some staff come to the Occupational Health Unit for counselling, they engage with the process. It's called cognitive therapy. They are suffering mental problems because of things they have seen and dealt with at work.'

'Shame, but it's what they get paid for.' He couldn't help it. *Shut up, idiot.* He bit his tongue.

Laura let it slide.

'When we went to the barbecue on Saturday, you talked to someone I work with. I'll call her Jane, but that's not her real name. I don't know what you said to her, but she worked out you were the guy who got stabbed and nearly died.'

Stallard smiled. Fame at last. The guy who nearly died.

'Jane has been treating somebody in the Unit for some time now. I will call him John. He has acute situational depression, arising out of his part in a traumatic incident at work. He may also be bipolar. The incident involved an officer being stabbed by a young woman.'

That narrowed it down. Wait a minute... Stallard screwed up his eyes.

'John feels responsible for the incident. He made a mistake. Instead of admitting it, he covered it up. Fortunately, the officer didn't die and is making a recovery of sorts. But John doesn't feel as though he can work in the same Unit as the officer again, because of the–'

'STOP. STOP IT... It's Frank. John is Frank.'

'You needed to know. None of what happened was your fault.'

'John is Frank... I'm going to kill the bastard.'

'Don't do anything stupid, and don't ever try to contact me in the future. I've applied for a job in another force. Goodbye Harry.'

He tried to say something, but she'd gone.

CHAPTER 37

'I'll follow you this time.' Stallard shouted through his driver's window to Maggs, and waited while the PI spun his car round. Then set off in convoy towards the east end of the city.

They climbed the ring road, then dropped down into the Don valley, where the steel factories once stood, and the back-to-back workers' houses. Now, most of it had gone. There were still odd patches of concrete scrubland, where demolition had taken place and nothing had been built, but the rest was regenerated. It had call centres, and modern factories and a new police headquarters that looked like an antiseptic office block for overpaid accountants.

The daily throng of commuters heading home was tailing off. A translucent veil of cloud had appeared in the sky, and there was still a heat haze shimmering over the valley, as you looked out towards the motorway. Stallard had rung Frank. He'd not answered. Five times. He'd also tried to catch up with Block, but the drug squad must have been busy trying to keep the lid on the latest moral panic.

Maggs swung left off the main road, and down a street that had industrial units either side. It was called Ganister Road. They were in clusters of half a dozen, each with their own car park and loading bay. After fifty metres, he pulled into the kerb. Stallard stopped behind and met him on the footpath.

'Which one?'

'That one.' Maggs pointed through the security fence. 'The one with the red sports car.'

Mmm, familiar. 'Wait for me here.'

'What are you doing?'

'I've not got time for static surveillance. I'm going route one.' Stallard set off walking.

When he reached the unit, he saw the roller-shutter door in the loading bay was up. A lad was sitting on the tailgate of a box van, smoking and Face-timing someone.

'Evening.' Stallard nodded and walked past him and through the open door.

The interior was racked out with metal shelves. About two-thirds had cardboard boxes. There was a forklift hooked up on charge just inside the door, and a pile of wooden pallets in the corner. There were three aisles. Stallard walked down the central one, and tried to make out the labelling on the boxes. They were addressed to Triangle Trading Ltd, at Ganister Road.

At the far end of the warehouse was a table and chairs. A few empty coffee cups and some rolls of packing tape. Stallard found a Stanley knife, and went back to the boxes. He slit the seal on the first one, and folded it open. There was a lot of bubble wrap. He pulled it out, and found some more smaller boxes. He cut his way in to one, and slid out a little steel case. He flipped the catches and opened the lid. It was a set of snooker balls. He picked one out, and jiggled it in his palm. Yep, definitely a snooker ball. Heavy enough to kill Goliath at fifty paces. The real deal. He put it back.

He took a few steps down the aisle, and tried another box. This one felt lighter. He cut the tape, and opened it up. More bubble wrap. He pulled it out, and found again some smaller boxes. He was trying to open one of these, when he heard a connecting door open. Footsteps.

Brandon Quinn appeared at the end of the aisle.

'I think you'll find you need a warrant to do that.'

'I think you'll find that I don't,' said Stallard. 'Not if I have the implied consent of the owner.'

'You don't.'

'Oh, so are you the owner?' Stallard smiled at him. *Bishop to King's Rook 5. Check.*

Quinn looked unsure. Sensing a trap. He didn't say anything.

'Thought so.' Stallard carried on opening the smaller box. It contained plastic bags. He pulled some out, and tore one open. They were socks. Thick, white sports socks.

Quinn puffed himself up. Took a few steps closer. The intimidator. 'Looking for something in particular?'

'An explanation for why Joey Doane went to Vietnam.'

Quinn laughed. 'You're crazy.' Another step. 'That's enough.'

'Back off, butterball.'

Stallard pulled another box down from the racking, and started to cut the tape. There were voices outside in the loading bay. Then two more men appeared. It was Baxter Quinn and his sidekick who looked like a boxer.

'There's been an accident,' said Baxter Quinn. 'Somebody call an ambulance.'

Brandon Quinn smiled. 'My batteries dead. What about yours, Woodsy?'

The boxer smiled. 'Sorry, mine's dead too.'

'But it looks really bad.' Baxter Quinn smiled. Something hilarious was happening.

Stallard dropped the knife and ran out of the open roller-shutter door. He saw Maggs at the entrance gate to the road. He was lying on his side with one arm at an unnatural angle. His head was hanging over the kerb. When Stallard got close, he could hear him moaning, half-conscious. His face was covered in blood, and there was a trickle of liquid on the pavement, where he had lost control of his bladder. Half throttled in the morning, fully twatted by teatime. The work of a PI is not all dancing girls and Dry Martinis.

As he waited for the paramedics to arrive, Stallard wondered whether baiting the bear had been the right tactic. The Quinns weren't stupid. They always made sure there was never any prospect of their personally appearing in court. Yet they'd just taken a risk attacking Maggs outside their own premises. Were they panicking because he was getting close, or were they confident nothing would happen to them? Was it a last-ditch attempt to ward him off, or did they genuinely believe they were above the law? Maybe they thought they had some protection? Money can buy most things.

Something was happening, and it all linked back to Joey's disappearance. Tyler and Mickey dying in quick succession can't have been chance. Just at the time when the case had been reopened? Too convenient. They knew something and had been silenced. The fact that it was by their own hand was a stroke of genius. Subtle and sinister. The opposite of what they'd just done to Maggs.

What if the Quinns were now raising the stakes? Shannon was the only Magic Rat left. What could be done to afford her more protection? Personal-attack alarms? CCTV? She'd probably refuse, but he ought to offer. And what about closer to home? Baxter had made a statement by turning up at the caravan. Was it still safe to live there? Fuck them. If they turned up there, they'd better bring an army.

Part of the problem was, he was having difficulty thinking straight and making decisions. The phone call from Laura had put him in a state of shock, and his mind was thrashing around for answers. There was something he needed to resolve first that might help.

At 9.05pm, Stallard tossed another empty beer can into the back of his Jeep. The house was in darkness. There was no car on the drive. He was going to give it until nine, but sod it, what's another few minutes, when there's just an empty caravan to go home to? He pulled the ring on another can. Hate can be a powerful emotion. He knew, because he was cherishing it right now. There was a tightness in his chest. It wouldn't go away, even when he closed his eyes and slowed his breathing right down.

When the car came round the corner, and pulled into the driveway, he was ready. A big, lumbering figure got out of the driver's side.

'Hey,' Stallard shouted. 'I thought we were brothers.'

Frank stopped. Slowly turned round. There was a look of resignation on his face.

'Hit me.'

'What are you on about?'

Frank walked up, until they were face to face. 'I said, *hit me*.'

'Piss off.' Stallard shook his head, and looked away.

Frank threw a rabbit punch that caught him on the back of the neck. He staggered, regained his balance, and pivoted in one movement. The right hook hit the side of Frank's jaw. He didn't go down. The man was a monster. He stood there looking blank. Stallard hit him twice more. The second one knocked him sideways. Frank fell, and his head hit the floor. There was a soft thud. He rolled onto his side, and curled up, expecting more. Blood started to drip from his ear.

Stallard stood over him. Fists clenched. After a few seconds, it was like a valve opening, and he started to breathe.

'Fucking hell, Frank. I could have killed you.'

'So what?'

Stallard helped him up. They went inside, and sat Frank down in the kitchen. Stallard ran a towel under the cold tap, and folded it into a square. Gave it Frank. 'Tell me about it.'

'I had an informant.'

'On the human trafficking case?'

'An Eastern European.'

'I'm guessing prostitute.'

'Sex worker.'

'Look at you.' Stallard drew a tick in the air. 'Our new lead on wokeness and diversity.'

'She was a victim for Christ's sake.'

'And you pumped her for information.'

'It wasn't like that.'

'Did you or didn't you make the beast with two backs?'

'Irrelevant.' Frank fetched two beers one-handed from the fridge, keeping the cold compress clamped to the side of his head. 'The thing is, Jared Finn found out that someone was grassing.'

'Did she specialise in catering to the debauched, larger gentleman?'

'Shut up. They took her back to Belarus.'

'Who did?'

'The fucking Jehovah's Witnesses, who do you think.' Frank snapped. He twisted the cap off a Bud, and took a drink. His hand was shaking. 'The gang who had smuggled her over here in the first place.'

'Isn't Belarus…'

'Where Karina's from. I know. It all fits.'

'Wait. If this is a jigsaw, I'm struggling. I've not even got the straight edges in place yet.'

'Her name was Maria.'

'Who?'

'Karina's sister. They killed her and it was my fault.'

'How?'

'Someone told them I'd got her pregnant.'

'Whoaaaa…' Stallard's turn to need a drink. He shook his head. Disbelief and disgust. 'You got an informant pregnant?'

'Don't be stupid. How many sex workers get accidentally pregnant, on a scale of zero to none?'

Stallard swilled the beer in his mouth. Frank was right about one thing. Maria would have been topped for giving information to the police, not getting pregnant if indeed she was. It didn't make much difference to her. But how come he ended up getting knifed by Karina in the Blue Butterfly? No doubt Maria would have been interrogated before being dispatched. Not by nice rules either. She would have talked. Torture is a great loosener of tongues. Especially when there's no loyal cause to protect.

So, the whole operation was compromised. When he had walked into reception and met Jared Finn and Stefan, he might as well have been wearing full police uniform, and shouting *Let's be having you*. Something bothered him.

'Finn took a massive risk.'

'She wasn't supposed to stab you.'

'I feel so much better.'

'They wanted her to play along. Try and find out what evidence we had on their operation, and then abscond.'

Stallard gave a little puff of disdain. He got the picture. The bad guys trying to run some counter-intelligence. Blaming Maria's death on the British undercover cops. Saying she was pregnant. Putting pressure on Finn to sort out his end of the business. Problem was, they wound Karina up too much. Never underestimate the strength of family bonds.

'It was you that rang Occupational Health, wasn't it?'

'I was concerned.'

'Were you fuck. You reported me mentally unfit, because you didn't want me back in the unit.'

Frank didn't speak. He sat there holding the towel. Some watery blood ran around his ear, and soaked into his collar.

'We're done.' Stallard stood up.

'I'll sort it. I'll speak to the DI and you'll be back in the unit in no time.'

'I don't want to come back. I can forgive you for what happened at the Blue Butterfly. Everyone fucks up. But not what you've done since.'

'It's made me ill.' Frank raised his voice. Pleading.

'I'll send a card.' Stallard turned and walked out.

He got back to the Jeep. There were tears in his eyes, and he couldn't see. One spilled out, and he smeared it away with the base of his palm. The hatred had gone, but the world would never be the same again. Something else had died.

CHAPTER 38

Shannon Doane was in her front room. She was curled up with her phone in an armchair, catching up on Internet messages and postings. The TV was on. She'd made a mug of hot chocolate, and set it on the coffee table, with her midweek treat – a bag of Maltesers. The lighter way to enjoy chocolate. When Joey went missing, it was one junk meal after another. No thought of nutrition. Now she was on a new routine. Eating more healthily and watching the calories. It wasn't easy, because some days she didn't care how she looked or felt.

Tonight, she was good. Better than she had been for a while. Mickey and Tyler had been a shock, but she was strong. She'd just spoken to her mum, and everything was fine in Kos. They'd just got back to their hotel room, after a meal in the restaurant and a walk on the beach. That was a relief. It had been a struggle to persuade them, because they always wanted to be home in case there was any news of Joey. Like they had to be constantly sat next to the house phone, because mobiles hadn't been invented. More like, they couldn't bear the thought of anything approaching enjoyment or the prospect of living their own lives.

Shannon knew she wasn't much better. Joey's disappearance was all-consuming. Was it her own guilt that powered her quest for the truth? Would she have felt the same compulsion if they hadn't quarrelled? She liked to think so, but wasn't sure. One thing she was certain of was the argument itself. She was right and Joey was wrong. What was he thinking of, cosying up to the Munday family? Selfish idiot. Couldn't he see what effect it had on Mum and Dad?

Her parents had not talked about Kate Munday. Shannon thought it was because it made their suffering worse. If they had lost their son, it was better to remember his good qualities, rather than dwell on his inconstancy and flaws. Her parents weren't great talkers, and that hadn't helped. At least they were now somewhere relaxing and far away, where words might come more easily. Words – little things that might help them come to terms with something enormous. Or maybe not.

The drive to the airport had been awkward. Shannon screwed her fingers up at the memory, and felt the nails dig in. Driving over the Snake Pass to Manchester in a frosty atmosphere. Before they left, Mum had been at the top of the stairs and overheard the conversation with DC Stallard. All of it. The part about Joey booking a flight to Vietnam, and the bit where she told the police officer that she didn't care a shit about what he thought.

The truth was, she did care. Stallard was different. Fancied the pants off him, the first time she saw him. But finding out what happened to Joey was the priority, and if that meant bending him towards doing what she wanted, so be it. She knew what most police were like. Unresponsive robots. She'd spent months trying to get them to follow up leads on Joey's disappearance, but they hid behind the same anodyne phrases. Further enquiries were *not in the public interest*, the case was *filed pending developments*, and it would be *subject to a regular and structured review process*.

She'd not known what to say to her parents about the flights to Vietnam. There had been an awful couple of minutes when they thought that Joey was still safe and well, and living over there. Shannon had been forced to repeat three or four times that he'd not taken the flight. She didn't know why he'd missed it, other than his car was found abandoned, and something must have happened to him. She had no idea why he'd booked the flight in the first place or why he wanted to go to Vietnam. For a while, it looked like Kos was off. It was touch and go. They'd all had to go and sit down in the kitchen and have a cup of tea.

When Mum and Dad had settled down, Shannon took a deep breath, and explained to them what she'd explained to them before. If Joey was still alive, there would be some things that he would definitely have done. He'd have taken his guitar; he'd have gone to the Foo Fighters gig in March that he had a ticket for; he'd have cleared out the last few pounds from his bank account, and he would have sent his mother a birthday card on the 15th of May. Joey could be thoughtless, but he'd not missed his mum's birthday since he was old enough to buy a card. This last point was always the clincher, and made Mum cry. They got in the car, but didn't talk all the way to the airport.

Shannon had a drink, and popped a few Maltesers. There wasn't much on Facebook, so she went onto Twitter. On TV, someone was talking about their in-laws, and there was canned laughter. Outside, she heard some car doors slam. Leo had Tweeted a few photos promoting tomorrow night's fundraiser at The Wild Tulip. One was a screenshot of the poster advertising the event; one was of Joey on stage at a gig, screaming into the microphone.

There was a loud knock at the door.

She dropped the phone and went to look. When she went into the hallway, she saw two figures walk down the alleyway to the back of the house. Strange. There was another knock at the front door. She froze. It wasn't locked. She didn't know whether to try and lock it or stay still and quiet. Try and tiptoe back for her phone. Which? The door handle turned slowly, and made the decision for her. She darted forward to try and turn the key. Too late. The door burst open.

Two men. One stayed outside and closed the door. The one in the hallway grabbed hold of her hair and pulled her into the kitchen. She didn't know whether to scream. She'd never screamed in her life, and didn't know if she could even do it. The force was tearing at her scalp, making the back of her head burn. She tripped backwards over the threshold, and onto the tiles. The man picked her up by the armpits and pushed her against the wall.

'Do you want to die?' He was early forties, dressed sharp, with a wide face. He smelt of aftershave and the leather gloves he was wearing.

Shannon looked him in the eyes. 'What do you want?'

'It's time you stopped looking for your brother. He'd dead. Call it a day.'

'Why should I?' She wasn't frightened.

'Because you should have respect for people's right to privacy. Nobody likes a snooper.'

'Tell Baxter Quinn to go and fuck himself.'

The flat hand came from nowhere. It hit Shannon on the side of her head, and knocked her over. She fell across the table, and onto her knees. Her brain was in shock. Spinning and senseless. A hand grabbed her by the scruff of the neck, and sat her down on one of the chairs. She felt sick.

'No respect. That's your problem.' The man towered over her.

She held onto the dining table and blinked. Blood was pounding in her ears. She couldn't talk.

'Call off the private investigator,' he said. 'Or you'll be in the same hospital, and stay away from the long-haired copper. He's bad news.' He grabbed her by the chin and drilled his eyes into hers. 'It's over. Do you understand. Leave it.'

She shook herself. 'Piss off.'

He squeezed on her chin and leered. 'If you're too stupid to care about yourself, just remember we know where Jim and Elaine live.'

He let go of her chin, and back-handed her across the face. She fell onto the tiles. Sprawled out, with her nose pressed down on them. They were cold. Her cheek was on fire. She heard him walk away and the front door open and close. There were voices and more footsteps came down the side of the house from the back. Then silence. Just a burble of canned laughter from the TV in the room. She curled up and cried.

CHAPTER 39

The streets between the cathedral and Crown Court were old and narrow. Some road surfaces had their original cobbles. The pavements were formed by huge wide stone slabs. One of these was called Wickfield Row. It had Georgian terraced buildings and Victorian street lamps and all the doors were painted black to match the iron railings that ran in front of the properties. They were all law firms and associated parasites.

Stallard stopped outside number 19. It had a discreet sign on the wall – *Palmer, Lees and Munday.* The blood brother of Joey Doane had done pretty well to make partner before hitting forty. Even if they were Division Two of the English Law League – Industrial Disease and Personal Injury. Fair play to him.

It must be hard to lose your father, and watch your mother go through a breakdown. The same trauma had driven sister Naomi into drugs, and crimes against art. No two people are the same. Identical twins have different fingerprints, and psychologically, they develop differently in response to the same experiences. That's life. It can't be reduced to a mathematical formula. Just get on and enjoy it while you can, because you never know what tomorrow will bring. Probably more shit.

The door was open. He smiled, said *good morning* to the receptionist, and walked straight through the foyer into the back corridor. No asking permission. He knew men like Oliver Munday liked to have their full name and qualifications etched into a brass plaque on their office door. It made their penises bigger. He found Munday's second on the left. The office door, not his penis. He knocked once and walked in.

He said, 'I'd like to make a claim against my employer. Is exposure to repetitive management bullshit classed as an industrial disease?'

Oliver Munday was at his desk, eating a bowl of muesli, and working on a laptop. It was a big, mahogany pedestal desk, with a red leather veneer. He looked up. Not fazed by the interruption.

'Good morning DC Stallard. Please take a seat.'

The receptionist came running in. 'Sorry, Mr Munday. He just walked past…'

'It's all right, Valerie.' Munday waved her away. Then he called her back. 'Wait, perhaps the officer would like a drink?'

Valerie gave Stallard a strange look. Like he was an escaped convict, who'd been serving life for killing kittens. Probably in a microwave and then eating them.

'Black coffee, please.' Stallard gave her his best Jack Nicholson psycho smile. It was the least he could do.

Oliver Munday pushed his cereal bowl to one side, and wiped his mouth with a napkin.

'I presume this is not a social visit.'

'I wasn't kidding about the repetitive management bullshit. If it's not already a listed workplace disease, it definitely should be.'

'Is it about Joseph?' Munday. Smooth and unflappable.

There were three framed photographs on the wall next to the desk. The first was a blonde woman with two young boys. The second was an Aston Martin DB9 in Arizona bronze, and the third was a whitewashed villa with a swimming pool and blue sea in the background.

Stallard pointed. 'They all yours?'

'My life goals – they're there to help me visualise.'

'You're partially sighted?'

'Every day I sit here dealing with misery and misfortune, detective. I need a constant reminder of what I'm doing it all for.' The voice was purring good this morning. Full Rolls-Royce.

'To motivate you?'

'Exactly.'

'It must be great to have focus.'

Stallard didn't go for this psychology nonsense. 'I went to see your sister.'

'How is she?'

'Good fun. I liked her.'

'She's been doing well for a while now.' Munday smiled. Oil ran everywhere.

'Yes, it must be a relief.'

'She told you, then?'

'The drugs? Yeah.' Stallard nodded. 'Isn't it strange that Naomi and Joey both became heroin addicts?'

'You mean was it a coincidence, or something genetic?'

'I don't know. Just strange.'

Valerie came back in with a black coffee. She gave Stallard the same disgusted look, and he gave her back the same Jack Nicholson.

, 'The other thing I find strange,' said Stallard, 'is why you didn't tell me about the money that you generously donated to Joey.'

'I was embarrassed.' Munday opened his arms. He had red braces beneath his pinstripe jacket. Nice touch.

'How much was it?'

'A little over £6,000 for a 28-day course.'

'He just rocked up and asked for 6K?'

Munday looked sheepish. 'It started lower, but seemed to snowball.'

'Junkies are upselling?'

'Once I'd said *yes,* it was difficult to back out.'

'I went shopping for socks once, and bought a pair of ankle-harness boots. Still love those boots.'

'It does appear a little naïve now.'

'But I would never give cash to a druggie. 'Stallard screwed up his eyes. 'That's crazy.'

'He needed help.'

'James Saville ever babysit your kids?'

'Listen. I know what good treatment can do – look at Naomi – and Joey was technically my brother. Our brother.'

Stallard had a drink of coffee. It was the real stuff, and tasted surprisingly good. He thought Valerie might have gobbed in it, but if she had, she'd done a good job of stirring it in. It was silky smooth.

'Why didn't you tell the police about the money when Joey went missing?'

'What good would it have done? It was too late. He'd committed suicide.'

'Perhaps with the money you'd given him, he could have staged his disappearance, skipped bail, and gone a long, long way away.'

Munday shrugged, and the red braces made another cameo appearance. 'I realised too late what the money was really for. It must have been a drugs debt.'

'The Quinns?'

'Who else? They were the only ones Joey mentioned.'

'So, you rang the police?'

'Yes. Ben Phillpotts told me he hadn't gone in for his appointment, and I read in the paper that he was missing.'

'Which solicitors does Mr Phillpotts work for?'

'He doesn't.' Munday's nose wrinkled, upset at being in the presence of such ignorance. 'He's a barrister.'

'He does coffee as well?'

'No, just criminal law.' Munday sighed.

'The old ones are the best, aren't they?' Stallard winked. *The comic detective, on stage here all week.*

Munday said nothing.

'Would you be happy to sign a financial-release form?' said Stallard. 'It gives the police access to your accounts.'

'I wouldn't be happy, but if you think it might help, then yes. I'll sign.'

'I'll have my secretary email one through.'

He smiled at Valerie on the way out. She pretended to be filing her nails, and ignored him. Some women. He stood outside on the pavement, and took a chest-full of fresh air. It felt good. The sky was clear peacock blue, and the sun was starting to heat up the city streets. It was going to be a good day. The only problem was Oliver Munday was lying, and Stallard didn't know why.

CHAPTER 40

It took a short phone call to the hospital to confirm what Stallard suspected – Maggs had told Baxter Quinn who he was working for. Definitely time to get *discreet and trustworthy* taken off his business card. He tried Shannon's mobile, but there was no answer. He left a message, and wondered if it was just because she was still angry from yesterday. Probably *yes*, he decided. But he couldn't be sure. What to do? Two bandmates dead, and the Quinns now knew she'd been spying on them. A dangerous cocktail. He made a U-turn on the dual carriageway, got flashed by a Gatso in the bus lane, and booted the Jeep towards her house. Better safe than sorry.

There was no answer at the door. He went down the side alleyway and looked in the off-shot kitchen. It was empty. Some pots by the sink that could have been from breakfast. Nothing else. He went back to the front, and looked through the living room window. Clean and tidy. He took a couple of steps back and looked up. The bedroom curtains were open. He went back to the front door and knelt down. Then he rang her mobile and lifted the flap on the letterbox. He clamped his ear right up to it, but there was no sound coming from inside. After eight rings, it tripped to voicemail, and he left another message.

At the station, Fay Nash collared him as soon as he walked in. It was Roger's retirement. Good ole Rodge, never heard of him. There was a *do* straight from work in The Moon Bar. It wasn't really called *The Moon Bar*, just the police social club where there was never any atmosphere. She was in charge of the collection, and it was twenty quid each. Stallard asked if for that price it included the Space Shuttle there and back. It didn't, but there would be a buffet, if the usual fat bastards didn't get there first. Unbridled joy. He couldn't wait.

Keith had prepped an application for a Section 8 warrant. It was to serve on Bell-Bio Inc, and order them to release the information they held on Joseph Noel Michael Doane. Stallard had to go to the Magistrates Court at 2pm and swear it out. It wasn't something he'd done in over eight years. He hoped they still had the oath printed on a laminated idiot card in the flyleaf of the New Testament. An *idiot card*, as in for idiots. What had he become?

Myers was in the usual position. Locked into the controls of the *Enterprise,* and staring at two giant monitors. He was pleased to see Stallard. The wise mentor and path into the grown-up world of detecting. The bleep-test results were getting better, but still not good enough. Stallard told him to keep trying and think of all the girls he could date when he got his warrant card. As inspirational speeches go, it wasn't Henry V at Agincourt, but it was the best he could do. Sometimes you have to know your audience, and your own limitations.

Stallard said he wanted a live cell-site trace putting on Baxter and Brandon Quinns' mobile phones. It was a potential life-at-risk scenario. The forms needed to get authority for this were twelve pages long. Would Myers mind doing them? Of course not. He'd love to. They'd be in the superintendent's inbox before lunch. Splendid. What about the Mundays? Had the research thrown anything up? Myers got busy with the mouse, and minimised a few windows of graphs and charts, until he found a Word document, and pressed *print*.

It was a summary of what the checks analyst had done and the results. There was no trace of the Mundays on any police system, so what intelligence had been gathered was open source, and graded 2/D/P. Stallard asked what this meant, and Myers said it meant he had searched the Internet. The kid had already learnt to speak police bullshit language. He was halfway there.

There were plenty of hits on Detective Google for Oliver Munday, but they were what you would expect. Ads for vibration white finger and hearing loss caused by noise in the workplace. Reports of some individual cases in the local press, and modest awards of compensation. Some charity function he had attended, and a charity golf day, where Palmer, Lees and Munday had entered a team. The firm had also bankrolled a food kitchen for homeless people, and donated to the local hospice. Stallard almost felt bad about thinking Munday was a worthless shit.

The only negative note was a piece last year in one of the monthly law magazines, which reported that

Caroline Stubbs had taken Palmer, Lees and Munday to a tribunal for unfair dismissal. The report mentioned Oliver Munday by name. There were no details of the case and no outcome. Stallard asked Myers if there was anything else on the case, but there wasn't. He'd checked the following month's edition, and there was no update. Stallard told Myers to find out where Caroline Stubbs worked now, and if she was young, free and single. Asking for a friend.

There wasn't much online about Naomi Munday. Mainly her own website, and a couple of mentions in articles about other people. One was about her mother, Kate Munday. It was on the occasion of her retirement as chief executive from the homeless charity, and told how she was going to return as a volunteer. It drew a short and uplifting pen picture of her career. Kate had been drawn into the homeless sector because of her daughter. Naomi Munday had lived on the streets for a time, when suffering from mental illness and addiction issues. It had been a terrible and testing time for both of them. Now Naomi was a successful artist. Everyone lived happily ever after. The end.

But not all the family were still living.

CHAPTER 41

S till no message from Shannon. Stallard put the phone down, and picked up his pint. He'd got a booth to himself, away from the cider drinkers, the weirdos and the gamblers who spilt over from the bookies next door. There were a couple of texts from Frank, but he didn't read them. The beer tasted of grapefruit. An over-hopped IPA from a brewery he'd never heard of, but under two quid a pint.

An hour later, he was joined by Dan Berry from the Border Force. They'd worked a couple of joint-ops together – people trafficking and gangmasters. Berry was an ex-cop, who'd been required to resign when his hand was fractured by a sex offender's cheekbone. The man hadn't wanted to press charges, but it had been filmed by a passer-by and posted on YouTube under the title, *Copper Smacks Paedo*. It got 300,000 thumbs-up. That didn't help Berry. The force's discipline tribunal gave him thumbs-down. So much for public support.

Stallard told him about the Quinns and the Vietnam connection. How there had been a recent upsurge in

Fentanyl deaths, and the suspicion that the drug was arriving into the UK by post. Berry wasn't surprised. There were two Border Force hubs where all foreign postal packets were processed and they were both massively overrun. One was at Coventry and the other at Langley, near Heathrow. The one at Langley handled anything under 2.2 kilos, which was 99 percent of the packets. Last year there was over 700 million. This year it would be shedloads more.

How many staff worked there, asked Stallard. About half of them, said Berry. Cop humour – he'd still got it. On paper, there were between 40 and 50, and some of those were short-term contracts or agency staff. It wasn't enough to scratch the surface. They relied on being sent intelligence on names, addresses and places of origin. Even then it was impossible to ensure things got followed up. At Coventry, the packets went along a conveyer belt and could be visually examined, but at Langley they were in steel caged trolleys called *yorks,* and the best that staff could do was dip sample at random. Stallard did the maths in his head. On those figures, he reckoned there were just under two million parcels a day. A workforce of 40 meant that only 30 would be working any given 24-hour period. That was 200,000 parcels per Border Force agent per day. How many seconds in a day? Not enough.

It all confirmed what Block had said. Parcelforce was set to be the biggest drug trafficker in the UK. Stallard bought Berry a drink. He asked if the addresses of Quinns' companies could be added to the intelligence logs at Coventry and Langley. Berry said he would make sure they were, for what it was worth. They reminisced about old times, because the present times were so depressing. Law enforcement makes you old before your time.

At one o'clock prompt, Stallard walked into The Gallery. It's an old department store that's had its intestines ripped out and replaced with street food stalls and coffee bars. It was rammed. He looked around for Caroline Stubbs, while his nose was assaulted by far away spice: Korean beef, Rajasthani lamb and Moroccan chicken. All here in the Steel City. It was hard to believe for someone whose dad thought Vesta curry was as exotic as things were ever going to get. The world was shrinking fast, and it wasn't all bad.

Caroline Stubbs was going to be difficult to spot with all the people milling around. He was looking for a frumpy woman, with blue worsted stockings and possibly hair she did herself with pruning shears. Wrong. She was smart and attractive, with a look of Hedy Lamarr. She strode up to him, immaculately coiffed.

'Excuse me, are you the detective?'

'Got me in one,' said Stallard, and smiled. *The detective.* He didn't know whether to be flattered or disappointed at being picked out. He went for flattered. 'Thank you for seeing me.'

He bought them coffees, and struck lucky with a table next to the window. A prime spot to watch shoplifters legging it from Boots, and a man selling DVDs from a sports holdall. The wooden chairs were little and hard. Probably a job-lot from a local primary school. Trendy, but uncomfortable.

Stallard said, 'How long were you a solicitor at Palmer, Lees and Munday?'

Caroline Stubbs said, 'I'm a paralegal.'

'Where's the wheelchair?'

'Is that a joke?'

'Obviously. I'm not a complete dummy.'

'It's not funny.' She didn't look amused. Not entirely convinced about the complete dummy bit either.

'Sorry. How long were you a paralegal at Munday's firm?'

'A year. It was enough.'

'What happened?'

'I can't tell you.'

'Why not?'

'I'm not allowed to discuss it.'

'Who says?'

'I do. I signed a document.'

'What document?'

Caroline Stubbs sighed and closed her eyes. When she opened them again, there was a look of frustration, mingled with contempt. 'Do I have to spell it out for you? N.D.A.'

'Non-disclosure agreement.' Stallard got there. A little tardy. Three pints of grapefruit IPA had slowed him down.

'I don't think I was the first. You might find one of my predecessors who didn't sign on the dotted line and take the money.'

Stallard took a sip of coffee, and considered the possibilities. If she'd been paid to keep quiet, then the firm had been in the wrong. They were solicitors. It was their job to argue a case in court. They wouldn't cough up unless they knew they'd lose. The problem was Caroline Stubbs had undergone the full humour bypass. Immune even to his wit. She was the sort of dry stick who could have taken offence to the slightest whiff of political incorrectness, and there was probably no shortage of that flying around in the male-dominated bastion of the law.

'Give me a clue.'

'For a detective, you don't seem quick to pick up on clues.'

'I'm rusty. Try me with another one.'

'I signed a document. I'm bound by the law.'

'Is that the clue?'

'No, that's me telling you I'm not at liberty to divulge details of the case.'

'Just a little clue. That's not like divulging.'

'No.'

Stallard sensed a change of tack was required. The charming ingénue was getting nowhere. Time for his tag-team partner to take over. The evil Count Nasty. Cue villain laugh, mwahahaha…

'Does it ever keep you awake at night?'

'The case?'

'Knowing that you took the money.'

'It's what I was entitled to, for what happened.'

'Then why sign an agreement not to talk about it?'

'I took advice.'

'You don't care that what happened to you might happen to other women?'

'I didn't say that.'

'You're complicit. Are you happy to be bought off and say nothing?'

'No, I'm not happy.'

Stallard let her dwell on it. Silence, the old interview technique. Not as old as violence, but we're talking twenty-first century now. Assaulting a female witness in a busy street-food hall was not appropriate these days.

'Okay, look at the date it happened,' she said. 'If you're a detective you'll work it out.'

'Sometime in September last year?'

'That was when the case went to the tribunal. The firm settled on the day, before it started.' She gave a little snort of derision, as though she was wasting her time. 'Look at the date of the incident. It's in the court record.'

She stood up and left. Not even touched her coffee or the free biscuit. That's gratitude for you. Good job he'd kept the receipt. It wasn't something that he was used to doing. In the undercover world you get expenses paid per day at an agreed rate, irrespective of what you've actually spent. As a UC, you can't stand at the bar buying an Albanian gun-runner a large vodka, and then ask for a receipt. It's like doing surveillance with two holes cut in a newspaper, or putting an anorak on over a full police uniform. Fools nobody.

There was an hour to kill. He ordered a Katsu chicken curry with noodles and phoned Myers. The date of the incident, which resulted in the NDA, was the 19th of December. Eighteen months ago. It didn't mean anything to him. The Katsu chicken curry arrived, and tasted wonderful, but didn't help. The noodles weren't too good with dates either. Guinness was what he needed. It has iron and is well known for inspiring great thinkers and grammatical outlaws like James Joyce. He tried two pints, but they didn't make any difference. Scratch that as a theory.

There's a kiosk outside the Magistrates Court that sells Trebor Extra Strong Mints for detectives and lawyers who have been drinking. Little gold mine. Stallard bought a packet on his way in. The usual rag-tag bunches of defendants and hangers-on waited in the corridor and seating area. Surly, in their best Sunday clothes. All innocent. They watched him walk past, trying to work out which side he was on. One or two nodded, like he was a fellow offender up before the beak. Little did they know.

Warrants are sworn out in private before the afternoon court sessions start. Stallard found the magistrate waiting for him in the back of Court 3. She was the headmistress type. Friendly and efficient. Everything went well, and the warrant was signed within five minutes. He loved magistrates. They're ordinary people who give up their spare time to help society be a better place, and don't expect to get paid for it. They also love the police. It's just one big love-in down there in the lower court.

On the way out, he squeezed past a cluster of suits in the corridor. Behind him, a woman's voice said, *thank you, Mr Phillpotts.* He turned back to see a red-faced man with messy blond hair in a double-breasted suit with thick pinstripes. He was surrounded by a family of five and two legal executives. Stallard waited until the barrister was on his own.

Ben Phillpotts was sorry, but he had to act in the best interests of his client. Legal privilege applied to any communications between himself and Joseph Doane. Stallard said what if the client had been murdered? Was it still in his best interest? How long did the client's family have to wait until something was in their interest? Phillpotts did a spot of soul-searching, and smiled. Said he had a bail application to make, which would take ten minutes, and then he'd speak. Just goes to show, sometimes barristers can be reasonable people.

Stallard sucked mints and waited. A man with an Irish accent offered him twenty quid for his tiger tooth earring. He declined. Half an hour later, Phillpotts and the family of his client came out of court. The family didn't look happy, so maybe the bail application hadn't gone so well. Dad's banged up for another week. There was a brief scrum, while they all discussed what happened next, and then Phillpotts came over. He was flustered and sweaty. He apologised again. Said there wasn't much to tell about Joseph Doane. They'd only had one consultation together, and were due another one the day he went missing. Mr Doane was going to attend his chambers, and then they would have gone to the police station together for the bail appointment. He never showed.

Not much help. Stallard knew where this was going, but ploughed on. Would Joey have been charged? Phillpotts thought he would. His advice was to co-operate with the police. Mr Doane had stressed how important it was for his career at that point that he didn't go to prison. If he'd pleaded *guilty*, there was nothing to worry about. Worst he was looking at was a community order. It would result in a criminal record, but better that than risk prison.

That made sense. Stallard nodded. You don't engage the services of a barrister to ignore their advice. They're not cheap. Joey would have had to pay for Phillpotts to represent him, because legal aid does not stretch to counsel, only solicitors. That meant one thing. Somebody was bankrolling his defence costs. The Quinns? Possible, but not likely. The more obvious candidate was the person who had referred Joey to Ben Phillpotts. Mr Oliver Munday LLB, of Palmer, Lees and Munday. The question was asked. Phillpotts confirmed it to be the case. Straight from the horse's mouth.

Stallard left the courthouse, and went back to Spoons. Something bothered him about Oliver Munday's largesse towards Joey. It was excessive. Yes, the two of them were brothers, but only technically. There hadn't been time for them to develop a bond of kinship, and yet there was an attraction between them. Misery acquaints a man with strange bedfellows. There was something dark and troubling that linked Joey Doane and Oliver Munday, and he had to find it quick.

CHAPTER 42

The police sports and social club was a concrete prefab, with football pitches and crown green bowls. The bar had a glitterball, and a dusty stage with velvet curtains and three rows of tables and chairs. Everything was half a century old, apart from the staff, who were older than Methuselah. Maybe it was to make the cold case team feel young. One of them pulled Stallard a pint of lager, and said the first one was on Roger.

He was taking the top off it when Fay Nash dashed up with a look of shock and wild excitement in her eyes.

'Have you heard?' she said.

'What?'

'Really? You've not heard?'

'What?'

'You won't believe it.'

'Try me.'

'Seriously, you won't believe it.' She blinked three or four times. 'Joey Doane just walked into a police station in Berlin about an hour ago.'

'Ugh. Berlin?' He almost choked.

'Yeah, Berlin.'

'You sure?' Stallard coughed. Lager had gone down the wrong way.

'Positive. Came into Force Ops from Interpol.'

'But, why...'

Nash was doing a mime. Like she was holding a rod and winding a reel. 'Think I've hooked a monster.'

'You bastard.'

'Should have seen your face.' Nash did a bit more winding. 'Priceless.'

'That's because I've inhaled half a pint of Carling.' He coughed again. 'It's still in my lungs. I'll get you back for that.'

Nash was doubled up. Crying.

Keith wandered over. 'Did I miss a good joke?'

Nash couldn't talk.

'No, you didn't,' said Stallard. 'Just our team leader being cruel and heartless. I'm a victim of bullying.'

'You should put a grievance in,' said Keith.

'I might.' Stallard thumped his chest. 'Let me ask you a question on the subject of grievance. It's about a workplace incident that resulted in a woman taking her employers to an industrial tribunal.'

'Fire away.' Keith put his spectacles on, as though this helped him think.

'The incident happened on the 19 December two years ago,' said Stallard. 'What could be significant about that date?'

'Christmas office party,' said Keith. No hesitation.

'Eh?'

'It was the last Friday before Christmas. Mad Friday,' said Keith. 'It's when most firms have their festive fun, and unfortunately it usually involves too much alcohol. Therefore, incidents of an unpleasant nature are more prevalent.'

Stallard drank some lager. This time he guided it down the oesophagus, rather than the trachea. Years of practice finally bearing fruit. Mad Friday was when people took their pants down and sat on the photocopier. Put cannabis in the HR department's cake. Mooned out of the window at passing buses. Or was that just the police? Then of course, there'd be the inevitable fight. Every year. Two drunks, taking offence to nothing in particular and rolling round on the carpet tiles in a heap of fists and mince pies. Then best of mates again.

Fay Nash was still drying her eyes. Stallard left her and went and sat in the corner. There was still nothing on his phone from Shannon, just another message from Frank. He ignored it. What Keith had said about the office party might be true. Whatever had happened to Caroline Stubbs, she believed that she hadn't been the first. Was it something that happened only once a year at Advent? How would he find out who these others were? The only way was to ask Palmer, Lees and Munday. Waste of time. They'd close ranks to protect the firm's reputation and bank balance.

The piped music was cut, and the room fell silent. Gerard Hardcastle made a speech thanking Roger for his long and distinguished service to the Cold Case Review Unit. They stood together on the stage, next to an electric golf trolley. The retirement present. Hardcastle's speech was long-winded and devoid of humour. If there had ever been a faintly amusing incident at some point in Roger's working life, it was to remain forever secret. In response, Roger meandered through a career of forty-five years. He'd worked with some great colleagues. Too many to mention, he said, before name-checking every single one of them. When he finished, there was a ripple of polite applause from those still awake.

Gerard Hardcastle stepped down from the stage, and looked in his direction. Turn away. Pretend you're not there. Avoid eye contact. Too late. The cold case manager had spotted him sitting on his own, and made a beeline.

'Not mingling, Harry?'

'Not my thing, really.'

'You're the maverick who ploughs his own furrow?'

'Interesting image.'

'Don't worry, good detectives come in all shapes and sizes. Look at Keith.' Hardcastle beamed.

Stallard followed the old man's stare. Keith was nibbling on a vol-au-vent. The golden child. He was wearing corduroy trousers, and a maroon cardigan. Okay, not exactly a child.

'I like you, Harry. You embrace the *meshuggah*.'

'Is that legal?'

'The *meshuggah*. Hebrew for craziness,' said Hardcastle. 'A military tactic for doing something so unexpected that the enemy won't have even considered it.'

'We had a saying in the undercover unit – you are only ever limited by your own imagination.'

'And the criminal law.'

'There are exceptions.'

'Boundaries have to be pushed in any conflict.' Hardcastle tapped his nose. 'Keith told me about the knickers.'

'Did he?'

'That's why I'd like to offer you a permanent position in the cold case unit.'

'To steal underwear?'

'Become part of the family.' Hardcastle's moustache flexed. Maybe it was a smile.

'Can I think about it?'

'I know you've put a request in to return to force. You could do worse.'

It hadn't taken long for the police jungle drums to let everybody know what was supposed to be a personal memo. Quicker than shit through a nervous goose. Some things never change. You want to disseminate something to every police and civilian member of staff, stick *confidential* on it, and send it to the HR department.

Workwise, he didn't know which way to jump. His head was a mess. There were worse postings than the cold case unit, but could he see himself in there long-term? He just didn't know. All that mattered at the moment was finding out what happened to Joey Doane. If he didn't, no one ever would, and was that something he wanted to carry on his back for the rest of his career, whatever that turned out to be? No. For once, he was going to see something through.

The party didn't go on long after the speeches. People started to shake Roger's hand and drift away in twos and threes. Sharing lifts or cabs. Stallard picked over the remains of the buffet, and was biting into a pickled onion when his mobile pinged. The message told him he had got a Snapchat video, and he pressed *play*. The phone-screen flickered and showed the inside of a part-derelict building. The windows were cracked and there was light coming through gaps in the roof. It looked familiar.

The camera zoomed in, and there was a man sat on a chair. No, not sat, tied. A man tied to a chair with electrical flex. His head was lolling to one side and blood ran from his nose, down his cheek and onto his shoulder. The floor tiles were herringbone. That was when something hit Stallard in the solar plexus like a guided missile. He recognised those tiles. That was his bungalow.

Another figure came into view. He was big, wearing a black ski mask and gloves. Stallard knew it was Frank straight away. Without a shadow of a doubt. The figure grabbed the seated man by the hair, and the camera moved in closer still. It was Jared Finn. Not looking as cocky as he had been at the Blue Butterfly. His eyes were puffy and almost closed. He looked unconscious.

The hooded figure slapped Finn across the face, and his head flopped the other way. There was no resistance in the neck. Whoever was filming it on the phone, said, *that's enough Frank.* Nice one. Bit of a *don't tell him Pike.* Waste of a good ski mask. Not that the video would be around very long for anyone else to see it. Stallard knew that as soon as he'd viewed it, the file would be deleted automatically from the Snap Inc servers. That's why criminals and terrorists used it. Sixty seconds of whatever evil you want to share, instantly consigned to the trash can of eternity.

Outside in the Jeep, Stallard phoned Frank.

'What the fuck do you think you're doing?'

'Settling the score. I tried calling, so you could be here.'

'Be there? Why the fuck would I want to be there, while you beat the crap out of someone?'

'Justice.'

'Sentence first, then the verdict. What about the trial?'

'We know he's guilty.'

'Start breaking the law, we're as bad as them.'

'Did I miss it?'

'What the fuck are you on about?'

'Your conversion on the road to Damascus.'

'Meaning what?'

'You're no saint. Never have been.'

'There's a line, and you just crossed it.' Stallard laughed. Sarcastic. 'Guess it makes a change from those times you snorted it.'

'Very funny, but who gets to decide where the line is, if it's already outside of the legal framework?'

'Don't try and philosophise your way out of this shit.'

'I did it for you.'

'You did it in my fucking bungalow.'

'Come on, I'm not stupid. Finn was hooded all the way here.'

'That's all right then.'

'Mates?'

'No. I'm not coming back.' Stallard ended the call, and switched his phone off. The end of an era.

He sat in the Jeep and stared at his hands. For the second time in as many days, he felt tears fill his eyes. Pathetic. He could hear his old man, telling him off – *thi' bladder's too near thi' eyes, that's tha' trouble.* Thanks, Dad. Always compassionate and understanding.

Stop it. He gave himself a mental jolt. Stop feeling sorry for yourself. There are millions of people out there with bigger problems than you. One of them was Shannon Doane. He switched his phone back on, but there were no missed calls or messages. Alarm bells. What was going on? He was running out of things to try. Then he remembered something. Who the fuck are The Magic Rats?

CHAPTER 43

The night was hot. Stallard badged his way into The Wild Tulip, and went looking for manager, Leo. He wasn't hard to find. The place was empty, and he was propping the bar up, chatting with a couple of staff. He looked different. The beard had been cut back to stubble, and the top-knot had slipped down the back of his head. Comic Book Guy from *The Simpsons*.

'Where is everyone?'

'The event's cancelled,' said Leo. 'No more *Justice For Joey* fundraisers.'

'How come?'

Leo shrugged. 'Ask Shannon when she gets here.'

'She's coming in?'

Leo shrugged again. He looked pissed off. 'Maybe. She said she'd call in to explain, but who knows?'

Stallard got himself a tin of Red Stripe and sat in the corner. Students drifted in. The DJ played some Northern Soul. *Do I Love You,* by Frank Wilson. Old-school dance music. An hour passed. The DJ played some reggae, and the

Red Stripe came into its own. He started to build a pyramid with the empty tins, and sing along under his breath. *Exodus. Movement of Jah people. Oh, oh, oh. Yea-eah...*

There were four tins on the bottom row, when Shannon walked in with a girlfriend. She saw him and quickly looked away. Strange. She took her friend by the arm and they rushed upstairs. What was that all about? He didn't know whether to be relieved or angry. How many messages had she ignored today? Just one reply to say she was okay would have been nice. But then Shannon didn't do *nice*.

When he got upstairs, they were sitting on stools at a bar table with a bottle of JD and an ice-bucket. He could tell from Shannon's body language that she knew he was there, but she didn't turn round. The friend, a Goth with long blonde hair and black lipstick, seemed to be giving her updates on his position. Talking behind her hand, as though he might be a fully qualified lip-reader. Maybe she'd seen football managers doing it on television. Maybe she ran her own team, Goth Rangers.

'What's happening?' Not his best ever opening line.

'Nothing.' Shannon kept her eyes down.

'I nearly circulated you as *missing* on the police national computer. If I hadn't made the effort and found you tonight, I would have posted you first thing tomorrow as a missing person.'

'Well done, you found me.' She looked up. 'Now will you leave me alone. I don't want to talk.'

'I'm only trying to help.'

She turned her back on him, and poured herself another drink.

'Fine,' said Stallard.

He walked away. Got to the top of the stairs, and the penny dropped. Mister Slow-on-the-uptake. Perhaps Caroline Stubbs was right and massive clues weren't his thing. He felt the anger spark up inside and went back.

'The Quinns have warned you off, haven't they?'

She said nothing.

'That's why you've cancelled the fundraisers.' He waved his arms around the empty bar. 'It was your private investigator, Maggs. They knew he'd been watching their warehouse.'

Shannon didn't move.

'What did they do? Did they come to your house?'

She stayed facing away, her head bowed. Stallard walked around the table, and bent down. She had her eyes closed. He saw the silent tears trickling down her cheeks, and pooling on her chin.

'Ring me if you have any problems.' He bolted down the stairs and out into the night. It was time to pay someone a visit.

The Jeep was parked just down from a 7-Eleven Boozebuster store. Stallard picked up a six-pack just as they were closing, and sat it down on the passenger seat next to him. Then he set off driving to nowhere in particular, and scrolled through the contacts on his hands-free until he found SPOCK. Not the half-Vulcan first officer with pointy ears. The Single Point Of Contact for police telecoms authorities. A 24-hour on-call facility.

A woman's voice answered. Tired and surly.

'It's Stallard. I need a favour.'

'It's been a while. Why should I help you out?'

'Because I'm taking you out to dinner tomorrow night. A little French bistro I know that does seafood to die for. Then I've booked us a penthouse suite at the only five-star hotel in town, with a magnum of champagne and the bed covered in rose petals.'

'Yeah, all right, Harry. What do you want?' The voice still sounded tired and surly.

'There should be a live cell-site trace on two nominals Baxter and Brandon Quinn. I want to know where they are right now. As close as you can get it.'

'That's a lot of work.'

'Champagne and rose petals.'

'One day.'

The streets were quiet. He followed the tram tracks down into the centre. You could feel the day's heat coming back up out of the tarmac, and mixing with the cooler air coming down. He parked up on a strip of wasteland, and cracked open a can from the six-pack. After a while, his phone rang and he got the information he needed.

The snooker club was called *Quinny's*. Very original. Must have taken days to think that one up. It was down the east end, not far from where Triangle Trading Limited had their warehouse. There was a big sign outside, *Quinny's Snooker*, with a picture of a snooker table underneath for people who couldn't read. Downstairs was a room with pool tables and gaming machines, and a kitchen that sold cheese and ham toasties, for people who didn't like food.

Upstairs was the snooker hall. There were eight tables, in two lines of four, and a bar at one end. Stallard didn't like the way his boots stuck to the carpet, or the smell of drains coming from the toilets, and he didn't like the fact that the jukebox was an Internet cabinet stuck to the wall, and not a pukka Wurlitzer or Rock Ola, with twirling bubble tubes and vinyl 45s. Hugely disappointing. All this would be going on his TripAdvisor review.

Brandon Quinn sat at the bar, and his younger brother was on the nearest table, playing a frame with his sidekick, the ex-boxer Woodsy. There were signs on the wall, *No drinks at the table*, but this didn't apply to owners of the club, because Baxter had a pint of lager balanced near one of the ball pockets. He saw Stallard, and shouted over,

'It's members only.'

'Is that why it's full of dicks?' Stallard put a tenner on the bar and ordered a single malt.

The barman was a young lad, who knew something was going on, but didn't know what. He froze, and glanced at Brandon.

The older Quinn humphed. 'Give him a drink. On the house.'

Stallard smiled. When the barman came back with his whisky, he folded up the tenner and stuck it in the pocket of his waistcoat.

'Buy yourself a drink or donate it to a good cause. Like the families of kids who've been killed by drugs overdoses.'

Baxter Quinn slammed his cue down on the table. 'What the fuck are you doing here?'

There were four Chinese lads playing on tables at the other end of the room. They stopped, and stood watching.

Stallard knocked back his drink, and put the glass on the bar. He walked over to Baxter's table.

'Don't threaten Shannon Doane again.'

'Or what?' Baxter stuck his chest out.

'I'll take that cue and shove it so far up your arse you'll be able to lick chalk off the tip.' Stallard stared him straight in the eyes. No fear. No blink of doubt.

Baxter puffed himself up even more. 'I'd like to see you try.'

'Then do it. Threaten her again and watch what happens.'

'Big talk, Harry. That's always been your trouble – the lippy kid who couldn't stop showing off to his classmates.'

'At least I wasn't a coward who hid behind his older brother. You're still doing it.'

'If you weren't a copper, I'd take you outside right now and mash you into fucking pieces. You know that, don't you.'

'*If.*' Stallard held up thumb and forefinger, a millimetre apart. 'That's a little word for a big man to hide behind. Let's go outside now and see who gets mashed.'

The Chinese players started packing away their cues. If there was going to be some scrapping outside, they weren't going to miss it.

Baxter huffed and sneered. 'You're not going to trick me. You're not worth it. Get back to your caravan, you fucking Pikey.'

Two tables down, the Chinese lads lost interest, and started playing again.

Woodsy came and stood in front of Stallard. 'Do you want me to throw him out, Mr Quinn?'

Brandon Quinn slid off his bar stool, and put an arm around Woodsy. He steered him away. 'It's okay. The officer can see himself out.'

Stallard left. Brandon Quinn followed him down the stairs, to make sure he didn't piss in the foyer on the way out. When they reached the door, Quinn stepped in front and held it open.

'Don't worry about what Baxter says. It's all talk.'

'Think I'm worried?' said Stallard.

'Maybe we can work with each other. Instead of against each other. If you know what I mean?'

'I don't.'

'We're legitimate businessmen…'

'Mmm…'

'But in our line of work, we come across all sorts of characters, and some of them do bad things.'

'Such as?'

'Bad things. Like selling drugs and stuff.'

Stallard folded his arms. 'What do you want?'

'Nothing,' said Quinn. 'I'm trying to help. If you knew who was selling drugs, you could make the city a safer place, and get in your gaffer's good books. You might even make sergeant.'

Yeah, when hell freezes over and fish climb trees, thought Stallard. He could see what Quinn was angling at.

'You throw me a sprat, and I stay off your case?'

'Something along those lines…' Brandon Quinn's hand made a see-saw gesture.

'That's not how it works. Detectives use little fish to catch the big ones. Not the other way round. We call that cheating.'

'The world's not that simple. Some of your colleagues understand that.'

'Not me.'

'Think about it.' Brandon Quinn let go of the door and went back upstairs.

Stallard blipped the Jeep open, climbed in and popped another can. Confrontation makes the throat dry. He pulled out his phone and messaged Shannon.

Is everything okay?

Two minutes later. *Not really. I'm scared.*

Where RU.

Still at club.

Wait there. CU soon.

A fancy saloon pulled into the snooker club's car park. Stallard guessed it was a Bentley, but he couldn't see the badge. The driver got out and opened one of the rear doors. Two men in suits and ties climbed out of the back. They were older than the average snooker player. Businessmen. The driver got back in the car, and the two men went into the club. They all looked Chinese. It could be a coincidence, thought Stallard. He took a photograph of the plate on the Bentley, and set off back to The Wild Tulip.

CHAPTER 44

'Detectives don't dance,' said Stallard.

Shannon tried pulling him up by the arm, but he refused to budge. She gave up and sat back down.

Stallard smiled. She didn't look scared any longer, just a little pissed.

The Goth was called Stacey, and she was fully pissed. She walked her fingers up his other arm.

'If you're an undercover officer, does that mean you do a lot of work under the covers?'

'I'm just an ordinary detective.'

Stacey puckered up her black lips in mock disappointment, then giggled. 'But are you still good under the covers?'

'I got an eight out of ten once.' Stallard deadpanned, and took a drink.

'Fancy showing me?' Stacey batted her lashes, big as a Friesian heifer.

'Oy.' Shannon leaned across. 'Your Gavin'll be here any minute.'

Stacey made an effort to focus on her watch. 'He's late, The useless shitbag.'

Bang on cue, as though he'd been waiting in the wings for a drum roll, a gangly lad bounded up the stairs, and stood in front of the table, panting. Ladies and gentlemen, the useless shitbag himself, at your service. Ta-da. He was a Goth too. There was a big debate about whether he should drop Shannon off as well, but she said she was okay. Stacey and Shannon did a lot of hugging and kissing. Then Stacey left with Gavin the Goth, who seemed to be in a rush to get away. Perhaps the Batmobile was parked on double yellows outside.

Shannon bought another round of drinks on the way back from the Ladies. She put a tin down in front of Stallard, and said, 'Quiz time.'

'Uh-oh,' said Stallard. 'I hate quizzes.'

She ignored him, and sat up straight with a serious face.

'Best American band?'

He shrugged. 'The Strokes?'

A nod. 'Best band from this city, not counting the Arctics?'

'Pulp. My dad went to school with Jarvis.'

'Lola or Layla?'

'Lola, definitely.'

Leo came over and put an envelope on the table. It was what was left in the Justice For Joey fund from previous weeks. Shannon refused to take it. She didn't want to talk about stuff and get upset, but it was over. They'd tried their best, but it was time to move on. Leo was consoled. No shame in it, he said. Joey would have been proud.

What about the T-shirts that were left and the rest of the merch? Give it all away, said Shannon. Or ask for a nominal donation to a local charity. What about a drugs rehab? Agreed. They hugged and Leo asked if they wanted another drink. The place was empty, so he was closing the bar. No thanks, they didn't.

'I'll give you a lift home,' said Stallard, after Leo had gone.

'I can't go home. I've checked into a Premier Inn in town. Stacey offered me their sofa, and I might go there tomorrow.'

'What did the Quinns do?'

'It wasn't Baxter or Brandon. Just some bouncer-type guy, who liked to throw his weight about.'

'I'll find out who it was. Teach him some manners.'

Shannon put a hand on his arm, and shook her head. 'Stop all this macho nonsense. It might make you feel better, but it won't change things.'

She was right. Joey wasn't coming back, or Tyler or Mickey. It didn't matter how many times Frank slapped Jared Finn, the same number of victims would still get trafficked and exploited. The Quinns would carry on getting richer by bullying and bribing anyone who got in their way. Sun keeps burning, world keeps turning.

The night was still hot. When they got outside Stallard could feel the perspiration on his skin. Judging by how wired he felt, it was probably twenty percent alcohol. Minimum. It might be a smart move to leave his trusty steed parked up. Traffic cops like nothing better than to breathalyse a detective. It's their second-best scalp after their own grandmother's.

They walked arm in arm down beside the deserted tram-tracks, and past the cathedral into High Street. One kid, who looked like a student, was bent double throwing up into the gutter. A homeless man in a shop doorway shouted, *go on, son*, and gave him a round of applause. A black-cab driver sat eating a kebab, and a couple of private hires cruised up and down, looking for fares, even though they weren't supposed to tout. Stallard waved one away, who looked hopeful.

When they reached the hotel, Shannon stopped outside the glass double doors, and looked him in the eye.

'Is this where I invite you in for a coffee?'

'I don't know. Ask me.'

'What if you say *no*?'

'Try asking.'

She put her arms round his neck and kissed him. He kissed her back.

'I'll take that as a *yes*,' she said.

He smiled. 'No quizzes.'

She smiled back. 'Not even coffee.'

They fell through the main doors, and fumbled their way through the key-card door in reception, sniggering like a couple of schoolkids. Alcohol. The miracle cure for fear, shyness and all society's ills. Everyone should try it.

The Happy Days Nursing Home had been rebranded. Someone had peeled off the sticker that covered *Cold Case Review Unit*, and put another one in its place: *Welcome to Purgatory – Twinned with Barnsley*. Nobody had bothered to change the sub-heading. It still said, *Department of Urology*. Stallard smiled as he walked in. It was 7.45am and his head hurt. So what? He still felt good.

Myers was already strapped in at the controls, multi-tasking. Chomping on a bowl of cereal, and knocking together the morning briefing for Mr Hardcastle. Stallard opened the gallery on his phone, and scribbled down the number of the Bentley he'd seen at the snooker club.

'When you've got a minute, check this VRM and any linked nominals.'

'Mmm, mmm, mmm...' Myers nodded, mouth full of Coco Pops.

Yesterday's dirty mugs were scattered around the office. He got a tray, and collected them up. Fay Nash walked in.

'What's going on? A Stallard brew?' She arched both eyebrows. 'Scarcer than unicorn shit.'

'It means you have to do the sandwich run. I'll have sausage and tom.'

'In your dreams.'

He pleaded, 'Come on. I need carbs and fat.'

'Hangover?'

'Either that or someone's put my brain in a vice.'

'Tough. Wait for Keith.'

'So cruel.'

He got the teapot and headed down the corridor to the kitchenette. The cleaner, Edna, was just coming out, leaving a smell of stale cigarettes in her wake. He put the mugs in to soak, and checked the fridge. There was only one container of milk. No surprise there. It was a large four-pinter, labelled *Marjorie's milk – keep your thieving hands off*. He lifted it out, and a deafening bell started to ring in the corridor. Shit. Marjorie must have had the milk wired up to an alarm, like the Mona Lisa in the Louvre.

Fay Nash came out of the office wearing a fluorescent bib that said *Fire Warden* on it, and said, 'Leave the building. Rendezvous at point 4 in the car park.'

Gerard Hardcastle stuck his head out of his office door.

'It'll be that silly cow in finance on the ground floor that's burnt the toast again.'

'Possibly, sir,' said Nash. 'But you know the regulations.'

Stallard joined in a conga of staff trudging down the back staircase. He milled around in the car park, making the most of the fresh morning air. It felt good. Unlike the bells mounted on the wall that wailed in a continuous high-pitched dringgggg, and made his temples scream in pain. Motorists drove past on their way to work, and pointed, laughing. Thick coppers have set fire to their own police station.

He checked his phone. There was a missed call from Shannon, and a voicemail. He wandered out onto the street, away from the noise, and clamped the mobile to his ear. She sounded a little down. Her parents had heard about the deaths of Tyler and Mickey and Rosie. Mum and Dad had never approved of Rosie, but they'd hoped she would make Joey happy. There'd been an article in the local paper and a friend had rung Mum. The holiday was ruined. They'd flown home.

Traffic noise from the dual carriageway made it hard to pick up every word of the message. Shannon's parents had tried to ring her last night, when she was in the club. They'd got an overnight flight that landed at Manchester at 6am, and she'd not been there to meet them. She felt bad about it. She was going to go home and get changed, then go and see them and try and smooth things over. She wondered what Stallard was doing later. It was a casual remark. She had a commitment, but maybe they could meet up. That's if he ever wanted to see her again. She sounded nervous and laughed.

Ever wanted to see her again? Come on. He was smitten. He rang her straight back.

'Hi'

'Hi'

'I got your message.'

'And?'

'I'm not doing anything later.'

'Cool.'

'So, what are we doing?'

'I'm playing on stage at The Leadmill.'

'Come again, you're what? The actual Leadmill.'

'There's a band called The Keys to Utopia. They were our main rivals when we were playing, but also sort of our mates. Now they've taken our place.'

'I've heard of them.'

'They've had it booked for ages, but have turned it into a memorial gig for Tyler and Mickey. They've asked me to join them on stage for a few numbers.'

'Wow.'

'I thought you might like to come. I can put you on the guest list.'

'No need. I have a magic shield with Her Majesty The Queen's crown on it. She's got me in to Elton, The Who, Stereophonics and many more.'

'Thought you didn't carry a warrant card, because it spoilt the cut of your jeans.'

'I can put it in a shirt pocket.'

'There's just one thing.' Shannon sounded hesitant. 'There's a good chance Baxter and Brandon will be there.'

'Does SIAM manage this Utopia band as well?'

'No. The Quinns are related to Mickey's family. Half cousins or something. That's how we ended up with Baxter as our manager.'

'I'll be there.' Even more reason.

'Thanks...'

'Are you home yet?'

'No, I've not checked out yet. I'm just having a full breakfast.'

'Mushrooms, hash browns and black pudding, as well as the usual? Mmmmm.'

'Yes.'

'Can you hear my stomach? That loud grumbling?'

There were some muffled sounds. 'I'm just chewing some bacon, with egg and a bit of toast.'

'Stop it. I could eat a cow between two bread vans. Have mercy.'

'See you later. We sound-check at six. On at nine.'

Back at his desk, he saw an email from Bell-Bio Inc had pinged in. They had received the Section 8 warrant, and were happy to comply with the request for information. All the material they had on the case was contained in the attached file. Stallard looked but there was no attachment. The force firewall had snaffled it. Who would have thought that the IT department could be so efficient? These guys were living proof of the saying, *if you pay peanuts...* It was like the Rock of Gibraltar down there.

He looked across the room and saw Myers at his desk. 'Were you after me?'

The analyst looked startled. He took a plate with a half-eaten jacket potato and closed it away in a desk drawer.

'It's that reg number you gave me this morning.'

'It doesn't exist?'

'It exists.' Myers wiped butter off his chin with a tissue. 'But it must have a hidden marker on PNC. Five minutes after I checked it, I got a phone call from the Head of Intelligence at headquarters, and as soon as I put the phone down, another one came in from someone in the National Crime Agency.'

'Who's the car down to?'

'Nobody. Registered keeper's just shown as a leasing company in London.'

Stallard rubbed his chin-stubble. It must be a high-end outfit to lease out cars like Bentleys. The Far East end of the Fentanyl operation?

He told Myers about the email from Bell-Bio Inc, and how the attachment hadn't come through. The analyst got straight on it. By the time he'd fetched a coffee and a Mars Bar from the canteen, there was a print-out on his desk. It wasn't exactly what he was expecting.

He read it again. Joey Doane had submitted a sample to Bell-Bio Inc for comparison against two other DNA profiles that were already held on their database. These samples had been previously submitted by means of self-administered mouth swab kits. The two other persons were Oliver Munday and Naomi Munday. The results were that all three were full siblings. The same biological mother and father. Why had he done this? Had there ever been any doubt? He was missing something.

CHAPTER 45

Jim Doane had been awake since before dawn. He'd watched the curtain edges grow light, and lain there next to Elaine, quiet and still, with the familiar strands of thought swirling around in his head. It had been the same for months. Over time, some had shifted and become more prominent, then faded, as others took precedence in the hierarchy of anguish and self-doubt. But it was always the same ones.

In the first weeks after Joey's disappearance, things were confused. Suicide was a word he couldn't bring himself to say. There was grief, frustration and anger, but there was no sign of a body, and so there was always hope. At times, he knew his son was gone forever, and that he would never see or touch him again, and this filled him with a terrifying emptiness. The endless void that only death can signify. The anger was directed at drugs and those who pushed them. There could be no other explanation as to why Joey would kill himself.

The frustration came from not knowing. There was no note left in the car, and no messages of goodbye. He remembered reading a report in the local paper of a man who had fallen to his death from a multi-storey car park in town. The coroner had recorded an open verdict, because there was no evidence the man had intended to jump. He could have slipped or there could have been another unknown explanation. Maybe that could have happened to Joey?

Shannon tried to help, but she often made things worse. Her obsession that Joey had been murdered made it difficult to draw a line and move on. Not that he always wanted to move on with life. Sometimes, he wanted to shout, *let him rest in peace,* but he couldn't because there was always the chance, he was still alive. It was a slender and diminishing possibility, but they had to cling to it.

More recently, the demons racing around his brain were all about guilt. What could he have done differently bringing up his son? Why didn't he see what was going to happen? How did the two of them grow so far apart? When did it start, and where was he, when his only son needed him? These strands of thought were the worst, because they ate away at his mental and physical health.

Jim got out of bed around 6.30, and left Elaine asleep. She'd been on tablets from the doctor for a while. They knocked her out, and even when she came downstairs in a morning, she wasn't *with it* until lunchtime. He got dressed and fed the birds in the back garden. They had a cedar bird table with hanging wire baskets that he filled with nuts and seeds. It was one of the small rituals that helped him get through the day. Rituals were all he had left.

Breakfast was porridge, made with water, salt and a splash of milk. Then he walked to the petrol station, a mile down the main road, and bought a newspaper. There was never any good news in the paper, but he liked to read the sports section, and the exercise helped clear his head. Another ritual.

Since taking voluntary redundancy, the days were too long. If the weather was good, he pottered in the garden, and if it wasn't, the hours dragged. He'd never been a reader, so it was either watch sports channels on TV, or have a run out with Elaine in the car. He was finding retirement difficult before Joey went missing, but now it was soul-destroying, and getting worse each day. Life wasn't worth living, and he had dark thoughts, but then there was Shannon…

She kept him going. He knew it should be the other way round, and as a parent he ought to be the one supporting her, but roles reverse with age, and he felt prematurely old. She wasn't perfect. He should never have let her persuade him to go to Greece. It was a disaster. He'd used the deaths of those unfortunate kids as an excuse to return home, but that wasn't the real reason. Without his rituals to perform, he was lost. He loved Elaine, but she'd changed. They'd both changed. They were distant, and couldn't talk about the one thing that had driven them apart. They couldn't talk about anything.

Just before 9.30, Elaine came downstairs, and Jim made her a cup of tea. Then, he jotted down a few items on a scrap of paper, before slipping it in his back pocket, and going into the garage. Once a week, he drove to a farm shop just over the border in Derbyshire, and bought some meat. Nothing fancy, just some chops or whatever looked good, and always a few rashers of bacon for Shannon.

He took Shelly out of the garage, and checked her tyre pressures and water bottle. She was a 1998 Ford Fiesta he'd owned since new, and kept immaculate. He filled her up on the way to the farm shop, and got all five things on his list, plus a pork pie, because they'd just been made and were still warm. Then he arrived at Shannon's terraced house.

Jim went down the side alley as usual, but the back door was wide open, and he saw broken dishes all over the kitchen floor. He went in, and shouted SHANNON, SHANNON, SHANNON, but there was no reply. The taps were running in the sink, and he went over and turned them off. The overflow had prevented a flood, but he couldn't understand what was happening. He had an awful feeling in his chest.

The pine bureau that Shannon kept so fastidiously neat and ordered was open, and all the files and papers were scattered on the floor. In the living room, the furniture had been tipped over, and there was a spider's web of cracks in the television screen. His heart was banging. He ran upstairs two at a time, but the bedroom was empty. Clothes were strewn on the floor, and there was a smell. The bed was made, but somebody had defecated on one of the pillows.

Jim gagged. He went back downstairs and burrowed for the phone in his trouser pocket. He rang Shannon from the back yard, and closed his eyes, praying that she answered.

'Hi dad.'

'Wh…where are you?' He couldn't breathe properly.

'At a friend's. Leave the bacon in the fridge, thanks.'

'Are you all right?'

'I'm fine. What's the matter?'

He froze. Didn't know what to say.

'Dad, are you okay? Please, what's the matter.' There was a frisson of panic in her voice.

'I'm at your house. I'm sorry, Shannon. I'm sorry. I wish...'

'Just tell me what the hell is wrong.'

'Somebody's trashed it.'

'Don't worry, dad. Break-ins happen – I'm just waiting for a taxi, and I'll sort it out when I get there.' She sounded relieved.

'What sort of burglar puts a laptop in a sink full of water instead of pinching it?'

'Are you joking?'

Jim was quiet. He was thinking about the answer to his own question. 'It's the Quinns, isn't it?'

'Dad, don't be daft.' She was pleading.

'I'll call the police, for all the good it will do.'

'No, dad, don't. Please. Let me sort this out.' The panic was back in her voice.

'Why don't you want to involve the police?'

'Nothing. I'll explain later. I won't be long.' She ended the call.

Jim Doane sat down on the back doorstep. What had she got herself into? She'd never messed about with drugs, like Joey had. Not that he knew of, anyway. She was strong and stuck to what she believed was right. That was a problem sometimes, just like when she'd had a go at Joey for getting in touch with his birth mother. It had never really bothered him and Elaine, but Shannon had taken offence on their behalf. It had caused a bitterness in the family at the time, and yet now, it all seemed so irrelevant and petty. Funny how death can put things in perspective.

He went back inside, and took the plug out of the kitchen sink. He let the water drain away, and lifted out Shannon's laptop. It was a MacBook they'd bought her for her 21st, and cost a fortune, but it was the only one she wanted. When she set her mind on something, there was no point trying to change it. She's been like that since the age of seven or eight. He propped it up on the draining board, and kicked away some broken crockery under his feet on the tiled floor. He looked down and saw it was part of a Peter Rabbit bowl that she'd had since she was christened, and he felt the water start to fill his eyes.

For a moment, he teetered on the brink of collapse. Part of him wanted to give up, and stop pretending that he could hold it all together. His life was a charade, and it would be easier to stop the constant battles inside his head. Perhaps he could get pills like Elaine's, that turn you into a brain-dead zombie, or try and pickle himself in alcohol, even though he'd never been a big drinker.

That's when he made the decision. There was another option that had always been there, and now he knew it was the right one. Shannon wasn't the only one in the family who could be stubborn. As soon as the choice was made, it was a weight lifted from his shoulders, and he felt at peace with himself.

The Quinn brothers were responsible. Whatever they'd done to Joey had driven him beyond the point of despair, and forced him to choose oblivion over life. Or perhaps Shannon was right and they'd killed him. What had the long-haired copper said when he caught him with the baseball bat? He was picking on the soft targets? Yes, but not this time. He was going to do what he should have done months ago.

Elaine was still in her dressing gown, watching TV in the kitchen. *I'm back,* he shouted, and went straight upstairs. The loft hatch was on the landing, and he used the telescopic ladder to climb in. He crawled to the far end, under the gable, and pulled back the wads of fibre-glass insulating roll. The shortbread biscuit tin was still there. He carried it down to the bedroom, and opened it. There was a familiar musty smell. He pulled out the bits of uniform that he'd once cut out with the Royal Marine Commando badges sewn onto them, and a couple of green berets. Then he carefully lifted out a cloth draw-string bag. It was heavier than he remembered.

Jim Doane took a deep breath, and took the gun out of the bag. It was a Ballester-Molina 11mm semi-automatic pistol, with two rounds in the magazine. For a few years, after he came back from the Falklands, he told his mates that he'd taken it from an Argentine soldier when a thousand of them surrendered at the battle of Goose Green. The truth was he'd bought it on the ship home from a lad in 2 Para. Lots of squaddies had them as the spoils of war, and he didn't want to be left out. It was a white lie that over the years he'd come to feel ashamed of. But now wasn't the time for regrets. It was time to find out what had happened to his son.

CHAPTER 46

The force's Covert Ops building was tucked away behind a razor-wire fence near the wholesale markets. A new-build with smoked glass windows, and an indoor garage big enough for thirty cars. The sign outside said *Diamond Logistics*. It was where the force drug squad, surveillance unit and organised crime unit had their base. Half the city's criminals probably knew, but so what? Better than advertising the place to all and sundry with flashing blue lights and sirens.

Block was sitting at a computer, typing up risk assessment forms. Bored and tired-looking.

'Why is *reducing bureaucracy* a force priority every sodding year, if all that happens is, we get more and more of the stuff?'

'To piss you off,' said Stallard. 'What's happening with the Fentanyl job?'

Block kept typing. 'Not our problem.'

'Whose is it then?'

'Do I look like Mystic Meg?'

'Yes, but uglier.'

'If you check the system, the intel has gone. It must have been red-texted.'

'Red-texted?'

'I forgot you've been out of force for years in La-la land.' Block stopped typing. 'The new intelligence system has levels of security, and red-text is beyond my pay grade. It's minimum DI in Force Intelligence, which probably means one thing.'

'It's NCA?'

'Yes, we can all rest easy in our beds. The UK's answer to the FBI is about to fuck another job up.'

Stallard wondered how many more young lives in the city might be extinguished, while the locals bitched about the NCA, and the NCA kept the locals in the dark? Some things never changed. Small-minded politics and mistrust always shaped the relationship.

Block beckoned him closer. 'Look at this.' He closed down the risk assessment form, and brought up a video on screen. 'We managed half a day surveillance before the plug was pulled.'

The screen showed Brandon Quinn hanging around near a statue in a park. He was joined by two men. They were late 40s, with button-down checked shirts and dad jeans of the one-size-fits-fuck-all variety. Baggy on the arse and then squeezed in by a belt beneath overhanging guts. Mufti for the middle-aged law enforcement operative. One did the talking, while the other made notes, and then they were gone. No handshakes or fist-bumps.

Stallard felt his back stiffen. The bastards. 'I recognise

the taller one. He's an ex-cuzzie, now in the NCA source-handling unit.'

'Quinn's a CHIS?"

'Might explain their charmed lives.'

'Doesn't help us, though.' Block closed his eyes, and ran both hands back through the greying mullet. 'That means they're going upstream.'

'After the source of the Fentanyl? The pill factories?'

Block laughed. 'They never actually get anyone at the source, but they make a few drug seizures. That's all that matters – seizures. It looks good in the newspaper and ticks the boxes in their performance matrix.'

'And the Quinns carry on, like they've always done?'

'Do I sound cynical?'

'I bet you get invited to lots of parties.'

Block yawned. 'Sorry I can't do more.'

Stallard cruised back into town with blood pounding in his ears. Going upstream – a euphemism for doing fuck all. The biggest bust in the world is always just on the horizon, but it never gets closer. Meanwhile, here's some analysis we've done to show what a good job we're doing. Tossers. He pulled over and calmed himself down. Anger wasn't going to help Joey Doane.

Oliver Munday was already waiting for him in the sushi bar. There were booths down one wall, but he was on a stool at the conveyer belt that horse-shoed round the middle. Munday had a matcha green tea, and Stallard had a 620ml bottle of Asahi to enhance the cultural experience. He asked why the little plates going round on the train were different colours, and Munday explained they denoted the price of each dish. He asked why some cost a lot more than others, and Munday explained rice was cheap, but fish was expensive, and so the ratio dictated the price. Then he asked, how did anyone know how long a dish had been going around on the belt, because if it had been going round at room temperature since they opened four hours ago, he didn't really fancy it. Prawns were notorious for going off and giving you the runs. Munday said he didn't know and didn't care, and that he had to get back to the office soon. Mr Impatient.

Niceties over, Stallard unleashed the big one.

'Tell me about Caroline Stubbs.'

'Wh… what about her?' Munday's Rolls-Royce engine had a misfire.

'Why did she take you and the firm to an industrial tribunal?'

'That matter is *sub judice.*'

'Don't try to fool me with your law-school Latin. The case never went under judicial consideration, and what's more, it's done and dusted.'

Munday's Adam's apple bobbed up and down. 'She signed a non-disclosure agreement.'

'I'm not asking her. I'm asking you.'

The Adam's apple did a somersault. 'Do I have to tell you?'

'No, but if you want, I can go to your house and tell your wife that you and Caroline played hide the chipolata at the Christmas party.'

'You wouldn't do that.'

'I'm a proper bastard.' Stallard beamed. The evil Iago about to dash the marriage of noble Othello and the fair Desdemona.

'It wasn't what you think.' Munday's face was grey. 'I thought I loved Caroline. I was going to leave home, but. well, you know how it is. It's a big step when you've got kids, and financial suicide…'

The lawyer talking. No contest when it comes to love versus money. Stallard brought up a mental image of the three photos in Munday's office. The life goals. If Mrs Munday went, so did the Aston Martin and the villa.

'I take it you changed your mind about leaving your wife, and Caroline didn't like it?'

Munday nodded, and took a drink to try and settle the Adam's apple that appeared to be in training for gold at the next Olympics. 'I told her on the Friday before Christmas, because I couldn't stand the thought of living a lie over the holidays. Caroline didn't take it very well, and when we went back into the office after New Year, she didn't show up.'

Stallard took a couple of plates off the conveyer belt. He lifted the clear plastic lids and sniffed. Gave them a suspicious stare. The cod-in-batter man, wary of raw fish.

'I saw Ben Phillpotts at court yesterday. You didn't tell me that you were paying him to represent Joey.'

'He's a dear friend. His fee was very modest.'

'And Joey paid £500 to get his DNA checked against yours and Naomi's. Did you pay for that too?'

'Possibly, probably, I don't know…'

'And then there was the cash advance for his drug rehabilitation course…'

Stallard tried picking up a roll with chopsticks. It kept slipping through. He stabbed it with one stick – a sushi kebab – and ducked his head down to just above the plate. Not textbook, but effective. 'Mmmm, not bad.'

Munday checked his watch. 'I really do need to get back to the office.'

Stallard tried another. It fell through the chopsticks half a dozen times. He gave up and used his fingers to dip it in a bowl of soy sauce. 'Mmmm. I like that one better.'

'Please...'

'All right. We're nearly done here.' Stallard licked his fingers. 'Just tell me what dirt Joey Doane had on you.'

'Dirt?'

'He must have had something on you to make you spend all that money.'

'Nonsense.'

'Was it bad enough to kill him?'

'Preposterous.'

'Did you kill him, Oliver?'

'That's enough.' Munday stood up. 'If you want to ask me anything else, I shall exercise my right to legal representation.'

'You never returned the signed financial-release form.' Stallard prodded at another couple of plates.

'If you want to see my accounts, then you'll need a court order.' Munday peeled a couple of £20 notes out of his wallet and slapped them down on the counter. 'That should cover it. I hope you enjoyed yourself.' He walked off, and out into the street.

'It was a revelation.' Stallard shouted after him.

A couple on the opposite side of the conveyer belt stared and gave him funny looks. Maybe they'd been blown away by his genius chopstick skills. He ignored them and finished the Asahi. Then he paid and left.

The light outside the manager's door was green. Stallard knocked once and walked in.

'Sit down, Harry.'

Something about Hardcastle's face was different. More sepulchral than usual.

'If this is touchy-feely chat about how I'm adjusting back into the work environment, I'm doing fine, thanks for asking.'

'Bad news.' Hardcastle shook his head. 'The result of the case conference is that you are not fit for duty at the current time.'

'WHAT?'

'You're on gardening leave with immediate effect, until one of the doctors at OHU can see you and sign you off.'

'What happened to you fighting my corner?'

'The Head of HR and the Head of CID out-gunned me.'

'I see.' Stallard's mouth was dry. There was a vacuum in his guts. 'What happens to the Joey Doane case?'

'It will be reviewed again in twelve months' time.'

'PLEASE.' Stallard tore at this hair. 'Don't let them do this. There are two scumbags called Quinn, who are importing powder from the Far East that's killing kids in our city. They've used Joey – I mean Joseph Doane – to facilitate this on at least one previous occasion.' Stallard swallowed. Throat hoarse, heart racing. 'And he was due to travel out there again on the day he went missing, but didn't make the flight. The money had come from Doane's natural brother, a solicitor called Oliver Munday, who he'd never met in his life until a couple of weeks before. The solicitor's dodgy. Doane must have had something on him and been blackmailing him for cash. I just haven't worked out the connection between Munday and the Quinn brothers yet. When I do, we'll know exactly what has happened to Joseph Doane's body and who killed him.'

'I'm sorry.' Hardcastle folded his glasses into a case, and snapped it shut.

'Is that it?'

'I did what I could in the circumstances.'

Stallard sensed a sub-text. Something he wasn't being told. Then it struck him, and his shock turned to anger. 'It's the NCA. They want me out of the way.'

'Come on, Harry.'

'Why else would our Head of CID go to my case conference? A lowly detective constable? They got him to go and make sure I was removed from the picture.'

'You're seeing conspiracies.'

'I know how they work, God's gift to law enforcement. They couldn't detect a fart in a spacesuit.'

Hardcastle's eyes softened. 'Remember, when this is all over, there's a place for you in the cold case unit if you want it.'

Stallard stood up. His cheeks were burning. There was nothing else to say.

CHAPTER 47

The afternoon was as bright and shiny as a guardsman's boot. It was as though the weather gods were mocking him. It should have been thick, black cloud and pissing it down at the very least. He drove away from the nick feeling numb, and not knowing what to do. The soundcheck at The Leadmill wasn't for a couple of hours, and what was he going to tell Shannon? Congratulations, the new man in your life has been deemed mentally unstable. And don't forget the best bit – nobody's trying to find your brother's killers any longer. Not for the next year anyway.

He drifted towards the town centre, and then dropped down to a little Irish pub that was an early-bar haunt of the local CID. It was an egalitarian sort of place. Circuit judges rubbed shoulders with binmen and bag ladies. It also served the best Guinness in the Steel City, which is what he needed. Four pints in, *Walk On The Wild Side* rang out on his phone.

'Hi, it's Dan Berry from the Border Force. Close your eyes, I've got a surprise.'

'Yay, I've won the EuroMillions rollover jackpot?'

'Close. Remember you asked me to send intel logs to the hubs at Langley and Coventry? You gave me two addresses?'

'Vaguely. The Quinns' businesses?' Thinking was an effort.

'There's been an interception. A postal packet at Langley was spotted with an onward address of Triangle Trading.'

'Clean or dirty?'

'Dirty. It was a box of pool balls with forty blister packs of pills taped inside the lid.'

'Tell me they didn't seize it. Go on, tell me they let it run. Please, please, please...'

'Don't worry. They let it run.'

'Yes.' Stallard hissed and punched the air. 'This could be my lucky day after all.'

'Not luck. I told them to let it run. Don't forget I'm ex-job.'

'I owe you'

'Big time.'

'Courier?'

'Parcelforce operating out of the Magna depot. Delivery time between 0900 hours and 1100 hours tomorrow.'

Stallard sat back and swigged his stout. Under normal circumstances, it would be good practice to control the delivery; use a surveillance team and contain the area, and have static obs in place to call *strike*. Then the arrest team would move in, and the premises would be secured for a dedicated search team to go in later. But this wasn't normal circumstances. Forget the fact he had been caseconferenced and relieved of his duties. He didn't want to give this intelligence to his own force, because it would get passed on to the NCA. They had primacy.

The problem was, the big, fancy boys wouldn't do anything with it, because they were too interested in what was happening way up stream to care about forty blister packs of pills. If these were pure Fentanyl, then ground down and bashed with a kilo of another white powder, you'd be looking at a street value of fifty grand. According to sentencing guidelines, if convicted the Quinns would get between nine and thirteen years. Nowhere near sexy or grand enough for the NCA, but good enough for him, and he guessed, many parents across the city. He knew what he had to do. Early tomorrow morning he would be waiting for the Parcelforce delivery at Triangle Trading. Fuck gardening leave.

The Keys to Utopia were already sound-checking when Stallard got there. They were an indie band. Jangly guitars and a girl on lead vocals. She had black hair that obscured her face most of the time, and a leather mini-skirt that showed off a swirling selection of floral tattoos. Shannon was standing behind a keyboard, and waved when she saw him. She was stunning. Fire-engine lipstick, and hair teased up into a beehive.

The band did a lot of starting and stopping, and one instrument at a time segments until they got the levels right. Then the same with the mics and vocals. The young guy on the mixing desk had hair down to the small of his back, and didn't believe in deodorants. Whenever he took his hands off the faders, and pointed to one of the band,

Stallard got a blast of rank body odour. It added to the general aroma of stale beer and cannabis. So, this is what it's like in the world of showbiz?

Eventually, Smelly was happy with the levels, and they played three numbers the whole way through. They were good. Better than good – the songs were powerful, melodic odes to the human condition, with catchy choruses and a driving beat that made you want to jump up and down and punch the air with the unbridled joy and despair of being alive. That's what music does. Fuck literature and painting pictures – that stuff's for sissies – this is real art. It touches a primordial g-spot in the soul and resonates around the body. Connects humans to each other and to the past, irrespective of race and class. It punches you in the face and takes you on a journey of hip-shaking, risk-taking greatness. And this was just the soundcheck.

There was a howl of feedback, and the sound check ended. Stallard stuffed two fingers in his mouth and whistled his appreciation. Everyone looked at him as though he just taken a dump on the dancefloor. He swapped his star-struck grin for an uber-cool, disinterested frown, which seemed to be what was expected.

Shannon climbed down off the stage and pecked him on the cheek.

'Thanks for coming.'

He risked a little smile. 'You were pretty good.'

'They're a great band. I basically just played three chords on a keyboard.'

'You played them really well, and you look fantastic.'

She blushed. 'Do you want to see back-stage?'

He followed her through a side door, and down a corridor that smelt of boiled cabbage and sweaty socks. The rest of the band were already back in the dressing room. It was a windowless rectangle, full of guitar cases and some battered sofas. Shannon introduced him and they all said *hi*. The rest of the band had girlfriends with them, including the singer. They all said *hi* too. Everyone settled down to chill for the best part of what would be three hours before they were back on stage.

One of the girlfriends was stoned. She came up and draped an arm round Stallard.

'Are you Shannon's boyfriend?'

Hmm, awkward. He smiled and looked for help.

Shannon picked up the baton. 'Harry is the detective who is leading the investigation into Joey's disappearance. He's a friend.'

'You're a copper?' The stoner's mouth hung loose.

'Yep. Size nine feet, hairy arse and everything.' He watched the band glance at each other. Holy shit. Then automatically look towards wherever their stash was in the room. He held up his palms. 'Don't worry. They don't call me Norman Pilcher.'

'Who the fuck?' A screwed-up face from the stoner.

'The detective who arrested all those musicians for drugs back in the day – John Lennon, Mick Jagger, Donovan, Dusty Springfield...'

Nobody looked convinced. They went into their own huddles and shot scowls in his direction. He sat in the corner of one over-stuffed sofa, and Shannon sat alongside him on the arm. There was something not right. She was distracted, and just when she looked like she was building up to telling him what was bothering her, she shook her head and blew the clouds away. The smile came back, and he was mesmerised.

There was a Bluetooth speaker on the floor pumping out *There She Goes* by The La's, and in the middle of the room was a table made out of old wooden pallets, with a case of bottled water and two boxes of Coors Light. Next to the beer were some family bags of crisps, and a selection of chocolate bars.

Shannon slid off the sofa arm, and tore open the shrink-wrap on the waters.

'Want anything from the rider?'

'The what?' Stallard's forehead made creases.

'The hospitality rider. It's what the promoter agrees to provide in the artists' dressing room. Have you never heard of Mariah Carey's kittens or Van Halen's M&Ms that could be every colour except brown?'

He shook his head. 'My band were lucky if they got a cupboard to put their guitar cases in.'

'You kept that quiet.' Shannon's face lit up. 'Tell me all about it. Name. Genre. Line-up. What instrument you played?'

'It was a lifetime ago.'

'So?'

'Another time.' His voice became wistful and solemn. 'There's something more important I need to tell you.'

'No. I want to know about the band.'

'I'm sorry, but there's been…'

There was a knock and the door opened. It was Mickey's parents and an entourage of relatives. Stallard melted into the background as best he could. The group shuffled in and went round the band, shaking hands and being diffident but grateful for the tribute to their Mickey. Stallard saw Baxter and Brandon Quinn towards the back of the huddle and gave them his best don't-mess-with-me stare. They didn't look too frightened. If anything, there was a gloating smirk on Baxter's face, that was asking to be wiped off.

Stallard felt a hand on his arm. Shannon had seen the looks, and been quick to react. She smiled and used her eyes to direct him towards the exit. He took the hint and slipped away. An unseemly brawl would be disrespectful, and besides tomorrow he was going to bust their fat arses for importing fifty grands worth of Fentanyl. He couldn't wait.

CHAPTER 48

The doors had opened. There were a few kids hanging out in front of the stage. He went to the bar before it became busy and got two tins of Red Stripe and a plastic glass. The PA was playing *Not Nineteen Forever* by the Courteeners. It made him feel old. He looked round at the punters who were now starting to drift in from the turnstiles on the main entrance, and saw a different generation. Fuck, he really was old.

He went into a side room, and found a booth hidden around the corner. Maybe Laura had been right when she said it was time he grew up and started doing what most people of his age were doing. But when people say things like that, what they mean is it's time you stopped having fun. Press the pause button on your life for twenty years and have a family. Go on, listen to your clock ticking.

Time is a never-ending mini-hamper full of surprises. So much had changed in the last week, both personally and professionally. His head was spinning. What did the future look like now? No Laura to babysit him through the next stretch of enforced sick leave. Maybe he'd get lucky tomorrow at Triangle Trading, and the Quinns would be eating prison food for a while, but where did that leave Joey's case? Nobody seemed to give a shit. Oliver Munday was hiding something, but he was smart enough to make sure whatever it was stayed in the shadows. The next few weeks were going to be tough, and there were going to be some dark moments. The only glimmer of light was Shannon.

When he went back to the bar, the place had filled up, and it took him a while to get served two more Red Stripe. Before he could turn round with the drinks, a voice rasped in his ear: *Hello Harry.*

Baxter Quinn stood there grinning.

Stallard ignored him, and went to squeeze past.

Quinn blocked his way. 'Does she get personal protection now?'

'Shift or wear a pint of lager on your face. Your choice.'

'Are you allowed to shag witnesses?'

'She's a victim after your thugs paid a visit.'

'I bet the victim always *comes* first with you? Always the gentleman.'

'Last chance.' Stallard raised his plastic glass.

'Can't be with her all the time though, can you?'

Stallard stopped himself. There must be a reason Baxter was winding him up. He glanced into the crowd and saw three or four faces watching. Body-builder types with matching tattoos and tight, black polo shirts. Rent-a-goon. No sign of his favourite thug, Woodsy. Maybe he was out keeping the trafficking side of the business on track. He lowered the pint of lager.

'Tell you what. Let's go and find Mr and Mrs Flint right now and tell them where their little Mickey got his Fentanyl from.'

'Don't push it, Harry. There's only one Magic Rat still around, and it would be tragic if anything happened to her.'

'Shall I get on that microphone and tell everyone here that you and your brother are registered informants for the NCA?' Stallard could see he'd hit home. 'Touch her again, and I'll make sure every scumbag in town knows you're a grass. Nobody likes a grass.'

'Very funny.' Quinn regained his balance. 'Go fuck yourself.' He laughed and swaggered off, like a gunslinger who'd just dispatched the sheriff. All chin and chest. He nodded to his posse, and they closed ranks behind him.

Stallard watched them disappear behind the mixing desk, and hoped he hadn't said too much by mentioning the F-word. No point deliberately spooking them when a delivery was imminent. He wished he'd not made the *grass* taunt either. It was an empty threat, because no police officer in their right mind would ever reveal somebody as an informant. It would undermine an invaluable, crime-fighting system, the integrity of which relied on absolute confidentiality. But he wasn't in his right mind, was he? They'd had a case conference and told him so.

The first support act came on, and a group of thirty or so thronged to the front of the stage. Everyone else ignored them and milled around, making the most of valuable drinking time. Stallard leant against a pillar, and once again the time-travel switch in his head clicked, and he was back at The Shapeshifter Club. He could see Joey, and feel the atmosphere. What he wouldn't give now to find out what had happened to that kid. Fast-forward and he saw the CCTV Myers had downloaded. Two cars travelling to the Humber Bridge and one coming back. Who was driving?

'Excuse me, Detective Stallard.'

The voice jolted him. It was loud and directly into his earhole. He looked down and saw Leo from The Wild Tulip. 'Oh, hi.'

Leo was agitated. He shouted over the music. 'There's somebody outside who wants to see you. He says it's urgent.'

'Who?' It got lost in the sound.

Leo had already turned and was leading the way. Stallard followed him down past the front of the stage, through some fire doors, along a short corridor, and out through another fire door into an alley way, which bands used to load and unload their gear.

Stallard couldn't see anybody waiting.

Leo stopped and turned to face him. 'They made me do it. I'm sorry.'

'Made you do what?' Stallard was still shouting, even though the music was now just muffled. Within a heartbeat, he realised what was going down. A sixth sense or some movement reflected in Leo's terrified eyes. He spun round, but not quick enough to do anything about the fist that crashed into the side of his head.

The lights in his skull flickered. He dropped onto one knee. Came back up swinging for his life, but they were on top of him. Three or four. Another fist came out of the night, and glanced his cheek. Someone behind grabbed his neck, and he snapped his head backwards. Bone on gristle. A roar of pain filled his left ear. It gave a chance. He dropped to the floor and rolled under a line of commercial waste bins. A black Chelsea boot came through the gap, trying to stamp on his head. Missed. Two more pairs came round the other side. He scrabble-crawled through grease and shit to get away. His elbow went in a foil tray of fluorescent curry sauce. He gagged and carried on. Chicken bones. Broken glass. Plastic forks. More chicken, with skin and fat. A puddle of liquid that smelt like piss. Then crunch. Straight into a brick wall. The bin shielding him was wheeled away, and he curled up tight. Only one thing left – protect the head and groin.

Nothing. What the fuck? Nothing, he could feel nothing. Was he dead? He kept his arms clamped either side of his ears, and opened his eyes. The boots were gone. There were lots of legs in the alley way, and they were moving fast. People were pouring out of the club and running towards the main road. Stampede.

Stallard stood up, picked some glass out of his arm, and batted some pieces of crap from his clothes. What was happening? Screams were coming from inside. The faces of those leaving were frozen with panic, and the music had stopped. He edged his way along the wall against the human torrent until he reached the fire exit. And that's when he heard the gunshot.

CHAPTER 49

The scene was chaos. The house lights were up, and the last stragglers were fighting for the exits. A few had been trampled and were being helped up or supported, arms around shoulders. It was the only evidence of altruism. There was no sign of any door staff or security. The main floor area was a sea of abandoned plastic glasses and high-heeled shoes, and the mixing desk was a Marie Celeste with headphones left dangling over the sides. A metallic buzz filled the room, coming from the support band's amps and mics still left switched on, and above that were the screams of those desperate to leave.

Stallard crouched by the side of the stage, and immediately saw what had ignited the hysteria. It wasn't hard. The only three figures not rushing for the exits were ten yards in front of him. Brandon Quinn was on his back, propped up on one elbow. His face was contorted. Baxter was standing next to him, with his hands half-raised, and a murderous look in his eyes. The third man was wearing a three-quarter length car coat – not your usual summer-night gig-wear – and holding a black handgun steady in a two-handed grip.

Stallard couldn't see his face, but knew it was Jim Doane. 'Police. Don't shoot.' He stood up and walked towards them.

Jim Doane never turned round.

As he got closer, he saw blood pooling under Brandon Quinn's leg. He was in a pair of military-style shorts, and there was a neat, little entry wound just above his left knee. The back of his entire thigh was probably ripped clean off, because that's what bullets do. They trick you with their kinetic energy. Brandon's eyes were closed tight in pain, and he was moaning.

Baxter saw him coming. 'Lock this fucking lunatic up.'

'Calm down.'

'My brother needs an ambulance.'

'Like Maggs did?'

'That's far enough.' Jim Doane turned to Stallard. 'Stand there. I want you to witness the confession.'

'How many fucking times? We never touched Joey.' Baxter's face was purple. He loomed closer.

'Get back.' Jim Doane didn't flinch. Kept the gun pointed at Baxter's chest. 'Perhaps you need some encouragement.' His finger curled round the trigger.

'NO.' Stallard took another step forward, palms up. 'Remember the cricket pavilion. We can sort this out.'

Baxter's eyes became big as saucers.

'Too late for all that.' Jim Doane squeezed on the trigger. At the last moment, his shoulders pivoted and the barrel switched direction. BANG. The crack was deafening.

Stallard froze in horror.

On the floor, Brandon Quinn screamed and convulsed. Right leg this time. Straight through the kneecap.

'Holy fuck. You're fucking mental.' Baxter was starting to lose it.

Jim Doane had the barrel straight back on Quinn's chest. 'If I'd shot you, there would now be two of you rolling around unable to talk, and I need answers.'

'You're fucking dead.' Baxter. Eyes wild, jaw clenched.

'That's enough, Jim.' Stallard took a couple of steps. Ears still ringing. 'Give me the gun.'

'Stay away, son.' Jim Doane glanced sideways, but kept the gun trained on Quinn.

'Dad. Do as he says. Please…' Shannon was standing on the stage. Her face and body pleading.

Jim Doane turned instinctively at the sound of her voice. 'Shannon, my love.'

Baxter Quinn saw his chance. He charged. Jim swung back. Too late to prevent the coming together. There was a muted explosion. The two men stood locked onto each other in a morbid waltz. In slow motion, they collapsed onto the dance floor in a heap. Neither moved.

Stallard heard a cry of anguish from the stage, and watched as a spent cartridge spiralled on the ground. An acrid smell hit the back of his throat.

Then Baxter Quinn rolled away onto his back, and Jim Doane gradually hauled himself to his feet.

'Now, it's over.' Stallard moved in and gently took the semi-automatic from the old man's hand. He unclipped the magazine, and checked there wasn't another round up the spout. Baxter didn't move.

A couple of security staff appeared in the main doorway. He shouted to them to get paramedics and the police, and did a quick triage on the Quinns. Baxter wasn't moving, so he started with Brandon. The older brother had lost a lot of blood. One of the bullets must have nicked an artery. Stallard whipped off his belt and tourniqueted one leg, then wrestled Brandon's own belt off and did the other. This Quinn wouldn't be making Team GB's giant slalom team, but he'd live.

When he stood back up, Shannon was hugging her father, and he was stroking her hair. Words were irrelevant.

Baxter's eyes were open, but non-responsive. Saliva was bubbling from the side of his mouth. Stallard knelt down. The chest was still rising and falling, but there was a hole in his shirt, between his sternum and clavicle. It was a white T-shirt, and there was black staining around the edges of the hole. He checked the airway, and it was clear, but when he turned the head to one side, some bright red blood, full of fresh oxygen frothed out. He thought about turning him over, but decided it would do more harm than good.

Nothing left to do. He took hold of Baxter's hand, and held it in his.

'It's Harry. I'm here to help you. Trust me, you're going to be all right.'

CHAPTER 50

Stallard couldn't sleep. He'd gorilla-taped an old office fan to the bedroom ceiling, but it was making zero difference. The caravan was hot enough to make pizzas. He kept going over last night's events in his mind, trying to work out if he could have done anything different. Something that might have prevented the carnage. Should he have known Jim Doane might do something crazy? Had he let his personal feelings for Shannon cloud his judgement?

Thoughts kept bombarding him from all different angles. Unresolved issues with nagging doubts, and random memories from the past. He kept deflecting them but some kept bouncing back. One was a very old joke, and he couldn't shake it out of his head.

Groucho Marx is sat next to a pretty woman at an elegant dinner party.

Groucho: Would you sleep with me for ten million dollars?

Pretty woman: Sure, of course I would.

Groucho: (wiggling eyebrows) How about doing it for fifteen dollars?

Pretty woman: (indignant) What sort of girl do you think I am?

Groucho: We've already established that. Now we're haggling over the price.

Stallard knew what it meant. He and Frank were one and the same. He'd not pummelled anyone unconscious, but he'd slept with a witness. They'd both crossed the line, and it was just a question of degree. Who in this material world is the line judge? Does it even matter? Once you cross the Rubicon, the die is cast and there's no going back.

He wiped the film of sweat off his forehead, and slid out of bed. Took his phone outside onto the paving-slab patio and messaged Frank.

I forgive.

Friends again? The reply came straight back.

Stallard checked the time. It was just after 4.30am. *Go to sleep. You're as fucked up as I am.*

Ha ha. Night, night. Again, the response immediate.

A mellow glow beyond the valley-sides showed the sun was stirring. He went back inside and put some coffee on to brew while he took a shower. The lump on his cheekbone was tender to the touch, and he fashioned a cold compress from a flannel Laura had left. Then he fixed his ponytail with a fresh rubber band, and sat down with some toast to plan the day. For someone who was off work, there was a lot to do. Most detectives in his position couldn't operate outside of their work environment, but he was different. He was used to being resourceful, and living on his wits. Years undercover had schooled him well.

349

At 7.40, Stallard met Chris Block, who drove them to Ganister Road in one of the drug squad's unmarked cars. Just the two of them, without any teams of surveillance officers or firearms unit. They parked up with a view of the entrance to Triangle Trading and waited. Eight o'clock came and went. No staff arrived to open up. At one point, a black 4x4 slowed down, then sped off. The word was out that Baxter was in an induced coma, and Brandon would be lucky to walk again. Perhaps the ragtag bunch who worked there realised the end was in sight, or maybe the Quinns didn't trust anybody but themselves with the keys.

Block scrolled on his smartphone. 'Hey, congratulations. You made the national news.'

'I'm thrilled.'

'The night the Bataclan came to Britain.'

'WHAT?'

'In scenes reminiscent of the French capital, gunshots caused mayhem inside the iconic music venue.'

'The stupid, disrespectful fuckers. How can they compare heavily armed Islamic State terrorists massacring innocent kids to a grieving father shooting a couple of scumbag gangsters?'

'It's called journalism, calm down.' Block scrolled some more, and tapped a link. 'Jesus. Someone's uploaded a video of the crowd surging out the doors. It looks scary.'

'It was scary.' Stallard yawned. 'Did you get the result back on the gear found in Tyler's flat?'

'Same as Mickey Flint's – one hundred percent pure Fentanyl pills.'

'I wonder if they knew?'

'They'd no idea or they wouldn't have injected or snorted those kind of doses, but so what, we'll never prove anything.'

Stallard nodded. It confirmed his suspicions. 'Listen, you're not going to get into trouble for doing this, are you?'

'Do I look like somebody who gives a shit?'

The Parcelforce van arrived bang on nine, and Stallard took possession of the three boxes to be delivered. The first one he opened was the snooker balls. Inside a false lid he found the blister packs, just like Berry had described. It would have been a better result if he could have got the Quinns hands-on with them, but sometimes you have to accept life isn't perfect. At least the pills he was holding wouldn't kill more young people. Chris Block filmed it all, then sealed the drugs in an exhibit bag. Someone in the NCA wasn't going to be happy.

Keith was waiting for him in the Marks and Spencer café, buttering a scone and looking nervous.

'Thanks for doing this.' Stallard sat down opposite.

Keith pulled a buff folder from his briefcase and nudged it across the table. 'Now we're even.'

'Your panties for my Joey Doane missing person file.'

'It's not the original – I took photocopies, so nobody can discover it's gone and become suspicious.'

'I'm not an offender planning to use it to commit crime, I just want to see if there's something in there I missed. Methodical and meticulous, remember?

'You shouldn't be working.'

'Remind me. What legislation gave me authority to break into that house for you?'

Keith's nose twitched. 'That's different.'

'I'm not letting this case sit gathering dust for another year.'

'What if Mr Hardcastle finds out?'

'Once on a UC job in South London, a one-eyed Turk threatened to cut off my testicles and make me eat them.'

'I see. So, the prospect of a written warning from Mr H is less concerning?'

'Say hello to Nash for me.' Stallard stood up and tucked the folder under his arm. 'Tell her I haven't forgotten Berlin.'

'Wait.' Keith called him back. 'Ring me if you need anything else.'

Back at the caravan, he set up office outside, using a knackered picnic table, and a John Smiths parasol. He jumped straight in and started wading through the pages of Joey's missing person file. It was dismally familiar. The same banal witness statements from people who had nothing but background information to offer. The paper actions allocated to detectives, directing them to undertake standard enquiries, and their stereotypical written responses. Coleman and Katz were the main culprits, but others were no better. A whole investigation just going through the motions, so they could tick boxes and move onto the next, more deserving case. One that didn't involve a junkie who'd topped himself.

Even the intelligence implicating the Quinns hadn't been explored thoroughly. No arrests or house searches. The brothers had been interviewed under caution after attending the police station voluntarily, and their alibis checked out. Big deal. That meant nothing. Except there was something in Baxter's face last night when he was staring down the barrel of a loaded gun, and claiming to have nothing to do with Joey's disappearance that was strange. Stallard believed he was telling the truth.

The day began to drag. Lack of sleep and the afternoon heat made his eyelids heavy. The soporific paperwork was never-ending: message logs, exhibits lists, phone records, personal descriptive forms, officer reports, analyst charts, timelines, interview transcripts, and the administrative debris that accumulates in the gutter of any major incident. Twice he woke up with his forehead resting on the table. Each time, he fetched more black coffee, and carried on ploughing through.

Shannon was never far from his thoughts. What must she be feeling? How long would it be before she recovered from the shock, and realised that her father might never see home again? Baxter was clinging to life, but for how much longer? Even if he lived, the penalties for gun use were severe. Losing her dad as well as Joey could break what was left of her heart. Stallard wanted to help, but now wasn't the time.

Three-quarters of the way through the file, he took a break. Word-blindness had kicked in. Nothing was registering, even though he re-read the same page over and over. There was nothing in the fridge, so he made do with baked beans mixed through a packet of noodles. Fortified, he pushed on. The remaining pile became thinner and he realised the end was nigh. Then what? Go back to the beginning and start again? Like a vinyl record player left on auto-return? Yes, he said to himself, that's exactly what you're going to do. Keep going. For once in your life, do something you don't enjoy and doesn't come easy. Finish it.

Planes flew overhead. Down the road someone fired up a chainsaw. The scent of jasmine came and faded away. Soon, he reached the bottom of the stack of papers and took a deep breath ready to start again. The last two sheets were nothing to do with the missing person file. They were Keith's that he had been photocopying, and lumped in with the rest by mistake. It was an update he'd prepared for his DNA case. Stallard managed a smile. He'd worked some hairy undercover cases, but nothing had frightened the living crap out of him as much as that time in the bedroom, just as he was seizing the knickers. Happy days. Before the dead kids came along – and the shootings.

He read Keith's typed note. The DNA from Amanda Paice's underwear had come back negative from the lab. She wasn't the killer. No real surprise there, because the victim in this case was a barmaid who'd been sexually assaulted and beaten to death. You didn't need to be the sharpest offender-profiler to know the murderer was probably a man. No matter, Amanda Paice still needed eliminating from the enquiry. Keith recommended that the cold case review should continue, as there was one further family member to trace, and at the present time there was…

Stallard stopped reading. Just a minute. What was the reason she was flagged up in the first place? Why exactly did he break into an innocent woman's house and violate her laundry basket?

The realisation when it came wasn't instant or by any means certain. There was no bolt out of the blue, or flash of Archimedean incision. It was more like putting together an item of Ikea furniture. You start with a picture and lots and lots of pieces. It seems impossible, but slowly you learn how certain parts can only fit in with others. When you know how it all connects to make the final ensemble, it's so simple. That's how he came to identify Joey Doane's killer. Flat-pack detection.

CHAPTER 51

Traffic on the ring road was light for rush hour. It was the last day of summer term for most schools, and holidays seemed to have started early. Stallard cruised to the south of the city, and picked up the old turnpike road that ran out towards the Peak District. The A625 is the Champs Élysées of the Steel City. The pavements were alive with bars and cafés, and folk just strolling up and down enjoying the sun. *Très bourgeois*. After the old toll gate, the road started to climb, and he dropped the Jeep down a gear, and gunned it up towards the edge of the moors.

The swanky cul-de-sac and house were as he remembered, and the same Range Rover was parked there on the drive. When Oliver Munday answered the door, he was wearing full Lycra and a gallon of sweat. The look on his face was hostile.

'What is it now?'

'I've got some bad news about your brother.' Stallard barged past him, and into the kitchen.

'Hey.' Munday followed. 'What are you doing?'

'Looking for evidence.'

'Get out.'

Stallard opened the fridge and peered inside. 'No, not in there.'

'I said, leave my property now.'

'Mmm?' Stallard hovered over some pots in the sink. 'Maybe, maybe not.'

'Right, I'm calling the chief constable.'

'You've not asked what the bad news about Joey is.'

'I don't need to, he's dead. How could it be worse?'

'If it was fratricide, not suicide.'

Munday gripped the island and bulged his eyes. 'Preposterous.'

'Fiver says I'm right.'

'This is absurd.'

'Shall I call you Cain, ancestor of all evil?'

'Don't try and make sick jokes. I'm not going to stand here in my own house and be insulted by an uncultured moron like you.'

'Get changed. I'll insult you down the police station.'

'Now I'm calling my lawyer.' Munday went over to a worktop where a mobile was on charge.

'Don't you want to know how I can prove it?'

Munday stopped and turned. His eyes betrayed a scintilla of panic.

'Everybody's got a secret,' said Stallard. 'Most people won't kill another human being to protect it, but you did.'

'Complete rubbish.'

'Your own sibling. That's a new low.'

'I don't know what you're talking about.' Perspiration ran down Munday's face.

'You couldn't let Joey answer bail at the police station, and get charged, because he would have been photographed, fingerprinted and had his DNA taken.' Stallard snatched one of his own long hairs from his head, and held the root up to the light. 'Incredible thing, deoxyribonucleic acid. Less than one in a billion chance that profiles from unrelated individuals will match.'

Munday didn't speak. He looked like he had a golf ball in his throat, and took a drink of his green vegetable smoothie to try and clear it.

Stallard said, 'You knew, that once Joey's profile went onto the national DNA database, it could be subject to a familial DNA search, and that process would reveal your terrible secret.'

'What secret?' Munday managed to talk.

'I don't know, yet,' said Stallard. 'But I bet there's an unknown DNA profile on the system from a serious crime in the past, and it belongs to you. Joey's profile would have been almost identical, and eventually led the police to you. That's why you killed him.'

'Where have you got this outrageous theory from?'

'He's called Keith. Bit of a legend in the world of cold case reviews.'

Munday's eyes fired up. 'So, there we go. You have no proof.'

'There's one easy way to find out. Let's go down the station and take your DNA.'

'I don't think so.'

'Please yourself.' Stallard reached across the island

and picked up the tall plastic beaker Munday had been drinking from. 'That's the evidence I was looking for. Saliva is good for DNA.'

Munday dived onto the worktop, and pulled a knife from a wooden block. His voice was cold. 'Put it down.' He stood in the doorway. 'Go on. Put the cup back on the side.'

Stallard's eyes fixed on the blade. It was about seven inches long, and glinted under the recessed LEDs in the kitchen ceiling. A ripple of electricity ran down his spine and then bolted off at ninety degrees to where he still had the scar from the Blue Butterfly. Strange how memory can stimulate a physical reaction.

He put the cup back down. 'You don't look like much of a music buff, Oliver. I bet when we check your computer, you were googling *Manic Street Preachers* at the beginning of February.'

'Do you think I'm stupid?'

'Absolutely. You're stood in your own kitchen pointing a knife at one of Her Majesty's finest. What's the next move? Any idea how much blood comes out of an artery? What time are the wife and kids home?'

Munday stood there thinking and sweating. His entire life was being ripped out from under him, and he was desperate. He needed a way out. Not a lawyer or a smooth-talker anymore. Just a cornered animal.

Stallard took another a peek at the blade. Getting stabbed twice in six months would be careless. The nurses might start thinking he was doing it deliberately for the bed baths. He tried to keep his voice calm and throw in some sympathy.

'I know you didn't want to kill Joey. You gave him the chance to skip bail and live in another part of the world. He chose Vietnam, because he'd been there before. You were going to fund it.'

'He was an idiot.'

'But you came to realise he didn't have the character. He would have come back, and you would have wasted a great deal of money.'

'It was never about the money.' Munday's bottom lip quivered.

'When he came back, the police would have arrested him. They'd have taken his DNA.'

'He was weak.' Monday sobbed.

'Joey was a junkie. It didn't seem fair. He wanted to be famous.'

'Why should a fucking drug addict have the power to ruin my life?' Spit and sweat flew from Munday's lips. 'Because of his selfishness?'

Stallard nodded. Quiet for a moment. Then, 'How did he die?'

Munday wiped his eyes with the back of his hand. 'He didn't suffer. He was overdosing on heroin, unconscious. I used a plastic carrier to help him on his way.'

'Tell me it was a Tesco bag for life.'

Munday screwed up his face. 'What?'

'Nothing. Don't worry, we'll edit that bit out.' Stallard bowed his head and spoke to his left breast pocket. 'Are you deliberately waiting until I get stabbed again?'

Five seconds later, a voice in the hallway said, *drop the knife, dickhead*, and Frank appeared. Oliver Munday let go of the knife, and it fell onto the kitchen tiles. His legs wobbled, and he slumped into a corner, up against a pedal bin.

'Got it?' Stallard raised his eyebrows.

'Every word.'

Munday was sobbing. 'I made one mistake when I was seventeen... he was never my real brother... what about my wife... the boys... work...?'

Frank hauled him up and cuffed him. Then dragged him out through the front door.

Stallard picked the knife up, and wrapped it in a towel. He still didn't trust blades. The sun was still shining when he got outside, and a pair of alpacas in the field next door were peering over the fence with cute permed hair and knowing looks. The air smelt sweet. Stallard knew he should be elated, but he wasn't.

Joey's death was a tragedy, but not in the classical sense. He had flaws and may have gone on to achieve great things, but it wasn't these traits that brought about his downfall. It was the fact he shared his DNA with a horrible bastard. You can't pick your relatives, or change the molecular structure inside your own cells. Stallard felt no catharsis at closing the case, just a lingering sense of waste.

CHAPTER 52

A purple-pink sky framed the gasometer on the side of the canal. It cast a cylindrical shadow over the red-brick factory walls, which lined the bank, and ran along to the lock gates. Stallard had a pair of Hiatt Speedcuffs in his hand, and used them to rap on the workshop door. There was an overpowering smell of skunkweed. On a rickety table between two deckchairs, were a load of decaying butt-ends floating in a half-full jam jar of rainwater.

Fay Nash wrinkled her nose. 'Gross.'

'Wait 'til you see the paintings.' Stallard knocked again.

There was a light on inside, but no movement. He tried the door, but it was locked. He banged again so hard it rattled the hinges.

There was the sound of deadbolts being pulled back, and Naomi Munday appeared.

'Come to show me your tattoos?' She tilted her head and smiled. Gave him the fence-post teeth.

'What do you think?' Stallard smiled back.

'Ooh, handcuffs, kinky.'

Stallard could tell she'd been on more than weed. Her eyes were hooded, but their pupils were big as black gobstoppers. Not for the first time, he thought about the likeness between her and Joey. Not just the appearance, but the gene that burdened them with a predisposition to certain substances. Or was that nothing to do with inherited DNA? Was it just a chance combination of circumstances and individual choice? Is it the stars that hold our destiny or ourselves? Too deep. He switched his brain back onto auto-pilot.

'Where's the car?'

Naomi Munday didn't look surprised. She walked back inside her workshop cum home, and nodded for them to follow. There was a battered oak dresser, and she took a set of keys out of the top drawer.

'He was dead. What could I do?'

Stallard took the keys. They had a fob with the three red diamonds grouped in a triangle – Mitsubishi. 'How about calling the police, followed by a reputable funeral director?'

'Oliver said it wouldn't look good. A dead junkie in his house.' She was unsteady on her feet. She felt her way along the wall and dropped into a leather armchair.

'So, you just went along with it? Because it didn't look good?'

Naomi Munday closed her eyes. 'He said I owed him, because of all the money he'd spent on my *issues*.'

Stallard saw that Fay Nash was staring at the artwork on the studio walls, and he gave her an eyebrow wiggle, *what did I tell you?* She wiggled hers back, *yes, it's all so weird and definitely not to my taste.* That's Nash – always a wider range of expression in the supraorbital department.

Naomi Munday let out a cry. 'Me and Joey were soul-mates. I knew it from the first time I met him.'

Stallard said, 'Tell us what happened.'

'It was so long ago. There was blackness and ice.' She opened her eyes, and stared at a spot on the wall in a trance-like state. 'Oliver called. When I got there, Joey was on the garage floor. We rolled him in carpet and lifted it into the back of his truck. Oliver drove, and I followed. Oliver had stick-on plates for mine. He stopped at the end of the bridge, and we carried him back to the middle. It was cold and murky. If anyone had seen us, we were just fly-tipping an old rug, but there was nobody about. We threw him over the iron barrier, and he went down into the darkness. Like a stone into nothingness. I knelt down and pressed my forehead into the girders, and prayed for forgiveness to the Higher Power, who inhabits all living creatures and plants.'

Stallard wasn't buying it. 'Did you sing, *He ain't heavy, he's my brother,* while you and Oliver were carrying Joey over the Humber, because if you didn't, you missed a great opportunity.'

Naomi Munday looked at him, and he knew. There was something in her eyes that confirmed his suspicion. He also knew she wasn't as stoned or smacked as she had been having them believe.

He said, 'Aren't you missing something out?'

'Such as?'

'Joey was sedated with an overdose of heroin. I don't think Oliver has the knowledge and experience to do that. But you do.'

'Did Oliver say I did it?'

'No.'

'Then I didn't do it.'

'I think you did.'

'Blood's thicker than water.'

'Except when it's in the wrong brother.' Stallard handed the Speedcuffs to Fay Nash. 'Let's go.'

There was no sign of the heatwave stalling. The sun pressed down on the pavement like the heel of a giant foot, and shoppers huffed along in shorts and floppy hats, with water bottles and mini, battery-operated fans. It was like Santa Monica, but with less sand and more cellulite. Stallard found Shannon in Bridge Street, round the back of the magistrates' court, waiting for the prison bus to leave.

They hung around for a while in the shade of an old lime tree, and eventually the gates opened, and a big, white meat-wagon nosed across the footpath and out onto the road. Shannon stood and waved, big exaggerated overhead crosses, like she was on the deck of HMS *Ark Royal* signalling to a landing jet. All the windows were black, and her dad could have been in one of the holding cells on the other side of the bus, but Stallard didn't say anything. She could have been waving to Mad Bert, a drunk of no fixed abode, and record-holder for most alcohol-related arrests. At least, she wasn't waving to Oliver Munday. He was subject to a warrant of further detention, and still in custody at the police station, pending official confirmation from the national DNA database.

It was a formality. He had already admitted the rape he had committed twenty-two years earlier. Not that he had much choice. He wasn't a fool, and knew that early co-operation with the police would lead to a reduced sentence. Stallard had been surprised at first when he discovered Oliver Munday's dark secret. The girl was a student, and had been walking back alone from a nightclub to her hall of residence. She'd been heavily intoxicated, and unable to provide many details. Then he'd remembered why Kate Munday had put Joey up for adoption – so she could try and save her two older children, because they had lost their moral compass following their father's death.

Stallard knew what it was like as a teenager to lose your dad. It hadn't turned him into a monster, but maybe that's where his occasional drive for self-destruction came from. Anyway, Freud and Jung, all bollocks. Fact is, Munday was a messed-up kid, who had problems with alcohol and women, and over the years he turned into a grown man with the same issues. He'd jumped on Caroline Stubbs after the firm's Christmas party, and then made out they were in a relationship. In his dreams. Shame the uptight paralegal hadn't spelt it out to him more overtly, but there you go. It was probably just him being dim, instead of his razor-sharp self. These things can happen to the best.

The bus carrying Jim Doane to the remand prison chugged away in a cloud of particulates, and the brave face that Shannon had been showing in front of it, cracked and collapsed. She let the tears flow and asked how long her dad would have to spend locked away. He chewed his bottom lip, but there was no point trying to sugar-coat shit. It all depended on whether Baxter pulled through. The bullet had clipped a rib, and ricocheted around inside him like a pinball. At the moment, he was still fighting, but at any time his body might go, *tilt, game over*. If that happened, Jim was looking at upwards of twenty years, because he took the murder weapon to the scene.

Should Baxter survive, it was a different ballgame. With the mitigation of Joey's death, and the fact Quinn was a drug trafficker, plus a following wind and friendly judge, then Jim might drop for a six-stretch. Be out on licence after four. There was a massive disparity between the two scenarios, and at Jim's age it could mean the difference between playing with his grandkids or dying in prison, all of which didn't make any sense, because the outcome was mainly dependant on the skills of an unknown trauma surgeon at the Northern General Hospital. Stallard shrugged – that's baseball.

He took Shannon's arm, and they walked uptown to find a coffee shop. At the start of the pedestrian zone, there was a ponytailed guy with a guitar and a three-legged lurcher. The guy was singing the old Cat Stevens' classic, *Father and Son*. The lurcher looked sad. Probably because his owner messed up the guitar part, and couldn't hit the octave-higher notes in the third verse. Stallard chucked a quid in the flat cap anyway, out of respect for the ponytail. He pointed out the travel agents where Joey had booked the flight he never caught, and Shannon grew quiet and pensive.

When they reached the Town Hall, she slowed down and asked why Joey had chosen Vietnam. Stallard explained it was where the Quinns had sent him last year to execute a Fentanyl importation. No reason other than familiarity, because he had been there before. She nodded. That sounded like her brother. A melancholy smile appeared at the memory, and lingered as she ferreted in her handbag for a tissue.

Stallard explained how Joey was the first. Then Mickey and Tyler. The Quinns always sent clean skins, who were the right age to pass for gap-year tourists. Only ever one visit each so as not to raise suspicion. What the Quinns didn't know at the time, was that the wet-behind-the-ear musicians were going to turn out to be such a great band. One that had the potential to make more money than they got opiate-peddling. The irony was painful.

Were Mickey and Tyler deliberately killed? Probably, but there was no way of knowing for sure. The police reopening Joey's case wasn't what the Quinns were expecting, and it had rattled them. It certainly suited their purpose if two more of The Magic Rats were no longer in a position to tell tales about what they'd once done. It was the headless body washing up on the Humber's north bank that had triggered the review by the cold case unit, and yet it hadn't even been Joey's remains. Another cruel twist. Maybe one day his body would be found, and he could be laid to rest too.

Shannon blew her nose and sniffed. She couldn't understand why Munday hadn't let Joey catch the flight and make a new life for himself over there? It was just so brutal and unnecessary to kill him. Stallard stopped and pointed down at the pavement. Every few feet were brass plaques set into the stone slabs, with a star on each like a sheriff's badge. Beneath each one, a name. The two nearest were *Joe Cocker* and *Def Leppard*. It was the city's Walk of Fame. Not exactly Hollywood, but who gives a toss about those plastic-faced airheads, and their stupid oversized sign on the hillside. He asked Shannon if she thought Joey would have wanted to be on the Walk of Fame, and she said *definitely*. Then she realised why Oliver Munday had murdered him. Both she and Oliver knew their own brother, even if in Munday's case it was only for a few weeks. No way Joey could have lived a life of anonymity on a beach somewhere. He wanted his plaque.

They found a café with a few outside tables under a canopy that fronted onto the Peace Gardens. It was a patch of grass in the middle of the city, with some sculptured water cascades to signify the flowing molten steel which had shaped its heritage. Drunks and little kids love it. They ordered iced coffees and bagels. Shannon was withdrawn and distant, as if the emotional journey had left her physically drained. She was grieving for her brother and her father in different ways, and the shock would take time to dissipate. Then there would be anger and guilt, and the usual entourage of anxieties that loss brings. All thanks to a random traffic accident twenty something years ago.

If Joey's natural father had taken a different route to work or left a few seconds earlier or later, none of this would have happened. He wouldn't have been put up for adoption, and his two natural siblings wouldn't have become the biggest bastards since Bonnie and Clyde. Maybe Joey wouldn't have developed a taste for self-centredness and heroin. Who knows? Fortune, the blind goddess and her fickle wheel. What a cow.

The fact was, Oliver Munday was a calculating, cold-blooded executioner. He had used Bell Bio Inc to be one hundred percent certain that he and Joey were brothers. He'd also engaged the services of Ben Phillpotts QC to check whether the police had already taken Joey's DNA – the power exists to take it on arrest, but often cops defer it until after charge. Once Munday knew that a sample hadn't already been taken, he needed to know from Phillpotts if there was any way of Joey avoiding the criminal charge. When it became clear that was not going to happen, there were only two choices: Joey could leave the UK or be killed.

Stallard finished his iced coffee and sat twiddling the tiger tooth earring between his thumb and finger. Nerves or plaintive hesitation? He asked Shannon if she would like to still see him when the case was over. He felt bad, but both she and he were witnesses. It could be prejudicial to the proceedings if they continued a relationship, which was increasingly more personal than professional.

Shannon took his hand. She was grateful for the support he'd given her. She'd enjoyed their time together, but everything had changed. One day she might feel different, but right now, she could only think about her mum and dad, and how to get through each day and night. One thing at a time. He nodded. The two trials would be tough and might not take place for months.

They left the bagels untouched, and walked down to the row of bus stops in High Street. The number 93 was ready to depart. Shannon thanked Stallard for discovering the truth about Joey's disappearance, even though it was painful. She smiled and apologised for ever thinking that he wasn't a real detective. Then she hugged him and got on the bus. He waved as it pulled away and felt an emptiness he'd never felt before.

Epilogue

The music blared out from a Bluetooth speaker tied to the gutter by a piece of baler twine. Sam Cooke was having a party and everybody was swinging. Stallard balanced on what was left of the bungalow's joists, and removed the last of the slates that were going to be reused on the new roof. Shorts, lumberjack shirt, steel-capped boots and a claw hammer. He shouted down.

'I give in. How should I know what the bloody B side was?'

Shannon shook her head in disgust. 'Bring it on home to me, obviously.' She was emptying bags of rubble into a skip. 'Your music education needs stepping up.'

'Yes, Miss.' He grinned down.

'What's the biggest oxymoron in the world?' She called up.

He closed one eye in studied deliberation. 'Jumbo shrimp or police intelligence?'

'Country music.' She laughed and pointed at his checked shirt. 'Here endeth the first lesson, cowboy.'

Shannon had moved into the caravan over a week ago, and all was going well. No bust-ups, mega-binges or petty squabbles. Even when Naomi Munday had been acquitted on the murder charge, they accepted it with a resigned stoicism, helped by seeing Oliver Munday dragged out of court in tears to start his life sentence. Shannon was even mucking in with the grand restoration project on site. He'd binned the plans for a fancy four-bedroom house, and gone for a more modest refresh of the bungalow's fabric to make it sound and habitable. No more unrealistic dreams. A card had arrived the other day from Laura, addressed to The Cliché, wishing him well and telling him of her new job in Avon and Somerset. The irony. All she'd ever wanted was for him to be something like normal, and now here he was, almost there. It was too late for them, but that's life.

A brisk south-westerly was pushing the clouds fast across the clear spring sky, and sparrows were scratting around in the garden for moss and twigs to build their nests. Stallard climbed down from the roof, and they sat on deckchairs for KitKats and Pepsi Max. They were quiet for a moment, then he said, 'Have you made a decision?'

'Not yet.' She looked at him, and then her gaze wandered off towards the green hills, searching for something. 'It's still too soon.'

It was three days since The Keys to Utopia had offered Shannon the opportunity to join them on their forthcoming tour of Europe. They were doing okay, and touring as the support act for another band that had already stepped up to the next level. If things worked out well on the road between the band and Shannon, then the chances were she'd become a full-time member when they came home.

Stallard put his hand on the back of hers. 'Come on, you've got to live your own life. Don't put it on hold for seven years.'

Baxter Quinn had pulled through. Funny how horrible lowlife always seem to survive, when good people can die young. It must be God's way of being mysterious, or showing us what a true non-interventionalist deism looks like. Quinn was confined to a wheelchair, and the doctors said he wouldn't be able to wipe his own arse for the rest of his life. That was something, but it hadn't played out too well with the judge, and he'd given Jim Doane ten years. It was a serious violent crime and he'd have to serve two-thirds before being eligible for parole.

A look of mischief began to sparkle in Shannon's face. 'What if you came with me?'

'What as, a roadie?'

'No, just hang around. Act cool and sound knowledgeable.'

'Be myself?'

'Come on, your turn to decide?' Shannon poked him in the ribs.

'Aaargh…' It was the side where he'd been stabbed, and he feigned severe pain. The Blue Butterfly seemed an eon ago. Maybe it had been the jolt he needed to move on with his life, or maybe she was sitting right there in front of him. 'Do I get a private Limo and a luxury suite in Europe's swankiest hotels?'

'It'll mean staying in the cheapest dives in the roughest parts of town, and then spending ten hours, with a hangover, in the back of a van driving to the next dump, where we play to a bunch of bored teenagers who've really just come to see the headline band. If we're lucky we might sell a few T-shirts to pay for the booze, and then get wasted.'

'Can't wait.'

Shannon laughed. 'It's shit, but hey, it's rock and roll.'

'I'm in.'

'Sure?'

He leaned over and kissed her. Maybe they'd get to Paris and Rome. Maybe they'd fight like feral cats, and he'd go back to being a lousy copper. Who could say? All that mattered was he was now free to be himself. No more pretending.

What about Joey? How would the original Magic Rat be remembered? A national broadsheet carried an obituary telling the story of his short life. Fame at last. It didn't focus on his song writing or singing, but more his death, and the motive behind it. Turns out he was the first person ever who was killed to prevent their DNA sample going on the national database. Maybe he'll be the last. Who to say? The thing is, lots of people will never look at their own brothers and sisters in the same way again.

And Shannon? How would she cope? Losing a brother and seeing a father sent to prison would destroy most people. But she was strong. There would be wobbles, but nothing that could stop her moving on with her life. There is no better balm for the brain than music – it relieves pain, lifts, inspires, heals and transports you to another place. Even if it's just a band of kids playing the back room of some shithole pub, and that's why music is the only true magic in this world. Think about it.

ABOUT THE AUTHOR

The author was a police officer for thirty years. As a Senior Investigating Officer (detective superintendent), he led numerous murder investigations, and enquiries into serious crime. The last seven years of his service, he was Detective Chief Superintendent, Head of CID, and had overall responsibility for specialist investigations, including covert operations and cold case review.

Acknowledgements

It takes time and perseverance to write a book. The distractions of everyday life can easily provide an excuse to lose concentration and walk away from the computer screen. Some people are able do this and then return with ease to pick up from where they left off, but I am not one of them. I need long, uninterrupted spells for day after day until the task is finished. For this reason, I am completely indebted to my wife Catherine for enabling this book to be written. Without her selfless and constant support, it simply would not have been possible.

The desire to write a book was something I had harboured for many years, and retiring from the police appeared to present the perfect opportunity. However, it seems these things can prove more difficult in real life than in the imagination. That's why I am grateful to Barry Nicholls, the tutor of Abbeydale Writers in Sheffield. It was his balance of encouragement and honest criticism that gave me the confidence to carry on writing and ultimately publish a book. Not only that, but his many and specific contributions to this manuscript are very much appreciated.

I also want to thank the colleagues I served with in South Yorkshire Police, some of who provided inspiration for this story. It was a pleasure to work with so many good people, and the memories will always be with me.

This book is printed on paper from sustainable sources managed under the Forest Stewardship Council (FSC) scheme.

It has been printed in the UK to reduce transportation miles and their impact upon the environment.

For every new title that Matador publishes, we plant a tree to offset CO_2, partnering with the More Trees scheme.

For more about how Matador offsets its environmental impact, see www.troubador.co.uk/about/